# SOPHIA

*For special friends*
*John and Beth —*

# SOPHIA

A Woman's Search for Troy

*Nancy Joaquim*

∞

*December 2005*

A NOVEL BY

NANCY JOAQUIM

Montrose Hall

*This book is for my husband, Richard, with love and thanks for always being there.*

# ACKNOWLEDGEMENTS

I WISH TO thank Patricia Gates for her assistance and to whom I am grateful for an unfailing sense of order and the ability to expertly juggle a half-dozen tasks with grace and good humor; Vanessa Joaquim whose computer skills and readiness to assist in meeting deadlines proved invaluable; and Buffie Joaquim whose companionship and loyalty inspired me.

I am indebted to Dr. John Silber, trusted advisor, author and scholar, whose interest in archaeology and faith in the Schliemann story were a source of encouragement; and to Michael Fleissner at Langen Müller Herbig, Munich, publisher of SOPHIA SCHLIEMANN, Eine Frau entdeckt Mykene; 1994, F. A. HerbigVerlagsbuchhandlung GmbH. München whose friendship and support are deeply appreciated.

I am grateful for Robert Fitzgerald's translation of THE ILIAD; Anchor Books, Copyright 1974 by Robert Fitzgerald.

SCHLIEMANN'S EXCAVATIONS by Carl Shuckhardt; MacMillan and Co., London and New York, 1891 was my primary guide to the Schliemann discoveries at Troy, Mycenae, Tiryns, and Orchomenos.

*Rule with me equally,*
*Share half my honor,*
*But do not ask my help for Agamemmnon.*

*The Iliad     Book Nine*

*Sophie Schliemann*

*As a seventeen-year-old Greek girl received a history prize in Athens, a forty-seven-year-old German gentleman purchased a gift in Paris.*

*They lived many miles apart and had never met, but their dance had begun, and later, as the carefree, young Greek beauty looked forward to a summer by the sea, the restless German gentleman was setting the boundaries of her future as if in stone.*

# CHAPTER ONE

## Rumors Of War

*PARIS*
*MAY 1869*

H E WAS STRUCK by the dramatic effects accompanying his signature: the supple texture of the paper under his fingers, the weight of the pen in his hand, the ample light.

"Is it a gift, Monsieur Schliemann? Shall we include a card?"

"No, no card. The usual wrapping will do," he snapped nervously but with a quick forced smile to the clerk as he put the pen down beside the bill of sale and placed his hands at his sides, hoping their trembling would go unnoticed.

Was Chaumet always this dazzling, or was it that he had never been this anxious before, he wondered, struggling to compose himself as he searched for distraction and glanced toward the long glass display cases, focusing first on the gloss of gold jewelry flashing inside them, then on the blaze of emeralds and diamonds set against soft folds of dark velvet. Even the well-dressed patrons of Paris' most exclusive jeweler appeared possessed of an arrow-like sheen that afternoon he thought, deliberately turning his attention to the elegant clusters of monocled boulevardiers and their gloved female companions engaged in hushed conversation as the clerk disappeared with the silver box he had just purchased without asking its price.

He was pale waiting in Chaumet's flattering light, a slim, meticulously groomed man of medium height, his best features, which were his charm and great wit when it came to observing his fellow man, well-hidden beneath a pair of overly serious brown eyes and a cautious, often hesitant smile that did not always convey pleasure. As far as the staff at Chaumet was concerned, Monsieur Heinrich Schliemann was prominent but not important, polite to a fault but intense, often ponderous and preoccupied, and certainly a man who had never rocked with laughter.

How could they possibly know that like an excited child he had thought about the silver box for weeks, since his return to Paris its hold on him so relentless that it had begun to consume his imagination, overtaking all else in life as again and again he had tried and failed to force the vivid image of shining silver out of his mind. Heart pounding and breathless, in recent days he had found himself returning more and more frequently to number twelve Place Vendôme, immensely relieved each time he entered Chaumet's bronze doors to see the gleaming rectangle of silver still lying there in the case. No one must purchase it. It belonged to him. It had always belonged to him. Once, fearing the box was about to be purchased by a passing stranger who lingered too long to admire it, he had confidently approached one of the clerks well known to him, intending to finally complete a purchase, but in the last fragile seconds he had quickly turned his attention to the contents of another of the long, velvet-lined cases, helplessly pretending to admire other objects he did not and could not see. At last though, the passage of time and its firm grip on his yearnings had ripened his resolve, and on an early spring afternoon, emboldened by visions of a lost, lonely hill, his courage had prevailed.

"This is an extraordinary piece," the clerk said as he removed the box from the case and placed it on a square, velvet pad, pressing a small, silver, bird-shaped knob to one side as he took a step back. In an instant, a small, golden-beaked bird rose out of the center of the box, spread its wings and twirled around and around as it chirped a cheerful song. At the completion of its song, the bird pulled its wings closed and quickly slipped back into the box, vanishing out of sight, concealed and undetected under the scene of its protective silver covering.

"Yes, extraordinary," Heinrich agreed, nodding his head, "but I knew it would be," he added in a near whisper, eagerly leaning forward to press the small, bird-shaped knob himself and watch once again as the golden bird rose out of the center of the box to pirouette atop its interior oval of gold filigree, twirling round and round and slipping back into its engraved enclosure at the completion of its joyful song, safely hidden away and lost under festooned borders and a center medallion etched in a design of musical instruments, a lute and horns on a booklet of musical pages.

"Have you ever seen such a box, monsieur? The maker's mark leads us to believe it was made in the Biennais workshops," the clerk said, proudly pointing out the small laurel wreath chaised into one of the underside corners.

"It was the silversmith, Biennais, who created the imperial insignia for the Emperor Napoleon's coronation ceremony, the laurel wreath like this one that became so famous. I'm sure you've seen it hundreds of times. Napoleon wore it as his crown in countless paintings and of course, Biennais would have been the only artisan in all France allowed to use this imperial symbol on his work. I've been told that the Empress Josephine collected 'tabatieres' such as this and that a good part of her collection still rests in private hands at a chateau somewhere near Chalandry. Of course, I cannot say with any certainty that this particular one was made for her, but anything is possible. Napoleon gave her so many beautiful things. Ah, such people were so good for business!"

The silver singing bird box was set into a velvet-lined green leather case along with its simple gold winding key. It was then placed in a Chaumet gift box and wrapped in the black and gold bee-strewn paper for which Chaumet was famous.

Heinrich Schliemann left Number Twelve Place Vendôme unsettled but well-pleased with his purchase and a few minutes later, sitting in the privacy of his carriage and in a manner which would most certainly have surprised the Chaumet staff, he began to laugh uncontrollably. His whole body shook.

He had actually purchased a gift for Helen of Troy and Napoleon had helped him to select it! This astonishing accomplishment successfully completed, he instructed his driver home to Rue Victoire and a short time later solemnly deposited Helen's gift into the lower left-hand drawer of his desk before departing for a few days in the French countryside visiting his good friend, Martial Caillebotte, at Yerres. There was so much to tell him.

ๆ ๆ ๆ

Yerres was a French country village in the district of Brie, its name taken from the river whose lower course flowed through it from its junction with Reveillon near the watermill of the Benedictine Abbey of the Sisters of Notre Dame d'Yerres. Martial Caillebotte liked to tell his visitors that the picturesque village of Yerres had sprouted up where the old Roman road from Paris to Sens crossed the river and as proof he proudly pointed out the ancient fiord located directly on his property's east boundary. Wooded Mont Griffon overlooked the town and on the left bank the land rolled away from the horizon in wide ribbons of green, extending deep into the gamerich Senart forest, for centuries the royal hunting preserve of a long succession of French kings. To come to the fertile Brie Valley was to come to the great wheat-producing region of France, and to come to Yerres, twenty-five kilometers southeast of Paris, was to come to the beautiful land of haystacks in the curve of the region's sentinel river.

The carriage approached Martial Caillebotte's pale yellow house from the north, in the bright sun of late afternoon, passing first through an open pair of black iron gates and then onto paving stones which formed a drive and ended at the courtyard entrance to the house. From his sitting room facing the drive, Martial had heard the unmistakable rasping of wheels rolling across the stones and as the carriage rolled to a stop he stood waiting at his open front door, the unobstructed length of the windowed foyer behind him unlocking the first glimpses of La Casin's remarkable gardens.

"Ah, here you are at last," Martial said, eagerly extending his hand in a warm welcome. "I was so happy to receive your letter. Celeste can't wait to see you. She's planning to serve you tea this afternoon and some of those macaroons you like. She made dozens. I hope you're hungry!"

Martial Caillebotte was a highly successful bed manufacturer who for years had supplied the French military under exclusive contract and although long retired, he was still a judge at the French Tribunal of Commerce through which he had met Heinrich Schliemann some ten years before. The Schliemann export licenses were renewed and recorded in both Berlin and Paris, and in Paris it was Caillebotte who reviewed the annual permit applications with the thoroughness for which he was widely respected. Over time he had developed an unusual interest in the immaculately groomed, well-spoken German gentleman who appeared before him each January, never failing to inquire after Martial's well-being and that of his family before presenting his precise, well-ordered documents. From year to year, Martial had welcomed Schliemann's piercing brown eyes, looking forward to the sound of the resonant voice, consistently impressed by the remarkable growth of his diverse business interests – food, textiles, dyes, paper goods. For some time it had remained a cordial, relationship between professional acquaintances, an occasional dinner in town or a walk in the Bois de Boulogne the extent of their socializing, but in more recent years, mutual and avid interest in the Paris art world as well as in the city's frequent furniture auctions which both men loved, had created social and conversational opportunities conducive to a particularly warm and respected friendship.

On the surface, the portly, seventy-year-old Martial might have seemed an unlikely companion for the forty-seven year old Heinrich Schliemann who was known as "Tag" to his closest friends, but the two men enjoyed one another's refined company, attending many of the spirited Paris furniture sales together where, always good-naturedly, they often vied for the same well-crafted pieces. Martial had married twice, his second wife, Celeste, a woman twenty years younger than himself, and in 1860, at the age of sixty-one, he had purchased the country property at Yerres. He had named it La Casin and lavished his attention on its extensive park and gardens, encouraging his three sons to know the property in all its natural diversity. Through childhood the boys had lived on familiar terms with spring ranunculus, celandine, and primrose patches on the edges of leafy fields where orchids grew wild. They had watched peach trees espaliered and carefully protected to the south by late summer, taught to notice the soft, splendid carpets of small seasonal plants growing untended under ancient oak in autumn, the subtleties of summer fern and moss comfortably nestled under ivy-covered tree trunks, and always spring's delicate Japanese iris tucked guardedly into deep shade nourished by the clean rushing water of running streams. Along the River Yerres, seven rows of poplars circled the great yellow meadow they had named the "Ha-Ha," and it was there that the boys had raced fastest and laughed loudest. Breathless and panting, they had rested on thatch-roofed benches by clumps of poppy and curves of hornbeam near the ice-house, welcome daily visitors to the Swiss chalet a few yards away that served as a dairy where they drank fresh milk from white porcelain bowls and complimented one another on the day's superb catch of grasshoppers, snails, and frogs, which they trapped in various sizes of grass-filled jars and proudly carried home.

Martial had looked forward to Tag's visit, eager to catch the satisfied glint in his discriminating eyes as they swept over the most recent choices he had made in his shrubs and young trees and the freshly planted varieties of annuals that Celeste had taken great care in selecting for the cutting beds. He had come to expect Tag's sharply detailed attention to every subtle change at La Casin, welcoming his astute comment on an added bed of tulips, a grove of young spruce, the dense, budded maples, and as impatient to show off the fine new varieties of young rosebushes he had secured from the teaching gardens at Lyon begun by Josephine as he was to hear news from Paris. Shortly after his guest's arrival, Martial suggested a stroll through the rose garden before tea and macaroons with Celeste.

The afternoon had warmed and sunlight shone down on Martial's well-tended roses, showing them off to best advantage. Some plants were in full flower, others tightly budded. Still others would blossom by mid-summer and continue on to autumn, rhythmically absorbed into the profusion of color and gentle fragrance that each year lingered from May well into October at La Casin. The two men walked leisurely along the smooth, well-tended gravel paths, mutual sensitivities willingly caught under the spell of Josephine's imperial roses residing in perfect harmony with arbors of rambling vines and hedge roses of no particular pedigree and later, in the gazebo by the riverbank, they sat side by side on one of the simple wooden benches, observing the far-ranging flow of the river under slowly shifting clouds as they shared news of city friends and recent events in Paris, commenting most often on the ominous threat of war, which on that tranquil spring afternoon in the idyllic land of haystacks along the curve of the River Yerres seemed little more than an absurd impossibility.

"I see a good bit of Lampierre these days," Tag said, responding to Martial's inquiry on current activity in Santini's, the popular Paris cafe they both patronized. "He draws a daily audience to his table and of course loves the attention, but his outspoken opinions of Louis Napoleon are beginning to worry me. He brashly announces that war with Prussia will be nothing short of an egotistical exercise for Louis, one sure to jeopardize the entire country unnecessarily, and just so that another Bonaparte can play at war, he insists. He even goes so far as to address complete strangers, inquiring as to whether or not they have received their engraved invitations to Louis Napoleon's new war. The Santini crowd usually laughs, but Lampierre's language verges on treason and I fear for his safety sometimes. I wish you would come into Paris for a few days and talk some sense into him."

Martial smiled, seeming unconcerned, his gaze directed toward the clusters of trees bordering the riverbank. "Our friend, Lampierre becomes dramatic over causes and has no fear of retribution," he said with the spare, candid patience for which he was well-known. "It makes him a successful journalist. Do you remember what he had to say about the incident with the Archbishop last year when Rauchet's novel was banned? You do know, don't you, that he was single-handedly responsible for the enormous popularity Rauchet has enjoyed ever since, a second printing necessary to satisfy the great demand for that dirty little book. By the time Lampierre had his say about its physical effect upon the Archbishop's private body parts, all Paris was clamoring for it and Rauchet was quickly becoming a wealthy man. Tag, I remember nothing about Lampierre fearing excommunication. In fact, he openly credits this incident with making him a devoutly religious man, and so much so that he continues to pray daily at La Madeleine for the Archbishop's more frequent intervention into the literary matters of Paris. Tag, everyone knows that Lampierre is outspoken and glib-tongued, but I can't believe he's in any serious danger, not even now, with the Prussians breathing down our necks."

"I hope you're right, Martial. In any case, Lampierre's monkey provides the required levity. He's been accompanying his master to Santini's every day. Lampierre says his table manners are greatly improved. Frankly, I see little change in Vincente, but he does unfold a napkin with a certain degree of flair and Santini's patrons seem quite fond of him. He drinks cafe noir along with the rest of us but as you know, prefers a glass or two of good brandy. One of Lampierre's lady friends made a blue military jacket for him. It's quite beautifully tailored and covered with gold braid. If he could be taught to hold on to a sword he'd look like an officer in The Garde de Seine."

It may have had something to do with Martial's age, more likely with his sage appearance, which the friend he would forever refer to as "Tag," found even more impressive whenever Martial reminded him that both he and Balzac had been born in the same year of 1799, but with Martial, Tag discussed matters closest to his heart, and with an open candor inconceivable with anyone else. Although Lucien Lampierre was most certainly his best friend and most frequent bachelor companion, full of fun and ready at a moment's notice to savor the many attractions of Paris, Martial Caillebotte was much more. To Tag he was a true confidante, that rare sort who had always defined his trust with unfailing faith and quiet honesty, keeping personal secrets to himself and sharing them with no one, not even Celeste. For all his reliably tight-lipped confidentiality, however, Martial listened little and talked incessantly when he walked through his gardens with a visitor he particularly enjoyed. There, he was the expert guide in his preferred world, the likes and dislikes of his various plants and flowers providing an endless flow of information and advice. This plant liked wet feet, and this one demanded full sun, and all the while no wilted leaf escaped his watchful eye, the offending petal or blade quickly plucked away and whisked out of sight into his pocket.

Martial was well-acquainted with Heinrich Schliemann's demanding, complex world and as was the case in their small circle of friends, also knew the range of his personal interests. Lately, however, Martial had become the only person in that circle made aware of Heinrich's growing interest in the ancient Greek legend of the Trojan War and his increasingly obsessive search for its related hill.

For years Martial had admired his friend's ease in the world of Greek myth, often stunned by the extent of his knowledge and his strangely passionate loyalty to The Iliad and to Homer's historic and geographic credibility, but unlike Heinrich Schliemann, Martial

Caillebotte was a staunch realist, a man of the soil who lived far away from the obsessions of dreamers, so of course his friend's increasingly stubborn fixation with the legend of Helen of Troy, Homer's Iliad, and his intensified search for the hill he believed to be Helen's link to historic reality had actually begun to worry him. They had resumed their walk and had reached a gentle slope where a stand of young trees had recently been planted when Martial stopped to busy himself with the examination of a young maple.

"The search is over," Tag announced quietly, watching the quintessential gardener's hands testing the resilience of young branches. "Martial, I think I could be on to something this time," he said. "This time I truly believe I've finally found what I've been looking for."

"Really?" Martial responded, turning to face him. "Your lovely, lost city of Troy?"

"No, not a city at all. Far from it," Heinrich laughed. "A barren, lonely place, miles and miles away from anything resembling civilization. But that's the magic of it. It's a hill in the middle of nowhere, not terribly high, not terribly long, with absolutely nothing on it. You can walk it end to end in two hours. But my God, Martial, it overlooks all the right things: the right islands, the right mountains, the right river, the right sea."

"But surely there's more than good geography about the place," Martial insisted to his restless friend.

"Of course. There's a city under all that geography. I'm sure of it. A wonderful, forgotten city. And I'm going to find it."

"But how? You mean you'd dig for it? Tag, what do you know about excavating? Nothing. You could spend a fortune on archaeologists and their lame advice. Now that's a field to stay away from. Adventurers, treasure hunters, the whole lot! It all sounds a little too far-fetched to me."

"No Martial, it's not far-fetched at all."

Tag's voice was steady and calm and remarkably untouched by passion as he spoke, his decisive statement made factually and with steady conviction, his manner successfully disguising the sudden rush of blood surging through his veins as he remembered a hill's view to the sea and a sprinkling of purple – tinged islands spread out in the distance.

"It conforms to everything I have ever believed about the site of Troy and what it must once have been. Martial, I've decided to retire and devote myself to excavating on that hill. Troy is there. I know it. I've never been so sure of anything in my life."

"And exactly where is this fantastic hill?" Martial asked, attentive once again to the inclinations of his maple tree.

"In a northwest corner of Asia Minor. Turkey."

"Maple trees are among mother nature's favorite children, did you know that Tag?" Martial asked as if his devoted friend's startling revelation had gone ignored or unheard, his steady gaze unflinching in the candid light of afternoon. "Maples are the endlessly gifted ones, capable of the most generous protective shade, given to strength and height, their branches safe enough for a young child's swing. They provide a sweet syrup too, a golden liquid with a fine-textured flavor, and of course theirs is not the common wood of idle winter fires. Their wood is distinctive and strong, a special, uncommon wood, suitable for furniture and decorations. You, Tag, are like the maple, strong and distinguished and intended for fine things. I would not be a very good gardener if from time to time I didn't occasionally prune back some of these maple branches so that my tree grows well-formed and full of robust good health, and I wouldn't be a very good friend if I didn't tell you what is in my heart, clearly and openly, to say what others might not say: that I wish you were not allowing yourself to be carried away by this strange idea of a hill and that I wish you were more concerned with directing your life into the glorious present and not into the imaginary past. Tag, what you need is a real person to fill your empty life in real ways. You pursue this dream, this Helen of Troy and her city, in place of things that could make you so much happier. Tag, you don't need an excavation into a hill in Turkey or a search for proof of a fabled woman who may or may not have lived thousands of years ago. You need a wife, a family of your own to love, human beings to touch and hold and share in all the pleasures you can easily provide. You need a real home like La Casin to care about and nurture, gardens like this to fret and fuss over. Tag, you're a rich man. Has the greedy Russian really spoiled it all for you?"

They walked together slowly and in thoughtful silence, the fragrance of pine in the air pungent around them as they reached a path thick with fallen needles.

"Martial, I appreciate your concern, really I do, and I value your advice," Tag said, "but I'm perfectly happy, alone as I am, content to do as I wish without restriction. Of course I suppose I would like very much to have had a family and a home such as La Casin, but it's too late for that now. I'm a forty-seven-year-old creature terribly set in my ways and I can't think of a single woman who would tolerate me for very long. I am simply not suited to family life. I tried it with Ekaterina. Surely you remember."

"Tag, La Casin, for all its beauty, would mean nothing to me without Celeste and the children. Selfish contentment is not enough. The right woman would make you happy and that kind of happiness is the important thing in life. And time has nothing to do with it. It's never too late. This business of searching for Troy is admirable, but what happens when it is over? And it will be over at some time or another. Then what will you do? Admire yourself in Paris alone, with your butler Henri serving your one o'clock luncheon every day? Or will you discuss your adventures in Santini's every afternoon until the boredom sets in and finally no one cares to listen? My friend, you have all the resources necessary to provide a style of life that far exceeds your present one, and probably mine as well, but the genuine well-being you come to find here at La Casin has to do with sharing the smallest everyday things with people you care about. There are countless obstacles in life, Tag, but every now and again, we must trust in someone, and that trust must be complete. You must allow yourself to look beyond your unpleasant memories of Ekaterina. She's in your past. Find someone else and put all this ancient history, Greek and otherwise, behind you."

Heinrich smiled pensively. "It might be a very pleasant way to live Martial, and you make it sound very appealing, but it isn't the right way for me. Not now. Not anymore. My own company suits me best, but if my lack of close companionship concerns you, perhaps I should consider a monkey like little Vincente. What do you think sedate Henri would have to say about such a thing at one o'clock luncheon?"

The two men laughed as they approached the gracefully set house, returning to broad emerald lawns and the afternoon activity of a family with a house in the country. Under an elm's outstretched branches, Celeste had prepared a tea table, and awaiting their return and sitting beside her in the leafy shade, Heinrich saw Gustave, one of the Caillebotte sons. Gustave leaned back in his chair, engrossed in animated conversation with his mother as she arranged a bowl of fruit on the table.

Martial suddenly stopped at the turn in the path. He wore the faintest smile. It gave his face an uncustomary touch of fancy, a capricious expression, unusual for him. "Do you think she was as beautiful as they say, this Helen of Troy?"

"More beautiful," Tag answered without hesitation. "She has skin of palest amber. Her hair is black. It shines like gleaming ebony."

"It does?" Martial exclaimed, incredulous.

❦ ❦ ❦

Gustave Caillebotte was twenty-one and had grown into a tall, full-bearded young man, well-mannered and polished. Having dutifully complied with his father's wishes that he train for the law, he had successfully completed his studies, earning a degree and recently passing the required examination with high marks, but it had become abundantly clear that Gustave's heart was not with the law at all. It was with painting.

"I have a studio of my own, monsieur!" he announced proudly to Tag as Celeste poured tea and passed a tray of the macaroons she had baked earlier in the day. "My parents have given me the small north sitting room. Would you like to see it?"

"Now, Gustave, let's give our guest some time to enjoy his tea," Celeste said as she smiled indulgently to the son whose enthusiasm for a home studio could hardly be contained.

After tea, Tag accompanied Gustave to the small room at the north front of the house, surprised to see that except for the trailing red geraniums drifting from freshly painted black window boxes outside in the forecourt, it was surprisingly austere. There were a few old tables and chests of drawers along the stuccoed walls. A black wood-burning stove stood at the far end of the room, a tall pipe ascending above it through the ceiling. Small oriental carpets and larger pieces of flowered cloth lay rumpled and bunched here and there into corners of the floor, and hanging on the walls and lying on old chairs were drawings, studies, and countless oil paintings, all of them scenes of La Casin, the flower gardens and the stream, the colonnade view of the house, the path through the Ha-Ha. They were marvelous pictures, full of spontaneity and disciplined style, pictures seen through the developing eye of a discerning young painter who with his father and brothers and through his most impressionable years had freely prowled the orchards and park of his own home. He knew its rustic meadows and pristine lawns and he had studied the patterns of its many moods. He observed the cyclical natural rhythms of its flower beds profuse with bloom and foliage throughout the seasons, trained from earliest childhood to place the fading plant next to the budded one, the lowest growing in outer rows, the tallest in the center, one variety setting off the other in an unerring sense of scale and balance, all in simultaneous contrast, one variety sparking against another in uncontrived pure brilliance.

Among the paintings were several scenes of the walled kitchen garden where Gustave liked to spend long hours sketching the gardeners in the two well-kept hectares that provided the household with its unlimited supply of fresh vegetables and fruit. In one, the barefoot gardeners watered their meticulous green rows from metal cans tipped to spray water like gently falling rain, and which they held in pairs, one in each hand. In another, they stood tending the wall trellises, where cucumbers and beans climbed in summer light. Tag became particularly enthusiastic about one of the paintings he felt so expressively depicted the activity of the kitchen garden as he himself knew it, a view of two of La Casin's gardeners covering a row of tender young plants with the inverted clay pots Martial called, "cloches," propped up ever so slightly from the richly colored brown soil with small stones. The barefoot gardeners wore narrow-brimmed yellow straw hats and had rolled up their trousers to the knee.

"I would like to purchase this painting, Gustave," Tag announced to the young, dark-eyed bearded man who stood tall in the room's cool light. "What is the price?" Gustave smiled.

"Monsieur, I cannot accept payment from my father's good friend! Please let this painting be my gift with the knowledge that I very much appreciate your interest in it. Father says you have many fine paintings in your Paris house."

"Yes, some are fine I suppose, but I only purchase what I truly love. Perhaps you will come to see them when you are next in Paris and let me know what you think of my tastes."

For a brief moment, Tag had lingered at another of Gustave's paintings, immediately recognizing the scene from one of La Casin's oldest gardens with its distant view across the river and the yellow meadow, beyond Concy and the Tallis hills and east to Montgeron.

"Gustave, would you save this one? On my next visit I shall come to see this painting again, but I shall insist upon a business transaction, so please be considering a price."

Well-mannered Gustave agreed, enormously pleased by this compliment of interest in his work, at the same time anxious to say good-bye, left free to return to his sketches and studies of everyday life at Yerres as the Caillebotte houseguest paused for a thoughtful moment outside in the courtyard and watched the lifelike bronze figure of the boy in the courtyard fountain who under the playful splash of water struggled to hold on to a squirming goose.

By the time he had settled himself into the large second floor guest bedroom, a servant had hung his clothes in the mahogany wardrobe cabinet. The books he had brought from Paris had been placed in a neat stack on the console table in the center of the room and he idly ran his hand over them as he walked past. Standing at one of the open windows he could see the gently sloping lawns sweeping in green bands from the borders of the drive to the distant poplars lining the river path beyond, and as the scented twilight breeze drifted into the corners of the room, he thought about the past weeks with a clarity he realized had completely escaped him until today. La Casin's peace and quiet would do him good, clear his head, focus his thinking. Martial's wisdom would help too. Perhaps now the voids would begin to fill and he would be free. Strange though, he thought gazing toward the river as he unbuttoned his white collar, how the same few troubled moments could be re-lived over and over again in a lifetime, clear as a bell anywhere you went in the world, the people, the voices, the inescapable shadows. Even here at La Casin. Even two weeks before, aboard the Argentan sailing out of Constantinople and into the Bosporous the old resentment had festered inside him, managing to stab at him and stir familiar old anxieties. But not for much longer. The memory he had never succeeded in escaping was about to die. He would make it die. From the heart of a hill in a northwest corner of Asia Minor he would kill it with sheer determination.

"Why must we leave our home? Could we not write a letter begging to be allowed to stay? What have we done?" he had asked as a small boy.

The years had never changed his anguished memory of those three haunting questions he had asked on that dreadful day before Christmas. Father had given him the book to quiet his tears, the small book filled with words the small boy could not read, the beautiful book filled with page after page of the pictures that had set fire to his shuddering heart as the world crumbled to pieces around him.

Of course, as a grown man at ease in the tranquility of La Casin's landscaped perfection it was all too simple a matter to realize that at that time he had been too young to notice unusual relationships between the people closest to him. But even then he had not been too young to notice that his family was a family only on Sunday mornings when the children and their parents walked the short distance from the rectory where they lived to the village church of Ankershagen in moments precious with hands touching and fingers entwined. And even now, at the age of forty-seven, he still remembered the feeling of his mother's hand around his in those moments, her skin warm, her fingers protective and strong. If only the touching had not ended so quickly. If only it had been allowed to continue on and on until it finally meant love. Much too soon each Sunday, Father left his wife and children at the front pew and disappeared behind the white door into the corner room where he reviewed his sermon and selected the hymns.

Young Tag had seen the room. Moving like a small phantom, he had sometimes opened the white door undetected, peering inside to assure himself that Father was there, safe and well enough for the following Sunday's precious family walk and the affection manifested by the comfort of his mother's hand. On winter afternoons the room was gray and full of shadows, but in spring and summer, golden sunshine streaked across the window, lighting the big soft chair near the fireplace where Father sat to read.

People came to visit Father in the room: Herr Fassbinder and Frau Bechler, Frau Lanz, and her sixteen-year-old daughter Elsa, who was the prettiest girl in the village. Elsa had a head full of wonderful shiny yellow curls and even on the coldest winter day she wore no hat, braving the elements as she devotedly walked to church in a long brown coat and the unprotected halo of beautiful yellow light he loved. In the lengthening shadows crossing La Casin's wide lawns he still remembered how Elsa's confident air of superiority had intrigued him and that although she was quite a bit older than he, she was the first girl to captivate his heart. He had admired her accomplishments and noticed with pride that of all father's parishioners she was the best singer. Elsa had memorized most of the hymns, a feat which could still impress him enormously whenever he thought of it. Once the new organ had been installed she had led the hymn-singing with unusual gusto.

The thought of Elsa could still cause his stomach to churn. He could still see her yellow curls crushed against the cushion of Father's chair and he could still see Father's fingers unbuttoning her white blouse, her long brown coat in a crumpled heap on the floor.

"Tag," his mother had affectionately called him. "Day," the best part of her life, her "Tag."

One afternoon in the middle of a bitter winter, his mother had held him close as huddled together in her bed they had turned the pages of the beautiful book Father had given him, admiring the pictures of the ancient hilltop city of fabled Troy bathed in sunlight and the beauty of the queen called Helen. Outside, in the German village of Ankershagen, the snow had begun to fall. He heard the blowing wind and felt the room grow cold as Mother's arm fell away from his shoulder.

Dear Tag. Dear Mother. Dear Ankershagen.

❧ ❧ ❧

Two weeks before, in Turkey, he had been one of the last to board the Argentan departing Constantinople. Unlike his fellow passengers he had seen no reason to pause at the rails for one last look at the magnificent fiery sun setting on the Golden Horn. Instead, he had raised the tip of his black walking stick to quickly scan the posted list of cabin numbers and the arrows beside them, proceeding directly to his assigned deck without so much as a backward glance toward the Turkish coastline he had vowed he would return to before year's end. There would be time for red sunsets on the Bosporous, he told himself, more than enough time to leisurely savor all the glorious color of Constantinople, but just then he was much too tired for idle reflection. Inside his cabin he quickly placed his worn brown leather satchel on the small corner bench and removed his coat and gloves. Exhausted as he was, he took great care with his fine worsted coat, meticulous as a London tailor as he expertly aligned the shoulder seams and with a swift flick of his hand straightened the sleeves before placing it on a chair, his gray gloves neatly paired beside it. Without bothering to remove his shirt or trousers, he slipped between the paper-thin sheets and stretched out on the hard mattress. As he closed his eyes, he promised himself the luxury of sleep on no fewer than four of the softest down-filled pillows to be found in the city of Paris. The thought made him smile as he pulled the blanket up around his shoulders and reminded himself that in just five days he would be in Marseilles and shortly after that, at home in Paris at long last. Soon he would be reading the daily newspapers seated at his favorite marble table behind Santini's beveled glass windows and a whole continent away from the thick Turkish coffee he detested he would drink Gabriel Santini's delicious cafe noir to his heart's content, all afternoon and late into the night if he wished.

He was asleep in seconds. And again, the dream of Helen, always the same, was repeated in his cabin aboard the Argentan with the same precision he had welcomed for years, its familiar fragments rippling over him as he slept. Back. Forth. Full. Voluptuous. She was close enough to touch, near enough to hold, the amber skin fragrant with myrica a mere breath away.

They dined by the burgundy velvet drape at Broussard where he watched the legendary face in the flicker of candlelight. Her loveliness had not been exaggerated. She was flawlessly beautiful, her shining eyes large and dark, her hair a sumptuous jet-black frame of curling ebony. A delicate luster of gold highlighted her cheeks and glistened along the length of her smooth, magnificently sculpted brow. She wore a dress of rose chiffon.

Napoleon came to sit beside her in a silver-studded chair. He sipped claret from a hollow crystal knot. They recited poems together, laughed as they challenged one another to rhyme, and ate pastry puffs light as air and filled with yellow cream. Her voice was a richly textured flow of lilting ancient music declaring her accessible, and as a waiter served warm macaroons from a silver tray, she said she was expecting a gift. She was a queen, she reminded him, Queen of Sparta.

Napoleon whispered into his ear. "Flowers, or a music box." "Yes! Biennais has made a silver box for me!

Flashes of silver. Thunder and lightening in the air. Her voice rustling in the night. A thousand leaves of autumn swirling in October winds. "My fault. All my fault" she cried out.

"No," he reassured her. "Yes, my fault," she insisted in the voice that burrowed through him, brimmed over him, swept past him to peaks of stark white mountains in a not-quite blackened sky. "I was entrusted to do all in my power to see to the comfort of the royal houseguest, but his comfort became my own, his desires my desires, and by the time Menelaus returned home to the watchfires of Sparta, I was gone. To Troy. With Paris."

Swirling. High. Higher. Highest. Calling. Dance with me. Sing for me. Silence. Sitting at the table by the velvet drape, Napoleon kept one hand inside his satin vest. "What have you in there?" Helen asked. "The message from Menelaus," Napoleon answered.

For a lonely, somber man, a secret dream was a clasp of comfort, the friendly, undulating fragments of beloved companions warmly welcomed, eagerly recalled, even in waking hours. Helen's voice, Napoleon's hollow crystal knot, flashes of silver, the flame of rose chiffon suddenly blazing in his brain. And always the wonder. What lay in the message from Menelaus buried and unread beyond Napoleon's last tantalizing image?

Lately though, there were times when the company of dreams became sheer torment, the repetitive visitors of night a relentless sea of swarming clouds filling with the rain of a thousand pleading voices. "Touch me! See me!" they cried out. And the message. So close he reached out for it, only to find himself awake, eyes wide open, his hand extended to Napoleon, his heart pounding. Repeatedly, he made every attempt to return to his elusive cover of sleep in the hope of restoring the sight of Napoleon about to produce his message from Menelaus, but he had never succeeded in claiming the secret that for years Napoleon had kept safely hidden under his heart.

Eyes closed, he had even hummed the Marseillaise in search of the most responsive route by which Napoleon would be reached, but the general held fast, well-acquainted with the disguised half-sleep of the vanquished, ever the demanding adversary, smiling smugly into the eyes of his opponent, pleased with himself and his undeniable victory over the man who attempted to breathe life into a hopeless dream.

❧ ❧ ❧

He lived alone at Number 2 Rue Victoire in an elegant pale gray limestone house designed with mullioned windows and a slate roof. It was filled with fine things: signed French furniture, bronzes, porcelains, giltwood consoles. A patron of several of the old guild craftsmen who had successfully survived the aftermath of the Revolution, he understood the function of ormolu galleries on chests and tables, the composition of pietra-dura, and the subtleties of furniture made of tulipwood, kingswood, and purplewood, in the distinction of the style called Régence.

Upon arrival from his Turkish travels and with little more than a passing nod to his housekeeper, he had quickly crossed the paneled foyer and barely touching the brass rail on the sweep of florid black iron had climbed the graceful, curving stairway to his study. He walked past his massive desk, past glass-enclosed bookcases lining the walls and across the fringed Levasseur carpet to the pair of towering doors at the end of the room which he opened in great haste, almost too anxious to get beyond them. But his intent was immediately clear, and anyone watching him and sharing his vantage point would also have shared his delighted impatience in returning to Paris and its astonishing range of pleasures, for through the pair of doors he had quickly flung wide open lay a fascinating view of life in this city he loved and certainly it was a spectacle unfailing in its power to intrigue and hypnotize him, this daily activity on the center stage of Paris, the Bois de Boulogne, great wooded park of the City of Light seen from the privacy of his balcony, a panoramic view of Second Empire Paris in pursuit of its endless pleasures, its dangerous games played through the gilded gates of the old Rouvray forest designed by Napoleon III to attract the inhabitants of the city's most fashionable districts.

From the safety of his secluded precipice he liked to watch the daily procession of gleaming black broughams, phaetons, and open landaus turning slowly in and out of the Avenue of the Acacias. He focused on their elegant occupants, the Second Empire notables who occasionally nodded or waved to one another in polite recognition as they were driven through the refined landscape of the Bois, along the new macadam-covered drives and around the flower-bordered lake by liveried drivers who held the reins of splendidly matched pairs of horses, their sterling silver bridles sparkling in the springtime sun. But those who struck poses of pampered anonymity interested him most, the Empire's eccentric leading figures who preferred to be seen and admired from afar, well-dressed and stiffly seated on velvet-tufted cushions, inviting the recognition and distant stares of other stylish Parisians in the Bois who practiced the art of the promenade, the women strolling lime-tree shaded walkways in long, full-skirted dresses and elaborate plumes, the men beside them wearing top hats, many of them monocled, most carrying walking sticks pommeled in silver and gold. The City of Light was basking in opulent Napoleonic splendor, its newly completed public gardens and broad, tree-lined boulevards designed by Baron Haussmann only enhancing its long-standing reputation as the most beautiful city in the world, the seductive city Heinrich Schliemann loved more than any other, and seldom more than on a sun-filled day in May.

Paris had become his mecca of indulgent, contemplative avenues, thoroughfares well traveled in style and dalliance, across high life and low and to the celebrated habitués of the cafes; Hugo at Closerie de Lilas, Dumas at the Bernay, Georg Sand with Chopin at the Royale. It was a cultivated, inquisitive, madly intoxicating city worthy of savoring, and savor it Heinrich did. He relished its abundant visual pleasures. He thrived on the dash and drama of its sound. He was nourished by the ease with which it issued licenses to dream, and the Paris Heinrich Schliemann loved was full of dreamers. In domed shadows along the Seine, the as yet unknown Pierre Auguste Renoir was dreaming his dreams of faces and figures caught in fragile sparks of undiscovered light, the rose-white light it seemed he alone had seen, the life-giving light that enabled him to forsake the outline of a face in a picture, while Flaubert, the great Hercules of a man from Rouen, dreamed fully costumed, in a long, gold-embroidered robe, putting pen to paper with the effortless delicacy of the bud burst noiselessly into flower. And there were other dreamers: Monet, Manet, Cezanne, Zola, du Maupassant, Victorien Sardou, even the young Gustave Caillebotte, all of them swallowing Paris life and obsessively developing the masterful styles by which they would set their indelible stamps upon Heinrich Schliemann's Paris. Few of them would ever achieve the degree of financial freedom he presently enjoyed, yet as unknowns many of them had already achieved a far greater sense of fulfillment. But that was about to change. He could feel it. He had found his own blank page, his own bare canvas.

The dream of locating Helen's fabled city of Troy had haunted him for as long as he could remember and now he knew where he would find it. Troy was not the creation of a poet's fertile imagination, its golden rooftops not mere pictures in a childhood storybook, absorbing and completely fictitious. The face that had launched a thousand ships was not merely a lyrical expression of prehistoric poetry, not merely the face in his dreams. Those eyes had seen the light of day, and in a northwest corner of Asia Minor, on a lonely hill surrounded by a vast treeless plain, he had seen the same light.

# CHAPTER TWO

## The Gathering

BY LATE SPRING of 1869, the search for Troy had taken Heinrich Schliemann to Turkey, first to Constantinople then on to the hill of Bali Dagh in Bunarbaschi, a village deep in the remote Turkish countryside where for years academicians had maintained the city of Troy was most likely to have existed, if indeed it had ever existed at all. The disagreeable French Consul in Constantinople had made every attempt to discourage the difficult journey, but Heinrich had persisted, and after securing the services of a guide the required travel documents had been grudgingly issued. The geographic isolation was by itself encouraging, but from the moment of his arrival in the hovel-ridden village of Bunarbaschi, he remained firmly convinced that it had been a waste of time to make the arduous journey so far inland. Bunarbaschi was not Troy and could not possibly be. It was too far from the sea. Bunarbaschi's hill of Bali Dagh looked out to the forbidding arid wasteland of inland Asia Minor, not to the shores of Homer's wine-dark sea, nor to his islands of Bozcada, Samothrace, or Imbros. Where were the breathtaking views from the Trojan citadel, the long, sweeping vistas to the wild sea that once foamed white with the soul deadening sight of a thousand enemy ships? Where was Zeus' lofty Mount Ida, and where the Sea of Marmara and the River Scamander? The mountains, the islands, and the waters had not vanished. They still appeared on maps. But why had Alexander and Caesar come to pay homage to the memory of Achilles here, in this vermin-infested hell? Did they know so little of the Iliad?

In spite of overwhelming doubt he had given Bali Dagh every chance, and for three days in the hottest May anyone could remember he and Murat Narjand, the guide he had hired in Constantinople, had wielded pickaxes alongside five Albanians hired in Bunarbaschi.

"Here!" he had ordered. "And here!"

Over and over again, chips of rock splintered into the stagnant, sweaty air but the ground remained unyielding and not a single attempt to break through the bedrock surfaces proved successful. There was not the slightest sign of an ancient city whose great stone walls and buildings he was so sure could not have disappeared – not ever, not even in an all-consuming fire. Troy, the Troy of his dreams, lay buried somewhere in deep folds of earth. He was convinced of it, but not at impenetrable Bali Dagh more than five kilometers from the sea. He searched the bleak horizon for recognizable landmarks, and again for the islands, the mountains, the river, the sea, but he found not a single element at Bunarbaschi to satisfy the driving hunger with which he had come.

The day he left Bunarbaschi, the storks continued to build their nests on the hovel rooftops, strikingly beautiful in their squalor and along with Bunarbaschi's human inhabitants calmly indifferent to the mood of the discouraged traveler who had come into their midst on a fine, white-footed horse for the sake of a dream and a golden city by the sea. Waiting in the pale yellow dawn, his gentle mare, suddenly skittish and unsteady, seemed to sense her rider's impatience to leave.

The guide, Murat, took up his reigns and turned the horses in the direction of Hissarlik. As Heinrich mounted and looked ahead, it was with little doubt that the day's ride would prove tedious and boring, the ugly landlocked terrain totally free of the inspiring beauty he had fully expected to find. His predictions proved faultless as the long dusty trail leading to Hissarlik became little more than a narrow dirt path winding through occasional patches of stunted, nameless trees that by some miracle of nature had managed to withstand the bleak severity of their landscape. By sundown, weary and unrewarded, they had reached Murat's farm in the Greek peasant village of Hissarlik where they would spend the night before resuming the journey back to the city of Constantinople.

❧ ❧ ❧

It was a small farm, comfortably nestled against a remote green hillside and Heinrich found himself looking forward to whatever peaceful respite it might offer. His disappointment in Bunarbaschi was immense and had weighed heavily throughout the day, forcing him into a dark mood and obliterating any attempt he might have made during the long, monotonous ride to concentrate upon more important things in his life, but in truth, nothing was more important. The search for Troy had become an obsession, the passionate, spell-binding temptress who stubbornly navigated his imagination through her tantalizing sea, the undisciplined old lover who could fill his heart with endless delight. Until now. Could it be that the temptress had finally become too demanding, he wondered in exhausted swells of doubt, all her eager answers compressed into too few empty words to be believed? Perhaps the time had really come to turn away and say good-bye.

"Tag," his mother's voice had called out. Dear Tag. Dear Village. Dear Ankershagen.

❧ ❧ ❧

He could see the twilight outline of barns and trees clustered in the distance and as he and Murat neared a stone cottage a woman stepped out of the door.

"She is Tessa, my wife," Murat said, climbing down from his horse as the woman greeted her husband with a wide, warm smile hinting at feelings of relief and reassurance. He smiled back.

The sounds of goats and sheep could be heard in the enveloping darkness, and out of the shadows a small boy came to tend the horses. Inside the cottage, Tessa quickly set out a supper of marinated vegetables, feta cheese, a pitcher of wine and a loaf of bread for her husband and his guest. She went about her tasks wordlessly and efficiently, in a room of stark simplicity. Watching her, Heinrich was aware of the immaculately clean table on which Tessa proudly displayed the fruits of her domestic talents, and in an easy, open spirit of generous hospitality for which he had been totally unprepared. Her table was worn and bleached from years of daily scrubbing, he noticed. The stone floor beneath it shone in the dim light of the room's only oil lamp and on one wall, a collection of mismatched plates and cups stood in impeccable rows, on two open shelves. The faded dress Tessa wore was equally neat and clean, her face serene and composed above its collarless neckline, her piercing eyes a clear and utterly frozen gray.

In Constantinople, Murat had said he was a Greek shepherd. Heinrich had thought him remarkably resourceful for a shepherd, appearing in Constantinople as he had, on the busy street outside the consulate, wearing a broad smile as he confidently declared himself to be by far the most reliable of Greek-speaking guides in all Constantinople and unquestionably the most trustworthy in all Asia Minor. He had driven a wooden donkey cart to the entrance of the Nomion Hotel where he had met his new Greek-speaking employer. The donkey cart was painted bright blue and could be spotted at a great distance. Its traditionally Islamic color had succeeded in attracting Heinrich's attention and although he had understood Murat's need for added distinction in a city with no shortage of unqualified guides eager for work, he had insisted upon horses for the expedition to Bunarbaschi. The conspicuous blue donkey cart had stayed behind in a friend's dilapidated barn, but Murat's more conservatively colored brown donkey had plodded behind the two-man expedition to Bunarbaschi, carrying supplies and proving quite indispensable. Now, at ease in the hospitable atmosphere of Murat's farm in Hissarlik, Heinrich determined that in every sense Tessa was the true shepherd in the family, plainly assuming all of Murat's responsibilities during his forays into Constantinople and fulfilling them with admirable dedication and skill. She was farm supervisor, dairy maid, and the mother of three. Her body was small and delicately boned, her diminutive size most clearly emphasized when she stood alongside tall, barrel-chested Murat. They spoke Greek to each other and to Heinrich

Schliemann, an accomplished linguist, who long ago had mastered Greek and spoke it fluently.

Although from the day of his marriage to Tessa, he had lived in the Turkish countryside, Murat Narjand had been raised in the Greek community above the Golden Horn of Constantinople. He was a man of deep loyalties, jovial and likeable, managing in spite of his modest station in life, to maintain many warm friendships among the residents of the long rows of wooden houses whose common walls provided only visual privacy between an endless warren of dwellings. Several times each year, he boarded the ferryboat at Canakaale for the short crossing to Eceabat and the journey on foot that took him to Constantinople along the wooded north coast of the Sea of Marmara and through Kavak, Gaziköy, Tekiridag, and Silivri. Once in the city, his first stop was at the small house above the Horn where he had spent his boyhood and where his mother still lived. He never failed to bring her some food from the farm; in summer a basket of vegetables, in winter, the cheeses Tessa had made, and sometimes a chicken he had managed to keep alive in a wooden cage during the journey. If the chicken proved robust enough to survive the severe jostling it suffered between Hissarlik and Constantinople, its fortitude and strength of character went sadly unrewarded, for after greeting his mother, Murat promptly killed his loyal companion of several days with great pride, expertly stretching its neck in his bare hands until he could feel its bulging throat bone which he deftly wrenched with both thumbs while his mother prepared the fire. As the chicken was methodically hung for an hour with its feet tied to a wall hook and the fire began to crackle and spit, entertainment was provided by one of the earsplitting domestic quarrels usually in progress in the long warren of dwellings around them, and over their hot meal, Murat and his mother could take great pleasure in effortless eavesdropping, venturing comments, cheering, or taking sides, and of course they were not alone. Detailed knowledge of neighborhood life in the close-knit Greek community above the Golden Horn of Constantinople was absolutely essential to setting the simplest dimensions of one's personal identity, which in Islamic Turkey meant survival. One's address was known not by street and number, but by the assignment of human attribute. One lived next to "the purple nose," or could be found between the houses of the "baked mouth" and the "woman who cannot have children." This labeling was neither casual nor was it haphazardly assigned, requiring as it did, a close study of personal idiosyncrasies and physical characteristics, to say nothing of wit and compassion for physical deformity. Murat had grown up in the house between "loose legs" and "small man," prostitute and dwarf respectively, the most popular the prostitute, the best loved the dwarf, both among the better known residents of the Horn, each as economically deprived as any around them, but none quite so sensitive as they, Murat knew from experience, to the richness of sunsets in which the Horn was bathed late each afternoon. The dwarf had taught a young Murat to name colors as the daily spectrum of the sky was miraculously transformed overhead, and as she welcomed her earliest evening visitors, the prostitute smugly pointed out there was no green in a sunset.

Later, leaving his mother, Murat affably called upon nearby friends and relatives, producing additional samples of his farm produce and Tessa's cheeses in sufficient quantity to guarantee his urban popularity and at the same time satisfy an insatiable curiosity. Beyond his fierce loyalties and with a sixth sense, Murat understood the daily preparation of food as a galvanizing ritual and in his own way he helped to perpetuate its tradition. The repetitious ceremony of commingling cooking odors emanating through paper-thin walls provided reassuring incense to the Greek residents above the Golden Horn and offered a desperately needed sense of community in the overwhelming Islamic world of Constantinople where five times each day the sound of the muezzin was heard, reminding every Greek within its range of the difference between the conquered and the conqueror. It was a sound the Greeks of Constantinople had heard for hundreds of years and it had continued to stir just enough bitterness to keep old traditions alive. Prior to his marriage to Tessa, Murat had heard the muezzin every day of his life, but things were very different miles away at Hissarlik which was far enough away from Constantinople for a small population of Greek peasant farmers and shepherds to have fallen out of step with the rhythms of daily Islamic ritual and over time preserve their own. It was, of course, impossible to totally ignore the existence of the Turks anywhere in Asia Minor when it came to religious tradition, but for many years the Greeks of Hissarlik had observed their own customs and religious holidays out of habit and with an intense dedication for which few of them could have offered explanation. Anticipating oppressive futures free of change, they looked to the reliable traditions of the past for strength and lived out their lives in a pattern of sameness that from one generation to another and of itself brought fear of change or anything new. They were wary of strangers, especially foreigners, and even Murat, one of the most progressive among them, was more than mildly suspicious about the distant, Greek-speaking German who had hired him in Constantinople, paid him well, and now sat across from him at his own table, sharing his wine in Hissarlik like a Greek neighbor. Murat had taken no one else to Bunarbaschi and had, quite uncharacteristically, asked nothing regarding Heinrich Schliemann's interest there. Even now, after spending considerable time with him, he knew no more about him and his intentions than he had at the start of their journey the week before, but after three cups of wine, Murat concluded that his guest was now an amiable companion and as he gained in confidence, his guest grew talkative.

"What is it you seek here in Asia Minor, Herr Schliemann?" Murat finally asked.

Heinrich answered wearily. "Murat, I seek a lost city, one that I am beginning to think I shall never find. I have often been reminded that my city is a great, impossible myth and never existed, and perhaps that is the truth I must face after all."

"Does your city have a name?" Murat asked, sipping more wine.

"It was called Ilium."

"You mean the Ilium of the Trojan War?"

"Yes, the Ilium of the Trojan War."

With astonishing accuracy, Murat proceeded to recount several of the ancient tales related to the legendary city of Troy he had called Ilium, the names of Priam, Paris, Hector, and Achilles spilling out with astounding ease. He smiled.

"At times I think of these grand stories as I drive my donkey cart. I have known the tale of Ilium all my life. Many of us learned it as children in Constantinople. We heard it from the storytellers who came into the city. They sat under a tree or at a street corner and began telling a story to just one or two people, but soon a crowd had gathered to listen. Some of the storytellers were famous and attracted large groups."

Murat's eyes crinkled at the corners and he smiled broadly, recalling one of his few happy childhood memories. He laughed when he said, "Many Greeks wish that Agamemmnon would return to these shores in his thousand ships today and change the way things are for us. Some believe that Ilium is right here, at Hissarlik. Not far away there is a hill. We could go to see it tomorrow if you like."

"How far is the hill from the sea?" Heinrich asked, his mind jarred and suddenly racing.

"About two kilometers," Murat answered. "It is a place that people here have known for many generations. There are old ruins there, very old. The word, `Hissarlik' in Turkish, means, citadel."

The ruins would not be prehistoric Greek, more likely Roman, Heinrich thought quickly to himself, but two kilometers from the sea was a reasonable distance, one easily in keeping with a system for running messages several times a day from a city's fortification walls to a large Greek army camped by the sea.

They started out at dawn the next morning. As they rode in the direction of the hill, the trail became littered with small white stones and pieces of broken red clay. They passed shepherds huts along the way, gnarled trees, patches of undergrowth, and occasional tufts of wild grass growing around clumps of large white rocks. But as the hill of Hissarlik came into view in a flash of sunrise, there were no shepherds huts to be seen, no grass, and no white rocks. They had reached a large, lonely mound of solitary earth surrounded by an open treeless plain that ran on and on until it reached the sea. Heinrich could see it. A sea of brilliant blue. For a few moments, he sat quietly on his horse, studying the long, sweeping vistas in every direction and then suddenly, he was off, his white-footed mare galloping boldly across the width of the vast, barren plain, her long silken mane ruffling in the wind ever more fragrant with the smell of the sea. She ran effortlessly, her powerful motion smooth and free, her steady stride carrying her willing rider in a magnificent, timeless rhythm of solid force and sheer pleasure as if with the conviction of some long, unfathomable consciousness she knew what her rider was thinking: that the Trojans were lovers of horses, the Plain of Troy the haven of their herds, Ilium's famous Hector a tamer of horses.

"What are those islands called?" Heinrich asked Murat a short time later as they stood together facing the sea from the hill's highest promontory.

"There is Bozcada," answered Murat, pointing, "and there Samothrace, and there, Imbros." Heinrich smiled into the bright sun, his eyes glistening. There was no need for Murat to tell him that Mount Ida rose to the southeast and that the Sea of Marmara and the river still called Scamander were to the northeast. He could see them. The search was over.

He delayed his departure for Constantinople and spent the next two days on the hill, returning at nightfall to sleep at Murat and Tessa's farm. In those two days he explored the hill's every inch, completely enchanted by the ancient chaos he could imagine taking place: bucklers with bosses tightly ground one into the another, the great din of arms rising, elation and agony of men destroyed and destroying, the earth astream with blood, Menelaus, broad in shoulder, once a guest in Priam's city, now his sworn enemy; Helen, weaving in the women's hall, "a double violet stuff," as Homer called it, woven with "images of Trojan horsemen and Akhaians mailed in bronze." And the voice of Alexandros ringing out: "Let Menelaus alone and me, between the lines, in single combat, duel for Helen and the Spartan gold. Whoever gets the upper hand in this shall take the treasure and the woman home. So death to him, for whom the hour of death has come."

He devoured the hill's every irresistible angle, measuring its length and breadth again and again. He walked its ground for hours. The ruins Murat had described to him were broken column fragments and had lain on their sides for centuries. He attributed them to a late Roman period and knowing that the Troy he sought predated Roman occupation of Asia Minor by at least a thousand years, he also realized that if this hill of Hissarlik was indeed the site of Troy, the original city must lie far below the surface of the earth. He would have to dig for it and he would need Turkish cooperation. Returning to Constantinople a few days later, he appeared at the Office of the Minister of Public Education to submit his written request for a permit to excavate, a "Firman."

"How long will the Firman take?" he inquired of the white-turbanned clerk.

"There is no way of knowing," he was told. He would simply have to wait for word, the clerk informed him, turning to carelessly rifle through stacks of paper for which a filing system seemed unknown.

"It must have the seal," Heinrich heard him mutter in Turkish as he plodded through the disarray of forms and documents on the shelves before him, searching for the requisite application form and delaying Heinrich's departure from the ministry at Mesrutiyet Caddesi by more than an hour until the elusive Firman application was at last located, the Argentan's final breathless passenger bound for Marseilles more convinced than ever that continuing study of the Turkish language was about to become essential.

# CHAPTER THREE

## Monkey See

T HE LUXURIOUS PROMISE
of sleep on four down-filled
pillows was soon kept as he quickly returned to the comfortable,
privileged routine of Parisian life.

Mornings were spent at his desk where he worked on
correspondence, read, and kept his accounts. Precisely at one o'clock
every day, he took his lunch at a small table overlooking the garden
in the windowed bay of the large dining room, his butler, Henri,
serving from freshly polished silver serving pieces which he held in
absolute silence. Heinrich neither addressed Henri nor acknowledged
his presence, eating his meal in an atmosphere of profound austerity
as he gazed straight ahead to the spring garden where blossoms of
scilla and narcissus bloomed under the gaze of a marble faun. His
meal completed, he left the house at Number 2 Rue Victoire and
stepped into his waiting carriage, directing his driver to Santini's. A
man fond of his habits, the routine never varied.

On the day following his return to Paris and just inside Santini's
door, Tag immediately spotted Lucien Lampierre. Santini's was filled
with a crush of noisy people, the sound of their voices a discordant
din behind the spotless beveled glass windows overlooking Rue

Royale, but undaunted by the competition, Lampierre held court at the center table under the chandelier, puffing on a cigar and vehemently denouncing Louis Napoleon in an unusually loud discussion he conducted with three men Heinrich had never seen before. For months in Paris there had been talk of war with Prussia and in Santini's it was clear that in a few short weeks more than just a few French patriots had actively renewed a taste for blood. The Prussian Chancellor, Otto von Bismarck, was said to be urging greater German unity, promoting a new expansive German patriotism, and he had clearly set his sights on France. In Paris, Louis Napoleon confidently welcomed the Prussian challenge, some thought too eagerly. Lampierre's face was flaming and Heinrich approached his agitated friend more in an effort to calm him rather than to join in heated debate.

"Ah! Here is a brilliant man returned from travels to far off Asia Minor!" Lampierre declared as Heinrich sat down at the table and ordered his long anticipated cup of Santini's cafe noir.

"Vincente, greet our good friend!" he said to the monkey perched on his shoulder. "Here is a man who, like myself, is opposed to war with the Prussians! But one of many!"

"You jolt my senses back to harsh reality, my friend," Heinrich said quietly, striking a match to light one of the three cigars he had placed neatly before him on the table. "Have we really begun to prepare for war in my short absence? It's difficult to imagine our beautiful city full of Prussian soldiers. Vincente will not like them at all. Of that, at least, I am certain."

Lampierre laughed heartily as Heinrich suddenly canceled his cafe noir and ordered a cafe serre, the very strong coffee Gabriel Santini prepared with just half the usual measure of water.

The monkey on Lampierre's shoulder rocked from side to side in the thick curls of cigar smoke he attempted to capture, but he was constantly distracted by the plates of food being carried past.

Vincente was a fat monkey, known for an insatiable appetite and a preference for soft cheeses, grapes, and bread, all washed down with sips of the fine brandy his master consumed every day in notable quantity. Santini's patrons found Vincente highly entertaining, especially amused to watch his quick little hands snatch anything that struck his fancy as it went past on the white plates carried by waiters who did not always manage to avoid his acrobatic maneuvers. He drew applause following his more lengthy and particularly daring attempts to outwit Santini's most agile, surefooted waiters, and his triumphs were always met with warm praise from Lampierre. Vincente had taken several sips of Lampierre's brandy. With each sip, he slowly ran his tongue over his perfectly straight teeth, exposing wide pink gums in the semblance of an enormous smile.

"Ah, it gives me such pleasure to see you enjoying the finer things in life!" Lampierre said to him affectionately.

"Dear Vincente has missed you!" Lampierre announced to Tag, "and you will notice a great improvement in his table manners. You will be pleased to see that he no longer relieves himself on my shoulder when the soup is served and that he has acquired some fine new clothes. You approve? Germaine made him this new military jacket covered with gold braid, most appropriate for what is surely coming to Paris don't you think?"

As easily as the discussion in Santini's had ignited national passions so had it successfully turned to the more lighthearted aspects of Lampierre's popular pet monkey, Vincente, who was just one of the many exotic pets in Paris regularly included in social gatherings and expected to appear as suitably dressed and groomed as any other guest. Pet lizards on leather leashes and jewel-collared lynx were not unknown. Prior to acquiring fat, incontinent Vincente, Lampierre had kept a toothless pet puma his wife named Dragon.

"Before Vincente, Dragon was the love of my life," Lampierre recalled tenderly, closing his eyes whenever he was reminded of the beast who in old age had developed a distracting tendency to bite. "And when he died at the age of ten years he was full of champagne and in a happy state of mind. Completely at peace at the end. I know this without a doubt because when I went to the taxidermist to claim his beautiful stuffed body, he said that he had never seen such well-preserved internal organs. And of course when my dear Dragon died there was the most serene expression on his fine face, which I must say the taxidermist did a fine job of preserving. I would have known my Dragon anywhere."

For some time the expertly stuffed Dragon remained Lampierre's most treasured possession, and after leaving his wife following several tumultuous and what he called "absolutely vicious" years, he took up residence in a small hotel room and transported Dragon there with great ceremony, riding in an open landau along Rue Royale with the preserved beast lovingly cradled in his arms, the newly acquired and at that time slender and sober Vincente, perched on his shoulder. On the way to his new home, Lampierre decided to take rest and refreshment at Santini's and in the company of both his pet creatures, one living and one dead, he succeeded in attracting from Gabriel Santini's patrons exactly the sort of undivided attention he relished most, the open-mouthed brand of instant recognition he strived for every day of his life, totally unprepared of course, for the sudden diversionary tactics of Vincent's dramatic Paris debut that day, which was made almost immediately as the lithe young monkey dove headlong and directly into the center of Gabriel Santini's freshly and quite artfully arranged pastry table.

"With his derriere buried in marrons glacé, raspberry ices and paté â choux, my Vincente introduced himself to Paris," Lampierre related to his amused audience. "It was a very expensive party!"

Heinrich had witnessed the famous debut and smiling as he sat back in his chair, attested to the validity of the story, politely avoiding discussion of the real reason for Dragon's toothless state, evidence of which Lampierre would bear on his meaty backside for the rest of his life.

How good it felt to be back in Paris. He had missed all this more than he had realized: Vincente, Santini's, and especially Lampierre living up to his reputation as a popular, successful journalist, still keeping company with many of the city's noted men of politics and reporting on their activity with the sophistication and clever wit that once heard or read was sure to be quoted all over Paris.

Lampierre said his territory began within the boring sanctity of the Madeleine and ended in the fascinating decadence of Santini's, and although it was true that he was one of the Paris men of letters who wrote his best articles while seated at one of Santini's marble tables, his presence within the sacred marble walls of La Madeleine typically followed an all too frequent appointment for a morning duel in the Bois with one of the Second Empire celebrities he had criticized. It was well known that Lampierre's pockets held an impressive assortment of bandages as he met his challenges at dawn. But it was also well known that as he lunged into action on the field of honor, he produced some of his best material, the explosively humorous and quotable remarks which led not to death at the point of the sword, but to spontaneous, often uncontrollable laughter, multiple brandies, and good-natured apologies in the comfort of Santini's, where a table was always set in optimistic readiness, with two glasses. Following particularly close calls with eternity, however, Lampierre faithfully stopped in at the Madeleine to light a candle, kneeling in everlasting gratitude to the Virgin Mother for having protected him once again, and although he had become famous for avoiding the point of the sword, he faithfully continued, in keeping with the established practice of many of the better known Paris journalists and drama critics, his Tuesday fencing lessons with Jacques D'Ange, the great fencing master of Paris.

In the weeks that followed, Heinrich was a regular afternoon figure behind the beveled glass windows of Santini's, where debates over war with Prussia intensified and where he first noticed signs of the spy-mania that had crept insidiously into the intellectual community of Paris. Lampierre was drawing a larger and larger crowd each day at the cafe where many of the more prominent men of letters now gathered and Heinrich felt his speeches against Louis Napoleon had become inflammatory. Someone jokingly suggested that a warrant would be issued for Lampierre's arrest by the end of the week and that he surely would be sent to Saint-Pélagie gaol. Although Heinrich had laughed heartily along with the others, he had suddenly feared for the safety of his outspoken friend who loved Paris as passionately as he did.

These concerns were successfully set aside, if only temporarily, at the late-evening suppers he enjoyed at Paillard's, frequently in Lampierre's debonair company, where vintage champagne and caviar were two distracting staples of the evening diet and where the undulating red velvet banquettes held a generous share of the expensive third, its grand horizontals. Prostitution flourished, and far from distracting from the intellectual and creative climate of Paris, was regarded as indispensable a part of life as were the city's cafes and grand boulevards.

"The purest of all French art forms," Lampierre often said, his eyes closed, his lips faintly curled into a dreamlike smile.

Like many other men in Paris, Heinrich was a regular client of several of the high-priced stars of the demimonde who were attracted to his money, and although he presently enjoyed no long-term alliance with any one of the cocottes who found him irresistible, he was on a priority list of sorts. Men with money were hotly pursued, their names whispered and treasured like maps to chests of gold, which in many cases they quite literally were, and only once had he fallen victim to the high cost of long-term easy virtue. For almost a year, he had kept the beautiful Marienne in a house of her own, showered with the things she most admired: clothes, furs, jewels, wine, and money. But Marienne had broken the cardinal rule. Not only had she confessed her undying love for him, she had made it clear that she intended to marry him. A member in good standing of the demimonde's hierarchy, one who had diligently worked on herself, and with quite satisfactory results, Marienne pointed out that adding to the delicate, blonde beauty she knew he loved, she had perfected the conversational skills he valued. She had learned about literature, music, and art, but just as he had never allowed Marienne to call him Tag, neither had he ever been able to bring himself to tell her that he had been married once before, and to a woman with equally cultured tastes.

They had attended the Monday night opera where Marienne found herself an object of great interest among the aristocratic ladies who focused their lorgnettes upon her, studying the cut of her exquisite gown and the design of her superb jewels, all gifts of the distinguished German gentleman well known in Paris, but a man no one really knew at all. He was known to have his friends and his favorite haunts, but in many ways he had assumed the role of the "flaneur," that skilled observer of the daily sights and sounds of Paris, a figure recognized yet unknown, a man few knew lived inside himself and terribly alone, in unreal places, so unlike the lively Lampierre who thrived on instant recognition and lived by his quotable wit and glib tongue.

Some said Schliemann was aloof, others that he was shy and lonely. All were correct to some degree, but whatever the impression he may have made overall, there was an undeniable aura about him. He was supremely self-assured, often more arrogant than charming, but always in control, his sharply defined jaw and straight nose splendidly chiseled under the serious brown eyes, and although he was not a tall man, his stride was that of a tall man, aggressive and deliberate, his shoulders constantly braced in the posture of confident authority that made him appear far taller than he really was.

Marienne had blazed in emeralds at the opera, but along her bare shoulder in the carriage later that night there was no warm brush of Tag's lips, nor was there the familiar husky whisper praising her pale beauty. She had been returned to her house and immediately left with a decidedly final goodbye. Moments later, Marienne drank the entire contents of a vial of veronal, but she would not fall victim to the permanent sleep of death she had so vehemently threatened at the door just moments before in the much beloved screaming tradition of the demimonde. The dose had lasted a mere forty-eight hours and after waking from a long overdue rest, totally free of interruption, Marienne returned to life, lovelier than ever in the purged, frail beauty the international set found so inordinately attractive at the Longchamps races, the site at which Marienne dramatically publicized her miraculous return from the land of the dead, dressed from head to toe in purest white, like the angel of mercy she vehemently insisted she had now become.

A few weeks later Heinrich saw her at Paillard's. Their eyes met and Marienne quickly looked away, freshly attentive to the handsome French count who had satisfied her newly discovered need to consort exclusively with the titled and who paid Paris' latest fallen angel by the quarter hour, unaware that across the room, the German gentleman whose eyes had met hers and with whom she was still so desperately in love was wanting her, vividly recalling the feel of her satiny skin on his and suddenly fiercely jealous of the handsome, tall French count who would be spending the night wrapped in her unforgettable arms.

That night, after seeing Marienne at Paillard's, the dream of Helen returned. Again, Napoleon's hand was in his vest, but this time when Helen asked what he held there, Napoleon announced that he clutched at his heart because Menelaus was in mourning for his mother. Huge tears glistened in Helen's eyes as Napoleon described Menelaus' return to his kingdom of Sparta and the rage he felt to discover that Helen had been kidnapped by the royal houseguest, Paris, Prince of Troy. Palace servants eager to incriminate Helen quickly told of the ardor that had flamed between the two, an ardor that had burned they said, from the moment of Menelaus' departure.

One handmaiden described long nights of passion on Helen's silver couch, another how Helen had taken her golden jewels and fled the palace with Paris under cover of night and in such great haste that she had not stopped to bid farewell to her child. The voice of Helen that for years had rustled in the music of Heinrich's dreams was silent now, unlike that of red-haired Menelaus who roared and thundered through his palace vowing war and revenge, the massive Greek chest fired with jealousy, the warrior heart deeply wounded and overflowing with betrayal, the memory of an ancient coalition restored, its urgent message unleashed through his every fiber.

"Yes, the coalition. Now!" he bellowed, "but first to Tyndareus, Helen's father. Renew the old alliance. Restore the honor of the coalition. Yes, hadn't Helen enjoyed the attention of her many suitors in her father's court? And as each was rejected hadn't Tyndareus extracted a promise, a pledge of honor that the departing suitor would defend Helen in the face of any future crisis, ensuring his daughter a lifetime of protection regardless of the choice made in her husband? The former suitors were now chieftains and kings in their own powerful domains. They must be reminded of their pledge. Agamemmnon himself had once sought Helen's hand but Tyndareus had given her to his brother, Menelaus of Sparta, saving his second daughter, Clytemnestra, for Agamemmnon, king of golden Mycenae."

"A brilliant coalition!" Napoleon conceded, the crystal knot of dreams filled with claret held high in one hand. "Perhaps the most brilliant in history! Ajax of Salmis. Odysseus of Ithaca. Idomeneus of Crete. Agapenor of Arcadia. Tlepolemus of Rhodes. Nireus from Syme. Ascalaphus of Orchomenos. A thousand ships!"

Napoleon drained the crystal knot of claret and smiled.

"Menelaus, call upon your brother, Agamemmnon!" he commanded, his lips huge and brightly aflame. "Send couriers, runners, emissaries! Inform him of the Trojan prince's betrayal and remind him of the coalition created for the sake of Helen. Tell him that at this moment Helen stands naked at her initiation into the cult of the goddess before the Palladion in Troy's Temple to Athena, her eyes unblinking and locked upon the graven image carved in the likeness of the goddess. She swears to secrecy before the priestess of the Liba Reguli and dedicates herself to the patron goddess of

Troy, Athena, goddess of wisdom and war, the owl her bird, the olive her tree! Tell Agamemmnon that in Helen's hand she holds the silver cask and that out of it rises the sweet song of the golden-beaked bird."

When he awoke in the gray dawn the linen sheets were twisted around him in a mass of wrinkles wet with perspiration. There were scratches on both forearms, his body felt sore and bruised, and later that day he found there was to be no further comfort in a familiar dream.

As if designed to deliberately torment him, small fragments of faces appeared to him in waking hours, lips, eyes, hands spinning out, one pressing at the other in a puzzling circle. Helen's sudden irrational presence could be so powerfully felt that he searched a room for her, certain that her delicate fragrance had at that very moment drifted past him, convinced he had just glimpsed a streak of rose chiffon in the shadows. At other times he awoke in the night, his breathing heavy, his chest heaving. The message. So close. He saw his own hand reaching out for it. And later, as he made every attempt to return to sleep he succeeded only in tossing and turning for hours as Napoleon smiled smugly before him, hollow knot in hand, a general pleased with himself and his persistent victory over the man who attempted to breathe life into a hopeless dream.

# CHAPTER FOUR

## Cake Walk

REQUIREMENTS FOR DIGGING into the hill of Hissarlik prompted a frenzy of activity. Letters were sent off to Henry Rawlinson in England, the British Army officer and experienced archaeologist who had recently deciphered a lengthy inscription discovered in Persia and attributed to Darius I.

Correspondence was renewed with J. J. Worsaae, curator of the Danish National Museum and the world expert in stratigraphic succession, or, as Heinrich came to call him, the Cake Man, Worsaae's stratigraphic succession theory based on the appearance of successive layers of material that accumulate in places man has occupied over time, his conclusions ultimately comparing the overall appearance of a prehistoric archaeological site to a layer cake in which the top layer is the most recent and the lower layers progressively older.

Unlike a modern bakery-style cake, however, Worsaae's theory allowed for some layers to vary greatly in their irregularity of depth and lack of clarity and uniformity, creating a very lopsided layer at some depths, most of the layers undulating unpredictably at every level, some having drifted down into completely unrelated lower layers. With this principle in mind, Heinrich approached the prospect of an excavation at Hissarlik knowing that whatever he might find closest to the earth's surface was datable to the most recent times. In return letters, Worsaae enthusiastically encouraged his study of archaeology in any way possible, emphasizing that experience on the site would ultimately be his best teacher and that in Athens he consider visiting the newly appointed curator of the Acropolis Museum, a young Greek scholar named Giannis Kolodji who was conducting studies and restorations on the site of the ancient Greek Acropolis.

Heinrich liked the idea of meeting Kolodji. He saw wide discrepancies within the infant science of archaeology, not only in theory but in method and practice, all exemplified by the convincing information that had taken him to Bunarbaschi. Although there had been no actual excavation or serious site study, and in spite of the fact that not a scrap of hard evidence had ever been found at Bunarbaschi to substantiate it as the site of ancient Troy, the most prominent world historians had concluded that there were enough geographic compatibilities with Homeric descriptions and with a number of related Greek legends to confirm the likelihood of this location in Asia Minor as the site of an ancient city such as Troy. Adding considerably to the weight of this academic argument were the writings of early Greek and Roman historians who had recorded the pilgrimages of Alexander the Great and Julius Caesar to Bunarbaschi where they had ceremoniously honored the heroic memories of Achilles, Ajax, and Hector, believed to have fallen there.

By assembling similarly fragmented pieces of loosely related information, history scholars traditionally remained secluded in their libraries, comfortable in vague anthropological studies and largely unscientific theories and rarely visiting a site for actual verification. Realizing this from the start of his earliest inquiries, Heinrich felt himself on equal footing and as confident in assessing the potential of the hill of Hissarlik as were the scholastic experts who argued in favor of Bunarbaschi, this attitude quickly serving to establish an unswerving mindset entirely compatible with his personal philosophy that under the proper circumstances, anything was possible. The prevailing skepticism among other academicians on the mere feasibility of a Trojan War was, however, another matter entirely, and one whose proof he knew would require the most carefully assembled body of indisputable evidence. But how was this to be accomplished?

He knew nothing about archaeology. More and more he liked Worsaae's suggestion that he visit Athens. According to Worsaae, Kolodji, the Acropolis curator, was knowledgeable and eager to involve qualified scholars in his studies on the Athens Acropolis. At the very least, discussions with the Curator of the Acropolis Museum would be helpful, informative, and to be in Athens was to be in the cradle of Greece's glorious long history, closer to the language of its poet, in the home of The Iliad. He booked passage to the Greek port of Piraeus for early June.

And it was to The Iliad that at this time he repeatedly turned his most passionate attentions, his vigorous interpretation of Homer's language breathing life into the crystal-clear picture of the citadel of Troy as he saw it and was certain it had once been. The Iliad's clearly named Trojan landmarks had, more than any other known factor, led him to believe that at Hissarlik he had indeed breathed the air of ancient Troy. Homer had named all the islands he had seen from the hilltop, every one. He had also named the River Scamander and the Sea of Marmara, and he had described Mount Ida in precise detail. Each landmark lay in exactly the direction Homer had described it, and now with time to dwell upon the suitability of Hissarlik as the site of Troy and to study maps of the region, Heinrich also realized that the straits he had seen connecting the Aegean Sea with the Sea of Marmara, called the Dardanelles, were the ancient Hellespont, the forty-mile long waterway through which the Greeks had come in the final stage of their voyage across the Aegean Sea to Troy. His maps showed a significant port city at that very point. It was Canakaale and it was in the exact region of Hissarlik, on the northwest coast of Asia Minor.

❧ ❧ ❧

Heinrich Schliemann had found Homer to be his greatest teacher and from him he had learned many things, most significantly, what to look for. The prehistoric poet of ancient Greece had taught him that the megeron was the central room in Priam's terraced palace, a ceremonial room where visitors and ambassadorial representatives were received; that stairways led to upper rooms and down to a lower chamber fragrant with cedar, where the royal robes embroidered by the women of Sidonia were stored, robes of glittering brocade that Paris himself had brought to Troy with Helen. He knew that Paris had lived in a beautiful, much admired house, built by the master-builders of Troy and located near his father Priam's own house and that of his brother Hector. Its walls enclosed a bedchamber, a hall, and a court, where each day Helen sat with her servants, directing needlework and weaving, in keeping with her sworn dedication to the goddess Athena. Prominent upon the acropolis of Troy and near to the great Tower, was Athena's temple, the shrine where Priam's queen, Hecabe, had taken her finest Sidonian robe to the knee of Athena and where prayers were led by the high priestess, Theano, in supplication to the patron goddess of Troy. He knew that Hector had walked the byways and walled lanes all though the town, meeting his wife, the lovely Andromache at the Scaean Gates. He knew that a well-known wild fig tree had served as the lookout point near the curving wagon road leading to the double springs that gushed fountains of hot and cold water into the wide pools where the Trojan women had laundered their linen in the days before the Greeks had come "to fill the plain with troops and flashing bronze on men and chariots as the whole earth reverberated underfoot."

He knew that Homer had lived in a world of beautiful things; silver and gold, bronze, blue enamel, and finely woven baskets. He had known vineyards and harvest and pastures in valleys wide with silvery sheep and huts and sheepfolds. He had heard the playing of flutes and harps, the barking of hunting dogs, the tumbling of acrobats, and the music of dancing across a splendid floor like that at royal Knossos made for the Princess Ariadne, young men and the most desired young girls linked, touching each other's wrists, the girls in soft linen gowns, the men in knitted khitons "given a gloss with oil," their golden-hilted daggers hung on silver lanyards. Trained and adept, they circled with ease, the way a potter sitting at his wheel will give it a practice twirl between his palms to see it run. "Magical dancing," Homer had called it, "and all around, the crowd stood spellbound as two tumblers led the beat with spins and hand springs through the company."

For years Heinrich Schliemann had studied The Iliad, dwelling on its lines and lyricism until he had memorized much of the epic, resplendent language, its mysterious allusions gradually revealing more and more of the substance for which he searched, teaching him what he must look for. Most of the leather-bound volumes lining the walls of his Paris study were related to the Trojan War, to Homer's Iliad, or to the history and geography of Greece. Editions of The Iliad and the histories of Pausanius and Thucydides in their original Greek lined the glass-paneled bookcases, their margins filled with myriad notes written in Heinrich's precise hand, and now his desk was littered with maps and the ever-increasing masses of notes he made every day as plans for a significant excavation campaign took shape in his mind and he eagerly awaited arrival of the Turkish Firman, his official permit to begin.

And in those weeks of waiting, Homer's only serious competition was the resonant city of Paris itself, the rhythms and sounds of its spirit essential to the pattern of every day as following one o'clock luncheon he called for his carriage and ventured out into the elegant boundaries of the Bois, a well-dressed, gray-gloved man in a top hat, carrying a silver-pommeled walking stick, stopping first for cafe noir with friends at Santini's and further nurturing his spirits with late afternoon visits to the shops that specialized in the elegant French furniture, carpets, and decorative objects he admired and collected. Magnificent pieces were to be seen, many of them from the splendid, abandoned chateaux of the Loire Valley; chests in richly crafted marquetry, salon suites of silk-upholstered chairs and settees, many bearing the stamps of Pluvinet, Levasseur, and Bauve. Occasionally, there were formal, day-long sales at the Hôtel Drouôt and auctions of superb pieces of furniture and clocks, garniture sets, porcelains, paintings, and garden pieces. Years before, he had purchased several important items at one of the Faugeron sales, among his prizes a fine commode-a-vantaux from Fountainbleau, its companion at the Louvre, and his desk, the massive Empire piece in fine walnut and intricate marquetry that for a time, Marienne had covered with red floor-length damask and used for painting.

The Place Vendôme, lined with grand eighteenth-century mansions, was a favorite stop, and on the first floor at Number 12, Chaumet, the jewelry establishment well known to affluent Parisians, had been in operation since the time of Napoleon. Heinrich Schliemann was one of Chaumet's many clients who over the years had purchased beautifully designed jewelry for a wife and an assortment of lovers. Marienne's superb diamonds had come from Chaumet, as had the thin gold band encircled with emerald ribbons she had frequently worn around her graceful neck and still owned. The founder of Chaumet, Etienne Nitot, had been court jeweler to the Emperor Napoleon, and it was Nitot who had designed the golden bee which became Napoleon's most recognized symbol. Searching out a replacement for the Bourbon Lily, Nitot had chanced upon the story of Childeric I, King of the Franks in the Fourth Century, B.C., whose tomb had been opened during the reign of Louis XIV. The body remains were found wrapped in fine cloth sewn entirely with small golden bees, representing Childeric's hard work and tireless attention to national order. So impressed was Napoleon with Childeric's symbol, that he immediately adapted it as his own, seizing upon its definition as one appropriate to the intended goals of his empire and creating unforeseen opportunity for Nitot who soon became famous for his Napoleonic bees usually sold in pairs and with or without diamonds, rubies, emeralds, sapphires, or pearls. Nitot had wisely enlarged upon related botanical themes, and in his lifetime the establishment of Chaumet also became famous for magnificent suites of brooches, necklaces, and bracelets formed of intertwining jeweled leaves, branches, and flowers.

Some of Chaumet's decorative objects carried these themes as well and Heinrich was among a discriminating group of Parisians who began treasured collections of assorted porcelain and gold boxes, or "tabatieres," painted in finely executed scenes of birds and vines, the most popular the enameled musical snuff boxes whose mechanisms were based upon those for small winding clocks, the rarest of all, the glistening silver boxes such as the one that lay in a bottom drawer of the massive desk in the study of the pale gray limestone house on Rue Victoire still wrapped in Chaumet's famous bee-strewn paper, a mere glance in its direction capable of stirring uncertain fragments of underscored memory and the whispered promise of a gift finer than flowers.

# CHAPTER FIVE

## Hellenic Dances

### *JUNE 1869*
### *ATHENS*

IN 1834 THE Greek War of Independence had created a new Kingdom of Greece. Athens was its capital and by 1869 was a city of seventy thousand inhabitants who could boast of a university and a respected government square, its new administrative buildings and royal palace a source of national pride where around the clock, corps of white-kilted Evzones stood guard in colorfully embroidered vests, red-tasseled caps, and red slippers.

Heinrich walked along Syntagma Square, returning to his rooms at the new Adelphi Hotel after meeting on the Acropolis with Giannis Kolodji as Dr. Worsaae had recommended, struck by the immense size of the hotel where he had registered the night before. The Adelphi occupied the entire south side of the square and many Athenians remained adamantly opposed to its prominent location, built as it was, directly across from the king's palace. With the Greek Parliament buildings bordering both its sides, Syntagma Square had become the busiest municipal area in Athens, giving rise to the prevailing opinion that a new public hotel like the Adelphi had been built in a highly inappropriate place, detracting from the square's more serious purposes. But, at its completion no one could criticize the Adelphi's architectural integrity, nor the handsome manner in which it had, more than any other building, enclosed the square with its distinctively Greek Doric columns and its impressive large friezes depicting mythical figures, recessed above windows and doors.

Though few of its more vocal critics had not realized it at first, the Adelphi Hotel had been built on one of the more significant pieces of land in all Athens and as Heinrich Schliemann now knew, it was not the columned formal view projecting so conspicuously onto busy Syntagma Square that was currently attracting attention. The most significant ruins of historic Greece, the ancient Acropolis itself, soared high above the city and the glorious pale columns of its Parthenon seemed only a stone's throw from the Adelphi's rear balconies and open terraces. It was a spectacular sight. From Heinrich's balcony the finest Doric temple in the world, the great hymn to Athena, floated high above the sun-bathed plain of Athens, soaring 270 meters into the sky.

Through nameless centuries the Acropolis had endured, steeply inclined, inaccessible from all directions but the west and conveniently blessed by a persistent stream gushing from the northwest into the Klepsydra Spring. In the Fifth Century, B.C. it had become a citadel representative of the democratic vision of Pericles, reconstructed according to his ideals for the new Athens he planned as a city of magnificent buildings and temples, theaters and halls, the Acropolis its unrivaled centerpiece, and under the direction of Phydias, it began. First to be built was a new temple to Athena Parthenos. The Propyleia and the temple of Athena Nike followed, and finally the Erechtheum was built, the temple to Athena Polias which would house the wooden image of the goddess, the "Xoanon," rescued by the Athenians in the last moments of their escape from the invading Persians.

The morning meeting with Giannis Kolodji had not gone well. Heinrich had learned absolutely nothing from Kolodji and hadn't liked him much. There had been no informative discussion concerning even the simplest of excavation procedures and try as he might to skillfully steer the conversation in that direction, Kolodji had displayed little interest in his project, pressing him for no specific details. As a result, there had been only the briefest, most frustrating opportunity in which to explain his intention to excavate at what he described only as a site of antiquity. Clearly, Kolodji was full of himself, overly impressed with having been appointed the first curator of the Acropolis Museum and entirely too self-promoting at this stage of things to be taken seriously, Heinrich concluded as he approached the Adelphi's broad steps. He assumed his stature to be equal with that of the great Worsaae!

Giannis Kolodji was in his late twenties and succeeded in appearing considerably older. He was ponderous-looking, soft-fleshed, and overweight. Cordial enough in his introduction, he had shared with his visitor a high professional regard for Doctor Worsaae whom he had never met, choosing to extend his welcome to Athens with a protective air of distant superiority. Initially, Heinrich Schliemann's ease in the Greek language had completely disarmed him and within a short time the added lure of his sophisticated charm had a positively unsettling effect on the unsophisticated curator whose own lack of charm did not blind him to its existence in other men.

In the company of Schliemann, though, whose well-developed talents for self-expression and gracious social behavior had successfully eluded him, Kolodji was uncomfortable and miserably aware of his dismal shortcomings. Wanting very much to impress his visitor, however, he had led him through a thorough tour of the Acropolis, authoritatively knowledgeable and deeply committed to the completion of the museum which he said would take years. Motivated by his own compelling interest in the Greek world, Heinrich had come to Athens on a number of past occasions and had visited the Acropolis, but to walk the celebrated ruins in the company of Giannis Kolodji was to see it all in a very different light. Kolodji could not put aside his resentment toward the Turks who had occupied his country until the War of Independence. He hated their ambitious appetites and he hated the permissive access they had allowed powerful people such as Lord Elgin, who as British Ambassador to the Ottoman Empire, had removed the finest pieces of Acropolis sculpture and the entire Parthenon Frieze depicting the struggle of the mythic Greek centaurs. The marbles quickly became famous and formed the spectacular collection sold to the British Museum in 1816 with the express stipulation that they be forever known as the Elgin Marbles.

"These are the most beautiful buildings in all the world, the most beautiful buildings conceived by man, and the Turks cared nothing for their history, their endurance, nor their meaning," Kolodji had said. "Barbarians! Ignorant vandals! They destroyed great artworks here, glorious creations in marble and stone, and they erected a monument to their brutality in that tall stone tower they built from which to observe the activity of the inhabitants in the city below."

"Why has the tower not been removed?" Heinrich asked.

"Everything costs money here. No one can afford to pay workmen for its removal, but I won't rest until it comes down. I'll find a way."

Kolodji had reminded him that the old Temple of Athena Nike had been destroyed by the occupying Turks and that they had built a mosque in its ruins. He also described in great detail the harem of the Turkish governor which had been housed in the Erechtheum complete with its famous porch of the Caryatides. In the course of his first visit with Giannis Kolodji, while Heinrich had learned precious little about excavating an ancient city, he had learned all he needed to know about Greek hatred of the Turks. He also learned about the legend of the Xoanon, the graven image of Athena known to have existed in Athens in exactly the same manner as had the fabled Palladion, the powerful symbol of war said to have been stolen from Athena's temple at Troy by the warring Greeks who believed its possession crucial to their victory.

He arrived back at the Adelphi at two o'clock, still engrossed in sorting out his mixed impressions of Kolodji and as he approached the Adelphi's polished oak door, Metrios, the well-mannered doorman, greeted him by name. Heinrich nodded to Metrios and decided he would take time for a few newspapers and a leisurely lunch in the hotel dining room before meeting Kolodji again later in the afternoon, for in a surprisingly gracious gesture highly unusual for him, Kolodji had invited Heinrich Schliemann to join his family for a sample of local hospitality.

They met promptly at four and together they walked the short distance from the Adelphi toward a narrow street of houses facing the northwest side of the Acropolis.

"Do you ever get used to these views?" Heinrich asked as they strode side by side, admiring the breathtaking sight of the Parthenon's columns against the flattering blue sky.

"No, not really," Giannis answered. "It's a wonderful thing, of course, to have those impossibly beautiful ruins in your everyday world, but to work among them in some meaningful way is the real privilege. I'm hoping I can begin to excavate soon and find some important pieces of lost marble, not only damaged fragments but whole works of ancient art that were an original part of the Acropolis, statues or friezes that could be buried under there. It would be so good for this city, for this country, to begin re-establishing its national pride and re-define its true heritage. There is simply no other place like this in the world, not with this magnificent rich history or influence."

Kolodji was more relaxed than he'd been earlier that morning Heinrich observed, more engaging and likeable. Perhaps he'd judged him too soon.

"Do you live here, on this street?" he asked.

"No," Kolodji said, "but my in-laws do. Their house is that one with the gate. I thought you'd enjoy meeting them and since my wife Niki spends almost every afternoon here it seemed a good idea. The Kastromenou family loves company."

The black iron gate looked freshly painted. It opened easily onto a gravel path which in a few feet had divided in two. In one direction the path was straight and led to the door of a white stucco house. In the other direction the path curved to the side where a high stuccoed wall extended beyond thick trees and a tall hedge. Through an arched opening in the wall he could see a few pots of flowers on the ground near a table. A cat sat beside one of the pots licking its paws.

"They're always out here," Giannis said as they approached the arch and walked through. "Sometimes I wonder why they need a house at all."

They had stepped into a cool, shaded garden protected from its closest neighbors by vinecovered walls and silver-leafed olive trees grouped here and there. A large plane tree stood at the center and under the shade of its generous branches three people sat at a rectangular wooden table on an assortment of mismatched chairs.

"This is the Kastromenou family," Giannis said as he and Heinrich approached. "Mamma Victoria, Papa, Niki, this is my guest, Heinrich Schliemann. He has come to visit Athens from Paris."

Papa Kastromenou rose to shake hands. The two women smiled. The older one brushed a few crumbs from the table while the younger one who Heinrich assumed to be Giannis' wife, Niki, had eyes for no one but her husband. She gazed at him with open affection and hung on his every word.

"Sit here," Giannis said, pointing to one of the chairs in the mottled shade.

"Have a glass of retsina," Mamma Victoria offered warmly. "And one of these honey cakes. Everybody likes them. What brings you to Athens?"

It was exactly the sort of obliging outdoor setting Greek families were known to love for the enjoyment of meals and visits with one another and he felt he had stepped into a secret world. That world was a garden and a terrace, but it was also a dining room, a waiting room, and an office, and nowhere could the dynamics of the Kastromenou family have been more closely observed than in that conducive space. Papa Georges Kastromenou always occupied the chair at the narrow end of the table against the thickest girth of the tree trunk. From this vantage point he could survey the length and breadth of his modest domicile without interruption, the sense of well-being it provided him an ongoing source of pleasure, the strength of family and loyalty to its members firmly re-defined in his eyes each time he watched a member of the household coming to take his or her seat nearby, drawn by some unexplained power of tradition to tree-shaded seating assignments no one could ever recall having been given.

They made polite conversation as Georges poured the resinated Greek wine which Heinrich had successfully managed to avoid during each of his previous visits to Greece but which had now assaulted his refined French palate with a searing shock of pine-flavored severity. Mamma Victoria immediately found that she enjoyed her visitor's complete ease with the Greek language and in a short time was rather taken with the interesting man who had come to Athens to consult her son-in-law on antiquities. He was attentive and asked simple questions about the things that interested her most: her children, their activities and educations. In turn, she had questions for him about Paris: the cafes and parks, the shops and boulevards she'd heard about but had never seen.

Mamma Victoria was a short, solidly built woman whose strong facial features gave her a determined, somewhat hardened look, but there was an admirable confidence about her whenever she spoke, and an aura of intelligence, a quality that Heinrich found appealing in the most unattractive women. She had just passed the tray of delicious honey cakes for which she was duly famous a second time when small, quick steps could be heard on the gravel path leading to the garden from the back door of the house.

A tall, slim girl with long dark hair hurried toward the table, her shoulders set into the resignation of one whose far more interesting activity had been interrupted by the social requirements of respectful family life and the hospitality being offered an afternoon visitor. She was young and strikingly beautiful. Her gleaming, long, black hair captivated Heinrich's immediate attention, but this was not unusual, for this was Sophia, vibrant and smiling, her dark, magnificent hair always the first thing people noticed about her. She smiled politely to Heinrich when introduced and sat in the chair closest to her father.

"I saw all of you from the parlor window," she said. "And before the last of Mamma's douloumas disappeared I thought I would come to enjoy one or two of them with you myself."

She smiled again as she helped herself to one of the pastries on the tray and bit into it, poised, self-assured and incredibly lovely in the shaded familiarity of the garden and the family she loved.

"Your mother tells me you have recently completed your studies at The Athenaeum," Heinrich said to her in flawless Greek. "You must be the daughter who wants to become a teacher."

"Yes," she responded quickly. "I graduated just last week. And with highest honors. Did Mamma also tell you I won the history prize? Where did you learn Greek?"

"Wherever I could," he laughed. "I'm really self-taught," he said, "but I love languages. My business requires me to speak and write in several."

"You use a lot of Vlachiki but your Greek vocabulary is good," she said as she sat back in her chair and with a quick sweep of her fingers indelicately brushed away a few crumbs from the corners of her mouth. "This can't be your first time in Greece."

She was an odd combination of amused self-confidence and startling elegance as she judged a stranger's fluency in Greek while she chewed and swallowed and thoroughly indulged her taste for the sliced pastries she devoured with great pleasure, but he was not at all offended. In fact, her startling poise and earthy lack of pretense had stirred an impatient strange desire to hold her attention and impress her further.

"No, this isn't my first time in Greece at all," he replied. "I was here a few years ago, in Ithaca. I saw the ancient palace ruins there and was so taken with them that I thought I'd try to buy the land and dig for traces of Odysseus."

"Oh, are you one of those who thinks all that ancient rubbish to be true? It's all mere myth you know, appealing as can be to the average imagination, but there is no proof," she interrupted. "That's what my paper was about. I argued against myth in favor of historic truth and cited the absence of factual evidence from examples of well-known Greek literature. I used the Helen of Troy legend as a good example, mainly because it's the most famous and there's so much marvelously fabricated material there which has just gotten better over time, but of course Professor Linus Ignatius Kadmus says that's the true power of myth, the way it settles down comfortably into our everyday thinking and over time becomes the truth as we know it. With that in mind it was quite simple really, for me to argue convincingly against Helen's impossible existence as part goddess, part human, and of course I had a wonderful time with that ridiculous tale of her birth out of the swan's egg. Her mother must have had a lot of explaining to do, don't you think?"

Victoria poured more retsina into Heinrich's glass, well aware that he had been unable to take his eyes away from Sophia and the gleam of her ebony black hair shining brilliantly even in the filtered silver shade of afternoon as like a fascinating raconteur she had taken full control of a few precious moments and allowed glimpses into the highly spirited corners of her quick, young mind which in spite of its strength and swiftness and unmistakable parallels with inherent factors, had of late become something of a hopeless mystery to the entire family.

ჽ ჽ ჽ

For as long as anyone could remember, Victoria Kastromenou had functioned conspicuously in her role as supreme matriarch. She claimed to be an expert in all things and her family believed her. Through twenty-two years of marriage she had managed her varied and entirely self-appointed positions as doctor, employment advisor, social director, and best cook in Athens with flair and little encouragement and although her powers may have seemed formidable to those around her, she never forgot for a moment that it was her husband, Georges, who provided the financial climate in which they could be exercised. Although the nature of his professional career in the drapery and upholstery business had never quite lived up to Victoria's expectations, the income from his endeavors did, and much to her relief provided a standard of living somewhat above that of her Athens neighbors. Victoria's ancestors were from Crete, a background of which she was immensely proud, Crete's legendary reputation as mythic birthplace of Europa, daughter of King Minos and namesake of all Europe providing all the emotional ammunition necessary to maintain and occasionally reinforce her superiority among the community of Greek matrons who lived on both sides of Andromous Street.

She loved the ceremony and mystery of upper class life and although she had little acquaintance with its function she identified more strongly with its manners and habits than she did with the realities of even the closest personal relationships in her own modest life. Queen Olga was revered, the royal palace on Syntagma Square a shrine, the regal life lived within its walls one about which she fantasized by the hour. In her own way she loved her husband, but in many ways Georges Kastromenou had disappointed her and although he had fathered her two daughters, as far as Victoria was concerned his major function within the family was to provide and if asked, to approve, both of which he did with abundant grace and few words.

A well-organized if somewhat dull man, Georges had started out in life as a young laborer in the marble quarries near Corinth and after a few years had saved enough money to buy a small shop in Athens where he could sell the handmade infant clothes and intricately embroidered skirts and blouses his two sisters made. In time, he had discovered a talent for textiles as well as a flair for selling domestic goods, ultimately finding he could make a good living in the manufacture of draperies and curtains as he provided good advice to his customers and a virtual lifetime of employment to a long list of Kastromenou relatives.

In all matters but those of a practical nature Georges was head of his family. He was loved by his children, accorded respect and held in high esteem by his wife, and although not wealthy, was thought of as prosperous and good-natured by his relatives and neighbors. It was Victoria, however, who made the meaningful, life-altering decisions of every day and it was she to whom Georges turned over his weekly earnings. Georges kept money for the taverna, the cock fights, and other small personal expenses but after that it was up to Victoria to handle the family income, which she did with a talent for saving as well as spending. Of the two it was Victoria whose limitless physical and intellectual energy motivated all those around her. She ran the household, the lives of her children, her husband, and much of the neighborhood with formidable decisiveness, and although all with whom she came into contact conformed to her demands with little or no resistance, most were intimidated by her. With enormous effort, Georges had managed for years to successfully conceal his own submissive nature and tendency toward deference from the children, but whatever effect Victoria's confrontational approach to life may have had on his own conciliatory nature, his gentlemanly air of infallible dignity was, like his friendly, ready smile, unfailing.

Victoria invited Heinrich to return the next day. She would, in his honor, bake special pastries. They would, without a doubt, be the best he had ever tasted. She would expect him at four o'clock. He thanked her and immediately agreed to both the appointment and the hour.

Early the next morning Victoria awakened early, baked, and carefully washed her best wine glasses before leaving the house for daily prayers at the Greek Orthodox Church of Saint Demetrios. Allowing herself the ten minutes it took to walk toward the dome of the neighborhood church easily seen above the red tile roofs on the sloping hillside, she opened the black iron gate facing Andromous Street and with a faint smile on her face breathed deeply of the morning air, fully convinced that what she was about to do took the kind of unwavering courage only she possessed. As the last benedictions echoed through the cavernous church and quiet settled over the icons and sculpted statues she hurried to find Father Spiro Tassos, a long-time family friend and one of Saint Demetrios' best loved priests. She found him greeting parishioners outside the church door and she waited for him to notice her folded hands as was the long established tradition assigned to those in need of special guidance.

"I am the faithful supplicant of old whose heart has come full circle," she recited in the ancient mode as he approached.

"Bless you, faithful child of God," he answered. "What troubles you?"

"I am contrite and unworthy but Father, God himself knows I am also a mother whose love for her children knows no boundaries," she added, looking deeply into his eyes.

"Father, help me to arrange a marriage. I have prayed for a suitable husband for my brilliant Sophia and my prayers have been answered. Like a miracle of the heavenly saints a fine gentleman has come from Paris directly to my house. What mother has not prayed for such a husband for her daughter? He is perfect for Sophia. Please come to meet him at four o'clock today and begin the procedure."

Spiro Tassos was one of Athens' most popular figures. He wore his black, Greek Orthodox cassock draped over his slim body with no particular distinction, but he was conscientious and inquisitive and over the years his devoted parishioners had come to expect his often uninvited intervention into the most inauspicious aspects of their lives. Nothing surprised him. Everything was of interest. He knew the city of Athens well and wandered its winding paths and alleys at will, his secular freedom and irrepressible curiosity not entirely free of frequent criticism. Those who may have expected more conventional behavior from this man of the cloth were often disappointed, but those in Athens who knew Spiro Tassos best and were most often in the engaging company of the peripatetic priest who wore his long hair pulled back and tied with a thin black cord rather than hidden under the traditional ecclesiastical headpiece were well aware that life in the priesthood had given a Greek child born to poverty the treasured opportunity to expand a brilliant mind and satisfy a natural inquisitiveness sacrificed throughout childhood to the daily struggle for scant survival. Now, in his early thirties, study had become a way of life and encouraged by his superiors, in addition to his clerical duties at the Church of Saint Demetrios, he also taught classes in Greek history and philosophy at the University of Athens. It was the calling to which he had truly been born. Teaching came easily to him and in a fresh climate of newfound national consciousness it was a talent for which he was being recognized by a community eager to define its leaders. Combined with a uniquely approachable and non judgmental manner which generated great trust among his parishioners, Father Tassos encouraged a very new sort of quiet confidentiality, one that enabled many to seek his advice and sympathetic counsel without fear of reprisal except from God himself and Victoria Kastromenou fit handily into this group who regarded him more as friend than pastor.

An arranged marriage was a widely accepted and highly respected tradition within the Greek community. Twenty-two years before, Victoria's parents had arranged her marriage to Georges and now she and Georges continued the custom with their daughters. Niki was the oldest and at nineteen, her marriage to Giannis Kolodji had been successfully negotiated by Father Tassos. Victoria intended now to proceed in a similar manner in arranging Sophia's marriage and she had targeted Heinrich Schliemann from the first moment of their meeting. Sophia was seventeen. She had graduated from a girls' finishing school. She wanted to pursue her studies and establish a career in teaching, but first and foremost she needed to marry properly.

"And what is the gentleman's name?" asked Father Tassos.

"He is Heinrich Schliemann, a fine German gentleman from Paris," Victoria answered proudly.

"Did you say Heinrich Schliemann?" Spiro Tassos asked, his tone one of astonishment.

"Yes, Victoria answered. "Heinrich Schliemann."

Spiro Tassos could hardly believe what he had heard. He questioned Victoria only to find that her hasty sketch of Heinrich Schliemann fit perfectly into what he vividly remembered about a

German gentleman he had met while studying in Paris who had a great talent for languages and an insatiable appetite for Greek studies. When Victoria told Father Tassos that Heinrich was at the Adelphi Hotel, he wasted little time in getting there.

"Shall I expect you later this afternoon?" Victoria asked.

"Yes, of course," Spiro Tassos called over his shoulder with a broad smile. "Herr Schliemann and I will arrive together."

The Adelphi would be a new experience for Father Tassos and he smiled to himself, wondering which of his parishioners he would see at the new hotel. He knew that some were employed by the British management, but walking along the square later that morning he had his first close look at Athens' latest architectural attraction. From the outside, the building was every bit as impressive as people said. He paused to admire the magnificent oak doors beside which the doorman stood, the uniformed Metrios one of Father Tassos' parishioners, and much to the priest's delight, respectably employed.

"Metrios, my son, you look like a great statesman!"

"Father," said Metrios, nodding respectfully to him as he removed his plumed hat and Spiro Tassos smiled as his young parishioner led him into the Adelphi's marble vestibule.

In the wood-paneled lobby, a few guests sat reading newspapers, their chairs attractively arranged on the thick, flowered carpet. Hotel attendants carried luggage to and from the wide doors where Metrios directed its placement in and out of carriages as Father Tassos approached the dark, gleaming desk prominently centered in the lobby and the formally attired desk clerk efficiently asked, "May I assist you Father?"

"Yes, thank you. I am Father Spiro Tassos and I would like to see Herr Heinrich Schliemann. I understand he is a guest here."

The clerk scanned the imposing leather bound register lying open on the desk. "Yes, Father Tassos," he said, "Herr Schliemann arrived two days ago. Shall I send a message to him?"

"No, I would like to see him right now if you will be so kind as to direct me to his room."

"Father, it is not our policy to allow unannounced visitors into our guestrooms. Please wait for just a moment and I shall be happy to send an usher to Herr Schliemann informing him of your request to see him."

"Yes, summon the usher," agreed Father Tassos, as with three sharp clicks of the desk clerk's gold ring upon the edge of the desk, the usher was summoned.

The usher, found to be yet another of Father Tassos' parishioners who also respectfully acknowledged the peripatetic shepherd, was not at all taken aback when he was followed to Heinrich Schliemann's rooms, Father Tassos close at his heels, having flatly refused to wait in the lobby as the desk clerk had insisted.

Through a small foyer and under the brass numbers "23" the usher knocked at one of a pair of double doors. With a newspaper under one arm, Heinrich opened the door and in an instant flash of recognition he welcomed his unexpected visitor with a broad, delighted smile.

"Spiro Tassos! How did you know I was in Athens? And here at the Adelphi? Come in! How are you?"

"Word travels quickly in Athens," Spiro said, his own smile restoring the sincerity and warmth of an esteemed friendship. "One of my parishioners met you yesterday, Giannis Kolodji's mother-in-law. We talked at Saint Demetrios this morning. I couldn't wait to see you! Heinrich, you look more prosperous than ever."

It had been ten years since they had last seen each other and but for his thinning hair, Heinrich Schliemann looked exactly as the Athens priest remembered him, the lean frame, the sharp brown eyes, the well-trimmed mustache, the imperious, almost defiant air, all of it just as he remembered.

Heinrich gestured him inside.

They had met at the Sorbonne in Paris. Already ordained, the young priest had been sent to France with a full scholarship for a year of advanced study in history and philosophy at the University of Paris and in exchange for housing expenses, he taught classes in Greek. Heinrich Schliemann was his star pupil and had impressed him from the very first day with his unusual facility in the Greek language and his burning desire to converse in it as often as possible. They had become fast friends and Spiro Tassos was one of the few people with whom Heinrich had shared his unique approach to learning languages without benefit of a teacher. First, he said, he listened to as many people as possible who spoke in whatever tongue he wished to cultivate. He then spent time studying textbook vocabulary. Following that, and without knowing what he was saying at all, he recited in a loud tirade what he thought to be the correct sound and rhythm of what he had heard and studied. This would go on for long periods of time and it often sounded as if he had gotten it absolutely right, when indeed, he was simply making a long combination of appropriate sounds with the drama of expression, his voice rising and falling in exactly the proper places. As he had traveled throughout Europe, he told Spiro Tassos, this technique had allowed him entree into any number of new experiences, the practice of which, however, had not endeared him to innkeepers or hostesses, who quickly discovered that Herr Schliemann talked loudly to himself in his room and often late into the night. Eventually, he had polished his language skills with admirable accuracy, but at the Sorbonne, with Spiro Tassos, Heinrich had, for the first time in his life, refined his language studies in a formal educational setting.

Of course, the urbane Heinrich Schliemann had been a rather unusual companion for a young Greek priest in Paris, Schliemann not at all a young student himself, but an established businessman, successful, worldly, and very serious. On several occasions Heinrich had invited Spiro to luncheon at his Rue Victoire home. He had accompanied him to the Louvre, to Sacre Coeur, Les Invalides, and to the Paris theater, hard-pressed to find an appropriate play that did not deal, as so many of the popular French farces did, with the eternal triangle, lovers without trousers, assorted husbands, servants, and elderly prelates who found themselves abandoned on less than hallowed ground.

Heinrich led Spiro Tassos into his Adelphi sitting room where they walked past chairs and settees covered in brocaded fabrics of blue and gold and arranged on a patterned carpet of deep cobalt. Tables held vases of fresh flowers and over the fireplace hung a gilded oval mirror. To one side of the room an opening revealed a bed with deep blue coverings. They sat down in the two chairs closest to the tall, glass-paned doors opening onto the balcony and its magnificent view of the Acropolis.

"Quite something up there, isn't it?" remarked Spiro Tassos with unmistakable pride. "I had no idea this view would be so splendid. Heinrich, the next time visitors to Athens tell me how surprised they are to see the Acropolis elevated so very high above the city, I shall recommend your balcony here at the Adelphi for a closer look at Greek history."

It was impossible to escape the visual impact made by the pale soaring ruins, and for many first-time visitors to the Adelphi's enthralling setting, Greece's history was dramatically emphasized in a surprising way. The spectacular view generated a reflective mood in Spiro Tassos.

"And what has happened to your own plans for exploring Greek history, Heinrich? I remember when I was in Paris you were fascinated by anything to do with Troy and the wondrous civilization you pictured there. Have you given up the search, or have your talents for making money taken precedence over adventure?"

"I'm more interested than ever in the search for Troy, Spiro, and I would like nothing better than to be able to spend the rest of my life pursuing that search. As a matter of fact, I'm now officially retired from business and I've taken steps to apply for an excavation permit."

"Excavation permit?" commented the priest with no little surprise. "If you have taken such steps, then surely you have pinpointed a specific location."

Spiro Tassos faced the man who more than any other, led the secular life to which he himself would have aspired under different circumstances. Schliemann had resources, enormous personal style and intelligence, and he was constantly learning, but why was he wasting his powers of concentration on such an unlikely search?

"Heinrich, you amaze me," he said. There may be a handful of people in the entire world who believe that Troy may have existed in some obscure time and place. I would dare to say that even here in the land of Greeks, few people would place a grain of truth in the story of the Trojan war."

"Spiro, the city of Troy did exist, and gloriously so, perhaps more gloriously than your Acropolis up there," Heinrich interrupted. "But, unlike your Acropolis, Troy is not presiding proudly in lofty ruin. It's buried and covered with earth somewhere. But it's there, along with the treasures of its king. I'm sure of it. Spiro, not only have I applied for a permit to excavate, I have studied the site. I have been there and my location conforms to all the landmarks in The Iliad, just as I knew it would. I intend to begin as soon as my permit arrives."

Recalling Schliemann's capacity for serious study, Spiro Tassos now found himself caught up in the contagion of his enthusiasm for a new project. It was not difficult to be swayed by the courage of

Schliemann's convictions once he had formed an opinion, but as the priest assessed his respected old friend's many fine attributes and allowed himself a momentary return to pleasant reminiscences of Paris, Spiro reminded himself that although he continued to admire Heinrich Schliemann, their relationship had changed and now, in Athens, it was the Kastromenou family whose interests he must serve. And justifiably, he concluded, Heinrich's serious preoccupation with irrational illusions of Troy did not suit the solid framework of the arranged marriage he knew Victoria Kastromenou had in mind for her daughter, but deciding to err on the side of caution, he bravely began the process she had requested by telling Heinrich that he was seldom comfortable in arranging marriages, associated as they were, with frequent dilemma and changes of heart. With some degree of wariness, Heinrich eyed him quizzically while listening to the suggestion that was to catch him completely off guard.

"I understand you visited the Kastromenou family yesterday and that you met the youngest daughter, Sophia. Heinrich, there is interest on the part of her parents to arrange a marriage. Victoria Kastromenou feels that you would make a suitable husband for her youngest daughter."

"She feels what?" That I would what? Make a suitable husband for whom? Spiro, now it is you who amaze me! How can you possibly come to me with such a ridiculous suggestion? The girl is a child! She cannot be more than sixteen! Surely you joke with me!"

"Sophia Kastromenou is seventeen. She is young, there is no question of that, but she is highly intelligent and comes from a good family who although not wealthy, are well-respected in the community here and value education. The father runs a successful drapery and upholstery business of his own and as I believe you already know, two years ago the older daughter married Giannis Kolodji, the curator of the Acropolis Museum. He attended the University of Athens and pursues his work with great skill and dedication. You would like the whole family once you got to know them."

"Spiro, I fear you have lost your mind in the years since I last saw you, and should you continue along these lines I shall be absolutely certain of it! I'm not interested in marriage and I am certainly not interested in a child bride. What is happening? There must be something in the air. I have just left a friend in Paris who was also trying to push me into marriage."

"You are invited to the Kastromenou home today, Heinrich, and I know you have accepted. Giannis Kolodji will be there. Victoria told me that you came to Athens expressly to see him. Heinrich, he could be helpful to you if you are truly serious about pursuing this dream of Troy. He knows how to expedite things with the Greek government and as you must know there is a highly charged interest in preserving Greek history for Greeks. I'd give it some thought."

"Spiro, Victoria Kastromenou invited me yesterday, and I could not find a way to decline graciously," Heinrich interrupted, beginning to feel offended. "Yes, I'm sure Giannis will be there, but my instincts tell me to make my excuses right now, this instant. While I wouldn't want to offend Giannis, to be quite frank, Spiro, he didn't seem at all receptive to my project, and I had no real chance to discuss it with him."

"Heinrich, keep the appointment with the family at four. I will come with you. See it through and then say good-bye if you wish. In the meantime, I will speak to Giannis. He has no idea that you and I know each other."

# CHAPTER SIX

## The Inevitability Of Rain

S ITTING AT THE table in the garden, Sophia and her sister Niki were grateful for a moment's peace after a morning spent beating carpets and moving furniture. Victoria had set her household into a frenzy of dusting and sweeping and rearranging of furniture in preparation for Heinrich Schliemann's visit later that day and after clearing the mid-day meal from the table, she had concentrated on the appearance of the garden. Her exhausted daughters marveled at her energy, watching in astonishment as she tirelessly straightened and re-straightened chairs and then removed a stack of empty clay pots awaiting the red geraniums she had intended to plant, but for which she now decided she had no time. Instead, she directed her efforts to tending the border of begonias which would be in Heinrich Schliemann's view, the background against which he would see Sophia once he occupied the seat she planned to assign him and judge under favorable circumstances the profile and the luxuriant hair of the daughter for whom she now confidently envisioned a bright future of wealth and prominence.

It hadn't crossed her mind that Sophia could be dreading the mere thought of Heinrich Schliemann's visit later that afternoon or that the young, contentious spirit was finding it could not reason its way to unconditional compliance and simply yield to parental decree.

"He is your opportunity! Find things about him to like and ignore the rest!" Victoria had adamantly announced as she had confronted a despairing Sophia that morning, in one hand the freshly laundered dress she was to change into later, in the other a hairbrush, the day's behavior code foremost in her mind.

"And remember, he speaks perfect Greek! That's something to like. Smile and look him directly in the eye. And Sophia, try to be a listener today and for once don't talk too much. Remember, this is your opportunity."

All day, Sophia had heard her mother's words spinning out in turbulent, insistent clouds. Opportunity. Concentrate. Listen. "He's such a fine gentleman, Sophia, cultured, refined. You can tell. I know how people are. And he lives in Paris!" By afternoon Sophia was feeling overwhelmed and disconnected from all life as she thought she knew it. All she could think about was the stern face of the man she'd been told she was to marry and as she looked to Niki sitting beside her she wondered exactly how she would possibly manage this loveless opportunity.

"I won't speak to him, that's all. He won't like that. I just won't speak to him." she announced decisively. "Why is Mamma doing this? He's such an old man, older than Papa I think. At least Giannis is your age. I'd rather marry a Greek peasant and live the rest of my life tending sheep in the hills," she said, struggling with tears as she confronted the dismal prospect of marriage to a foreigner, a complete stranger, and a much older man.

"Sophia, Mamma wouldn't force you to marry some dreadful man," Niki said, attempting to relieve her younger sister's anxieties. Herr Schliemann seems very nice, even if he is a little older. I liked his smile. And he's not too stern-looking at all. Some people are just difficult to judge at the beginning. You'll feel very differently about him after his visit today. I'm sure you will."

"Niki, I'm seventeen. He's thirty years older than I am. What do we have in common? Nothing. All Mamma sees is a rich man with a house in Paris. And you needn't try to make him something he isn't. He's a toad. A nice smile does not hide thinning hair and an old man's ways. Did you notice how he sips wine with his lips puckered up like a hundred-year-old prune? Imagine what it must be like to kiss him! You'd pray to die. He's probably a button-fumbler. And a groper, whispering silly love words into your ear while he hovers over your portal of Sweet Esther like a floppy jellyfish. His mushy little pauley must be the size of a grape! No. This can't possibly be the husband God intended for me. Maybe I'll talk to Father Tassos. Maybe he'll help me. He's my friend and the only person Mamma listens to. He could convince her."

She had pinned her hair up into a careless knot for the morning's cleaning and in the garden's unfurled midday light the outline of Sophia's chin and jaw revealed a determination that Niki recognized as unshakable, one she silently respected in the same way she respected sun and wind and the inevitability of rain. Sophia was the strong one, Niki reminded herself, the uncompromising, implacable, determined one.

Sophia Kastromenou had been the first baby baptized by the young Father Spiro Tassos when he'd arrived at Saint Demetrios and he had watched her grow into an unusually bright young woman, often struck by her quick grasp of skills and her disciplined habits. It was Father Tassos who had suggested to Victoria and Georges that tenacious Sophia be enrolled at the Athenaeum, an expensive private girls school in Athens whose tuition the family could barely afford. With his encouragement somehow they had managed it, and Sophia had excelled in history and languages, graduating, much to Father Tassos' delight, with highest honors and the school's coveted history prize. Academically, Sophia was first in her class and much to her chagrin, always last in line because of her height. In one confession to Father Tassos she had revealed her envy of the more diminutive girls in his religious classes that year, those dainty bodies always chosen to be first in line and seated in front rows. In her own eyes Sophia saw herself as something of a giant, but of course she had no way of knowing that this distorted self-image was in sharp contrast to that held by most of the boys in her class, several of whom in their own confessions to Father Tassos, told of lustful fantasies and deep, sinful passions ignited by the merest glance from the tallest, most beautiful girl they knew.

As the hour of four approached and Sophia was reminded it was time to change, she made her way up the narrow flight of stairs to the room she and Niki had shared until Niki's marriage. It remained familiar and comforting, the two beds covered in white scalloped cotton, the cambric window curtains washed and rehung just the day before, the lingering fresh scent of soap filling the room with an air of fastidious cleanliness.

She looked at herself in the mirror over the chest of drawers and stared into her own troubled eyes as she took a white linen towel from one of the drawers and slowly began to tie it around her head, knotting it very tightly under her chin so that none of her hair showed.

This is how it would be. This is how she would look as the Bride of Christ, one of the "Kologria," the Greek nuns who sacrificed themselves to poverty as they tended convent farms and aided the poor. She stepped back and stared at herself, tightening the knot even tighter, until her chin stuck out and her cheeks were pushed in close to her nose. She made faces at herself in the mirror, first squinting her soft brown eyes into narrow slits and then raising her eyebrows as high as she could. This is how it would be, wrapped in a wimple and no hair. She loved the outdoors. She would make an excellent farmer. The lump lodged in her throat had grown, but she fought it off. How she hated the way tears made her eyes puff up!

The linen towel came off and the curling black hair tumbled back to her shoulders in a shining cloud. She brushed it slowly, arranged it neatly, and then she patted her face, checking herself closely in the oval mirror as she replaced her hairbrush on the length of soft white lace lying across the dresser top and dutifully changed into the dress her mother had selected for Herr Schliemann's visit, a dress that Victoria herself had worn and a favorite until added inches had made it impossible to button. The limp, cream-colored cotton was fashioned with long lace sleeves and a high neck. The sleeves, although ruffled at the wrist, were too short for Sophia, and the set-in waistline was well above her own natural waist, but the intricate stitching and floral embroidery at the neckline were ornate enough to draw attention to her lovely face, just as Victoria had planned.

Sophia was still secluded in her room when she heard voices downstairs. They were all there she realized, assembling like vultures to watch her anguish – Niki, Giannis, Mamma and Papa, and Father Tassos, whose distinctive voice she recognized with surprise and a terrible sinking disappointment. Mamma had gotten to him first. She could hear them making their way through the house and out to the garden.

"And have they given you a lovely suite at the Adelphi?" Victoria asked in the grand, arm's- length tone she used when she wanted to impress. "I do hope the management knows you're from Paris. Father Tassos says everything in Paris is perfection. And he should know. He taught at the Sorbonne."

Sophia wished her window overlooked the garden and not Andromous Street, so that she could watch them swarming over Herr Schliemann, but what difference did it make? She had decided to hate him, no matter what, and somehow she would find a way to let him know how much she hated him. Were the Kologria allowed visitors, she wondered as she imagined in which of the chairs Mamma would seat him. There were only two chairs on what she and Niki had always called the visitor side of the table. Surely he would sit in one of those. Mamma would smile and serve a tray of her delicious honey cakes to the horrid old man while Papa poured wine into the good glasses.

Leaving her room, she paused at the top of the stairs as if preparing for an entrance in a school play. Miserably embarrassed, she wished it were suddenly tomorrow, or better yet, next week, with all this over and magically in the past, but somehow she managed to move slowly down the stairs, trying to swallow away the uncomfortable lump still lodged in her throat.

Standing at the door to the garden she looked out, the distance to where they all sat appearing endless. But she did exactly as she had been told and dutifully walked toward the garden table with her head held high, staring straight ahead, the silly ruffles mid-way up her arms billowing like limp curlicues as she moved. They all watched her, all but Niki who had quickly turned away, unwilling to let her younger sister see the tears that just then had begun to glisten in the corners of her eyes.

Heinrich was far more uncomfortable than he had expected to be in the Kastromenou family circle assembled as it was, to have a better look at him and he deeply regretted having allowed Spiro Tassos to convince him to return. The girl was lovely, but she was a child, and obviously as miserable in the situation as he. All of it was ridiculous, but as Spiro Tassos had advised, for the sake of his project and for whatever future assistance Kolodji might be able to provide, he would make the best of things for the moment and that would be the end of it. The retsina Georges Kastromenou poured with characteristic generosity was tasting better by the second.

Hardly oblivious to Heinrich's discomfort and sensing Sophia's distress, Spiro Tassos looked to Giannis for diversion, eager to focus mutual attention on a relatively neutral subject. His efforts could not have been more transparent, but in keeping with his intentions to address first things first and test the suitability of the marriage Victoria had proposed for Sophia, it was not long before his desire to open dialogue on what the future might hold succeeded quite well in generating new relationships between all the parties concerned.

"Giannis, you must have a look at the Acropolis from Heinrich's balcony at the Adelphi. What a spectacular view!" Tassos began, seeding his clouds of neutrality with touches of allure. "Has he told you he has plans for restoration and discovery not unlike your own up there? It could be that he could be of some help to you. Now that I think of it, perhaps you could be of assistance to each other. Like you, he too is searching for a missing part of our little-known Greek past and although his search will likely take him many miles away from Greece, I think his intentions could be very much in keeping with yours."

"What exactly is it you hope to locate?" Giannis asked, opening the door to discovery with some reluctance. "Perhaps I really can be of some assistance. We uncover new things almost every day in the Acropolis debris so generously left us by our barbaric Turkish conquerors. I did tell you, didn't I, that they used the buildings on that hallowed ground for their municipal offices and headquarters?"

Heinrich fell silent, the expression on his face suddenly rigid, his eyes intense and almost fiery in the flattering light, Giannis' intolerance for the cultural differences now integral to his life beginning to take a toll on his patience.

"I have found a hill not unlike your Acropolis here in Athens," he said, eager to open his own dialogue. "It's not as high, but I believe it could be older. It's fifteen kilometers in length and about two kilometers from the sea. Sunrise flashes up in a shock of white light at dawn and that's when the views are best, extraordinary in every direction, a sprinkling of islands to the north, mountains massed to the southeast, and a wide, treeless plain reaching west to the sea."

"Your hill clearly casts a spell on you," Giannis reflected with an indulgent smile. "Why?"

"I believe it is Troy," Heinrich answered.

"Troy?" Giannis responded. "You mean the Troy of old Homer, his Troy of Priam and Paris and Helen?"

"Yes, that Troy."

Giannis laughed.

"You cannot be serious. And if you are, my friend, you shouldn't be. The legend of Troy is exactly that: legend, the fabric of imagination and vague symbol, pure fiction created by a blind poet! Surely you know that!"

"I know no such thing," Heinrich responded calmly. "I believe the Trojan War was a real war waged at the gates to the Acropolis of Troy as Homer described it and waged for the same reasons war is waged today: land, trade routes, natural resources, and independence. I intend to prove it took place. I have applied for a permit to excavate."

Giannis shook his head.

"Have you truly read The Iliad, Herr Schliemann?" he asked wearily, not really expecting a reply. "Wonderful, isn't it? Wonderful fantasy of poetic imagination, one of the most glowing of all Greek tales told and retold over centuries in that never quite forgotten tradition so well established by the oral poets long before we had a written Greek language. And aren't they beautifully cast characters? Perfection. Helen, the kidnapped protagonist, not just lovely but the most beautiful woman in the world; Prince Paris, her reckless lover and handsome abductor; Agamemmnon, the great Greek general conveniently married to her sister, Clytemnestra, and Menelaus, the sadly injured party, a poor dolt of a husband bent on classic revenge. With such a cast of characters I think I too could have created a lively tale. And that's exactly what was done. Homer and others like him were the celebrity entertainers of their day, famous for their talents in holding an audience spellbound in the palm of a hand, immensely gifted in their ability to describe events and breathe life into the colorful part god, part human characters such as those who have succeeded perhaps too well in deluding you into believing them to have been real people living a real world. Remember that by Homer's own account he told the story of the Trojan War at least six hundred years after he said it took place. How accurate could he be?"

Giannis laughed again, concluding his discourse with an air of self-satisfaction and the reinforced conviction that foreigners really had no business in the world of Greek antiquities. They were misinformed and misguided, better suited to the ranks of supportive observers, fortunate indeed to gain a mere glimpse into the true Greek expertise.

"Herr Schliemann, could I not convince you to deal with us in uncovering the more realistic Age of Pericles? Many in our academic community think that even Homer himself was a fabrication and that here in Athens lies the unquestioned truth of history. If archaeology interests you, join us here."

Heinrich sat quietly, having listened patiently during Giannis' discourse, as he had so often done in the past when his passion for Troy had been challenged either by suggestion or inference. Giannis Kolodji was no child, but he reminded Heinrich of those youngsters in Ankershagen who years ago, after his mother's death and during his last days there, had taunted him with anything they could think of to tarnish his dream of the golden city. Well-practiced in self-defense by the strict lessons of life and the isolation he had never escaped, the curator of the Acropolis Museum did not intimidate him now, and Heinrich defended himself with a steady discourse of his own.

"I intend to prove beyond any doubt that Troy was a real city and no poet's fabrication," he began. "I believe that Troy existed just as Homer describes it in The Iliad and I believe its king was Priam. I also believe Priam had a great treasury of gold and that I will unearth it. I believe there was a long and difficult war at the gates of Troy where the Greeks, led by Agamemmnon the King of Mycenae, fought long and hard to enter and seize the city. On the other hand I do not believe that the war at Troy was fought merely for the sake of beautiful Helen. Her kidnapping likely brought to a boil some long festering grievances, forcing the Greeks to take action. We must remember Helen was not of Troy. Helen was the Greek Queen of Sparta, wife of the Spartan King, Menelaus. A royal kidnapping on that level could incite a war even today. And Agamemmnon, a king, a general, and the brother of Menelaus, would be the natural leader of a large coalition of allied Greek forces such as those of the thousand ships described by Homer. Giannis, I am convinced the Trojan War was fought over the same things for which war is always fought: land, natural resources, seaports, and trade routes, and I intend to find out why."

In the tinted twilight of that afternoon, the Kastromenou garden was alive and fairly pulsating with a wide range of unexpected and controversial thought. Was the idea of a real Trojan War to be taken seriously? Like two contenders for the same superior post, Giannis Kolodji and Heinrich Schliemann had fallen into contest and neither really wished for a simple emotional victory just then, but Heinrich Schliemann had decided that whatever the future might hold in these new relationships, he would stay the course and clear the air in whatever manner necessary. He was an expert at setting his own pace, unwavering in his conviction, and even faced with the opinions of the well-qualified curator of the Athens Acropolis he advanced his proposal with accelerated energy, and there was more.

"My studies show that neither The Iliad nor any other epic poem is entirely fiction, Giannis," he said. "I believe The Iliad is an accurate geographic guide, and I intend to use it as my primary source. In fact, I'm prepared to gamble whatever reputation I have on its premise."

Giannis had begun to write Heinrich Schliemann off. It was easy to patronize a foreign amateur, and why should he turn the family away from this rich man who could very well become his brother-in-law if Victoria had her way. Time would bring him around and Giannis would be waiting patiently. Let him go on. More confident than ever, Giannis decided to play the Schliemann game of chance and he asked with the trace of sarcasm that left him wide open to the final assault, "Where do you expect to find the ancient City of Troy, Herr Schliemann?" Heinrich did not flinch.

"In a northwest corner of Asia Minor," he stated simply and directly to Giannis.

"You mean in Turkey!" exploded Giannis.

"Yes, Giannis, in Turkey!"

※ ※ ※

Resentment for Turkish rule, was nothing new to the Kastromenou family or their Athens contemporaries. Although Greek independence had been won more than thirty years before, old wounds remained. At the Athens market stalls, Victoria was but one of the Greek housewives who commonly asked if that day's fish were from the Turkish side of the Aegean, and like many others she frequently consulted one of the superstitious old market women said to have inherited an ability to recognize the "cold, worthless eyes of Turkish fish."

Giannis' disbelief had now invaded them all and the peaceful Greek garden had been pierced with a rare note of discord that Father Tassos sought immediately to quell, knowing better than any of the others that the discussion had gone too far and that historically, the Greeks had really never wanted to love their enemies. They still found positive pleasure in their hatreds and in the heady prospect of eventual revenge. It was an ancient outlook and it always began in the intimate family unit, sometimes as an entirely harmless brief discussion, but in many cases the issue of revenge had eventually become the source of savage feuds in and with neighboring families, even leading to war between cities. Giannis Kolodji's explosive attitude had little to do with national pride or unity, but had everything to do with family loyalty and family pride. As first curator of the newly developing Acropolis Museum, he lived every day with reminders of Turkish destruction and now, to realize that a family member who might actually marry Schliemann could conceivably be asked to support the hope of excavating a Greek fairy tale in Turkey, was overwhelming. Family and friends were required to share personal hatreds as well as affections. Impressive as he was, Schliemann would never be a friend and he would certainly never be accepted, not by this family. The disappointment was written on Victoria's face. She had expected too much. They all had.

"Giannis, I well understand your concern here," said Father Tassos in an effort to mediate and smooth over an adversarial situation. "But Herr Schliemann is not searching for Turkish treasure. He is searching for treasures of Greece. And are we Greeks not far beyond vindictive anger? Giannis, the Turks have shown us no evidence of animosity for years, and as a matter of fact, they may welcome a cooperative opportunity such as this."

It was an admirable, if hopelessly feeble gesture on the part of Spiro Tassos, and although Giannis had calmed down, he stubbornly maintained his confrontational attitude from the safety of his innermost self.

Of those gathered in the garden, all but one came away with uncertainties regarding the wisdom of a marriage between Sophia Kastromenou and Heinrich Schliemann. The curator and his wife feared Schliemann's domination. For two years, as the only admired son-in-law, Giannis had enjoyed a uniquely prestigious position, but now his rigid Greek sense of honor had been threatened, only hardening his own conviction that it was his due to be the first among sons-in-law.

The scholarly priest had wisely begun to divide the Kastromenou family into the three classes of which Pythagoras had spoken: the seekers of knowledge, the seekers of honor, and the seekers of gain. In comparing human life to the categories of the Olympic Games, Pythagoras had matched the first class to the spectators, the second to the competitors, and the third to the hucksters. Other uncertainties had presented themselves to the members of the Kastromenou family, and in each mind, regardless of age or experience, were questions none had ever before thought to ask as the fascinating, unconsidered possibility of the Trojan War took hold, finding a guarded and strangely disturbing place, the afternoon visit Victoria had planned as prelude to the future becoming something else entirely as for one of the few times in her life she felt confused.

Sophia herself had not spoken a single word during the encounter in the garden but she had understood the power of its premise and from somewhere deep inside she felt its burning message. With her range of natural curiosity, she knew questions begged to be answered, solutions explored, and far from being confused herself, she knew she had witnessed a unique event. Its quality and conditions may have mystified her, but the attitudes and human posturing of those involved had commanded her full attention, and later, just before falling asleep in her bed in the room at the top of the stairs, she smiled.

Sophia had watched Heinrich Schliemann as he left the garden, his final departing footsteps like deliberate, audible markings in the otherwise silent passage of time. There was something about him, something about the rigid set of his shoulders as he walked, something about the way he moved, as if like herself, he knew better than anyone else that he was an intrinsic part of the world's churning velocity, innately capable of stirring its most time-honored dust.

She knew she didn't like him, but she also knew she had met a man who, if he chose to, could lay waste to the north wind. There was an odd, unflinching power about him that was true, but the dark abyss created by Heinrich Schliemann's dream loomed far too wide and too impassable to suit her Greek family. There would be no marriage. That was the knowledge that pleased her, its potency more than she had hoped for, and breathing a deep blissful sigh of relief before closing her eyes, she thanked God for Father Tassos' successful intervention into yet another development in her young life.

That same night, asleep in his bed at the Adelphi, the dream returned to Tag. More beautiful than ever before, Helen came closer, looked into his eyes, and again her voice rustled like dry leaves under ashen skies.

"My fault, all my fault."

Swirling. White passages spinning, the voice filling him, covering him, streaming through his ears, into his throat, pausing there until he swallowed it away and set it leaping through his veins. She was close enough to touch, near enough to hold, the sheen of pale amber skin a mere breath away.

"Tag, dear Tag," she whispered, warm in his arms. They were lovers. Sealed, one upon the other. Bones, skin, flesh together, sing. Suddenly, he was awake, temples throbbing. The voice, the eyes, the pale amber skin, the hair.

It was the girl in the garden, the girl whose ebony hair had shone in the silvered shade, the girl called Sophia.

# CHAPTER SEVEN

## Belonging

### *SEPTEMBER 1869*

ALTHOUGH THE PARIS garden had maintained the leafy dark green of late summer, from the dining room's windowed bay, he could see early signs of autumn. A border of bronze and yellow chrysanthemums had been planted that morning, the brown soil under them still wet from the gardener's tending, the blossoms rigidly proud and as yet unaccustomed to their new surroundings. He rarely walked in his garden and until recently hadn't taken much notice of it at all. Year after year it had grown and flourished quite free of his concern, left to his butler Henri's supervision, this practice over a number of years resulting in an annual abundance of flowering trees and seasonal flowers, lovely, and immaculate, and entirely heartless.

"Henri, are the stone benches still at the far end of the garden?" he asked. "Are they in good condition?"

"They are, monsieur," replied Henri, startled by the unusual sound of monsieur's voice during one o'clock luncheon. "In perfect condition."

"Do you think a lady would like the garden, Henri?"

"It is a lovely garden, monsieur. A lady would be most happy walking there, or reading on a lovely afternoon."

"Henri, I shall be traveling to Athens. Tomorrow. See that the garden receives attention. More flowers perhaps, more color."

In the morning mail, he had received a letter with an Athens postmark. It was from Spiro Tassos and it disclosed news he had hardly dared anticipate two weeks before when he had written with his proposal of marriage. The parents of Sophia Kastromenou were agreeable to a marriage between their daughter, Sophia, and Heinrich Schliemann.

It had not been easy to overcome the challenging obstacles apparent to all concerned, but Heinrich had persisted, and in notes and letters he had written to Sophia from Paris that summer he had succeeded, just as he had hoped, in appealing to her curiosity about the world outside Athens. At first she hadn't answered, but her interest piqued, eventually she had written back, by midsummer her letters filled with comments on his observations, her thoughts and opinions simply stated at first but soon amusing enough to delight him and often catch him by surprise as in novel new ways, he began to feel humanly connected to the world through another being. By late summer, when Victoria received formal word of his marriage proposal, he and Sophia were friends and Victoria found that her own renewed interest in Heinrich Schliemann's potential as a son-in-law was met with significantly weakened resistance.

" . . . . I have traveled the globe and I think the tropical landscape in Java is the most beautiful I have ever seen," he had written to Sophia in late June, "but parts of India are much more dangerous. I hope you see India someday. Every year, in the Sunderbans, a dozen or so tribesmen are killed and eaten by tigers and the crocodiles are three times the size of a man. One must exercise great care when traveling the jungles of India."

"We are broiling like fish on the fire in Athens this summer," she had replied after a week, "so Java sounds cool and green to me and I would love to see it some day. The Sunderbans, on the other hand, does not interest me at all. I have never thought jungles fit places for humans, as evidenced by the behavior of tigers, who apparently share my opinion."

"Egypt is a place of enormous mystery and intrigue" he wrote in July. "On one of my journeys there I sailed up the Nile to the Second

Cataracts. One day we will know a good deal more about the complicated geography of Egypt, but of course the burial tombs of the pharaohs hold the world's greatest interest right now. Have you ever seen a mummy? There is a fine exhibition of Egyptian mummies in the British Museum. One can spend hours in those rooms, lost in the perplexing spirit of that ancient legacy."

"I would never want to see a mummy," she wrote in quick response. "The dead should be left in peace. I'm glad that the ancient Greeks did none of that sort of preserving of the dead. I would have hated to take part in such a ritual or know I might one day be its subject and perhaps hundreds of years after my death be discovered and put in a public place where people could see me at my worst. How lucky we are to live in the modern world and have cemeteries."

In August he was at Trouville.

"You'd love it here," he wrote from l'Hotel des Roches.

"The sand along the shore where the ladies sit under striped umbrellas every day is pearly white and the shallow waters where the children wade is blue as peacock feathers."

Not to be outdone, she promptly wrote back to him from Corinth.

"It's lovely to be by the crisp sea air in Corinth. We've spent the month of August here since I was a child. Our house is but a short walk from the shore and although the beach is rocky, the view from the isthmus to the Peleponnese compensates nicely. My Aunt Stephania is visiting. She loves to pick the periwinkles from the rocks. We cook them in a pot of boiling water with lots of salt and pepper and eat them sitting outside. Do you know how to remove a periwinkle from its shell?"

"I understand Corinth's strange charisma," he wrote before leaving Marseilles, "and I have studied the effects of the earthquake which destroyed Old Corinth. Did you know that modern Corinth where you spend the month of August every summer was founded where the isthmus is flat and the air currents now healthiest? The earthquake was a blessing since at one time, Old Corinth was famous for its infectious fevers. In answer to your question, one should never eat periwinkles. They are assigned to the family of barnacles and are known to cause severe headaches so I suppose if I were forced to eat a periwinkle I would attack it with a hammer."

The Avillar sailed into the Greek port of Piraeus on the morning of September eighth and a few hours later Heinrich was settled into the Adelphi's second floor suite, number 23. Later that same day, in the Kastromenou garden, he watched Sophia, his betrothed, in the mottled light, firmly convinced that at that moment fate and destiny stood hand in hand at his shoulder and that his life was truly beginning at last.

The next morning, much to the dismay of the Adelphi's desk clerk, Father Tassos made yet another unannounced visit to Heinrich Schliemann's spacious rooms.

"No need to click for an usher, thank you," he said, his black cassock billowing up around him as he breezed past. "I know the way!"

"Heinrich, I am required by sacred and civil law to ask if you have ever married or divorced," he asked, barely inside the door marked number 23. "If the answer is yes, this is the time to tell me." "No," Heinrich lied. "I have not been married, nor am I divorced." It did not feel like a lie.

And so the courtship began, Heinrich visiting the Kastromenou garden every afternoon for the next two weeks and always in the presence of a chaperone, usually Victoria, who busied herself with needless garden tasks, all the while observing the couple who stole glances at one another in the afternoon shade of a late Athens summer, each forming opinions and impressions to be culled out later, for more careful deliberation.

One day he brought a backgammon board and taught Sophia how to play the game, happier and more contented than he'd ever been in his life to simply watch as she rolled the dice and made her moves, absolutely delighted, once she became comfortable with the rules, that she also became a formidable opponent. He loved the way she took the time to plan and execute each move, her strategy seriously focused on one thing: winning, which she often did. An accomplished player for years, victories in backgammon could not have interested him less that September. It was what the game provided him in a secluded Athens garden that really mattered: the opportunity and time to grasp the idea that he was a man in love. Seated across from Sophia at the shaded table where they sat each afternoon he could study everything about his beloved at will, her hands, her facial expressions, the sound of her voice. For her part, Sophia was remarkably at ease in his company, secure in the knowledge that she was at the center of his attention, and although she knew she didn't love him she also knew she was enjoying the daily rounds of intellectual jousting he provoked and which she handled with the natural wit and unpretentious freedom that had appealed to him during their first meeting. At the same time, Sophia's dramatic change of heart regarding her arranged marriage to Heinrich Schliemann was a mystery to the family, especially to Niki who had expected great flares of continuing resistance from the strong-willed younger sister who initially had confessed her disappointment in his potential as a suitable husband. Something had happened to change Sophia's mind and whatever it was, she kept it to herself, even then, Sophia's true state of mind understood only when she anticipated future events and tested her likely role in them.

"Sometimes I wonder what it will be like to leave this house alone with you," she said to him one day as their game of backgammon was concluded. "Perhaps you will become bored with me when you see me away from here and in a place where I do not belong."

"No, you could never bore, me, Sophia," he said, surprised and touched by the candor of her self doubt. "You are blessed with great gifts," he added quickly, "the greatest being your talent for belonging anywhere in the world you might choose to be. I have no doubt of it. And that leads me to something I want to talk to you about."

He had leaned closer to her, the outer corners of his eyes crinkling as he smiled across the table and faced her squarely.

"I know you must be apprehensive about the future and I'm well aware of the reasons for your worry," he said. "For one thing Sophia, I know I'm not the husband you've been dreaming about all your young life. You needn't answer. I know. You're afraid I'm too old, too set in my ways, too out of touch with your world."

She sat back in her chair and smiled reluctantly.

"Then there's the search for Troy," he went on. "That must worry you too, and it probably doesn't meet with your expectations for the future either, so you should know something important and remember it always. More than I've ever wanted anything in my life I want you to be my wife. I'll give you everything I can and I'll try to make you as happy as possible. I'll take care of your family, provide for them as we've agreed, and in return I'll ask just one thing of you.

Be there with me in the search for Troy. Give me time with it and try to understand my need to find it. Just be on my side and help me try. Once you see the hill, you'll understand. I know you will. We'll go there together in the spring. You'll see it then. You'll understand. Oh, and one more thing. Call me Tag. I'd like that best of all."

"You're very different from what I expected," she confessed in her straightforward, open way, grateful for the opportunity at honesty, "but I'm not disappointed," she said, "not at all. When you came here with Father Tassos I could see you weren't afraid of doing as much or more than any younger man. And your age doesn't matter anymore, not at all. It did at first, but I watched you with Giannis. I saw your courage and your resolve. It's stronger and more energetic than his own. But most of all, I felt your excitement for the search, your unyielding loyalty to it, and although I don't fully understand and I would fear the prospect of a journey into Turkey as much as any Greek in Athens, I want very much to see what drives you to find Troy and for what reasons you are so determined."

"Then we could go there together, you and I?"

"Yes, take me to see it. I want to see what you see. It's all so far outside the realm of any truth I've ever known and so remarkable to me that you, so intelligent and sophisticated a man could attach truth to a legend. No, I'm not disappointed. I'm intrigued. Can you forgive me for that?"

"Of course," he said, reaching out across the table for her hand, which she did not withdraw. He nodded his head in affirmation.

"We'll see then, won't we, Tag and Sophia together there on the hill? Good."

They sat there, staring at one another in silence, aware that they had formed a strange pact and that because of it now they shared a bond. And it was a secret between them, the sort of intrinsic, unvarnished secret shared by those who alone and of their own making understand the depths of a secret's meaning and the risks inherent in its revelation. It was the kind of secret that made a man know it would be good to have someone, a woman. It was the kind of secret that made a girl want to rise out of herself and become that woman.

❧ ❧ ❧

Victoria now added one more item to her forgiveness list. In her daily prayers, she now not only begged God to forgive her sins of omission and commission, she also begged God to forgive Sophia's love of backgammon, having stored away in the far recesses of her mind a sinful relationship between the dice and the devil. She shared her fears with Sophia, who one afternoon suggested that Tag teach her mother to play backgammon. Victoria fumbled with awkward excuses about so much to do in preparation for the wedding that her mind could not possibly absorb another thing and in spite of her protests to Sophia, the backgammon continued as each afternoon Tag watched the ebony crown of hair, the skin of palest amber, the face he'd loved for so long.

Other details bothered Victoria, not the least of which was Tag's insistence that there be no traditional Greek wedding feast in the church square following the wedding ceremony. He had made arrangements for a small wedding banquet to be held at the Adelphi Hotel and although Victoria cooperated outwardly with the terms of his wishes, in private she complained bitterly to Georges, who remained typically ambivalent, assured in the knowledge that Victoria would assume her customary role as family decision maker and that whatever her decisions might be, he would, as always, be in complete agreement. Secretly, though, Georges admired Heinrich Schliemann's firmness with Victoria and the manner in which he managed her, allowing for levity and a bit of compromise, but getting exactly what he wanted in the end.

None of this helped to soothe Victoria. A small wedding banquet at the Adelphi Hotel would reduce by considerable numbers the long guest list she had eagerly prepared, making it impossible for her to invite all the people she had planned for. Pity, her daughter was marrying a wealthy, worldly man and all Victoria's friends would be kept away. They would all come to the church, however, along with her relatives from Crete. She would see to it. Everyone would see what she had accomplished for her baby daughter, and in the presence of Almighty God.

On September twenty-third, Tag and Sophia were married by candlelight in the Church of Saint Demetrios. Wearing the nuptial robes of the Greek Orthodox church, Father Tassos stood before the life-sized icon of Demetrios framed in lustrous hammered gold and set with precious jewels, and together before him the couple sipped the wine that sealed the plighting of their troth. Sophia wore a handmade dress of white silk satin, its bodice beautifully woven with embroidery, her shoulder-wide collar fashioned of white lace, as was the small cap she wore on her magnificent shining head from which a cloud of veiling fell to the floor. Tag was handsomely turned out in dark formal dress, a small white rosebud tucked in his lapel. The long, candlelit table at the templum was covered with a white cloth and on it were a chalice of wine and two gold wedding rings. The Gospel lay on a silver stand in the center of the table and on the heads of the bride and groom were placed the traditional Greek stephanion wreaths of fresh orange blossoms. The two wreaths were connected with slender strands of white satin ribbon which Giannis, the best man, exchanged from one to the other three times during the course of the ceremony, and in the church she had known all her life, Sophia stood tall and radiant as she made her promises and recited her vows.

Strange, this new bond with a family, but the structure was one to which Tag readily responded as he watched Sophia at the celebration dinner later, his beautiful bride at the center of her family's affections, completely at ease and basking in their love. She had belonged, been connected to something solid all her life, and she carried her bold confidence casually, almost carelessly. He had never known that luxury. She knew no flood of fear to overwhelm the lonely night, no hollow memories to stir old pain. He remained the rootless burrower, disclosing almost nothing of his past, protective of his secrets, answering only to direct questions concerning aspects of his background, his origins vague, his lineage obscure, his business interests diversified and varied enough to defy accurate description, the extent of his education the greatest mystery of all, the whole of him clouded by dull, perplexing mystery, as if there was little to tell about his forty-seven years of life. And that was exactly as he wished it, for only now, in mid-life, had he really begun to live, dependent not on sagacity or practicality, but on the reality of his dreams.

He had never hidden the fact that he had been born into a poor family, proud of being a self-made man, but by the wedding day, he and Sophia had spent many hours together and all she knew was that he had been born into a German family in Ankershagen, a village in the district of Mecklenburg, near the Polish border, and that his father had been a Lutheran minister with a small parish church. He had skimmed lightly over the very real fact that he and his mother and two sisters had lived at the mercy of parish support in the form of outright charity and that his mother had died at an early age, malnourished and in a state of chronic exhaustion. He had attended school, he told Sophia, and had learned to play the organ in his father's church. The truth was, that although he had displayed a talent for music at a young age, his formal schooling had fallen far short of the educational background that was always associated with the highly intelligent, socially polished Heinrich Schliemann.

He was eleven years old as the family unit disintegrated after his mother's death and he still could not read, but apart from his lifelong discomfort with this fact, he had never been able to find the words to tell anyone how it had felt to abruptly leave his childhood home, abandoned to strangers and painfully separated from everything he knew. How would he have explained family humiliation and the meaning of disgrace to someone so secure in the love of a family committed to the safe support and honor of its members? Sophia had never seen white doors to corner rooms or yellow curls pressed against the cushion of a father's chair and she would never understand how such memories could feed on themselves over time and keep hate alive. And so, the picture he painted early on, although weighted heavily in favor of those events for which he felt little passion, also dwelled upon the irony and humor of events in his early life as he chose to recall them. Skilled storyteller that he was, his darker secrets remained concealed from Sophia for quite some time.

He revealed his gifts for storytelling to her in two memorable episodes, his account of the church organ Sophia's favorite. At her request, he recounted it to her on many occasions, and although in each telling yellow-haired Elsa's name was never mentioned, her clear soprano voice rang in his ears whenever the tale unfolded.

*"Break forth, o beauteous heavenly light,"* Elsa had sung.

"A former parishioner who had become a successful merchant in Berlin decided to gift his childhood church with an organ, his recollection of the church's size somewhat distorted once the organ was ordered sight unseen. It took an entire winter to install the organ and its bellows. The pipes were enormous and completely dominated what had once been a small, simple sanctuary. For some time the congregation enjoyed its massive new organ only visually, proud indeed to have its impressive grandeur in its midst but sadly lacking the skills of a local organist who could bring it to life, so hymns continued to be sung a cappella every Sunday as the congregation looked up to the organ pipes and prayed for a miracle."

*And enter in the morning.*

"Finally, pink-cheeked Herr Fassbinder came forth, shyly confessing to only a rudimentary familiarity with the flute and the piano, so, of course he was immediately appointed church organist. Some said that Herr Fassbinder had been sent by God. Others thought God could have sent a better musician."

*Ye shepherds shrink not with affright.*

"Every Sunday, Herr Fassbinder struggled with hymns on the huge organ, but no one complained about his many mistakes because the church reverberated with new music and new life and before too long a new repertoire of hymns was becoming familiar to the congregation as Herr Fassbinder became better at playing them."

*But hear the angel's warning.*

"Encouraged to train a successor, Herr Fassbinder courageously gave organ lessons free of charge. I was his best pupil. A girl with yellow curls was also one of Herr Fassbinder's pupils, but I put in the most practice time, living more conveniently and with greater access to the organ as I did, in the nearby rector's house."

*This child now weak in infancy.*

"I loved sitting at the organ bench in control of the keyboard before me. And I loved pulling out all the stops to make my music as loud and powerful as I could. One of my friends could always be counted on to handle the bellows. The church fairly shook at times and often father would come in to put a stop to the loud music he said could be heard not only in the rectory but in every one of the houses lining the church square. Since I had not anticipated so large an audience I was deeply complimented and thanked father, certain I was destined to become a great church organist like Johann Sebastian Bach, of whom Herr Fassbinder spoke with the greatest reverence."

*Our confidence and joy shall be.*

"The girl with yellow curls called me a show-off. She said that my father had told her my lessons would soon stop and that she alone would be allowed practice time on the organ. She said that one day she would replace Herr Fassbinder. Father had promised her."

*The power of Satan breaking.*

"One Sunday morning, Herr Fassbinder did not appear at the organ bench as was his custom, and father delayed the start of the service until someone could fetch him. Herr Fassbinder had died in the night. From the pulpit, father asked if I would play a hymn for the service. I chose one I knew well and when it was announced to the congregation, I played the introduction with no mistakes. As the singing began, I continued beautifully, repeating the hymn four times so that all four stanzas would be sung. Herr Fassbinder had always played only two stanzas. That day, I was appointed church organist by popular demand, successor to Herr Fassbinder. Afterwards, the girl with yellow curls said she would get even with me. Father had promised her that she would succeed Herr Fassbinder when the time came."

*Our peace eternal making.*

"For a wonderful, all too brief period thereafter, music was my life and by the time I was eleven I was quite an accomplished organist, or so I thought. I had learned to play every piece of music that Herr Fassbinder had left stored in the organ bench and I had taught myself to vary stanzas of the hymns with bass notes I improvised on the foot pedals. I was told I had a great talent. Then, suddenly father was transferred to another parish and overnight my life changed. There was to be no organ at our new church. We knew nothing of the reason for our sudden transfer from Ankershagen, but within weeks, my mother had died, and my sisters and I were parceled out into the homes of strangers. The separation was terrible. My sisters went to distant relatives in Münden and I was sent to live with a family named Schwann in Glückstadt, a small town along the northern banks of the Elbe. The Schwanns took in homeless boys and put them to work on their farm. The pay consisted of a roof over a boy's head and enough food to stave off hunger. The Schwanns were known as good caretakers. There were no whippings and no harsh physical punishments, but a boy caught stealing, fighting, or talking while working was immediately forced to leave. Herr Schwann took the offender to the dirt road at the bottom of the hillside pasture and introduced him to the long walk to Hamburg. I felt as if I had fallen into hell. When I arrived, there were ten boys at the farm. We ranged in age from five to sixteen and we all slept in a hut near one of the cow barns. As a newcomer, the older boys told me that the work would become easier as time passed. They laughed and said that soon the Schwanns would be the only family I would remember."

Heinrich had not told Sophia everything about the Schwanns. How could he? How could he tell her that he had arrived at the farm late one night, frightened, confused, and that early the next morning he was summoned to the house where Frau Schwann introduced herself and ordered him to strip down for examination. There, in the same room where she cooked and served meals and where waves of nausea swept over him as he breathed in the strong unfamiliar smells of that day's meal in its early stages of preparation, he stood naked while Frau Schwann slowly examined him for parasites. She then took him by the hand and led him to her bedroom where she served as his first sexual partner, clinically instructive, consummately female, hugging him, holding him and rocking him in her arms. Warm and accepting, Frau Schwann's body was round and sensuous. He remembered she was full breasted and fair, and that her hair fell into cascading blond ringlets around her face, framing her constantly damp forehead and flushed cheeks. Throughout the following year, they met in Frau Schwann's bedroom on a regular basis, and each time he left her to return to the hut where he lived with the other boys, he was filled with loathing and routinely vomited along the edges of the path.

Soon he discovered the truth about his father's indiscretion and the reason for his misery. One afternoon, keeping an appointment with Frau Schwann, he entered her bedroom as had become habit, but this time he found her standing beside red-eyed, roaring drunk Herr Schwann, blood trickling down the corner of her mouth where she had been struck. Herr Schwann had discovered the truth about his wife's trysts and he shouted loud angry obscenities, ending with repeated and graphic descriptions of the real reason for the boy's banishment to the farm. Heinrich heard Elsa's name as well as his father's. He heard Herr Fassbinder identified as the informer and he also heard that Herr Fassbinder had died shortly after a violent argument with Reverend Schliemann.

Herr Schwann had held Tag's arm in a powerful vise-like grip, his eyes inflamed as his venomous tongue blurted out the whole story in an ugly scorch of suffocating poison. Struggling to free himself, the boy ran. He ran out of the bedroom, out of the house, out into the air sweet with the smell of high summer's grass and young cornfields. He ran on to the velvet green hill pasture, confused and sobbing in a shattering rage of humiliation, and even when he had reached the dirt road leading away from the farm he kept on running, rushing as fast as he could to escape the savage demons that had suddenly been let loose upon him.

At first, he could not bring himself to believe such terrible accusations. But Herr Schwann knew so much. He had described the demoralizing effect of shame on Tag's helpless mother, and how it had quickly led to her illness and death. Tag remembered back to how he had tearfully pleaded with his father. "Why must we leave? Could we not write a letter begging to be allowed to stay? What have we done?" Those three questions came back to haunt him again and again in waves of bitter disappointment. He had offered all manner of childish suggestions to his father, all to no avail, all of it falling on deaf ears and at least one broken heart. It was true, he decided finally. His father was the cause of all this separation and misery and the root of this evil. He had failed his family and abandoned them. He had caused his own wife to die. And he had more than likely caused Herr Fassbinder to die as well.

And as he ran toward the city of Hamburg, needing no direction from Herr Schwann, the truth took hold and with every step, hatred for his father grew.

"He is dead!" he told himself over and over again. My father is dead!" he shouted. "Yes, dead," he shouted to trees and to birds and to clouds in the blue skies he would never again think of as heaven as lost in the clutches of alienation and loneliness he plunged into a life-long disagreement with God.

In this frame of mind he traveled along the wide banks of the River Elbe, surviving on summer berries and the shellfish that washed ashore. Penniless and haggard, for a while he made his home in one of Hamburg's small public parks, sleeping under a juniper bush, and every day he walked through the crowded market stalls where he stole food in the deft, quick moves that produced apples, tomatoes, and occasionally, scraps of the chocolate he loved. He looked for work, but his disheveled appearance and grim presentment conveyed characteristics of mistrust and suspicion. Despondency set in and he became more exhausted with each passing day. One morning, too tired to move, he sat under the bush he called home and idly examined his hands, turning the palms up and down, amazed at the black grime that had accumulated under his fingernails and up into the small lines at his wrists.

That afternoon, deciding to make one last attempt at finding employment and restoring some semblance of pride before returning to the Schwann's farm and begging to be allowed to stay, he entered a shop where behind the counter, a gray-haired woman stood reading a newspaper. He approached her and asked as politely as he could if she had work for him. Peering over her glasses, the woman looked him over and without a word pointed to a nearby broom and then to the floor. She went on with her reading and Tag took the broom, noticing as he swept that he was in a bookstore where row after row of neatly kept shelves were filled with hundreds of volumes in varying sizes and colors. When he had completed the sweeping of all three book-lined aisles, he returned to the woman, expecting to be handed a few coins, but still silent, she pointed in the direction of the back of the shop, and as he began to walk, the woman walked behind him. They reached a pair of dark colored curtains which she pulled aside, and for a brief moment he thought of Frau Schwann and her damp forehead, his stomach suddenly churning.

But, as if being rewarded for his long ordeal, behind the curtains, he entered a small room and the first things he saw were brightly colored pictures of cheerful mountain scenes hanging on the walls. Their simple beauty brought tears to his eyes. There was a round table with chairs around it in the middle of the room. Still silent, the woman motioned once again, this time for him to sit down at one of the chairs as she placed a whole loaf of fresh dark bread and a dish full of butter before him. She turned to one of the cupboards as he hungrily tore into the bread and scooped big chunks of it into the soft butter. The woman then produced a pitcher of fresh milk and with it, a metal cup. She then disappeared through the dark curtains, returning to her post behind the counter as he was left to satisfy his ravenous hunger, finishing off every last crumb of bread, the whole dish of butter, and every drop of milk. When he returned to the woman she was once again absorbed in her newspaper.

"Do you know what this says?" she asked him. "Read it to me." Tag looked down to the paper she had turned towards him on the counter.

"I cannot read," he said quietly, clearly embarrassed.

"Come back tomorrow," the woman said to him pleasantly and without a shred of judgment in her voice. "Early in the morning."

When he arrived early that next day, the woman introduced herself as Frau Mueller and with no further exchange of words, she sent him up the flight of stairs leading from the bookshop to the rooms over the store where she lived. It was there that Tag met Frau Mueller's husband, Herr Franz Mueller, who showed Tag to a small bedroom in which a wooden tub stood half-filled with warm water. He was told to leave his old clothes and after a bath to dress in the fresh shirt and trousers that lay in a neat bundle on a chair. He gratefully sank into the tub, watching the water quickly grow gray as the layers of dirt he had worn for so long began to wash away. There was a cake of soap and a washing cloth on an iron rack beside the tub. He lathered his hair, his face and ears, refreshing the tired young body that ached with loneliness and long neglect and after his bath, he eagerly dressed in the crisp, freshly laundered clothes.

The trousers, too full for his lean frame, came close to fitting, but looking down at his feet, he realized he had no shoes. Was he to go barefoot? As he tried to decide this matter, Herr Mueller appeared, a pipe clenched in his teeth. He was carrying two pairs of worn, but shining black boots. "Which pair do you think will fit?" he asked. Heinrich pointed to the larger of the two pairs and sitting on the Mueller's spotless parlor floor he put them on. The boots were a bit large, but he could walk comfortably in them, and thanking Herr Mueller, he excitedly rushed downstairs to find Frau Mueller, suddenly possessed of a great desire to express his thanks to her as well.

It was the beginning of a long and loving relationship, the Muellers kind to Tag in any number of ways, allowing him to sleep each night in the curtained room behind the shop and providing not only good food every day but also a few coins each week in return for his work in the shop, which included sweeping, keeping the bookshelves in order, and packing and unpacking the many books that came in and out of the popular Hamburg booksellers' shop called Mueller's. Tag loved the atmosphere: the smell of leather bindings, the texture of paper, and Frau Mueller set a splendid example at a time when it meant most. She was an avid reader and as she stood behind the counter between customers, she could invariably be found reading a newspaper or engrossed in the pages of a book. She soon encouraged Tag to attend the local school so that he could learn to read and write. She made a special visit to the district church school herself, assuming responsibility and guardianship for him and enrolling him under her name.

School in the city of Hamburg was very different from school in Ankershagen. Here Heinrich found an organized routine and a roster of teachers and classes that interested and motivated him. He found in particular, that words fascinated him, and that reading, once he caught on to it, came easily, as did writing and then history, which eventually he found he loved most of all. The Muellers allowed him free access to the books in the shop that interested him, knowing he would be as careful as they were in handling them, never forcing a binding, and always replacing a book just as he had found it. Between school and work at the Mueller's shop, the orphaned boy gradually came out of his shell, thriving on the rudiments of encouragement, interest, and most of all, the genuine affection of the Muellers and their community of friends and customers. He stayed until he was eighteen.

Johann Kimmel, one of Frau Mueller's brothers, operated a successful logging business. He had come to know Tag as a reliable and honest boy, and at his sister's suggestion he hired the dependable eighteen-year-old as his assistant. The good-byes were difficult. Tag had grown to love the Muellers as if they were his own family and Frau Mueller was often more like a mother to him than a generous employer or mentor. But she wisely advised him that he must go on to find his own new experiences, his own new ways to grow and learn. "It is your time," she told him. And in the autumn of his eighteenth year, he set out for the largest logging camp in the Black Forest, beginning his career with Johann Kimmel as a logger at one end of a double-handled saw. He made new friends among the group of itinerant loggers who constantly came and went, and he also made money. Housing and meals were provided at the camp, along with clothing, heavy boots, and gloves. Expenses were minimal, and with his frugal tastes he was able to save almost everything he earned. Johann Kimmel was his first banker and the man he entrusted with all his earnings except for the little money he kept for the taverns to which he was introduced at the end of his first season, the rugged lifestyle of the logger a drastic change from the gentle, intellectual environment he had come to know with the Muellers in Hamburg, but he thrived on its contrast, and when the season was over, he also thrived for a while on hard drinking and womanizing, usually searching out, along with an encouraging band of rowdy friends, the nearest brothel for evenings that often ended in fistfights and brawls and not just a few tales of passionate lovemaking with ravishingly beautiful tavern girls eager to share their creative talents with the persistently well-mannered young man many of them said stood out like a true gentleman.

Between logging seasons, he usually returned to the Muellers in Hamburg who welcomed him affectionately and listened eagerly to his tales of adventure deep in the German forests, captivated by the dramas he recounted to them in tales of dark, foreboding forests and crops of huge trees felled amidst the excitement of warning calls and the splinter and crack of falling timber. When he left the Muellers it was always with a parcel of his favorite foods and a few new books Frau Mueller had set aside for him, well aware that he was more than likely the only logger who traveled and worked in the Black Forest with leather bound books. After one visit to the Muellers in 1844, the titles included in his backpack were Jeremias Gotthelf's Book of Swiss Folktales and the German translation of the bestseller of that year which Frau Mueller recommended highly to her customers, The Count of Monte Cristo.

The spartan outdoor regimen and hard work agreed with him and by 1845, a good appetite and vigorous physical activity had turned the hungry, frightened boy who had first appeared at Frau Mueller's bookshop into a healthy, full-bearded young man content with his life and anticipating his future with great optimism.

That same year, with Johann Kimmel, he delivered an exceptionally large shipment of pine to a cutting and finishing mill in Berlin where he watched with fascination as the huge logs were cut into smaller and smaller sections and prepared for further refinement into a vast number of products. He noticed that the many wood scraps were saved in large wooden barrels.

"What happens to the scraps?" he asked.

"They go to Stossel," someone laughed.

Stossel was a huge burl of a man who worked at a machine with a revolving steel disk where he hand-chopped small wood scraps until they were diced into bits of fiber to be used as the base for the manufacture of paper. Heinrich watched Stossel wield his heavy sharp axe as he hacked away at the scraps in the revolving disk and casually suggested to Johann Kimmel that if Stossel mounted a few knife blades onto a revolving interior disk, the dicing might go much faster and with little or no need for the hand held axe or risk to Stossel.

With that simple suggestion, Heinrich Schliemann had invented the early automated process for the manufacture of wood pulp paper. It was the first mechanical process for grinding log scraps into a fibrous pulp and it changed the course of his life. In the next few years, Johann Kimmel helped him with early revisions of the revolving steel disk, making valuable alterations and testing and retesting. He also helped him to advance the later process that would come to include wood fiber separation in a solution of sulfurous acid. Johann spoke with great pride to his friends about Tag's innovative wood pulp process, becoming his mentor and essentially launching his career.

For centuries, rags had provided the raw material for the manufacture of paper, but the wood pulp process changed that, and as diversified demand for paper grew, Heinrich Schliemann found himself at the forefront of a new industry with world-wide markets. By the time he was thirty-five, he was manufacturing a variety of sophisticated machines, including one that brushed wood fibers and cut them into pre-measured lengths. It was called the Jordan machine and he licensed the apparatus to paper products manufacturers throughout Europe and America, collecting a royalty for its use. But by far, his most successful enterprise came about with the creation of machinery by which the earliest folding paper sack was made. Up until 1850, flour and sugar and other staple items were sold and shipped in bulk. If a customer did not bring his own container, a clerk made a paper cone. The paper sack became one of the world's most useful products. Just three years before meeting Sophia, Heinrich had sold his folding paper sack machine to Atlas Paper, Incorporated, an American company headquartered in Philadelphia, thus adding considerably to his existing fortune and enabling him to diversify his interest as he considered retirement and the pursuit of dreams.

In the years between 1845 and 1866, the boy born into poverty had, by the hand of providence and his own intelligent resourcefulness, become a very rich man. His fortune had grown with wise, well-managed investments, including a highly successful export business specializing in the shipment of specialty foods and grocery items such as coffee, tea, cheese, biscuits, jams, and chocolate throughout Europe and America. In spite of a demanding business schedule, however, he never stopped learning. He learned the languages of the countries with which he had business dealings, at ease in German, French, English, Italian, and Russian. A life-long fascination with Greece and its myths and legends resulted in numerous trips to the Greek mainland and to the Greek Islands. He became proficient in speaking and writing Greek and had read The Iliad in its original Greek, having almost memorized it in its entirety by the time he was forty. Following Frau Mueller's example, he read daily newspapers devotedly, becoming well-informed and articulate about world affairs and expanding his horizons in countless ways. Aware that he lacked personal refinement, he had learned about fine food and wines. He developed aristocratic table manners and visited a London tailor several times each year. He became popular within a small circle of influential European friends, entertaining and being entertained in Berlin, Paris, and London, but despite his wealth and success, he lived in a reclusive, solitary world of his own creation, enjoying only from afar the personal pleasures he was content to observe in the lives of those around him. But now, with Sophia as his wife, personal pleasure was highly prioritized. She was the key to unlocking the sense of his life and to fulfilling his dreams, and as the new decade began, he realized he had never given much thought to another person's happiness until now.

# CHAPTER EIGHT

## Fault

T HE WEDDING FESTIVITIES over, toward sunset they sailed out of Piraeus aboard the Valois bound for France and Sophia's new home in Paris. Fortified with wine and champagne, the Kastromenou family had cheerfully waved them off and the newlyweds had waved back from the passenger gangway, Sophia feeling oddly cherished by her new husband who had immediately proceeded to attend to every small detail of the boarding process: the luggage, the steward, flowers for their cabin, not letting on for a moment as he busied himself with an unusually long list of personal requirements that he was as aware of her mounting nervousness as he was of his own.

As Sophia unpacked her things in their cabin's small dressing room, Tag rang for the steward and ordered a light supper to be delivered later in the evening, further delaying the wedding night's sequence of events which now that they were alone were rapidly unfolding in moments drenched with mounting expectation. The lengthy details of this evening repast completed with the steward at the cabin doorway, he then turned in the direction of his young bride and in the imperceptible half-darkness Sophia heard his footsteps.

In the dressing room where she had nervously begun changing into a robe he wordlessly came to her and far from Athens, far from doubt and endless waiting, took possession of his dream. He unfastened her hair, her robe, and gathered her to him, the slim waist in his hands the only reality he knew in the slow, surrounding music of the night. Hands gliding to her back, he gently kissed the long-loved amber cheek, again traced the sheen along the jaw curved hard, and found the lips no longer out of reach. Virgin bride. Trusting him. Dear Tag. No time left for wondering and blurred pavilions. But his body was warm, his touch so prolonged, so tender, it churned her blood to hot, mulled wine. And on a cloudlike bed, her body came unplaited, freed, unbound, soft as eiderdown under summer stars. She smelled spring rain and linen towels dried in April sun. Her arms closed him in. Long legs, long hair. Silence on the raven waters. Fingers across his face, clasped around his neck, smooth silken hands tightening across his back. Hard. Harder. Hardest. His legs on hers. Again. Again. Sleep. Peace. Tag. And all the world in lovers hands, the lifetime of dreaming at an end.

Now he knew the hovering wind's intention at the shores of Ilium, knew the compact citadel of doves, the grassland where Poseidon's grove glitters. He was not old. She was not tall. And like the battle-weary son of Ares, he lay beside her, his heavy armor shed at last at the strand of Dion by the massive fortress wall.

❧ ❧ ❧

"He has come home with a bride!"

"A what?"

"A bride!"

"Whose bride?"

"Monsieur's."

"Which Monsieur?"

"Our Monsieur! Our Monsieur has come home with a bride! She is asleep in his bed! They arrived in Paris late last night and he told me!"

The Paris household was in shock.

"Our Monsieur? A bride? Impossible!"

At one o'clock luncheon Henri and Marie Durez, Tag's butler and cook, had their first look at Monsieur's bride.

"Une girafe!" Henri whispered to Marie in disbelief, returning the silver soup tureen to the kitchen and expertly collecting the warm platter she held for him. "Une girafe?" she asked, puzzled.

"Oui, une girafe!"

Marie peered through the narrow crack in the door opening with a view to the table where the bride and groom sat. She had never seen Monsieur so animated at luncheon. He looked like a young man she had never met. He laughed and tossed his head as he talked. She had also never seen him with a more beautiful companion. Sophia's face had caught the afternoon light streaming through the windows. She was absolutely radiant.

"Belle girafe! A beautiful giraffe," whispered Marie to her husband. "Trés belle girafe. Very beautiful giraffe."

"We shall never be apart, never," Tag whispered to her again and again at every turn, at every opportunity. "I want you with me always. Where I can see you. Here. Always."

Precious days. Precious hours. Paris, a cornucopia overflowing with high spirits, a mellifluous torrent of parties and waltzes, noise and dazzle. There could have been no better place to begin their life together and Sophia was receptive to it all, quickly warming to new friends who gave countless luncheons and dinners to introduce her, anxious to meet the new bride. Days and nights were filled with concerts, galleries, gardens. The Champs Elysees, the Bois de Boulogne, the Louvre. Rembrandt and Raphael by day. Offenbach, elegant restaurants, clever new friends by night. The theater, the opera. Tutored in French, practiced in food and wine. Petits pains au chocolat, paté a choux, madeleines, poulet au chasseur, pômmes lyonnaise. Lampierre with his neat mustache, the banker, Charles Demours, thin and cricket-like, his hair parted straight down the middle of his head and a fine line where his lips were supposed to be. The attractive, refined Caillebottes, their son, Gustave's brooding eyes. Vincente, Lampierre's monkey in his perfectly tailored Garde de Seine jacket and matching cap. And as if by design, the weather cooperated, bright, clear, an autumn warmer than usual, luring lovers into an open landau, to the flower stalls, the shops, the windmills of Montmartre.

She dazzled him, choosing her daily costumes from the new array of dresses quickly purchased, matching jackets, soft leather gloves, feathered hats. In the evening, Marie helped her into jade green silks and rustling ivory taffetas with tulle overskirts from Worth. For tea, white satins with sashes of blue at her slim waist. Fur wraps in the cool of the evening, diamond clips for her hair, ostrich feathers, pearls. Thunder and lightening, crackle and peal. Bells, chimes, music of the night. And in mid-November she began to fade. A few days rest was all she needed, Tag said. But the dark circles under her eyes remained.

Sophia loved the Paris house, and at first was reluctant to leave it, even for an afternoon. In a letter to Father Tassos she wrote, "the day we arrived, our carriage stopped at an arched passage just inside which I saw a small stone building with a sign that said, 'concierge.' A man in handsome livery stepped out to greet us and then our carriage proceeded through the arch into a large curving gravel courtyard. There are four houses in our courtyard. Tag tells me that the houses in France are always built around the courtyard. The entrance to our house is most attractive. Our door is black and we have a stone hall floor. The mirrors on the entry walls are held in quite fancy panels of white wood with gold decorations. We have a drawing room, a dining room, a library, a sitting room, two bedrooms, and a large kitchen with two servants rooms. Much care had been taken for our arrival. The bed linens were crisp and fresh, there were vases full of flowers, and small bars of the most wonderful smelling soaps at the washstands. I wanted nothing more than to run about from room to room, but you would have been quite impressed by my dignified manner. But, really, Father, our Paris home is quite the most wonderful place I have ever seen. A French couple named Henri and Marie Durez live on the third floor and take care of us." The letter was signed Sophia Schliemann, Paris."

What Sophia could not bring herself to tell Father Tassos was that Henri and Marie Durez, so like her own parents, did the cleaning, the cooking, the marketing, the sewing, the washing and ironing. New territory, and not one she had been raised to understand. She had already begun to miss her family and the easy interaction she had always enjoyed with them. Life in Paris was far removed from anything her parents understood and she began to realize it would take time to understand it all herself.

Fortunately, both Henri and Marie went beyond the boundaries of conventional domestic roles in welcoming "la belle girafe." They adored Sophia almost immediately, quickly aware of the miraculous change she had brought to their world, the once somber master of the house suddenly a man of bright new dimensions: talkative, charming, welcoming friends to his home every day, making plans for outings, and busy shopping, ordering stationery, purchasing jewelry, flowers, wine. Sophia would have a great deal to learn, but from the day of her arrival on Rue Victoire, the entire household had taken on a surge of new life and Henri and Marie found themselves needed as never before. A flurry of people came and went at all hours. There were guests for luncheon and guests for dinner, and morning tutors and wardrobe fittings and small emergencies and endless deliveries of dresses, jewelry, flowers.

From his customary post beside the pastry table, arms folded across his chest, Gabriel Santini had stared at Sophia in disbelief, the proprietor of Tag's favorite cafe intrigued by the sudden arrival in Paris of the very beautiful, very young Madame Schliemann. Lampierre was absolutely spellbound and could not explain why.

"At a loss for words, Lampierre?" Tag laughed. Recovering with a glass of brandy, Lampierre said he would teach her French. He knew a little Greek. They would get on perfectly. Greek had been an ingredient of his gentleman's education, he proudly announced, and was not a dead language at all, hardly dead he thought to himself, from the looks of the lively Greek-speaking Schliemanns, he observed. Lampierre the Tutor. He loved the idea and he and Vincente soon became a morning fixture on Rue Victoire. By the time he rang the bell at Marie Durez' kitchen door every morning precisely at nine-thirty, Lampierre had already spent more than an hour at Santini's, several of its marble tables serving as conveniently located offices for the growing number of Paris writers and political activists he debated daily. Seated at the kitchen table, he drank a cup of hot coffee with Marie, which he favorably compared to Gabriel Santini's café noir, commenting, between sips, on the day's weather prospects, the expected high and low temperatures, and the increasing likelihood of war with Prussia. It was the same each morning, weather reports and local news, but by ten o'clock, he was settled in the first-floor library, Vincente patiently occupied with examination of his tail or recovering from the previous evening's excesses, fast asleep on a fringed green brocade pillow, Lampierre seriously prepared for the morning lessons with Sophia, papers laid out in readiness. Shortly before eleven, Marie interrupted the lessons with a tray of coffee, an assortment of biscuits, and warm macaroons, the small passion Sophia found she and Tag shared with Lucien Lampierre, but not with little Vincente for whom, although she made no secret of the fact that she did not approve of animals in the house, Marie thoughtfully included the grapes she knew he favored.

Sophia became conscientious in writing long letters to her family in Athens, diligent in describing the sights of Paris in great detail, and equally diligent in glossing over the luxuries to which she was being introduced at an increasingly frantic pace. In her first letter to them she said very little concerning the Paris house which she had so enthusiastically described to Father Tassos. To them she said, "I wonder if you know that the Sabbath is a very festive day here in Paris? People dress up grandly and are out in the public parks which are very beautiful and completely open to them. There are large crowds to be seen and whole families can spend the day eating a luncheon and listening to band music. Tag says that no nation has ever done so much to create amusement for its children. Today I watched some of them riding in small painted wooden carriages connected to one another in a circle. They can also ride in little boats that are connected in the same way. It must be lovely to be a child in Paris. Many of the little boys wear sailor suits and hats and the little girls' dresses are made with white collars and bows. I have also noticed that the French love the open air, both day and night as much as I do. People read quietly by themselves in the park, while others play games and some ladies sit with needlework. There is always eating going on and endless chatter on all matter of subjects. I think about all of you, my beloved family, and with wishes that you could be here to enjoy this with us." The letter was signed, Sophia Schliemann.

In Athens, Victoria read Sophia's letter again and again, but it was her signature that made the greatest impact. It looked so regal and impersonal, and it was from Paris, which to Victoria was one of the grandest places in the world. She read the letter to Father Tassos one afternoon as they visited together in the small sitting room of the Kastromenou house and when she had finished reading, her eyes were filled with tears.

"I miss her," she confessed, "more than I thought I would. The marriage to Heinrich Schliemann seemed so special, so good for her. I didn't even think about the separation. He has taken her away from us, and will keep her away."

"Oh, no," Father Tassos gently reassured her. "He won't do that, but this is their time," he reminded Victoria, in his kind, understanding way. "They must be alone now, get to know each other. They are husband and wife."

"Yes," nodded Victoria, "but he'll change her. She's seeing another side of life. I know it." Of course Sophia was seeing another side of life. And its extremes were difficult to absorb and comprehend. She saw women arrested for smoking cigarettes in the Tuileries Gardens. Lampierre subscribed to La Rondine, a rubber, waterproof newspaper he said he read in the bath. The Tsar came to Paris to waltz with Eugenie. There was a wonderful little new invention called the electric light bulb, immensely complimentary to opulent jewels and the most extraordinary military uniforms in the world. There was drought, farmers prayed for rain, the Army sold horses for lack of feed, and syphilis was epidemic, virtually incurable, the plague of Louis Napoleon's empire. Baudelaire, du Maupassant, and Manet would eventually die of it, and it was all Louis Napoleon's fault. "The Empire is Peace," he had promised, waving the most powerful scepter in Europe as under enchantingly beautiful French surfaces, lay the stenches of discontent, death, and decay. All His Fault. Fault danced with Queen Victoria at Windsor Castle and a few days later stood beside her as she laid a wreath before the Tomb of "Bony" and the Les Invalides organist solemnly played God Save the Queen. From Legitimists to Orleanists and all the shades of Republicanism between, His Fault. Blanquists, Proudhonists, Anarchists, and Internationalists, His Fault. At no particular level of Fault's responsibility, however, were the intellectuals, especially the writers and journalists like Lampierre who unabashedly loathed the interference of His Regime. Likewise the painters. Manet, Pissarro, Renoir, for whom Establishment was philistine, the bourgeoisie who had no taste for the new art. And then there was Courbet who had angrily flung back the medal of the Legion d'Honneur presented him only to find that the young garret-bound "grenouilleres" loved him for it. He became their hero and dissension grew. Malcontents, angry young men, worried old men confronting their Menace from across the Rhine as Goncourt insisted Auteuil was at the end of the world. It was Autumn, 1869, and the last of the opulent Imperial Masked Balls was held at the Tuileries, Eugenie magnificently costumed, tastelessly wigged as Marie Antoinette. Drought. Poverty. Destitution.

Fear. Penal Colonies. Menace from across the Rhine. Come closer. Waltz with me. La Gloire.

And what would Kastromenou Athens have thought of French societal hinges not yet quite rusted enough to suppress its legend of hauteur, a pervasive French hauteur the Greek daughter examined closely, daily, deeply impressed by its exclusivity and as yet uncertain of her role within it as she watched the French Gratin, the upper crust of Paris, turn its comely head away from the nasty inconvenience of Menace From Across the Rhine and continue on, to dinner parties and to lavish balls where handsome officers in full dress uniform and decorations escorted ravishingly beautiful women adorned in magnificent jewels and gowns, decorating by their mere presence, the grandest, most influential houses in Paris.

Pearls, diamonds, silks, satins. She had them all. Quickly, almost magically, almost immediately, Sophia had acquired a collection of beautiful jewels and wardrobe cabinets filled with beautiful clothes. Tag saw to it that her evening dresses came directly from the fashionable atelier of Charles Worth who was himself exemplary of the French hauteur, in his eyes nothing quite good enough unless he had put his own exclusive hand to it. An Englishman in Paris and the first of the great French couturiers, he lived and worked as a self-appointed arbiter of style to the titled and affluent, designer to the Empress Eugenie, and first to sign his dresses with his name and attach inside the ornate royal crest that carried with it inestimable international prestige. But quite apart from his affectations and tyrannical moods, Worth was a true expert. Some called him a genius, unwavering in his seeming unlimited capacity for creating beautiful clothes, and not only for the wealthy clientele who attended Eugenie's candlelight balls almost nightly at the Tuileries place. He also understood the need for appropriate daytime ensembles and for clothes that suited the expanding lifestyles of wealthy European women like the young Sophia Schliemann who were traveling more and more and being seen in the elegant public settings of grand new hotels and resorts being built in European capitals. He was the innovator of the early art of pattern-making which allowed the same basic dress design to be cut repeatedly as a base to which any number of various ornaments and decorations could be added in a range of endless possibilities restricted only by imagination. Martine Durez was the first seamstress he engaged to experiment with the pattern idea. Her success with the procedure brought Worth great fame and forever changed the course of fashion around the world. Martine, the only child of Henri and Marie Durez, a simple girl of twenty, married to a baker and the mother of two children, was immensely talented and although kept busy by the demands of private clients, did most of her work for Charles Worth. Tag had wisely engaged Martine's services to assemble an appropriate wardrobe for his bride and she accompanied Sophia to her first Worth fitting at Number 7 Rue de la Paix.

At the time, Paris women of fashion were wearing the long, full-skirted dresses that defined small waistlines. Charles Worth's departure from this silhouette was creating a stir. He had done away with wide crinolined skirts and created a new silhouette, flat and narrow at the front, fullness drawn to the back, and ending in what would be called a bustle. Not only did this new silhouette reveal the lower contours of the female torso which for years had remained successfully hidden under vacuous yardage, but Worth made it in black, which was a dramatic departure from the traditional whites and creamy pastels being worn by the gowned ladies of the French court who were his best customers. One of the very first of the new black Worth gowns was created for Sophia as Worth scowled, scrutinized, and gestured in any number of physical configurations during her fitting, but when he said, "Formidable!" as he did to her, it was an assurance of the perfection guaranteed by his prices. Without that utterance, women left their fittings feeling they had not gotten their "money's Worth," a pun that thoroughly delighted his large British clientele.

"The dress needs nothing else, no further touch of the needle," he said to Martine in the fitting room. "She wears clothes magnificently! But the hair! Martine, perhaps you could style it for her. The color is superb, but it is a bit too wild, I think."

The black silk Worth would go down in history, soon copied by every amateur dressmaker in Paris, Sophia's hair quite another matter, remaining distinctively unique to its owner and staunchly resistant to Martine's repeated attempts at taming it into the fashionably smooth styles being worn by many of the sophisticated Paris women Sophia had begun to admire.

❦ ❦ ❦

Martine and Sophia quickly became good friends. They were close in age, and although Martine spoke no Greek and Sophia struggled with French, it mattered not at all. They were two women united in a language requiring no established vocabulary. The smiles, the sighs in the mirror were enough, and Worth was right. Sophia wore fine clothes magnificently and Martine had immediately seen that potential. The height, the good posture, the fine, slim figure, all contributed handsomely to what gradually became a more and more attractive picture. Martine took Sophia's measurements and a dressmaker form was made, one of the third floor rooms in the Rue Victoire house turned into a well-equipped sewing room where Martine spent many long hours adorning Sophia's dress form with yards of silk and velvet, a sash pinned here, a lace cuff there. She purchased all Sophia's new underclothes and made two beautiful dressing gowns, one a rose silk, deeply ruffled at the wrists, the other a dark blue satin, very full and flowing to the floor. The blue satin gave Sophia allusions of grandeur, and much to Martine's amusement, opportunities to practice her walk, her head held high, her hands out at her sides, palms up, in the dramatic manner of the actresses she had seen and admired in the Paris theater.

Tag told her that the women of ancient Greece were tall, that she was like them, and that she should be proud of her height, carry herself with pride, and practice a walk that would set her apart from other women. His comfort with her height provided much added confidence and an assurance Sophia handled not only gratefully, but with increasing poise, and as was the case with so many of her girlish concerns, his opinions now became the yardstick by which doubt was measured, Tag's the only opinion that mattered to her, as one by one, her insecurities were set aside by his gentleness and replaced by a feeling of total safety she could not possibly have anticipated. Nothing would ever hurt her. No obstacle would ever come between them. He would protect her forever. He said so, and she believed him. From the very beginning she loved her life with him. She loved the Paris house, the city of Paris and everything about it, the new people, the food, even the pace. Trust, gentle touches, gentle voices, laughter on the stairs, across the hall, in the garden, but the dark circles under her eyes remained and unknown to him the lump in her throat was a secret but daily companion.

Rest, Tag said was all she needed, and for a few days they stayed in quietly; reading, talking, and talking came easily to them, their running stream of conversation a constant interlocking dialogue offering immediate color and shape to their exchanges and the interpretation of events as they occurred. They concentrated on each other with care, listened to each other with care, and in Tag's study, surrounded by evidence of his lifelong interest in Greece, their conversations frequently focused on long discussions lasting well in to the night, most dealing with his intention to breathe life into The Iliad and bring reality to Troy. She asked questions, wondered openly and aloud, and as she did so he knew it would take optimal convincing before she would believe wholeheartedly, with him. But once she saw the hill, she would believe. He knew it, he said. At first glimpse she would hear the din of arms, and the shouting voices like cranes in clamorous unison before the face of heaven. She would understand it all then. She would come close enough to touch the leopard skin worn by the Trojan prince, the bow hung on his back, the sword at his hip, the two spears capped in bronze. And she would see the hungry lion fall on heavy game, Menelaus down from his chariot with all his gear to confront the prince of the realm, the great lover, the gallant sight. For now, though, Sophia still insisted that the Trojan War was a war of fantasy, of its very nature a suitable topic for the exaggeration accompanying its lasting popularity. Sophia believed, as others did, that war intrigued people, its unspeakable horrors, a source of public fascination.

She had read and now re-read The Iliad, but her interpretations remained at considerable variance with those of her husband and as aware of this as he was, it became increasingly important for her to understand the origins of his obsession and in the course of conversation during one of those few quiet days away from the lure of Paris, he told her the complete truth of his childhood, sparing few of the details that all his life he had withheld from others. Content and secure in the loyalty of her love, he revealed all that he had ever hidden about his father and Elsa, Herr Fassbinder, the Muellers, Frau Schwann, and for the first time, Sophia was told about the Christmas gift, the book his father had given him, full of the words he could not read and the pictures he had never forgotten.

"In the corner room, behind the white door, we sat close together in his chair, father and I alone in a rare moment. He read to me from my beautiful new Christmas book, turned the pages of pictures, and told me the story of the golden city of Troy. Of Paris and Helen, of Priam in his great palace surrounded by objects of gold. How wonderful it would be to find Troy and all its golden treasures, I said to him. We would be able to keep our home in Ankershagen. My father smiled to me and said it was just a story, but I could see the pictures, all the proof I needed of rooftops and temples and walls of stone in flame. Time and again I said that such a beautiful city built of stones could not have been invented or destroyed by fire and I told my father that one day, when I grew to be a man, we would go to find Troy and all its gold together, he and I. We would no longer be a poor family and we would be happy and remain together forever."

Years later, when she faced the German Emperor, Sophia understood with great clarity just how deeply and irrevocably the roots of her husband's romantic spirit were tied to the rich tradition of the German folktale. He had been born into the very heart of its medieval origins, in that same area of Germany from which the Brothers Grimm had drawn their rich inspiration, and he too was a natural storyteller, full of imagination and idealized imagery. And even during those magic months in glamorous Second Empire Paris, ancient tales were still being told by stone-faced, bent old women near the village of Ankershagen who still lived on edges of the forest and recounted legends set in misty clearings, tales of wooded darkness where they said tiny enchanted stone cottages stood, or where just a short distance down the winding path a cavernous dark castle held a beautiful princess captive under an unbreakable spell. A legend was attached to every pond and every lake. Mysterious creatures of the deep resided in these watery kingdoms, emerging only on blackest nights or in the whitest moonlight, a pair of transparent hands bearing the silver wands and golden chalices that if possible to capture, brought riches, true love, and eternal happiness. How natural for an impoverished, frightened child to dream long dreams of struggle and victory and to imagine himself the prodigal, securing fame and untold riches and the love of the most beautiful princess in the land.

Sophia's own concept of Greek legend held no such metaphor or background, her interpretation undeniably tied to the ancient tradition of the oral poet and an understanding which combined elements of fact and fiction. Tag saw this dramatically and for the first time when he asked how she, a Greek, had learned the classic Greek tale of the Trojan War. Although the simplicity of her answer may have surprised him at the time, he would, in their first months together, recall this incident many times over, and always with the clear recollection of how Sophia had first taken the time to settle herself comfortably into the chair closest to his, collecting her thoughts carefully, then deliberately creating an unmistakable mood and finally making every attempt to focus with as much accuracy as possible. It was an ancient posture, one indicative of the instinctive need for human preparation and reflection, and it was a trait of Sophia's which would always appeal to Tag's own more analytic nature.Sophia said that the story of the Trojan War was one she had heard told by her mother, at home.

"It was one of the very first fables Niki and I heard as children, Mamma telling us the tale of the most beautiful woman in all the world who ran away from her home in Greece with a Trojan prince named Paris, her point always to emphasize to us that the Greeks wanted Helen returned to Greece where she belonged, this the reason they had sailed the sea in a thousand ships to the shores of Troy where they fought a great war and outsmarted the Trojans by leaving a wooden horse inside the gate as a ploy to enter the city and finish off their enemies."

Victoria Kastromenou's interpretation of the tale of the Trojan War was not an unusual one. Countless generations of Greek families had told his same story to their young children in a similar way. For Sophia, however, the grandiose fable of childhood would eventually become refined in a more mature study of the Iliad at school, where a more complex set of circumstances were revealed and analyzed, and not so much with an emphasis on a motivating love story as on a great war in its final tragic stages. And now, more and more, Sophia was realizing that like it or not, this war, real or unreal, could become the central issue in her life, and for the time being she decided to treat its conditions in the same manner her mother had suggested she treat Heinrich Schliemann at first. She sought out only the elements she could deal with and ignored the rest. What she found she could deal with was the tempting thought of real people who could just possibly have inhabited a city such as Troy and before too long that tempting scope of mortality created the most basic of classifications that to the very end, remained fundamental between Tag and Sophia. For Tag, the major concerns were geographic proof and historical verification. For Sophia it was the people; their feelings, their motivations, the emotional impact of their successes and failures.

The brief rest did little to restore Sophia's energies and by early December she was seriously ill. The pace, the pressure to always be at her best had taken its toll and she could no longer cope with the demands being made of her. The exhaustion and feelings of malaise were overwhelming. The physician called in to examine her said it was a simple case of neurasthenia, or nervous fatigue, normal for young brides in Paris and nothing to worry about. Marie and Martine said Sophia needed her mother.

"Of course," Tag said. "I shall send for her immediately!"

"No, Tag. Take me home. Please take me home to Athens." Sophia begged.

❧ ❧ ❧

It was a dreadful voyage. Sophia was weak and seasick, and by the time they reached Athens, the lovely pale amber face was gaunt and ashen. Victoria gasped when she saw her. Georges' eyes filled with a fog of tears. They were sure their beautiful young daughter was about to die.

In a surge of anxiety, Victoria immediately put Sophia to bed in her old room where she stayed for more than a week, left to cycles of sleeping, crying, and vomiting, her face a constantly mottled mass of red blotches. Tag slept close-by in Niki's former bed, or tried to sleep, worried and unable to close his eyes for more than a few minutes at a time, Sophia's tears more than anything else, a great mystery to him.

It wasn't long before Victoria said her daughter was homesick, not pregnant as she had initially thought. Overtired and homesick, that was it! Curiously, and with vicious adversity, she blamed Tag. He had snatched her unwilling baby Sophia away and carried her off. "Sneak!" she called him. He had exposed Sophia to unspeakable depravities. She should have been more careful with her baby.

The tensions that developed between Tag and Victoria erupted suddenly as if in the surface winds of a violent storm. Hardly a full day passed without a thunderous explosion between them as Victoria methodically concocted a long list of reasons for Sophia's unexplained illness. She did not hesitate to remind Tag of the difference in their ages, that he really was too old for her baby daughter. What had he done to her? Beat her? Worse? Tag refused to respond, soon convinced that his mother-in-law's temper had been ignited by nothing more than maternal concern. And all the while, Victoria nursed Sophia back to health, forced her to eat, to drink fluids, to get out of bed, to walk and be well. She was an excellent nurse, she said. Of course. Victoria could do anything. Climb a mountain, cook for fifty, deliver a baby, tame a horse. Anything. Anything but make Sophia stop loving Tag. Victoria insisted upon an immediate annulment.

"Please, no," Sophia pleaded.

Father Tassos was informed of Victoria's wish. He was waiting for Tag. The documents he had requested from Paris had finally arrived. Tag could not deny it. He remained legally married to one Ekaterina Petrovna Lyshin, resident of the City of St. Petersburg. There were signatures, certificates, seals. It was all there.

"You are a forty-seven year old man," the priest said to him, "and it seemed questionable to me that you had never married. Before the wedding, to reassure myself that all was as you portrayed it, I sent for certificates of birth and I also requested marriage or divorce certificates, proof that all was as you said. These arrived just a few days ago. It took some time. How could you have betrayed us, Tag; deceived Sophia this way?"

The documents were spread out on the scarred pine table that served as Spiro Tassos' desk and aware of how deceptive they made him appear, Tag told the whole story and unfolded his heart.

"I secured an American divorce," he stated. "You know that I have traveled to America several times but Spiro, do you also know that I hold American citizenship? Yes, I happened to be in America on business when California attained statehood. That September 9th of

1850, anyone who happened to be in America became a naturalized citizen. Spiro, please understand that Ekaterina and I had lived apart for years. She wouldn't agree to divorce me and refused any terms I offered, no matter how generous. Finally, the only way I could free myself was to take up residence in the United States for a few months, which I did, in Indianapolis, Indiana. It is a perfectly legal divorce. I have the documents."

"No Tag, according to what I have here, you are very much married, and not to Sophia Kastromenou. There is no legal document of divorce from Ekaterina Lyshin Schliemann enclosed here. Are you sure you can you produce it?"

"Of course, I can," Tag said. "I'll have it sent from Paris as soon as possible. But please, Spiro, don't say a word about this to Sophia or her family. That's something I must do myself. And I will. Somehow, I suppose I knew this day would come. I should have been better prepared for it."

"I cannot conceal this, Tag" the priest said after a long, thoughtful silence. "It would be against all I stand for. But why didn't you tell me you were divorced? I made it a point to ask you. Don't you remember that day I came to see you at the Adelphi?"

"Give me a few days, Spiro. Just until the document of divorce arrives and I can talk to Sophia with something to support me. Please, Spiro, help me this much. I didn't tell you I was divorced because I thought it would affect the way Sophia's family would feel about my marriage to their daughter and it was all going so well. I just couldn't risk it. There was enough about me in question as it was. Please try to understand. Spiro, I love her."

Spiro Tassos neither agreed nor disagreed, but a week later, when the requested document had arrived from Paris, he reviewed it carefully and concluded it to be both legal and binding.

"I think the problem is a matter of interpretation," he said to Tag in the privacy of his small office. "The American decree of divorce you hold is not seen as being altogether legal here in Europe and that must be why nothing about it was included in the materials I sent for. Annulments are still more widely accepted, and especially here in Greece because of their obvious religious connections to the sanctity of marriage, but I would advise you to do whatever you can to legalize your divorce here on this continent, Tag, and as soon as possible. Do you think you can do that?"

Tag thought for a moment and then nodded his head. "You mean a substantiating or reciprocal document, don't you? Yes, I know exactly how to do that and now I can't imagine why I didn't think of it before."

"I must return to Paris for a week or two," he said to Sophia later that afternoon in the garden. "There are a few unexpected business matters to clear up and you shouldn't travel right now. By the time I'm back, though, you should be your old self. Promise me during that time you'll try to rest as much as possible and try very hard to get well, my darling."

He promptly booked passage aboard the D'Almare and arrived in Marseilles on the fifth of December. That same day, he rode the train directly into Paris and at the Gare de Lyon boarded the evening's last rail car bound for Montgeron and points south. It was well after dark by the time he arrived at the deserted village train station and quickly engaged the only available carriage driver who by some uncommon stroke of good luck had been waiting for the late mail delivery from Paris. On the last leg of his long journey he looked out from the carriage as it veered on to the Crosne road, grateful for the clear, cold weather and the starlit sky, knowing, as the carriage turned onto the familiar gravel drive and stopped by the splashing courtyard fountain that never before in his life had anything mattered so much to him and that even in the event of the worst blizzard or freezing rainstorm he would have continued on to this final destination at any cost, on foot if necessary.

The house was dark as he quickly paid the driver and approached the door, but as he knocked and waited he heard a dog barking and soon saw a flickering candle at the threshold to La Casin. A light sleeper, Martial Caillebotte had been awakened by the sound of carriage wheels crunching against the driveway gravel. Celeste's small spaniel had heard them too, and close to midnight was as eager as Martial to investigate. Wearing a thick woolen robe and leather slippers, Martial stood at the door, a candle in hand and Celeste's spotted spaniel yipping at his heels, utterly shocked by the sight of Tag standing on his doorstep.

"What on earth has happened? I thought you were in Athens. Has someone been hurt?"

"I had to see you as soon as possible," Tag blurted out as Martial led him into the foyer and closed the door behind him. It's an important personal matter."

"Here, let's go into the study," Martial offered. "I think I can stir up the fire in there. It was blazing when I went to bed. What time is it?"

The room felt pleasantly warm, and even in the half-darkness was inviting to its midnight visitor as he removed his coat and gloves and explained the reason for his unexpected visit.

"I need your help, Martial. As a member of the Tribunal of Commerce could you please expedite an official document that attests to the validity of my American divorce? I don't know who has to sign or how many signatures are required, but you know how to go about these things. Martial, I want to go through the proper legal channels but time is of the essence. I must be able to present the approved, substantiating document within a few days. Apparently, my American divorce decree may not be regarded as a legal document in Europe."

"Sophia must be upset," Martial said as he stirred at the embers of the fire and added another log.

"She doesn't know. Neither does her family. The priest there in Athens, a family friend, took it upon himself to check on my background and only now, two months after the wedding, has he received confirmation of everything as I represented it, everything that is, but my marriage and divorce."

"Sophia knows about Ekaterina and the divorce doesn't she?"

"No, she doesn't. I never told her. I should have, I know, but it was the one thing that could have stood in the way of our marriage. I couldn't risk alienating her parents at the time. Now, it will be more difficult but I can do it with the necessary document in hand."

The two men left for Paris on the early morning train. Arriving at the Gare de Lyon by ten, they stopped first to see Charles Demours, the banker who held all Tag's personal documents. With the American document of divorce in their possession, a short time later they then went on to the international offices in one of the Commerce buildings on Boulevard Saint Michel and by late afternoon Tag carried the officially stamped substantiating French documents of divorce in his worn brown leather satchel.

"Thank you, my friend," he said warmly as he and Martial parted in the crowded Gare de Lyon after an hour spent at Santini's. "You've saved my future for me. I won't forget."

"I'm glad I could help," Martial replied as the two shook hands. "Let's hope the next step in your plan works as efficiently. I truly hope it does, since it's the most important. Sophia seems like a reasonable, forgiving girl, but perhaps you should think of bringing her some flowers or a gift. That's what I would do. Chaumet's is not so far away. You have time don't you, to drop in there before leaving for Athens?"

Tag watched as Martial boarded and he smiled, now grateful for more than his old friend's official assistance. He waved and waited on the platform until the train steaming south toward Montgeron and Yerres was a small dot against the horizon, knowing there was just one thing left to do before returning to Sophia. Martial had made a most sensible suggestion. Flowers, or a gift, he'd said. Yes, of course, a memorable, symbolic token of his everlasting love. On Boulevard de la Gare he hailed a carriage and gave the driver his Rue Victoire address, Marie Durez as surprised to see him in his own house as Martial had been at La Casin the previous night.

"But where is Madame?" she inquired, fussing over him at the door as she took his coat. "Please tell me she is recovered and well."

"Oh yes, Marie. Thank you, Madame is doing very well. She is in Athens in her mother's care. I'll be here in Paris for just a few days before returning there. I really came to pick up something I've had upstairs in my desk drawer for a while. A simple dinner will do for tonight, Marie. I'll be leaving on Saturday."

Three days later he left Paris for Marseilles and the voyage that would return him to the blue harbor of Piraeus, the silver singing bird box he'd purchased at Chaumet in the spring and still wrapped in Chaumet's famous bee-strewn paper tucked safely into his leather satchel next to the documents that in spite of the explanation they would require, had once and for all time severed him from Ekaterina and the past.

"May life's hidden treasures be those of greatest joy to you always my darling Sophia," he wrote on the small white card he placed under the ribbon's fold as from the deck of the D'Albert the land mass of the Greek mainland came into view, more beautiful, more promising, and more welcoming than he could remember. The confession that followed in Athens was met with surprisingly inconsequential results, the passionate reunion between Sophia and Tag, in spite of his revelation of a previous marriage and subsequent divorce, one significant enough to ignore the existence or relevance of any past at all, the news of Tag's divorce, although rancorous at first to Victoria, a condition which upon reviewing the documents presented to her in Spiro Tassos' presence, she attributed to little more than not at all surprising behavior from the son-in-law she had begun to mistrust and doubt with mounting indignity. Of course, it did not go unnoticed or entirely unappreciated that the first of Tag's annual stipends to Victoria and Georges had, coincident to his confession and contrition, arrived in the form of a first generous check drawn on his Paris bank and payable immediately, allowing Victoria to deposit 10,000 French francs into her Athen's bank account and a healthy, happy Sophia to anticipate conditions ahead as Tag eagerly planned their spring journey to the Dardanelles.

# CHAPTER NINE

## Welcome To The Dardanelles, My Darling

### *MARCH 1870*

"E VERYTHING WAS SO green that spring," Sophia wrote from Paris years later, "and I the greenest of all in my fine new Paris hats and dresses, better prepared for an idle holiday with my husband than for ambling on foot over the ragged pits and furrows of a hidden hill. The one truly practical or useful thing I had with me was a pair of thick-soled, flat-heeled shoes which at the last minute Tag insisted I pack and how I hated them, preferring to believe I would best be prepared to appear ready at a moment's notice for a garden party in delicate little shoes and a big hat. But, in the rural Turkish countryside, no one had the bad manners to chastise my grandeur and I'm glad of that. Had my feelings been too badly hurt right then, I would have asked Tag to take me home, but of course at that time we really had no home to go to. It had become impossible for us to stay with my family in Athens for any length of time, what with my mother's constant criticism of Tag and travel to our home in Paris was out of the question because war with Prussia was imminent. It became an easy thing, really, to go ahead with an open mind, making my own mistakes and learning my own lessons as I went."

Escaping the unpleasant atmosphere on Andromous Street and encouraged by the dramatic improvement in Sophia's health, by February the newlyweds had taken up residence in a suite of rooms at the Adelphi Hotel as they awaited news from Paris. Hopeful they could soon return to the house on Rue Victoire where they had decided to make their permanent home, they were equally hopeful that current rumors out of France were indicative of little more than impotent war cries from across the Rhine. By mid-February, however, those hopes were dashed and all plans to return to Paris were clearly abandoned as war with Prussia became inevitable.

Lampierre had written to say that people were leaving Paris in droves, the trains to Britain filled to overflowing every day, and mostly with foreign diplomats and their families. With no choice but to attempt to restore a semblance of normalcy to their lives, Sophia agreed with Tag that the Adelphi become at least a temporary home as with increasing vehemence Mamma Victoria's behavior became impossible, her position abundantly clear that Tag's presence in the Kastromenou household had created an intolerable domestic situation.

Tag and Victoria could not live under the same roof. That much was clear, but at the same time Victoria was embarrassed to have it known that her daughter was living in a hotel and not in the family home just two streets away. It was a peculiar situation. Although she had not persevered with her original plan to effect an annulment, Victoria had turned against Tag for reasons he could not fathom and armed with Victoria's formidable episodes of mood and aware of Tag's disfavor, Giannis gloated, thrilled that the opponent had found disfavor, and so quickly. Unlike Victoria, however, Giannis' feelings were kept well below the surface, held in insidious secret and expressed in confidence only to Niki, who through her attempts at objective impartiality had only succeeded in raising suspicions concerning her own loyalties as dutiful Greek wife, devoted Greek daughter, and dependable Greek sister, all three of her greatest talents waging a miserable war within her. But, again, ignoring all family problems and with Sophia feeling well, Tag optimistically looked ahead, convinced that the spring journey to Asia Minor could indeed take place. With a departure date set for late March, a month at the

Adelphi seemed more like an extended honeymoon than the escape it really was, and confident that the Franco-Prussian War would be of brief duration, it was reasonable to assume that by the time they returned from Asia Minor, Paris would be back to normal and that life would go on there as before. And in the comfort and ease of their new privacy, their lovemaking grew ever more ardent and spontaneous, the range of warmth and tenderness so vital between them now that a touch or glance could instantly change, or delay by quite some time, the day's intended plan. So it was, on March twentieth, alienated from family members and for all intents and purposes homeless, that Sophia and Tag departed Athens for the nearby port of Piraeus, boarding the French ship Honoré bound for the Turkish coast and an appointment with a lonely hill that would further galvanize their fresh, courageous love and set the boundaries of that love as if in stone.

In a speech she gave much later in life, Sophia reflected on this period more poignantly than any other, recalling the voyage aboard the Honoré and attaching great significance to her first arrival in Asia Minor and the hill that would transform her life.

"The Hellespont's white caps were what I noticed first. Renamed the Dardanelles in modern times and navigated by a long list of captains and conquerors, these are the critical straits through which all boats and ocean liners still navigate when approaching the mainland port of Canakkale which lies to the south of the great capitol city of Constantinople by some 128 kilometers. It was through these same historic straits where at one point the land masses of Europe and Asia are separated by a mere mile and into Canakkale that as a bride I sailed with my husband aboard the Honoré in the spring of 1870, thus beginning my acquaintance with the many moods of the hill that had captivated his imagination. It was also in Canakkale that I set foot on Turkish soil for the first time in my life, an equally memorable experience for a young Greek girl from Athens at the time. My Greek homeland had been free of Turkish occupation and independent for little more than thirty years, a short time for a country with such a long history, and although by the time of my arrival in Canakkale I was well aware of the fact that many generations of Greeks had lived in Constantinople in the crowded communities above the Golden Horn and on peasant farms in the outskirts and villages of its rural countryside, in 1870, a citizen of Athens was still reluctant to venture into the land of his acknowledged Greek conquerors, and in fact was not encouraged to do so. Even as they had waved us off at the port of Piraeus, the troubled expressions on the faces of my Greek parents told the whole story of unabated fear and anxiety. Enormous tears rolled down my mother's cheeks and my father's normally cheerful, smiling face had turned to stone, but three days later, standing on the Honoré's deck in the gray-black light of early dawn, I saw the dramatic approach to the famous Hellespont. This was the moment I'd anticipated for months. Barely awake I had quickly dressed in our dark cabin, fumbling for shoes and a warm cape, enormously proud of myself for feeling well enough to have taken an active part in every aspect of the journey thus far, but it was cool and windy on the deck and I found myself wishing I had remembered my gloves. I thought about quickly returning to the cabin for them, but Tag was already standing at the rail studying something through his binoculars."

"There must be thousands of them," he said slowly, a broad smile on his face as he passed the binoculars to me. "Welcome to the Dardanelles, my darling."

"I took the binoculars from him and attempting a smile to match his own, peered through them to see nothing but a dark blur. I heard him laugh as I brought the lenses into focus and in a sudden flash of daybreak saw I was being welcomed to the Turkish world I'd been taught to dread by a natural phenomenon so breathtaking that I felt my own heart racing."

❧ ❧ ❧

In the pale soft light of morning the Honoré slipped through one of the world's most densely populated wild bird migration routes and in the annual tradition of unknown centuries, thousands and thousands of waterfowl had paused to feed and rest in the coves and marshlands of the Dardanelles during their long return flights to northern Europe. It was a magnificent sight, the resonating waterscape set against the background of nature's white morning blaze, the beaches and bogs fairly pulsating with calls and squawks and the agitated flutter of wings. Some of the larger native birds, the elegant wild ibis and long-legged cranes, preened and groomed themselves in the shadowed seclusion of rushes and reeds while nearby, smaller birds soared overhead, occasionally diving for fish. Sophia could identify clusters of bitterns and greyling geese at rest by the edges of a lagoon, and as the ship slowly maneuvered the famous serpentine straits there were spindle-legged sabine and immense noisy flocks of small ink-black cormorant and jaeger so numerous that they dotted their own private stretches of sandy white beach like dark, careless markings on strips of parchment.

"Thermal conditions above these straits allow the birds to reach extraordinary heights. They can soar for miles without a single wingflap," Tag said, standing close to her as she lowered the binoculars and passed them back to him, relieved to be able to plunge her cold hands under his warm, worsted wool sleeve and watch the activity of the unfolding scene. Testing the theory, she watched fascinated as many of the largest birds ascended with remarkable ease to resume the northward journey, confident in their instincts and spreading their wings as they allowed themselves to waft aloft and enjoy the ride. She and Tag watched spellbound, until the port of Canakkale came into view and the Sea of Marmara gradually narrowed as the Honoré approached the legendary one-mile width of water separating the continents of Europe and Asia, where both land masses lie visible to either side; to the European west, the peninsula of Gallipoli, and to the Asian east, Lapseki, Abydos, and Canakkale; crossed by Alexander and loved by Lord Byron who swam them: the spectral staits of antiquity. The Hellespont. Glossy, fluid depths of cherished tides, venerable depths murmuring of azurite and sapphire, Poseidon depths at which Tag stared long splendid stares.

There, the massive Greek flotilla, spotted from the Tower of Troy! A shout! Five ships! No twenty! No, one hundred! Now, two, three, four, hundreds of ships! Glorious! Godly! Prepare! To arms! Greaves, sword hilts! Scabbards and baldrics! A helmet, double ridged, with four white crests of horsehair nods savagely, the Mycenaean! Agamemmnon. Menace from across the sea! Prepare! To arms! Alert the great goddess, the owl her bird, the olive her tree. Athena! She rests too long, all in accord on peaceful Troy. Wisdom, naked wisdom, wake! See Cassandra run! Hers, the gift of prophecy. Never believed, never trusted. Sister of Paris running from her agonizing vision into infinity and the vapors of escape! No, to the vapors of Hell! Fire, she sees fire! Smoke, black smoke, screaming, black screaming. Mother. Father. Hers, the gift of prophecy and all the future seen in Helen's face. That face! Menace from across the sea.

A few sailboats bobbed up and down and outlined the horizon with color. Large cargo ships and ferry boats filled the harbor, and as the Honoré drew closer to its berth and prepared to drop anchor Tag and Sophia watched Canakkale's busy port activity. Barrels of tannin and crates of the terra cotta for which the area was famous were being loaded onto vessels bound for European and Mid-Eastern ports as gaily dressed continental day visitors disembarked ferry boats, eager to enjoy the views from the leisurely vantage points of Canakkale's numerous seafront cafes. Tag stared ahead, oblivious to the noise and activity and to the more important fact that the Honoré had dropped anchor, prepared to unload its small cargo of flour and tobacco and discharge its thirty-two passengers.

"The Greeks came from the opposite direction," he suddenly remarked, his eyes squinting into the sun. "But they were here, right here in these waters."

Even as he engaged a ship's porter to collect their luggage he was preoccupied, his jaw tightly clenched in the hard, unbroken line Sophia had only recently come to recognize as his way of locking out the interruptive cadence of the world. They had been married for six months and she still wasn't accustomed to this side of him. He had confided in her and told her his secrets. She knew about his childhood, his dreams, and how he'd felt the first time he'd made love to a woman. He had taught her to play backgammon, to whistle, and wonder about the world in a hundred high spirited ways, but he could also affect her happiest mood with episodes of silent gloom that suddenly descended out of nowhere to impose an abrupt uneasy barrier between them, leaving Sophia feeling quite alone. It was in this frame of mind and feeling somewhat neglected that she ventured onto Turkish soil for the first time, as on a sunny day that had turned warmer than she would have predicted from the cool deck of the Honoré, both she and Tag were quickly absorbed into Canakkale's bustling activity.

It was a town crowded with warehouses and shops, coffee houses and waterfront cafes, and it was impossible not to be drawn into its rich, mellow rhythms. Dogs barked at every corner. People shouted to one another from door to door, and in Greek, which astonished Sophia. Donkey carts filled with wood cages of live chickens and baskets of eggs were everywhere. Ox-drawn wagons lumbered along the main street, deepening its brown ruts as they splashed through the wide puddles of muddy water accumulated from recent rains. They registered at the waterfront Dardania Hotel, where much to Sophia's amazement, even the proprietor who welcomed them spoke Greek.

"You thought you'd be the only Greek in Turkey, didn't you?" Tag teased as they settled into their corner room, his mood much improved in the short time it had taken to reach the Dardania, "and that as soon as you stepped off the Honoré you'd be arrested and locked in irons! There she is! There's that Greek we've been waiting for! Get her!"

He smiled, held her close, and kissed her.

"I love you, Sophia, and I will never let anything hurt you," he whispered against her cheek. "I promised that to you the day we were married and nothing will ever change. You mustn't worry. There is absolutely nothing in Turkey that can harm you. Everything is in order. And times are different now. You must believe that and enjoy this visit. It means so much to me that you're here and that you'll see the hill at last. Now, are you ready for your first taste of Turkish food? I hope you won't be disappointed to find it's real food, just like food anywhere else in the world."

They unpacked, changed their clothes, and seated in the Dardania's outdoor cafe with an unobstructed view of the Dardanelles, ate a delicious lunch of "menemen," eggs mixed with green peppers and cheese served hot in a pan with small buttery buns called "pogaça." Sophia loved the various kinds of cheese "bores," which were delicious layered pastry leaves baked in the oven. For dessert there was "sutlac," a tasty rice pudding which she also found delicious.

From Athens, weeks before, Tag had sent word to the Dardania's proprietor requesting his assistance in securing the guide services of the same Murat Narjand who had taken him to the hill of Hissarlik the previous year. He had inquired about him as soon as he walked through the Dardania's doorway but there was a vague hesitation about Narjand. It was doubtful. No one knew. Who wished to see him? Why? The next morning, Tag and Sophia strolled Canakkale's main square and as they passed the clocktower sounding the hour in a deep, resonant ring heard throughout the seafront, a blue donkey cart came rumbling along the square's tree-lined roadway. Tag recognized it immediately and waved its driver to a stop. It was Murat, affable, smiling, and genuinely pleased to see the European gentleman he remembered so well, and now a young wife with him.

"Yes," he said, enthusiastically. He would be happy to take them to Hissarlik that day. Two more stops to make and he would return to the Dardania in one hour. The blue donkey cart held eggs and cheese. Six live chickens in wooden cages cackled and clucked beside him.

Tag and Sophia continued their walk, taking time before meeting Murat to see the Sultaniye Fortress built in 1452 by Mehmet the Conqueror and returning to the Dardania to order a food basket for the ride to Hissarlik. The Dardania was kept to a high standard where food was concerned and fresh eggs, poultry, fish, and vegetables were in plentiful supply, well-prepared and simply served. But the Dardania was best known for its delicious bread, which Sophia later learned was baked fresh three times each day. Of course, this meant that the aroma of baking bread was in the air almost constantly, and as they waited in the Dardania's dining room drinking coffee and eating a few of the fresh hot buns from the basket on their table, the fragrant air was as familiar to Sophia as that in any Athens bakery, the sense of well-being it aroused in her a pleasantly surprising condition.

"As we rode away from Canakkale," Sophia wrote to Niki several days later, "the countryside was covered in the fresh green of earliest Spring. Now and then I saw a rocky white hillside, but then the grass went on and disappeared into patches of white and yellow meadow flowers growing wild in the distance where sheep and goats were being herded out to Spring pastures."

The well-traveled roadway out of Canakkale soon became the dirt trail Tag remembered, but now, young shepherds and goatherds waved to Murat as he passed in the familiar blue donkey cart. Near noon they had arrived at the farm where Murat kept the horses Tag said were better suited to the coarse, rocky terrain at the hill of Hissarlik. Tessa greeted them warmly, courteously inviting them inside the cottage before they went on. At her table, she sliced into a loaf of dark bread, setting the slices onto a plate which she brought to the table for her guests along with a bowl of "patlican receli," a delicious eggplant jam she had made earlier that morning from miniature eggplants she had soaked in sweet syrup. It pleased her to watch the elegant young woman enjoying her jam. Could she really be Greek?

Murat and Tessa had three small children. The oldest, a seven-year-old girl named Leda who had her mother's gray eyes and her father's full cheeks, appeared enchanted by Sophia's hat with its cluster of pheasant feathers. She tugged at Sophia's hand and Tessa smiled as the child led their visitor through a wooden doorway and into a sheepfold that was attached to the cottage on three sides. Built of rock piles from the nearby hill which over unknown long years had bleached and whitened, it provided satisfactory winter shelter for the sheep and now, in spring was a nursery where lambs were born almost every night. Leda, speaking Greek, delighted in telling Sophia that each morning she awakened to the thought of baby lambs born as she had slept and she confessed that in the early light of dawn, before anyone in the cottage had awakened, she ran to the sheepfold to see if new babies had come in the night. Every day she counted them and now she brought her new friend to share in her delight and check the accuracy of her count. Lost in the wonder of new life, the two petted and nuzzled nine small creatures until Tag impatiently reminded Sophia that they must be leaving. Sophia promised Leda that she would return, and mounted on a young mare, she set out for the ride to the hill, waving to Leda until she was completely out of sight.

The winding trail through the rolling green countryside slowly gave way to a narrowing path. Tag warned her of sharp stones and bits of broken clay and although she understood how one of the horses might pick up a stone at any moment, Sophia was at ease on a horse, and of course there was nothing to fear when she was with Tag. They rode one behind the other, Murat in the lead. She could feel Tag's mounting excitement. He had barely slept the night before.

The sunny spring landscape at one moment gaily bordered by tall, errant clumps of oxe-eye daisies, in the next grew darker and narrower as the three rode deeper and deeper into the forest. An eerie quiet hung in the air. Now and then the cry of a bird pierced the graying stillness as to each side of the path the roots of enormous trees began to encroach. Soon the only sounds came from the horses hooves, but in an instant, as suddenly as the path had narrowed and darkened so did it abruptly widen and clear at a small, sun-filled hollow where she smelled the sea.

"There, Sophia! There it is! Look!" Tag pointed, quickly bringing his horse alongside hers. "Do you see it?" he shouted, his face awash in sheer joy, his horse suddenly breaking into a full gallop at the fringes of the broad expanse of treeless plain lying directly ahead.

She watched him ride toward the hill beyond under the cloudless blue sky, feeling a flare of infectious excitement welling up inside herself, its sharp hot pulse filling her with both delight and dread. For so long she had tried to imagine how it would feel to be here, to share in her husband's bright hopes as she was asked to judge the potential of his dream, but now that she was really there to confront the hill at last, it came down to simpler terms and the unadorned assessment of a human being unabashedly responding to a world there was no doubt he preferred above all others.

Tag was an excellent rider, in control, at ease, his shoulders squarely set in the unassailable posture she had come to know, but to see him come magnetically alive and transformed in the aggressive light of this alien world was to see him as never before. He was almost boyish, and as he stopped at the foot of the hill in the distance and turned his horse, waiting for her, inspired and unrestrained as she rode toward him, he could not for a moment have dreamed that with every advancing hoofbeat Sophia grew more and more apprehensive, not with disappointment in what she saw, but with fear for the power she knew this spellbound place, a continent away from Athens, would exert over their lives.

The hill jutted up from the fallow boundaries of its forsaken plain into the brilliant daylight like an oddly massed surplus of grayish brown earth, ascending gradually and almost unnoticeably, masses of white pebbles lining its bottomlands, larger rocks and irregularly shaped bits of broken red clay its inclines. A stiff breeze blew up from the sea, ruffling the horses' manes as they began the ascent, the smell of salt and sandstone perfuming the air as the party of three filed through an invisible corridor of time, their earlier procession through the winding wilderness like a demanding ritual of old, Sophia's lingering fears suddenly swept silent by the increased stirring of winds as they reached the hilltop and dismounted at the curving northwest promontory to face the unfurled panorama of the sea. Murat watched them standing there, the horses nearby. Tag held her close to him and they laughed delightedly, like lovers in a secret. He pointed to the sea, to the River Scamander, to Mount Ida. Again he held her close to him and again Murat watched them, the lovers in their secret.

What a simple matter it had been to discount the likelihood of Homer's royal city from faraway Athens. And in Paris, to luxuriate in idle conversations with Tag that had never succeeded in convincing her of Troy's existence. And how different to be here, victim of the vice-like grip of grandeur and stark, abandoned time, overwhelmed by the sight of legendary sea and sky and struck silent by the spectacular sight of sentinel islands spread out in the ocean-locked distance, the same purple-tinged islands Homer himself had named more than a thousand years before: Imbros, Bozcada, Lemnos, all in plain view of the defiant geography Sophia could not ignore.

Embracing four natural elements: the river, the mountains, the islands, and the sea, the Aegean Sea and the River Scamander had flowed unstoppable through unrecorded currents of time and caprices of man, Mount Ida presiding in white-capped splendor, the mythic summer residence of the gods reaching up slim and fingerlike to touch the sky as Sophia's imagination flew in ten directions. She blinked and scanned the islands and the sea, and she attached meaning to each compelling sign. It was impossible to do otherwise. There, below, on the Troad, lay the Greek encampment massing at the foaming beachhead. She could hear its great roar and din, the Greeks imposing their gigantic will, trampling freely across Homer's smoky battlefield, under his baleful summer stars, might and man and urgency spinning into trembling ground. She smelled the circling fires and counted tents and huts. She prayed for warrior faces out of Aulis outnumbering Trojans ten to one, and there, where she identified for Priam the best Greek warriors, beautiful Helen herself stood silver-gauzed and radiant in the sullen light, her husband, red-haired Menelaus, within her view, vowed to retrieve her, no, to kill her, and in the smoky air all round the voices of old Priam and his counselors, the crusty peers of the realm observing the war's daily progress from safe vantage points above the Scaean Gates. He stood beside Helen, pointing ahead, his arm wrapped in the royal tasseled cord of gold, Priam, aged rich ruler of golden Troy, his jeweled kingdom by the sea coveted by Egypt, known to Ramses, to Kodor, to Seti, and to young Moses.

❧ ❧ ❧

In just a few days the hill became theirs as in long, addictive hours spent exploring the length of its twelve miles and comparing lines from the Iliad to the landscape they were magnetically drawn to a growing list of endless possibilities. For a time Sophia fought it all valiantly and with a steady resistance of which Tag was well aware. She searched for the slightest justification, the smallest reason by which she could intelligently argue against the potential of the hill, but when she rode alone to the edge of the wide northwest promontory and looked beyond the plain below to the beauty of the glistening sea leading back to her homeland, she not only saw the past, she envisioned the future.

"When Troy is found that will not be the end, will it Tag?"

She had needed no answer. Mycenae lay across the Aegean, already known as an age-old Greek fortress clouded in mystery and myth. Every day she gazed in its direction, shielding her eyes from the sun's bright rays. If there was a Troy, so must there be a place from which the Greeks had come, and that was Mycenae, home of Agamemmnon and his queen, Clytemnestra.

The King of Mycenae had come to Troy with a thousand ships leading Greek kings, brave warriors, and golden heroes in a gigantic armada. They had gathered at Aulis, from all parts of the Greek archipelago to set sail in the great ceremonial pageant appropriate to their reputations, appropriate to their cause, and at Aulis waited for a favorable wind, one to speed their battalions, their horses, chariots, weapons and slaves across the sea to Troy. It did not come, and after weeks of waiting it still had not come. The men grew impatient, bored in their beach encampments. They fought. They argued. Food needed replenishing. Some died. The endlessly placid waters became the harshest of enemies and in a last desperate plea to the gods for a strong wind, Agamemmnon sacrificed his daughter, the beautiful young Iphegenie, stilling her voice and smearing her blood on the temple altar to find favor and prove the serious mindset of his mission. The gods accepted, and by morning had provided a swift and steady wind for the tall billowing sails of Menelaus, Odysseus, Ajax, Achilles, and all those listed in the Catalogue of Ships. Thousands of white caps crowded the sparkling blue waters of Aulis, carrying the thousand ships in a majestic send-off. But Clytemnestra, Agamemmnon's wife, mother of Iphegenie and sister of Helen, had screamed long into the night, inconsolable in the loss of her beloved child, vowing revenge, watching the great Agamemmnon and his thousand glorious ships depart through bitter tears of hate.

❧ ❧ ❧

There were more than enough Homeric comparisons to make identification feasible, but beyond that, the geographical contours and context of the hill of Hissarlik appeared absolutely irrefutable. Its landmarks conformed to ancient legend and commanded the appropriately spectacular panorama, but more than any other consideration, Tag's conviction that proximity to the sea remained paramount to proving his theory that this was Troy, made the fact that both the Hellespont and the Aegean Sea were found to be equidistant at just under one and one-half kilometers from the hill, the most decisive factor.

"Homer," he reminded Sophia, "said that Priam went in the night to beg from Achilles in the Greek camp, the body of his dead son, Hector, returning to Troy with Hector's body long before the sun had cast its first rays, even taking time for supper with Achilles in his hut. The gates of Troy were close enough to the sea to make Priam's pre-dawn mission possible."

Tag's excitement had reached fever pitch and he made an impulsive decision. On April 19, without the required Firman, he began excavating with Murat and one other workman. Four days later, the crew of three had dropped a shaft to a depth of eighteen feet, exposing a stone wall six feet thick, Tag immediately concluding it to be a part of the ancient city walls of Troy. It was a rash assumption with no basis in fact and one that Sophia found embarrassing. But, apart from her sensitivity to Tag's impulsiveness, she immediately knew that overnight the project had been dramatically defined with evidence that there really could be something of consequence under the hill of Hissarlik. For days, that thought disturbed her deeply.

Word spread quickly through Canakkale, and largely as a result of Tag's own promotion. Within the next week, news of his findings became a popular topic of discussion in the cafes dotting the waterfront, and headquartered at the Dardania, the Schliemanns were suddenly local celebrities. Continental travelers hearing of the recently discovered stone wall approached them to inquire as to the nature of the evidence of an ancient city at Hissarlik. Was it so? "Absolutely!" Tag confirmed, without hesitation, taking every opportunity to explain to curious bystanders that after a lifelong search, he had at last located the site of the Trojan War.

He wrote a detailed letter to Lampierre, full of enthusiasm, and he drafted a lengthy letter to the London Times with a complete accounting of his first days on Hissarlik and his plans to continue a major excavation. Once again, he contacted the ministry in Constantinople, stating that his early findings had proven highly significant. Why wouldn't the Turkish Government wish to have him continue under such circumstances? He was ready to do all the work, pay all the expenses, and Turkey would gain worldwide acclaim as the home of the legendary City of Troy. The Firman would come any day now. He was certain of it. So certain in fact, that the proprietor of the Dardania was alerted to its imminent arrival by official messenger from Constantinople. He also wrote to Adam Dreiser, the German Consul in Constantinople, advising him of his exciting early findings and suggesting the important role a son of Germany was about to play in the unearthing of the site of Homer's Trojan War. And he began to reinvent himself.

Yes. It had begun then, the lifelong craving for respectability at last within his grasp. Sophia was always sure of it. She had overhead him in conversation with the Dardania's proprietor, enchanting the man with spellbinding tales of his adventures along the Nile and completely captivating him with detailed descriptions of long months in China, the Great Wall, and his meeting with the Shogun. Later there were tales of Japan and America, all yarns of high adventure which Sophia had not heard before. New York had many fine public buildings and was clean and orderly, she heard him say. California was full of gold and he had made a fortune in mining there. In

Washington, D. C. he had called on the President of the United States and had met his wife and daughter. Their name was Fillmore and they had escorted him to see the marble obelisk being erected in memory of George Washington, the first American president. Every individual state had contributed one piece of building marble. It would take more than twenty years to complete. A great fire had taken place in a California city called San Francisco in which he had almost died.

The digging had progressed for three weeks when a Turkish official appeared, asking to see Tag's Firman. Of course he could not produce it, and was told that without it, "this destruction of the land must stop!" The Turkish Government owned the land, Herr Schliemann was told, and it had been officially designated as a site of Roman antiquity. Herr Schliemann was also told that new rules governing the granting of excavation permits were in place since a new Turkish Archaeological Museum was being built "to keep Turkish property in Turkey." The official summarily dismissed the small excavation crew Murat had collected and Tag and Sophia were left no choice but to plan their departure from Canakkale. But now, Tag decided he wanted more than a Firman. He wanted the land. He had decided he would own Hissarlik. He would buy it.

Even then, Sophia had realized that the digging could have continued for some time, had Tag not divulged the news of his early findings so impatiently, boldly sending word to the Ministry in Constantinople and directly into the hands of the very officials responsible for issuing the elusive Firman. Of course it was also true that some of the local peasants had complained, bitterly opposed to the invasion of their recreational privacy at the hill of Hissarlik, the romantic setting having served as a popular rendezvous for many pairs of lovers. The story spread that one eager adolescent had seriously injured himself in the dark of night, falling along with his female companion into a deep hole that had been dug at their favorite trysting place, remaining imprisoned in the damp cool earth all night long, until Murat had found them in the morning.

A week later, Tag and Sophia arrived in Constantinople, Tag's first inclination to descend upon the Office of the Minister of Public Education venting indignation, maintaining the integrity of his intentions, the validity of his findings, and demanding immediate cooperation. At the last moment, he proceeded instead, in a calm, precise manner, wisely inquiring first as to the status of his Firman and second, into the procedure for purchase of government owned land located near Canakkale. He was told by a clerk that he would be required to see the Safvet Pasha and signing his name to the form the clerk placed before him, in the upper right hand corner he noticed the date on which he had applied for the Firman. It had been one full year.

Prior to making an appointment to see the Safvet Pasha, Tag engaged a Greek speaking Turkish interpreter, unwilling to trust his own rather impressive Turkish vocabulary. He sent the interpreter, Melik Seljuk, to make the appointment, sending along with him a one thousand lire note to be given to the appointment clerk. Whether or not the bribe ever reached the hands of the clerk, Tag told Sophia he was fairly certain that the appointment would be made and kept, even if Melik held on to most of the money himself and shared a smaller amount with the clerk. The appointment was for Thursday of that week and at the appointed hour Melik met Tag at the Nomion Hotel and they departed for the Ministry on foot, walking along Sisane Square and past the British, German, and American Embassy buildings. Later that same day, Tag discussed subsequent events with Sophia.

The chambers of His Excellency the Safvet Pasha, he told her, were on the second floor of the central ministry building. He and Melik had climbed the stairs and waited for thirty minutes, he clearly recalled, sitting side by side on a long wood panel-backed bench set against a stuccoed wall. The military presence was obvious, two well-armed soldiers standing guard, their holstered pistols in plain sight, but at last, the clerk came to direct them through the doorway, past the guards, and into the chambers of the Safvet Pasha.

The Pasha, seated at his imposing desk, faced them. His dark military style coat was heavily braided and lavishly embroidered in gold, oversized epaulets at each shoulder. Standing beside him was his assistant, a small man wearing thick eyeglasses, a well-tailored European suit, and a red turban wound close to his head.

"We understand that you wish to inquire about a piece of ground near Canakkale," began the Safvet pasha's assistant.

"I wish to purchase the piece of ground called the Hill of Hissarlik," answered Tag through his interpreter.

"Half of the ground at the Hill of Hissarlik is under lease at the present time," stated the assistant. "The other half is owned by the Turkish Government, as I believe you already know."

"I would like to purchase the land from whatever parties hold ownership," declared Tag to his interpreter, who repeated his request.

"The Turkish Government owns all the land at Hissarlik, but we cannot cancel the lease which is presently in effect," responded the assistant. The Safvet Pasha and his spokesman exchanged comments.

"If you would like to lease the government's half of the land, perhaps we could consider such a thing." Melik passed this suggestion to him and Tag reached into his breast pocket for the down payment he had brought with him.

"Please tell the Safvet Pasha that I will lease the government's half of the land if I may buy out the existing lease on the other half." He held the brown envelope conspicuously as the interpreter explained his proposition.

Again the Pasha and his spokesman conferred.

"If Mr. Chadwick will relinquish his lease on the land in question, His Excellency will consider such a plan. If you wish to see Mr. Chadwick personally on this matter, you will find him at the British Embassy."

Tag stood to thank the Safvet Pasha, handed the brown envelope to the assistant, and left the ministry with his interpreter.

That same day he called upon Benjamin Chadwick at the British Embassy, as the Pasha's assistant had suggested. Chadwick turned out to be the Ambassador's Deputy and a British society portrait suddenly come to life. Every inch the privileged gentleman, from his elegantly tailored morning coat to his well-trimmed beard, his manner and demeanor were imperious and totally self-assured, but he was soft-spoken, witty, and completely fascinated by Tag's theory. Chadwick confessed to an affinity for Roman antiquities and fancied himself more than an amateur archaeologist.

"The Turkish countryside is a never ending marvel to me," he confessed. "As a boy I came to Constantinople with my father and I was taken with him to an excavation site where marble Roman figures were being excavated. Before my eyes, these wonderful, carved, life-sized statues were being lifted out of the ground! Their glorious impression never left me and I knew one day I would return to scratch the surface here, myself. I'm sure you know that there are hundreds of ancient sites in Turkey. One lucky shovelful can turn up something of enormous interest, Greek or Roman, and that incomparable feeling of being connected to the past. I hold a few renewable leases on several parcels of Turkish land and I may just turn something up one day. I keep hoping for something like those wonderful Roman marbles I can still see so clearly. Of course the way things are now, I shall probably have to turn everything I find over to the government for their museum, but for the time being it works out nicely and I'm able to pursue my favorite pastime."

Tag was honest and to the point in expressing his interest in the hill at Hissarlik, explaining as well, his lifelong fascination with a search for Troy to a decidedly spellbound Chadwick.

"Pretty place, isn't it?" Chadwick had commented to Tag. "And you really think something like a city is under there? I've never thought of Troy as a real city or for that matter, as anything conforming to reality at all." And continuing for the next moments in an easy banter peppered with pride of authority, Chadwick readily agreed to transfer his lease on Hissarlik, pending Turkish approval. He assured Tag that his Firman would be forthcoming once the transfer got into the system.

"System?" asked Tag.

"Yes, system," Chadwick repeated.

Tag had come to this meeting prepared, and shaking Chadwick's hand, he left an envelope on the desk. It contained two, one-thousand lire notes. Chadwick picked up the envelope and as he placed it into his inside breast pocket, he invited the Schliemanns to join him at dinner that evening.

Chadwick was a charmer and a relaxed, delightful companion. He spoke a bit of Greek, British boarding school style, but Sophia understood him and was appreciative of his attempts at making her feel comfortable, to the point where she felt brave enough to try out a few English phrases on him, "how do you do" and "thank you so much" greeted with abundant praise. Chadwick and Tag conversed in English, a language in which Sophia had rarely heard her husband speak. After dinner at the Nomion, Chadwick took them to his favorite cabaret, and Tag soon adopted his manner of attracting the waiter's attention with two claps of the hands. They drank ouzo and the men smoked hand-rolled Turkish cigarettes. There was loud music and dancing, and in the corners of the room men in red tasseled fezzes played backgammon at small tables. The rhythms of Turkish, Greek, and Russian music filled the room in exotic fusion, punctuated by the delicate sounds of finger cymbals worn by olive-skinned dancing girls with waist-length hair and almond shaped eyes who danced to the music of Russian balalaikas being played by rail-thin men in full-sleeved shirts who watched the dancing as they played, eyes languid and sultry, seeing and at the same time unseeing.

Tag was prepared to remain in Constantinople until the Firman was approved and he fully expected it within a few days, but the next morning Chadwick contacted him by messenger to say that they must meet once again. The Turkish Government would not approve a third party lease transfer on Hissarlik, nor would it consider a sub-lease of any kind. Tag was furious and suggested they go together to see the Safvet Pasha.

"I have credentials. I have the ability to finance an excavation. I do not understand," he repeated to Chadwick in the embassy's paneled office.

Chadwick made another proposal. He would continue to hold his lease on Hissarlik and Tag would pay lease fees privately to him. Benjamin Chadwick and Heinrich Schliemann would have an understanding between gentlemen.

"I will say that I am your advisor while you excavate the land. The Turks know me and are aware of my interest in antiquities. I am, in fact, the British representative for the new Turkish Archaeological Museum. When my lease on Hissarlik expires in two years, if your findings have proven worthwhile, the government will certainly lease the land directly to you, wanting you to continue, and even if they don't, you will still have your Firman. If, on the other hand, you find nothing, you just walk away. All we must do is to get the government to agree to your holding a lease on their half of Hissarlik." Chadwick said that he would make an appointment for them to see the Safvet Pasha together.

Tag's first instinct was to decline Chadwick's proposal. Why should he pay Chadwick's lease? They could have the same kind of gentlemen's agreement whether or not the government thought that Chadwick was advising or participating in the excavations. Although Tag didn't like the idea of theoretically being in Chadwick's employ at Hissarlik, it carried less risk. But then, on the other hand, lease payments to Chadwick would insure his influence and official support in whatever mysterious role he played with the government here. Besides, Tag told himself, the quest for Troy had absolutely nothing at all to do with business or its risks. He agreed to Chadwick's terms.

At the ministry, the same white-turbanned clerk wordlessly directed them to the same paneled wooden bench as the armed military guards remained at attention. The brief meeting went smoothly, His Excellency acknowledging Herr Schliemann almost ceremoniously this time, his red-turbaned assistant immediately agreeable to the request for both a lease on the government's half of the land at Hissarlik and to the necessary Firman. Chadwick personally presented Tag's letter requesting the Firman and signed as his reference. After signing the leasing documents which would remain at the ministry, Tag paid the fees required in full for one year. Again, Chadwick invited the Schliemanns to join him at dinner, assuring them several times through the course of the evening that the Firman would be forthcoming now. With no exchange of documents between Benjamin Chadwick and Heinrich Schliemann nor between the Turkish Government and Heinrich Schliemann, the application for the Firman was processed through the system. Tag had asked for no further documents, nor did he ask Benjamin Chadwick why he leased only half the land at Hissarlik. He was far too excited about getting started to consider such details.

Sophia did an admirable job of hiding her mixed feelings. Relationships had become more complicated, and she did not fully understand the circumstances, but Tag was happy, telling her repeatedly that their biggest hurdle had been overcome. Her most serious doubts concerning Troy's very existence remained, however, and although she kept these doubts to herself, now she questioned the direction of their lives as never before. She suspected she was pregnant and more than ever she wanted the security of a permanent home and a conventional life.

❧ ❧ ❧

These personal concerns, however pressing, did not prevent her from enjoying the city of Constantinople as she sought to understand its complex traditions and their impact on her Greek heritage, and as was the case with all her new experiences as a bride, she invariably thought of her family in Athens. Her participation on forbidden Turkish soil would likely never be forgiven, she had decided, not entirely, but no Greek she knew had ever seen Constantinople, not with Tag, not in his rarified orb and with his sense of sheer joy at the sight of enchantingly beautiful skylines along jewel-like shimmering waterways, the warm welcome of the familiar Greek language spoken at every turn; in shops, in street bazaars, in the cafes, and at the Nomion Hotel where she had waited while he negotiated with Chadwick and met with the Safvet Pasha. And how would she describe to Mamma and Papa the muezzin's call to Moslem prayer, its power over the many Greeks in Constantinople confusing to her at first, but a force she soon realized had been assimilated into their lives as she also realized that Greek religious tradition had not been irretrievably swallowed up by Islamic conquerors after all. Through generations since Grennadious, the Greeks of Constantinople had learned to weave in and out of a bewildering labyrinth of Islamic holidays, which added to their own and those of the Jews and Albanians of Constantinople occurred daily, often simultaneously. And everywhere, she saw the symbols of Islam, the emblems and banners of crescent moon and stars. They were hung in the shops and cafes, in the Nomion Hotel, and from the rafters in the Hagia Sophia, the once great church of Byzantium transformed into a mosque, its Eastern Orthodox loss a legend in itself.

On a May night in 1453, the last Christian liturgy was heard in the Hagia Sophia as the Emperor Constantine prayed alone on horseback and all the next day struggled valiantly to stem the massive tide of eighty-thousand Turks who bore arms against his seven thousand men. The Emperor's imperial insignia disappeared when he dismounted in the carnage all around him. His body was never seen again and in the Hagia Sophia that night, the conqueror, Mehmet I, prostrated himself on the altar, proclaiming himself Sultan, proclaiming Islam throughout the land to the glory to Allah, and bringing to an end the Eastern Orthodox theocratic era the world knew as Byzantium. Drunken soldiers paraded the streets in the days and nights that followed, plundering and destroying precious icons. Among richly embroidered vestments in the sacristy, priests were brutally assaulted and murdered, most of them left bleeding to death from stab wounds and slashed throats as the great Byzantine libraries were burned to the ground and private homes were sacked and looted. The Greeks of Turkey were slow to learn about the religion of their conquerors, but over time, as minarets and mosques continued to change their skyline, they began to recognize the solemnity of Friday Sabbath, the observance of Rhamaden, and the many meanings of Allah Akbar. Earthquakes, fires, and all manner of civil disasters had taken their toll throughout the centuries, but the Hagia Sophia had evolved as the Ottomon Court's grandest mosque, its glorious dome and arched sea walls which had once provided access to sailing vessels at a ceremonial stair, implemented to suit Moslem worship and remaining symbolic for Turks and Greeks alike.

The artistry of Constantinople's many mosques and minarets intrigued Sophia, the interiors of the smaller mosques covered with Nicene tiles, some set entirely with fine mother-of-pearl inlay, an endless visual delight. She discovered that the Blue Mosque of Sultan Ahmet I contained twenty thousand flowering faience tiles, including fifty variations of the tulip specimen alone and this too, delighted her. She had seen the giant Egyptian obelisk of Karnak, erected by Thutmose III in 1471 B.C. and she had returned again and again to the Column of Constantine originally composed of nine porphyry drums, the joinings concealed in full circles of pure gold metal wreaths. She had quickly developed a taste for the thick Turkish coffee Tag detested and before too long she would become accustomed to the sight of turbaned men in white jellabas, as through six excavation campaigns at the hill of Hissarlik, the Land of Five Pillars would become her unlikely ally.

ॐ ॐ ॐ

They returned to Athens in early May and attended several family gatherings in Victoria's garden. Niki and Giannis brought their infant son, named Thomas, born the month before, and Sophia and Tag announced that by Christmas there would be another grandchild in the family. Sophia's pregnancy had been confirmed by an Athens physician on June fourteenth and the next day, the Turkish Firman arrived addressed to Tag at the Adelphi Hotel. It would be effective in two months, on August 12, 1870 and it carried three major provisions. In addition to granting permission to excavate, it stated that 1) all finds must be divided, one-half designated to the new Turkish Archaeological Museum, the remaining half to Heinrich Schliemann; 2) all uncovered ruins must be left in the state in which they were found; and 3) all expenses connected to the excavation must be borne by Heinrich Schliemann, including fees to a supervising Turkish official who was also to be provided with living quarters.

Excluding the presence of the proposed Turkish supervisor, Tag knew he could live with the provisos and he decided he would take up the matter of the Turkish supervisor with Chadwick later. With another envelope full of lire, perhaps another miracle could be wrought in The System. In the meantime, he wanted to concentrate totally on the work at hand since nothing could really outshine its importance or his now official, written opportunity to pursue it.

The early stages of Sophia's pregnancy did not go well. She felt ill for much of the time and was easily fatigued. Victoria said this was entirely due to the variety of ill-prepared foreign foods she had eaten in the past months. Sophia decided to agree, hesitant to argue or to share her doubts and apprehensions about the coming year and too tired to understand the toll being taken by the emotional demands being placed upon her.

For Tag, life had truly never been better. Thoroughly delighted by the prospect of fatherhood and content in his relationship with Sophia, the chance to fulfill his dream of finding Troy completed a picture very much to his liking. Adding substantially to the satisfying mood of this period, was the purchase of a two-story house on fashionable Vintrous Street which would be freshly painted, redecorated, and ready for occupancy by Fall.

The house, just four years old, had been built by Harold Rimes, the famous British architect of the Adelphi Hotel, and was far more English than Greek in architecture. Although the white, exterior stuccoed walls and red tile roof blended successfully into the neighborhood's overall appearance, the house rambled, its large rooms formally laid out in the continental style, its thick, carved moldings, sweeping stairway, high ceilings, and polished oak floors serving to create an environment that although comfortable, also demanded attention. For some time Sophia remained in awe of the spaces which were so different from those of any other Athens house she knew, but with typical expediency Tag quickly set about ordering furniture and carpets to fill them, a particularly large French Savonerrie purchased for the gleaming floor of the dining room through the Paris antiques dealer, Claude Archambault, who was also asked to ship three hundred bottles of French wine and champagne to fill the shelves of the wine cellar.

They passed the early summer quietly, living comfortably in their rooms at the Adelphi, checking progress on the Vintrous Street house, and occasionally enjoying simple excursions into the Athens countryside, luncheon packed into a wicker hamper, awaiting exactly the right grove of ancient olive trees under which to eat and rest and discuss what lay ahead. With Firman in hand, however, it was impossible for Tag to concentrate on much else and it was decided that on the fifth of August he would leave Athens for Hissarlik. In no condition to travel herself, Sophia understood his driving need to go and encouraged the journey. Mamma Victoria did not, and made no secret of her disdain for a man who would leave his wife alone and pregnant to go off to a place as dreadful as Turkey must surely be.

As it turned out, Sophia was hardly to be left alone. It had been planned that she would remain in her parents' house and in their care until Tag returned, but shortly after Tag's departure, Sophia found her hard won independence quickly dissolved. At home, on Andromous Street, she was once again the baby daughter, subject to all the old rules, and it was soon clear to her just how far away from the old ways she really was. She loved her family, but she felt like a caged animal, panting for freedom, wanting to be off on her own, her attentions focused on the very things Tag had brought into her life, the stimulation of conversation, ideas, dreams. She missed him terribly, far more than she had ever expected. In just a few months, everyone around her had paled into a dull sameness, content with their predictable pursuits and patterns of existence and to escape she often withdrew to the solitude of her old room, to thoughts of Tag, as undisturbed in absorbing reverie she reconstructed events of the past year into a methodical chronology complete with vivid mental illustrations. Tag's letters became the best part of any given day and she read and re-read them with a longing that began to teach her all she needed to know about what he had come to mean to her.

"I can see your face here beside me," he wrote. "I have heard that when you truly love someone and are parted from them, that it can be difficult to recall exactly what they look like; that features never arrange themselves correctly in the mind's eye. I shall write about that myself one day, and say it isn't true, for I can see your lovely face, every expression, every smile and frown, exactly as it has been through all the days I have loved you."

Hundreds of miles away in Paris, as Tag arrived in Canakkale, Lucien Lampierre watched the beautiful mature trees in the Bois de Boulogne felled for barricades as the siege of Paris began, Vincente perched on his shoulder, the smoke from his now eternal cigar circling in the stilled air of late summer. Two-hundred fifty-thousand sheep and forty-thousand oxen were enclosed as the elegant wooded park in which he no longer dueled at dawn was transformed into the Paris food bank. Cabbages, onions, leeks, and squash had come into the city by the wagonload from Normandie and Touraine and in the forests around Paris daily public hunts were being conducted to gather game. Most of Santini's loyal afternoon patrons remained secluded in their homes. Many others had left for London and Venice to escape the advancing Prussians. But those like Lampierre, who largely out of emotional necessity continued to use the cafe as a home, ordered cafe au lait as usual, and seated at the marble tables in those closing days of summer, discussed totally unrelated matters having little or nothing to do with war, a commonly exercised diversion, it was noticed, as passionate theory and supposition concerning a conflict with Prussia had overnight exploded into all too factual circumstance.

In Athens, with Tag away, Sophia desperately needed something to occupy her time.

"I would like to take some language classes at the University," she announced to Father Tassos during a visit to his small office. "I want to continue my French and English while Tag is away and I would prefer to attend classes rather than having a tutor come to me. Can you tell me who it is I should see to arrange this?"

"Sophia, what a wonderful idea! Let me make inquiry tomorrow," responded Spiro Tassos, impressed by Sophia's decision to study during Tag's absence when she could easily confine herself to homebound activities, hand-sewing and embroidering infant layettes as other expectant Athens mothers did. But in the recesses of his mind the priest wondered exactly how the university would take to the prospect of an expectant mother in its midst, especially as her condition became more obvious.

"Sophia, you could be one of the few women taking classes at the University, and very likely the only one who is expecting a child. Have you thought of that?"

"I have thought about it Father, of course, but it would just be for a few classes. It is not my wish to enroll as a full-time student."

Her eyes conveyed resolve and a firm persistence, yet at the same time Spiro Tassos saw in them a plea for intervention in helping her to achieve this new goal.

"I imagine your mother may not think this is a good idea in your condition." he began, planting the seeds he knew would expose the deeper root of Sophia's reasoning.

"I have not told her yet, nor have I told anyone else, not even Niki."

She had bristled, Father Tassos noticed, as he realized he had indeed touched on the real reason behind Sophia's decision to study just now.

"Sophia, you have always confided in your mother. She expects it to continue that way even now that you're married."

"Father, if my mother could just be patient right now, it would be fine," Sophia interrupted, unable to contain herself, "but she is not. She criticizes constantly. In her eyes nothing about my husband and me is right. She says she sees changes in me she doesn't like. She doesn't like my new clothes or my new airs, as she puts it. She certainly won't like my idea of studying languages, especially now that I am going to have a baby. Father, Mamma thought Tag was perfection when she first met him. She said he was my opportunity and she scolded me for being the reluctant one. Well, I did exactly as she wanted me to and now I'm happy and she isn't. What went wrong?"

Sophia's voice had become thin and hollow as she spoke, lacking its customary color and depth, its emptiness and futility disturbing to the sympathetic priest who prided himself on his ability to promote the comfort and well-being of his parishioners.

"Sophia, sometimes people resist change, even when they know its for the best, and the biggest changes can be the most uncomfortable, especially when it comes to one's children. Your mother sees you moving into a world that is foreign to her and she may feel left out. She doesn't like being left out of anything. You know that. Your wealth and growing ease with it frighten her into thinking you may become a stranger, and of course the expedition to Turkey may never be acceptable to her regardless of its potential, but there really is nothing to be done about that for now. Once your child is born, you may all feel better about your relationships. Sophia, I think you are adjusting remarkably well to your marriage and it is true you are becoming a different person, but this is as it should be and as God intended. It has nothing to do with new clothes or access to fine new things or even opportunity. It has everything to do with your own broadening view of the world and the path and place you must make within it for yourself, and for Tag and your child. Your mother sees you racing far ahead, so perhaps it is you, my dear, who must be the patient one right now."

Victoria behaved predictably when Sophia announced her intention to continue language studies at the University of Athens, but Sophia had begun to determine her own position.

"And how are you to go back and forth? On a horse? In your condition?" Victoria had confronted her daughter with more than a mild trace of disdain.

"No, Mamma, I shall engage a carriage," Sophia retorted emphatically.

She not only engaged a carriage, she also engaged Metrios, the doorman from the Adelphi Hotel, to drive her. She took three classes each week in French and three in English and did remarkably well, enjoying particularly the class conversations in French and English with the added opportunity for describing what she had seen in pre-war Paris to an often fascinated group of male colleagues, but as her language skills blossomed, so did her girth, and as she joked openly with Father Tassos about this correlation, she was also aware that her condition was not altogether admired.

Contrary to local custom, Sophia did very little sewing and embroidery for the baby, creating a small stir on Andromous Street, but she did write to several of the London shops listed in the address book Tag had left for her, ordering all manner of English and Italian infant wear and supplies, including one of the beautiful dark blue baby prams she had admired in the Paris parks. They had such a proper dignity about them, she thought, with their four white wheels under a spring-balanced carriage, shining and topped with a dark blue canvas landau that could be folded down or rigidly snapped up into place, hooding precious contents from drafts or too much sun. There was nothing like that in Athens.

The late Greek August remained stifling hot and early September brought little relief. As Sophia's body thickened and the lovely French skirts and dresses from Paris no longer fit, she created her own maternity clothes by having a local dressmaker make long skirts with wide soft elastic waistbands and full overblouses with matching flared jackets. She also had some full dressing gowns made in light cambric cottons, and in the heat of that late summer she wore those at home most of the time. But when she left the house for any reason, to attend classes or enjoy a simple outing, she took pains to dress appropriately, regardless of the temperature, and this was duly noted by Victoria, who admired her daughter's unfailing sense of refinement in secret.

Far from the siege of Paris and an ocean away from Sophia, a new stage in Tag's life was initiated that August. At long last, he could pursue the life he had longed for, all the pieces in place, the very existence he had often pictured his to savor, and it began in the blistering late summer heat of northwest Asia Minor, the realization of his dream launched in the humid pestilential environment that every year brought swarms of mosquitoes and epidemics of deadly malaria. But he had come prepared. Every day he methodically took five drops of quinine and as a matter of course also administered five drops to Murat, now hired officially as his assistant. Murat had never heard of such a wonder as quinine, resigned as he was, to still another summer of raging fevers resulting in at least one death within his circle of friends and relatives. But a new life was also beginning for Murat, an assistant as yet uncertain of his responsibilities, but one fascinated by the idea of excavating for the city of Troy, for unlike many of his Greek contemporaries, Murat found nothing at all astonishing in such a pursuit, well aware, apart from this unique opportunity to attempt breathing life into legend, that for the first time in his life he was part of an undertaking requiring thought to the future and at least some strategy. It was a novel responsibility which he took seriously, affecting an indomitable will and tapping a natural talent for organization that had never before been tested.

"How long will it take to assemble a good crew?" Tag had asked him shortly after his arrival in Canakkale.

"A day, maybe two," Murat answered without hesitation. "I can pass the word in the villages here and in a few days I will go to Constantinople. My Greek friends there need work. They will come."

And they did come. Between the Greek community of Constantinople and the peasant villages nearer to Hissarlik, Murat efficiently assembled a thirty-man crew in one week's time. In two weeks there were eighty. Huts and tents were set up on the far north side of the hill, and several small cabins were hastily erected, one of which became Tag's Hissarlik home and office.

That August, Murat was not only Tag's trusted assistant, he also became his highly agreeable and almost constant companion, ready with an infectious smile and a good word when it seemed needed most. This amiability quickly made him a leader among the crew and his familiarity with life circumstances in the Turkish countryside went further yet in building early loyalties among the men. Murat knew which of them had suffered most at the hands of the "zaptieh," the Turkish police, and he knew which of them had seen meager farm profits eaten up by excessive taxes and prohibitively expensive farm equipment and supplies. In Murat, Tag saw a convincing portrayal of Greek poet and peasant, a man plainly possessed of an admirable talent for survival in his suppressive world but one also capable of assuming his serious responsibilities with enormous pride.

Under his intimidating hulk, Murat Narjand was tender-hearted and surprisingly sentimental. That he was also jovial and likeable were small miracles to Tag, given the suffocating conditions under which he and his neighbors lived, but the endurance and patience that allowed for perseverance also formed the most identifiable hallmarks of his personality. It was impossible to account for his sense of humor, or for his positive attitude and persistent faith not in the past, but in the future, and without fail, those very characteristics permeated the perceptions of all those with whom he came into contact. At Hissarlik and even in Constantinople, it was well-known that he had killed two men, one for stealing a horse from his barn, the other in a brawl over a wager in a cock fight. As a result, with most of his contemporaries, he carried an aura engendering fear and in many ways it was clear that he used this reputation to great advantage in assembling the working crew. In spite of the strength of his convincing personal demeanor, however, no one was as certain as Tag that Murat's greatest weakness was Tessa and that his greatest failure lay in his complete inability to let her know how deeply he loved her. He had a way of looking at her, his eyes wistful and soft, but he was never able to communicate the great depth of these feelings and it was clear that Tessa never expected him to, both of them understanding fully and privately that the circumstances of life had necessitated a particular ordering of human priorities which the world at large would never see or appreciate. But apart from his sheepishness and moments of shyness, now and again he thoughtfully brought her a gift, an embroidered bag of incense from Constantinople or a comb for her hair.

Although analytical about Murat and everyone connected to his hill, it never occurred to Tag that his life hung fragile as a thread in those hot August days. Quinine could not have protected him from the thugs and dissolute young men of the crew who, uncertain of his motives or their own futures, might have turned on him for any one of a number of reasons, but from the beginning, he was "Effendi," their leader and patron. They immediately looked to him as their confidante and mediator, and above all, he quickly became the one person in their lives who personified the word "planning," by example defining it, the very term itself alien to the vocabulary of Hissarlik and its peasant farmers who planned only for annual planting and harvesting, leaving all the remaining events of life to unfold, governed only by the seasons and by the Turks in power, whose interpretation of "what is written, is written," had successfully sifted into their thinking.

Tag's example was noted with great interest and with particularly high regard for its consistency. From the first day he awoke at dawn, dressed quickly, and mounted his horse, riding the short distance to the Hellespont where he quickly undressed and swam for half an hour, enjoying his daily bath and morning exercise enormously. By the time he had returned to camp, the crew was assembled and the digging began with the sound of the day's first clinking pickaxes and the roll of wheelbarrows behind which the small basket boys came in two long rows, each of them carrying the stacks of baskets with which they relayed the soil removed by the older men. From the start, Tag established his presence on the hill with a strong commitment to routine and schedule, disciplines not easily enforced in northwest Asia Minor, but before too long, there was a time set aside each day for eating and resting, and a time set aside each morning and afternoon for smoking. They all smoked, even the small boys. Every day, clouds of strong Turkish tobacco smoke hung in a thick haze over the hill, often motionless in the hot, stagnant air oppressive with late summer's humidity.

At first, he insisted upon seeing every basketful of soil and every small pile of pottery shards, in perpetual motion from morning until night as a result. Long hours in the hilltop sun quickly turned his face, neck, and arms a rich golden brown and in the weeks that followed his hair grew thicker, longer, and quite unruly under the brimmed hat he wore most of the time. But, apart from missing Sophia, he had never been happier and very quickly, Murat began to share his excitement and sense his deep conviction.

"I brought you to this place myself, but why are you so sure that this is the right place for a city such as Troy?" he asked, his interest and natural curiosity piqued and more intense each day as Tag directed the somewhat haphazard frenzy of activity and did his best to focus the crew's attention.

"It fits Homer's descriptions in The Iliad," Tag had answered simply.

"But surely someone else has read these descriptions and has tried to find the city," Murat insisted. "What does Homer tell you that is so different from what he tells others?"

"Homer does not draw a map for us in The Iliad, Murat. He does give us many clues, however, but we must work at comprehending his meanings. For instance, he says, 'as migrating birds, nation by nation, wild geese and arrow-throated cranes and swans, over Asia's meadowland and marshes around the stream of Laystrios, with giant flight and glorying wings kept beating down in tumult on that verdant land that echoes to their pinions, even so, nation by nation, from ships and huts, this host debouched upon Scamander plain, filling the flowering land beside Scamander as countless as the leaves and blades of Spring.' Murat, Sophia and I have seen the migrating birds, the wild geese and arrow-throated cranes, over the marshes here in the Dardanelles. Their annual migration pattern is unchanged over thousands of years. Homer is telling me that the Greeks came here, to this place, in that same undaunted spirit and he makes mention of the same landmarks we can still find here today. The Scamander flows, Mount Ida rises, and the plain below the hill of Hissarlik is of a size still generous enough to accommodate the assembled Greek armies. Look down there for only a short time and you'll see them too."

"Then what is it we search for?" Murat asked him.

"We search for signs of a city; for buildings, walls, fortifications. We look for signs of life within that city, for objects that would tell us human inhabitants have been here. We look for fragments of pottery, for household vessels that could have held their water, wine, and grain."

And so it began, the daily digging tedious, its progress clumsy. For all his concern with planning and order, Tag really had no idea where to begin his excavation, so with little else to guide him, he began at the site of the eighteen-foot stone wall he had unearthed the year before. After that, it became a matter of digging one hole, then another, and then another. He was tireless, his focus never wavered, and he never doubted the eventual outcome of his efforts, but his thoughts often turned to Sophia in what was to him, a preordained connection between his work at Hissarlik and the significance of her Greek heritage. Thoughts of the coming baby only strengthened this fusion in a uniquely manifested flood of energy propelling him on in the face of overwhelming odds as dirt was removed from the worksite by the wheelbarrowful and deposited onto the piles of brownish-gray soil that grew daily. At first, pottery shards, which were the terra cotta of Canakkale, came up in great profusion. The shards were sifted out of the soil and piled separately from the soil. Tag sometimes attempted to reassemble several of the clay pieces into a vessel, all without success. He was unprepared for the piles of garbage. After three weeks of digging at four worksites, it came up in huge heaps of unidentifiable mass, but soon, fishbones and mussel shells, thousands of them, appeared. The shells were found layer upon layer, most of them large enough to suggest a once generous edible morsel and certainly larger than any mussels he'd seen anywhere. In some places the soil had calcified around them, the still glossy shells appearing as textured collages, jagged around the edges and quite beautiful. At a depth of eighteen meters, stone lance points were uncovered, and shortly after, heaps of bronze nails. These findings were attributed to Roman occupation and caused him no excitement, but within six weeks, Dr. Worsaae's stratigraphic succession, or "layer cake" theory had begun to ring true. In all four sections under excavation an irregularity in the levels of debris and potsherds revealed an unmistakable lack of orderly erosion in what had become open areas of sliced earth and Tag astutely determined, just as Worsaae had suggested, that the ancients would not have displayed any great concern in rebuilding their cities. Of course. There was no time. Remains would not have been neatly swept away, the land neither leveled nor cleared before rebuilding. Remains were left where they had fallen, along with accompanying debris, a new city founded directly over the many undulating and irregular mounds of whatever lay there, towns and villages hastily erected for shelter and immediate protection from a rapid succession of marauding invaders. Of course, this would have resulted in wide variations of foundation and roof lines, roadways and walls, which along with forces of nature such as the frequent earthquakes known to occur in the area, left no clear markings in their wake. But if anything at all was becoming clear, it was this: If the hill of Hissarlik was the Pergamus of Troy, there could be many layered settlements and cities to uncover before Troy itself was found. How, among them, would he possibly recognize his golden city by the sea?

Characteristically, such probing questions seemed not to worry him at all. All problems would be solved, all questions answered, somehow. His confidence was such that he began periodic reports to the London Times, announcing that after the first, short excavation season, his findings revealed indisputable evidence of the existence of a well-established prehistoric civilization at Hissarlik in Asia Minor, one that he believed likely predated the Homeric period. He sent off similar dispatches to German and French papers, beginning what was to set off a world-wide and long lasting interest in his work on a remote hill in the northwest corner of Asia Minor, his early conclusions enough to prompt his first letter to the Institut de France and to the Berlin newspaper, Ausberger Allemeine Zeitung. He also wrote directly to Dr. Worsaae in Denmark and this was among his wisest communications.

"I believe I have discovered irrefutable evidence of a large, prehistoric settlement," he wrote to Worsaae, describing the potsherds, piles of debris, and the bronze nails. The bronze nails got Worsaae's immediate attention. He had been investigating the Three-Age course of Human Progress through prehistory, and was able to show that the Stone Age had preceded the era in which most tools and implements were made of bronze. After the Bronze Age, came a period in which everyday implements were of iron, bronze then being reserved for ornaments of luxury. Worsaae was the first to propose that the Three-Age system of Stone, Bronze, then Iron, was valid for all of prehistoric Europe. He said that findings of bronze nails in Asia Minor could mean one of two things: trade with or occupation by Europeans who could have brought bronze tools with them as early as three thousand years before the birth of Christ or earlier.

In September, much to Tag's surprise and delight, Dr. Worsaae made the arduous journey from Denmark to Canakkale and on to the hill of Hissarlik. In a letter to Sophia, Tag wrote, "Dr. Worsaae is most helpful and a most likeable and energetic gentleman. He thinks our hill could indeed be a prehistoric layer cake and that there may be several confusing layers with which to deal. He is neither discouraging nor is he entirely encouraging, facing the project here as he does every project, objectively and realistically. But since he did not dismiss my work completely, suggesting that I pack up and leave for home immediately, I must conclude that he senses some potential here."

J. J. Worsaae was a dignified, methodical man with a reputation as a fastidious researcher and his counsel and encouragement could not have come at a better time, his suggestions carefully noted, his advice carefully followed. Among other things, Worsaae advised Tag to avoid haste in digging and removing soil; to first be on the constant lookout for subtle stains in the soil, for impressions that could indicate the one-time existence of vanished fragments of cloth or wood. Guided by this advice and Worsaae's experience, Tag now worked out several logical approaches to his excavation, determining with Worsaae the possible horizontal layout and general vertical limits of the hill. These were the first real beginnings of a working plan.

Benjamin Chadwick also visited in September, impressed to meet Worsaae, well aware of his distinguished reputation within the small world community of archaeologists. Worsaae's presence was enough to convince him that the excavation on the hill of Hissarlik was not merely a rich man's recreational activity, and for the first time he assessed Tag's project seriously. For a fleeting moment he even seriously considered implications for its success.

As a result of Worsaae's visit, several major factors were put into perspective, but his remarks following one of Tessa's well-prepared evening meals left the most lasting impression. "Do not lose sight of the objective that has brought you here," he said to Tag. "If you believe that Homer has brought you, do not allow yourself to be distracted. Focus on that in your study and research and make note of everything you see and find. Add your conclusions and suppositions, no matter how unrelated or insignificant they may seem at the time. You will go back to your records again and again, and in the end, they will form the truest, most accurate picture of what you do here. Realize also, that what you are doing could very well fill in some important gaps in history. After the fall of the Roman Empire for example, history went largely unrecorded as civilization fell into the Dark Ages. The true splendor of Greece and Rome was all but forgotten in the desperation of a people struggling to remain alive. If just a fraction of what you seek is here, you will redefine the meaning of the word archaeology as a study of the remains of the past, and I for one, hope that you do."

Although greatly encouraged, it was disappointing to Tag that Dr. Worsaae had drawn no substantive conclusions on the bronze nails, his suggestion only that additional evidence would be required to verify their meaning in Asia Minor. Of course, Tag had desperately wanted to hear that his bronze nails had been brought by an army from across the sea, specifically a prehistoric Greek army camped on the Troad long enough to have made repairs and modifications to weaponry and fortifications. On October first, the London Times reported that Herr Heinrich Schliemann had begun excavations at a site in Asia Minor which he judged to be that of the Trojan War. A few days later he closed down the excavations for the winter and returned to Athens with very little to show for almost three months work. His hair had grown long. It curled softly around his ears, giving his sun-bronzed face a distinguished silver frame. Sophia waited for him in their suite at the Adelphi. They flew into each other's arms.

"We will not do this again," he whispered against her cheek. "We will not be separated like this, not ever again. I want you with me all the time, at my side every minute of every day."

Andromache Schliemann was born on December 18, 1870, in her grandmother Victoria's house, in the same small bedroom her mother had known for all eighteen years of her life. In that same house, she spent her first Christmas with her parents, her grandparents, and her baby cousin, Thomas, and on January 8, 1871 she and her parents moved into the large, airy house on Vintrous Street.

# CHAPTER TEN

## 1871

T HE WINTER OF 1871 was idyllic. At home in Athens. Settled. A beautiful healthy child. Happiness as never before. But that winter, their thoughts frequently turned to wartorn Paris, to concerns for Marie and Henri in the Paris house on Rue Victoire, to Martine, to Lampierre, and to the Caillebottes. And as Sophia and Tag at last began to carve out the meaningful dimensions of a life in Athens, Tag's beloved city of Paris endured the greatest of hardships under conditions it seemed the rest of the world had failed to notice, for while he had been digging into the hill of Hissarlik, Turkish Firman in hand, war had indeed come to Paris, and under the harshest conditions. It was impossible to know with any degree of certainty exactly what was going on. No accurate news came out of France as the Paris press became little more than a rumor mill, publishing reports based upon completely unfounded gossip and conjecture. On one day Bismarck was dead and on another, dead also was the Prussian Crown Prince. Nothing could have been farther from the truth as comfortably headquartered in the Rothschild's magnificent Chateau de Ferrières, Bismarck held fast and set his terms: Alsace and part of Lorraine. By October he had moved into the Palace at

Versailles where the Prussian King had hastily established his court. Bismarck requested personal use of the vast art galleries but they had quickly been converted into hospital wards for the German wounded and an apartment was prepared for him in another part of the palace. He passed the art galleries every day as he busied himself with appointments and meetings with the Emperor. He hated the stench emanating from those coveted chambers. By November he hated the cold even more, his persistently watery eyes growing ever more lacteous in the icy temperatures the king thought appropriate for the proper care of his new collection of paintings which hung on the walls above the maimed and dying. But there were compensations. Fine food and wine for example, and the satisfaction of Bismarck's gluttonous appetite, for as the war progressed so did his girth. By the time his king was proclaimed Emperor at the Palace of Versailles, according to well-publicized plans, the Iron Chancellor had become famous for a belly over which his custom-made military frock coats simply would not button. The tailor brought from Berlin found it amusing that such a large man would possess such a thin, high-pitched voice.

"Another button here, idiot!" the shirtless Chancellor impatiently shrieked, pointing to his nonexistent waistline as he attempted to stuff himself into the black frock coat whose hand-turned buttonholes simply would not support the strain placed on the fine gold Roman coins he had ordered sewn onto the wool as fasteners. His bare chest, partly visible under the open coat was snow-white and covered with black hairs that could quickly be counted, his bare, trouserless legs surprisingly well-shaped and muscular under his ballooning middle, but just under each knee a deep red welt could be seen, penalty of the fashionably high-cut, close-fitting leather boots his vanity demanded.

"It must be perfect for tomorrow!" the bullying tenor coarsely insisted as he flung the coat to the tailor, envisioning as he spoke, the sartorial splendor of his Emperor and the Crown Prince wearing their own impeccably fitted coats and vests in the Hall of Mirrors. And even in the privacy of his Versailles apartments, the Otto von Bismarck-Schönhausen born on All Fools Day was ever the insufferably demanding autocrat whose rudeness to underlings and parallel limitless courage enabled him to stand stark naked and alone, equally at ease whether confronting a single Berlin tailor or the judgment of the entire world.

And as Bismarck feasted, Paris was severed from the rest of Europe, a city under siege, its summer storage of food rapidly depleted, the livestock collected in the Bois all too quickly consumed. Caught unprepared, Parisians were introduced to the stringencies of rationing, its accompanying chaos, and the outrage that descended suddenly with the realization that theirs was a starving city. They had prepared for eighty days, not four months. That summer, under carefree sunshine, the mood had been recklessly optimistic. Let the Menace come. Let him dare. And on leisurely summer afternoons, through monocles and shaded under parasols, elegant Parisians had reviewed the impressive fortifications enclosing their city in the same placidly superior frame of mind that had so recently accompanied them on drives through the leafy Bois. Soaring fountains still sparkled in the elegant sun when the first canons were heard at Meudon and the streets filled with the first of the terrified French Army deserters who spilled into the city with unbelievable tales of French officers abandoning their troops in fear after having witnessed the overwhelming sight of one-hundred-thousand Prussian troops massed in the Bois de Meudon. And as the Prussian armies drew ever closer to the city, well-disciplined and inspired by their experienced soldier-king, French blood was boiling with indignation, but in column after column, down the three main roads leading into Paris they came. Overnight, the city of summer was occupied and cut off, the chill of French daring as useless as its irretrievable past.

Lampierre predicted a terrible winter and as he suffered the indignities of Prussian occupation, he was lonely and disoriented by more than the shortage of food, more furious over the unforgivable ten o'clock curfew that had been imposed on Paris cafes than over the disappearance of beef and cheese. For an insomniac such as he, the nightlife of Paris had been brilliance and balm, but now the opera and the theaters were closed and at night the streets were dark and deserted, not even a streetcleaner to observe or engage in conversation. Not to talk late into the night, not to exchange ideas, not to progress. It was unthinkable for his Paris. But it was so. Early to bed was His fault, the result of Louis Napoleon's irrational, inflated visions of glory.

In September, Louis Napoleon was captured at the battle of Sedan. As Bismarck's prisoner at Wilhelmshohe, Lampierre heard that Louis passed his time rather constructively, writing a detailed treatise on beet sugar production and a timely, if somewhat inappropriate essay on unemployment. It was the political fodder of which even Lampierre had not dared to dream as the hopeful and ambivalent struggled on, Manet and Degas joining the newly formed French National Guard, while Pissarro and his family fled to London, as did Monet. Cezanne successfully avoided conscription and continued painting at Aix and L'Estaque but both Renoir and Bazille were conscripted. Tragically, Bazille was killed in action at Beaune Rolande, but Renoir obtained a pass enabling him to move freely between Paris and Louvecienne where he frequently lunched with his nearest neighbor, Alfred Sisley. Later that Spring, both Monet and Pissarro exhibited at the International Exhibition in London's South Kensington.

And to the bucolic countryside at Yerres, in the land of haystacks at the curve in the river, came, that September, two heavy columns of Prussian infantry. They camped on the borders of the Senart forest and hunted in the game-rich royal hunting preserve, and at nearby La Casin the windows were tightly shuttered as the Caillebottes imprisoned themselves in the rooms of their country house while outside in their lovely landscaped park, Martial's young maple trees were cut down to fuel the Prussian fires blazing on his immaculate green lawns; fires on which the soldiers cooked their freshly killed wild partridge and crown pheasant, Josephine's prize late summer roses the decorations on their military lapels, the colorful, ruffled petals cascading gaily about in the warm September breeze as if to herald a long-awaited country celebration.

At the same time in Paris, looting went unchallenged, hostages were taken, and food shortages worsened. As supplies of fresh meat were exhausted, first horsemeat found its way onto the menu, many a champion of the turf butchered, as were the prize jumpers given to Louis Napoleon by the Tsar and valued at 56,000 francs. Lampierre may have been one of the first to notice the sudden culinary appeal of the many cats of Paris, impressed as he was by their agility and heightened aloofness when approached by kindly human admirers. The National Guard specialized in rats, which became the fabled creatures of the Siege. Rat hunts became quite popular with the Guard, but there remained an overriding fear of the diseases they were known to carry and it was said that the sauces required to make the meat of rodents palatable were overly time consuming for men at war. After eating horsemeat, which Gabriel Santini learned to prepare in an endless variety of clever ways, Lampierre said he would never again understand how people could eat cows, and when told that horsemeat was known to provoke wildly erotic nightmares, he compromised nobly, maintaining that the nightmares brought on by the flesh of light grey horses were preferable by far to those brought on by browns or blacks. And in the process, Paris grew frantic. Desperate young mothers substituted horse gelatins for non-existent milk and as supplies of flour dwindled, bakeries closed their doors and bread, the basic staple of the French diet, became a disappearing luxury.

At last in March there was a letter from Martine. Sophia tore it open, the grim truth it revealed hardly the news she had expected. "Although we were told that the occupation was to be of brief duration, it continues to bring much grief to us. Our food supplies are greatly reduced and we stave off hunger as best we can, keeping body and soul together on the carrots and potatoes that were stored in the cellar. The Prussians have brought much destruction to Paris. Its beauty is greatly marred. The Tuileries Palace is in shambles but it is the hunger that is most difficult for the people to bear. Children search and beg in the streets for the smallest morsel of food. Many have died. By the Grace of God, the courtyard at Rue Victoire has been spared serious damage. Time seems to have stood still here, and for that we are grateful. There are many broken windows on the first floor of the house, but my father says that these can easily be repaired. All inside is in good condition and just as you remember it. Both my parents are well and send you their affectionate regards. We were saddened to hear that Monsieur Lucien Lampierre lost his life one night as an innocent bystander in an exchange of fire. Against repeated advice from his many friends, Monsieur Lampierre was often out late at night. He died in the street at the entrance to the Avenue of the Acacias. His monkey, Vicente, was killed with his master, the blue military jacket he constantly wore still buttoned around his little body when he was found."

Tag had to read the words for himself. See them, touch them. And as the warm rush of memory overcame him, he secluded himself in his study for the rest of the day, its dark paneled doors tightly closed. Sophia could see Lampierre so clearly, the curling mustache, the small round spectacles he wore, and she could still hear his enthusiastic agreement with her that second only to a good glass of brandy shared with Vincente, warm macaroons were absolutely the world's most delicious creation.

From the beginning, the Athens household on Vintrous Street ran smoothly, its functioning needs met by a young Greek couple who performed the service of Marie and Henri Durez in Paris. They cooked and served meals, and with the help of two servants, kept the house clean and orderly. The routine was easily maintained. Tag determined it, insisting that a daily schedule be observed, regular times set each day for meals, work, and rest. Since there was little deviation from this norm, the household staff worked within its definition in a clear understanding of what was expected. The midday mealtime was set as it had been in Paris, at one o'clock each day. A five o'clock teatime was established, usually served outdoors on the broad terrace, but at times in the sun-filled drawing room. Andromache was brought down to tea every day at five, fresh from a nap, and for the next hour she was the center of attention, regardless of the importance of any single houseguest or visitor. Tag thoroughly enjoyed these times with his baby daughter. She was a phenomenon to him, a constant fascination. He held her securely in his arms, talked gently to her in a steady stream, and watched delightedly for her smiles and laughter, concluding from her attentive responses that she was not only the most beautiful of children, but unquestionably the brightest and most gifted as well. Her accomplishments and development became topics of serious conversation, amusing his visiting colleagues and charming them with a rare glimpse of his vulnerability.

The large house had quickly provided a solid base for private life but it was also a suitable setting for a growing circle of friends and a few genuine admirers. Sophia and Tag began to entertain formally, hosting dinners and receptions of a continental style that many still thought entirely too sumptuous for the Athens of those years, but the Schliemann house responded almost magically, and so did they. Visitors came from London and Berlin, and after the war, from Paris. Tag avidly courted the attentions of a long list of scholars and scientists, a few of whom, such as Worsaae, were established archaeologists. With them, in his own library, he discussed and often argued his case for the existence of Troy not as a mythic citadel, but just as Homer had described it, and in the comfort of his own home in Greece, he began to establish an important critical audience, a coterie of experts who listened to him with a mixture of admiration and reserve. Sophia relished it all and just as she knew Tag had thrived on the social and intellectual stimulation of his Paris, she now thrived on the accomplished people who came to her Athens with much to say about the world. She found herself never happier than in the midst of this lively activity within her own home as during many gatherings she participated in conversation and listened to the controversial views of her many guests, Andromache's blue pram seldom out of her sight, becoming a familiar fixture on the long terrace overlooking the garden as afternoon visitors to the Schliemann house on Vintrous Street took particular pleasure in looking in on the beautiful child asleep under its protective hood. Except for having inherited her father's warm brown eyes, Andromache was a small version of Sophia, down to the thick curling hair that had quickly replaced soft, flat infant hair with a thick mass of dark ringlets. She was a happy, smiling baby, showered with attention and constantly supervised by her doting parents and by her capable British nurse, Phillips, who had been hired just after the move to Vintrous Street.

Supper was at nine and there was usually one guest, often more. Sophia adapted with increasing poise to the new social demands made of her, meeting people with an easy charm and a natural elegance that never failed to impress. More extraordinary were her developing language skills which had improved to such a degree, that by March she and Tag were frequently engaged in French conversations which she handled comfortably and with an impressive vocabulary. English continued to be a more difficult challenge, but in addition to tutored lessons twice weekly, many opportunities for English conversation were presented by a long list of English visitors and by Andromache's Nurse Phillips, of whom Sophia was extremely fond.

Nagging issues with her mother began to take second place in a subtle but inevitable preference for a life on Sophia's terms. Recognition of this preference was not without its margins of guilt, however, and as a result, greater efforts were made to encourage family visits. Andromache facilitated matters by providing a welcome new interest for Victoria, but the devoted daughter who had dutifully married Heinrich Schliemann just as her mother had wished, was rapidly maturing into a young woman of such security and strength that when it came to her demanding mother, she found in herself ample patience as Andromache and Tag became her whole life. Preparations for her second visit to Asia Minor were met with resignation, and although she was heartsick at the thought of leaving her child, she did so with complete confidence in Phillips and in her parents who had agreed to visit every day and occasionally to remain overnight until she and Tag returned.

Sophia also asked Spiro Tassos to look in on Andromache from time to time, and she asked the same of Niki and Giannis, suggesting that in her absence the young cousins, Thomas and Andromache, have as many opportunities as possible to play together. Giannis was not particularly enthusiastic about this idea, but he did, in fact, enjoy the prospect of privately inspecting at his leisure, his brother-in-law's lavish Athens home. Outwardly, Giannis and Tag had found the means by which to deal with one another, remaining polite in the extreme, and although Tag's unswerving perseverance continued to grate at him, Giannis behaved impeccably at the family gatherings which, as a result of Sophia's urging, had become more frequent, thoroughly delighted by Victoria's continuing and open disdain for the man she could not bring herself to call, "son." This exclusion had not escaped Tag's attention, but since he was unable to call Victoria, "mother," or for that matter, Giannis, "brother," it was an acceptable standoff, and ignoring Giannis and Victoria for the most part, he proceeded as if they did not matter in the least. All that really mattered was Sophia and the dream.

In 1871, Sophia began keeping a diary. The house on Vintrous Street had provided the stability for which she'd yearned and for the first time since her marriage more than a year before, she not only felt like a normal wife and mother, she was also taking the pulse of Europe, her diary entries during the course of that pivotal year revealing much more about the woman she was becoming and less about the girl she was leaving behind.

30 January: Paris has fallen. Tag is stunned. He says news of an armistice at Versailles is news of humiliating capitulation. How he hates all this about the war, disturbed most of all to know that at the Versailles meeting with Bismarck, General Favres begged for Paris to be allowed the final shot of the siege, his wish granted. Begged indeed!

2 February: Tea, visitors, Andromache, the center of attention for one happy hour. Tag is wonderful with her, holding her, talking baby talk to her, cooing and whistling in artless ways I'd never thought possible for him.

10 February: Three guestrooms in use. Carl Wesser from Dresden, Louis Lartet from Brussels, and Professor Neumann from Vienna. Meals to plan. Downstairs a constant cacophony that lasts late into the night. Lartet changes subjects as if he isn't listening to anyone, says he's not at all fond of Greek food, "too spicy, too many tomatoes." He likes our figs in mavrodaphne, though. This is his second visit in a month. It must be the figs. The mavrodaphne?

11 February: Professor Neumann is the one I like best. He's kind and good-natured, and although just as opinionated as Lartet, he remains calm and never raises his voice the way Lartet does. Why is everyone under this roof so in love with argument? Of course Tag loves the confusion and creates most of it himself. He doesn't plead for their support but I know it's what he wants. I hear that urgency in his voice, that simmering anxiety. I sense his desperation and I want to tell him to take them there, to the hill, where far from the comforts of their paneled libraries they will see and feel what I have seen and felt; be moved and touched by the vastness of their own imaginings, as I have been moved and touched. It would be different then. Lartet is the truly obstinate one, stubbornly clinging to the belief that Troy lies not at Hissarlik, but at Bunarbaschi, on the landlocked inland hill of Bali Dagh. D'Illio Santos seldom leaves Madrid, so of course he agrees. Varnesse too, atop his smoky Roman hill which he tells me boasts a fourth-century temple and a charming belvedere. In ruins.

13 February: Who is this German Iron Chancellor? The papers say he occupied the Rothschilds' Chateau Ferrieres and became fat as a pig, his huge appetite for the estate's abundant game and fabulous store of wine impossible to satisfy. He has joined his emperor at Versailles to set his terms: part of Lorraine and all Alsace.

28 February: The German newspapers report that on February 23, units of the French National Guard led a demonstration in Paris. None of the Guard bore arms but each battalion marched with its own band, its colors draped in black. Some three-hundred-fifty-thousand Parisians joined them, and from the Place de la Bastille leaders of the Guard wearing red sashes across their chests made impassioned speeches to all who would listen in attempts to restore French pride and patriotism.

2 March: News from Paris is all Tag cares about. Every day he sits with a stack of newspapers for hours. Now we learn that the Prussian Hussars rode through the Arch de Triomphe, thus beginning their triumphal march through Paris, thirty-thousand troops passing in review before the Prussian Emperor.

6 March: Attired in the prestigious white uniform of the White Cuirassier, complete with plumed helmet and a chestful of medals and looking "vigorous and robust and every inch the victorious Iron Chancellor, Bismarck has left Paris for the Fatherland." London Times.

10 March: No one seems to know when it will be safe to return, but it's reported today that Paris turns on itself, the French Communards responsible for the terrible February fires, by nightfall of the 24th the skies over Paris clouded black with thick billowing smoke, the air suffocating as thousands of fragments of charred paper floated down from the windows of the blazing Finance Ministry. By next morning the Tuileries Palace, parts of the Palais Royal, and the Hôtel de Villes were gutted.

12 March: London Times: The Communards, or Red Sashes, have formed a committee of Public Safety, its newly appointed police chief a known hater of the church, his first official act to arrest the Archbishop of Paris. Also arrested was the seventy-five-year-old Abbe Deguerry of the Madeleine, the Empress Eugenie's own confessor, both men charged with hostility toward the Communards.

❧ ❧ ❧

They arrived in Canakkale on March nineteenth, too early for the dramatic welcome of migrating birds at rest in the Dardanelles, but Sophia saw the result of Tag's work first hand and now focused on a range of new considerations that Spring as at the same time she grew sensitive to a number of new influences. The colors of the Turkish countryside fascinated her and from the isolation of the cabin on the hill which had quickly become her Hissarlik home, she quickly learned she could escape bouts of fear and longings for home and Andomache, however briefly, by focusing on the far-ranging hues of glowing sunrises and sunsets over waterways and across horizons which in Turkey are unlike any in the world. From her open door, in the blink of an eye a disordered universe could become an enormous palate of solid tint and shade secured and unified by carpets of polished purples and flashes of buttery golds that left their magnificent scars on an unclouded sky for hours. The simplest sounds came to mean something, as did the humblest human acts. Two, perfect unblemished green peppers left at her cabin door by unseen hands. A bouquet of timothy grass, a basket of potatoes. These elements were basic to the land, sacred to its people as she came to know them, and eventually they connected her to the spirit of Hissarlik and the secrets of its ancient hill in ways that Tag himself would never understand.

In late March the deep trench on the hill of Hissarlik was begun, the great slice into the cake that would run from north to south in the hope of exposing the layers of several prehistoric periods, one of which would surely conform to the Troy of Homer. And as Tag directed his incision into the earth, Sophia was distinctly aware of a sense of anticipation on the hill as well as a growing sense of community among the participants. Faces quickly became familiar. Voices became recognizable as the habits and rhythms of the hill were established. Roused from sleep before dawn in the small hillside cabin as Tag left for his swim, the first sounds she heard were those of the crew assembling and immediately after, the shouts of the small boys in their daily game of securing the tokens they collected for every basket of soil they deposited on the growing mounds. There was great competition among them to accumulate the greatest number of tokens, since at the end of each day they were paid according to the number they presented to Murat. Some of the little ones were at a great disadvantage when it came to walking in the long strides of which the bigger, long-legged boys were capable. Running was not allowed anywhere on the hill, but when it came to choosing which of the boys would work on the wooden platforms erected for the deposit of soil once the trench had reached a depth of twenty feet, the smaller boys weighed less and happily scampered along the narrow lengths of platform, a few of them more frequently managing to accumulate the day's greatest number of tokens.

They were beautiful children, healthy and bright-eyed, most full of mischief and ready at the slightest provocation to display examples of physical dexterity on the platform edges, often frightening Sophia so thoroughly that she gasped and had to look away, certain that one of them had fallen to his death. Once this effect on Sophia's nerves was known and circulated, and as the depth of the great trench progressed, there was no end to the creative measures the boys devised to terrify her. From precarious footings on the platforms they pirouetted and performed the acrobatic leaps and dangerous balancing acts that left her numb with fear. Miraculously, no one was seriously injured as steadily and day by day the cutting into the hill grew more enormous, Tag's incessant labor, the gigantic canyon that changed the once bucolic mound of earth overlooking its placid plain into the scarred terrible beauty of slow and dangerous progress she hated in silence, by mid-May a descent into the very heart of the hill, Sophia's new daily companions the dreaded sounds of life-threatening rockslide and landslide.

In early April, the equipment ordered from London arrived. One hundred wheelbarrows, three hundred spades, shovels, pickaxes, and an assortment of baskets had been purchased from Wesson and Durleigh. There were boxes of brushes in all sizes, magnifying glasses, lengths of heavy canvas, storage crates, rope, and quantities of building materials. Wood planks arrived with boards of varying widths and lengths, nails, saws, hammers, and long rolls of black rubber sheeting all stored in several shacks. Pairs of heavy canvas gloves, black rubber boots, and two fine English saddles were unpacked along with crates containing the luxuries of silver flatware, china, glassware, table linens, candles, blankets and pillows.

The port of Canakkale was one of Hissarlik's few conveniences and as such, the shipment and arrival of equipment was uneventful. Its transport to Hissarlik, however, was another matter, a major undertaking requiring a caravan of ox-drawn carts and horses inching along the narrow dirt trail and once at the foot of the hill, a relay system among the crew who handed up, then carried crates and boxes from one man to the other until all the cargo had reached its hilltop destination. The unpacking took a full week and Sophia noted in her diary that not one piece of china or crystal had broken on the long journey to the middle of nowhere.

In one of the smaller cartons, Wesson and Durleigh had included two complimentary boxes of pencils and pads of paper. On each pencil, the name of Wesson and Durleigh was imprinted in bold black letters and at the bottom of each box, wrapped in thin brown paper, Sophia found one of the small new hand-held pencil sharpeners. She immediately sharpened one of the pencils and handily stuck it into her thick hair, which she was wearing neatly drawn back from her face into a bun. Several of the boys watched as she sharpened another pencil and jotted idly on a pad of paper. Unfamiliar with the function of a pencil, word quickly spread among them that a new invention had come to Hissarlik, its powers activated by contact with human hair. In a short time, Sophia realized the magic of cooperation wrought with the gift of the pencil and pad she made to any of the boys who asked, and although she taught some of them to write their names and a few made excellent drawings for her, she noticed that their greatest pride came in wearing a coveted pencil in their hair, or more securely, behind one ear, as she sometimes did. A few of the boys made gifts of their treasured pencils to their mothers and the name of Wesson and Durleigh was seen sticking out of the heads of many of the peasant women of Hissarlik as they milked cows and tended sheep in the type of advertising promotion Wesson and Durleigh could hardly have anticipated in Asia Minor.

In a strangely structured way, the many different sounds on the hill defined the hours of Sophia's existence as she became increasingly sensitive to them. Awakened as she heard Tag dressing quickly at sunrise, she listened for the hoofbeats of his horse on the well-trampled ground as he set out for his daily swim in the Hellespont, the clinking pickaxes and shouts from the boys setting the earliest rhythms of the morning, the idyllic fresh sky and the tranquil views surrounding the hill in bright contrast to the dark life seething beneath the soil. Found teeming within its depths were snakes and gigantic worms winding through mazes of timeless concealment. Several times each day, rats exploded out of their dark shelters. They were black and red-eyed, some the size of contented old cats. They scattered in a mad frenzy, their high-pitched voices decrying this trespass of human flesh brandishing shovels, spades, and the ruthless instruments of pain and death brought to invade their timeless seclusion.

In early morning the air smelled pungently rich as the brownish-gray soil was turned over and sifted, but as the morning wore on, dry musty dust rose from every working shaft and pit. Soil slid away from shovels and spades and formed a brown, air-born cloud permeating everything in its path. Dust fell into the smallest openings, into hair and into ears, under fingernails and into nostrils. A sneeze into a handkerchief left a dark residue. But determined not to hate being outdoors, and regardless of the circumstances, Sophia devised her own unique means for combating the choking dust. In her skirt pockets she took to the habit of carrying squares of white cotton fabric that she could tie quickly into a triangle over her face, covering her nose and mouth. This was a source of great amusement to the little boys who laughed heartily as they watched what they decided must surely be a disguise aimed at discouraging evil spirits adrift on the hilltop. At first, Tag laughed too, and said she looked like one of the masked highway bandits who had terrorized the countryside just outside Athens the summer before. But his humor aside, he admired her resourcefulness, and eventually he complimented her on it, well aware that above all, Sophia never once complained during that long, difficult spring. Not about the dust, not about the dirt, not about the appalling living conditions, not about the isolation, and not about the owls who mated and screeched all through the long spring nights.

Delighted by the novel abundance of small rodents and succulent worms grown more plentiful as the trench grew deeper, the owls of Hissarlik multiplied as never before, feasting and mating in a nightly chorus of atonal gorging and promiscuity. And by the time the sated owls fell off to what Sophia was certain must be an exhausted sleep at dawn, the storks took over in their own disorganized flurry of house hunting and feeding that brought long pointed beaks to carry off many of the morsels the owls had left behind. Sophia was fascinated by the storks and wanted a pair for pets. She repeatedly tossed bread scraps up onto the cabin roof with hopes of enticing a pair of residents, but after cautiously stopping to devour the bread and then assessing the low level of the cabin roof, they always flew off, beating their wings in a rapid flurry as they extended their long, saffron-colored legs behind them.

"Our surroundings become dismal now," Sophia wrote in April, "even in the fullest sunlight of the clearest day the earth lies piled high around us in mountainous brown deposits channeled through with white rocks and inky sand. Worst is the blowing dust, the smell of dank, fresh-turned soil our distinct perfume. Sometimes, looking outside my cabin door, when the air smells raw and mazes of sifted dirt and rock are piled for as far as I can see, I catch myself trying to remember how fresh cut flowers look in a vase or what it feels like to be making love. By the time darkness falls each day to conceal the hill's coarse ugliness and I can dream my own dreams, he is too exhausted to think of reaching out for me, his mind and all his senses captive of that secret sovereign world where I think warm bodies once lay sleeping but now rest cool and unattended, captives of time, untouched and uncontaminated by the smallest efforts I make to restore the memory of their passion."

By the end of May, the Great Northern Trench had reached a depth of thirty feet and had taken on the appearance of a great divide in the earth. Little of consequence had come to light except for huge white hewn stones, indistinguishable debris, and immense quantities of pottery fragments. In the first trial cutting, a few workers had come upon the large white hewn stones, some held in clay and extending for fifty feet. Tag took them to be foundation stones similar to some he had uncovered the previous summer, likely those of an ancient Roman building of about 100 B.C. he assumed. He had them all removed, taken out of the way and into the rock piles that grew on the far east side of the hill, but he grew impatient with the time it took to remove the stone to the rock piles and soon he instructed that they be allowed to roll down the steep slope and over the side of the hill. The men pushed the rocks to the edge of the hillside and took turns at the final thrust, watching the huge stone masses hurtling down in a thunderous splitting crash, delighted as children in a forbidden noisy game. The white stone accumulated so rapidly that nearby peasants built new stone huts and sheepfolds from the enormous supply piles that could be freely collected from several mountain deposits. And there were other enormous accumulations.

"Why do we save all these fragments of pottery?" Sophia had asked Tag. "There's no end to them."

"Pottery tells us a great deal about the people who once lived here, Sophia," Tag explained. By reassembling a pot we can tell how food was stored, how water, wine, and many other items may have been used. There were no kitchen cupboards, certainly no crates for storage, and I had not yet invented the folding paper sack!" He laughed so freely, so genuinely, asking nothing of her but to be there with him. And he had begun his meticulous record keeping, noticing each day's events and tracking progress in one of several journals he read and reread during the journey home.

With little to show for three months work they returned to Athens, eager to be reunited with Andromache and happy to be returning to the many luxuries of the house on Vintrous Street. During the first week at home Sophia soaked in two foaming soap baths every day, all her Hissarlik clothes left behind with Tessa who would hand wash the cotton dresses, skirts, and undergarments in readiness for the next visit in the Fall. Tag had hoped to maintain excavation activity on Hissarlik the year round, but the drastic seasonal changes in northwest Asia Minor prevented this. It was quickly determined that Fall and Spring were definitely the best of times, and unwilling to risk malaria in the heat of summer and pneumonia in the chill of winter, he decided to make the most of those few good months. Once they had left the hill, Tessa had indeed washed Sophia's clothes with extraordinary care, soaking away the grime and hanging each garment to dry in the open air. Tree limbs served as convenient perches from which to drape the wet garments and Tessa carefully positioned the skirts and blouses in such a way, that when a breeze came up the fabrics filled out, suggesting a headless, footless human form floating about in the gently moving air. She took extra care with the undergarments, intrigued by the intricately fashioned camisoles and matching pantaloons and petticoats, all in matching suites of creamy ivory and snowy white, suddenly aware that under her serviceable outerwear, Sophia wore the most feminine undergarments of fragile laces and satins, some ornately appliqued, others re-embroidered and trimmed in laces and ribbons. Tessa laid these out to dry on a large white cloth she spread out in the small grassy patch near the cottage and she kept a watchful eye on them, determined to protect them from the appetites of aimlessly wandering sheep and her constantly ravenous goats.

❦ ❦ ❦

In the Fall of 1871 they returned, and at a depth of forty feet, Tag began his east-west horizontal trench, his crew cutting still another gigantic canyon into the hill of Hissarlik. He also continued to erect the work platform essential to excavation at lower depths. The combined trenches would eventually measure two hundred thirty-two feet in length and forty-eight feet in depth. Tag took to pipe-smoking that Fall. He said he liked holding the pipe in his teeth. Sophia liked the smell of the pipe tobacco.

"Why must pipes be lighted repeatedly?" she laughingly asked him one evening as they watched the stars emerge. Tag struck several matches to the bowl of his pipe, smiling toward her. "Is it like the fireplace that must have logs added?" Sophia had continued to tease as Tag continued to ignite the stubborn tobacco in a series of lights and puffs. She watched him. His hair curled over his collar. He held the pipe in his long fingers, his hands disturbingly expressive and immaculately clean for a man who spent virtually every waking hour digging into the heart of a hill.

At last, in October. Something. Masses of coagulated debris. Fishbones. "Shark," Tag said. Following the fishbones came immense quantities of mussel shells, also massed in debris, and a vile odor, sour and rancid. Later in October there was diorite in odd black shapes, along with hundreds of coins belonging to the First and Second Centuries B.C. Of greater interest were some boars tusks which Tag determined had likely been used as primitive tools or household implements. A few stone lance points appeared. Their appearance disturbed Tag and actually worried him for some time. If Dr. Worsaae's stratigraphic theory was to be followed, these lance points suggested a primitive Stone Age civilization and not some later age that would have succeeded it. It would mean that remnants of a Stone Age civilization so close to the surface of the hill predated anything that could be found beneath it. Tag's only comfort lay in the unrelenting appearance of pottery fragments being found daily and in increasingly tremendous quantity. They were also of increasingly fine and elegant workmanship and he remained highly optimistic.

The hill of Hissarlik stood at 162 feet above sea level and was twelve miles in length. Tag could walk it in two hours. He had laid it out completely, following Worsaae's suggestion that he label strategic areas in an overall plan that staked out the location of at least two important landmarks. The first was the place where he believed the Great Tower of Troy would have stood. The second was at the very highest point of the hill where he expected to find the Temple of Athena. He roped off these particular areas as a guideline, certain that once he uncovered the Great Tower, he would also uncover below it, the entrance to the city at the Scaean Gate, the gate to which the Greeks had brought their gift of a wooden horse to the horse-loving Trojans.

The stone lance points were not his only concern at this time. The size of the hill was another disappointment. The Hill of Hissarlik was not the large luxurious city Homer had led him to envision, but he forced himself to remember that Troy had been a royal citadel, the exclusive enclave of its king, his fifty sons, twelve daughters, their wives, husbands, children, and all the royal attendants, their horses, livestock, and servants the personal support system of one of the most discriminating strongholds of the time. The agricultural community on the surrounding plain would have made up the larger extended city, dominated by royal life on its citadel and not unlike the relationship of the Athens Acropolis to its densely inhabited city below.

As Tag became increasingly preoccupied, Sophia felt bored and lonelier than ever that Fall. She craved companionship and took to the almost daily habit of riding down from the hill and to Tessa's farm. She enjoyed the change of scenery, the sharply winding dirt path she traveled now packed hard and well-trampled from its recent onslaught of men and wagons bearing equipment headed for the hilltop. At the bottom of the hill the air became blessedly free of dust, fragrant and sweet with the scent of fresh hay being gathered for the coming winter. She took deep breaths, mounted gracefully in the fine new English leather saddle that matched Tag's, never seeing herself as others might have, a strikingly beautiful rider moving through the austere countryside like an apparition, glistening ebony hair full and loose and matched exactly to the color of the mare she rode.

In two years there were noticeable changes in Sophia. Childbearing and a love of fine continental food had softened the girlish angles of her body into attractive contours enhancing the long-legged frame. The lovely face had taken on more distinctive characteristics, the once childishly full cheeks now defined, planed into beautifully chiseled hollows below noticeable high cheekbones. On horseback she was especially refined, the figure fuller, the posture forthright and secure. Her height continued to create an unusual physical presence that she knew smaller women lacked, and at Tag's suggestion, she used it to advantage, having learned to rise slowly from a chair, unfolding herself in a gradual ascent that never failed to command attention. Tessa was always startled by the sight of the beautiful young woman who came to visit and approached her modest cottage like a smiling queen.

Tessa had never known anyone like Sophia. Not a woman with this mobility and freedom. Not a Greek woman. She quickly became devoted to her, assisting in every way she could without being asked, and Tessa's abilities in housekeeping and cooking were greatly appreciated during the long periods of isolation. At first she appeared early in the mornings with food in a basket. She swept the cabin floor and then disappeared. At other times she appeared late in the day with the ingredients for a soup or a stew which she wordlessly prepared in the cabin's tiny cooking area. Appreciative of her skills and at the same time cognizant of the fact that Tessa provided Sophia with help as well as female companionship, before too long Tag had put Tessa on his kind of regulated schedule and she came and went at the same morning hour each day, paid for her day's work along with all the members of the crew.

The Schliemann's Hissarlik home was as far removed from the elements of luxury and comfort of the house in Athens as was Hissarlik itself. It was cramped, sparsely furnished, and provided only the basic necessities; a bed, a wooden table, two chairs, and a wood-burning stove in a cooking alcove. It had been hastily assembled of the leftover wood from three shacks built the year before as sleeping quarters for the crew. But it did possess one extraordinary feature. Murat had added a small stone terrace, made entirely of stones he had collected from the hill. The stones were very white, uniform in size, and Murat had laid them quite artfully, creating the pleasantly smooth surface on which Tag and Sophia liked to dine and watch the sunset. The cabin had no convenient access to water and there was no source for it. Every day a fresh supply was brought in wooden buckets from one of the nearby farm wells, and three times each week, Sophia rode her black mare to the privacy of Tessa's cottage where she enjoyed a bath in the metal tub that had come from London along with Tag's excavation equipment. Tag's own bathtub was the Hellespont, one in which he frequently tried to convince Sophia to join him, but her preference for complete indoor privacy while bathing remained unconditional and unaltered through all six campaigns.

From the beginning, visitors to the site, Chadwick in particular, were amazed at the level of formality Sophia and Tag observed in their daily lives on Hissarlik, in the midst of an excavation campaign, miles away from civilization. Returning from her bath and wearing a fresh dress, Sophia often invited him to join in their early evening meal at the table on the stone terrace outside the cabin, for regimented as he was in the work schedule, when the last tools of the day were stored away and the crew dismissed, Tag returned to the ridiculously crude cabin on the hillside as anxiously as he might have returned to his elegant house in Paris, anticipating the pleasure of his beautiful wife's companionship and looking forward to a thoughtfully prepared meal complete with china and crystal wine glasses set on a white linen cloth under the stars.

In a short time there was great curiosity among the peasant women of Hissarlik regarding the Greek-born woman who was living on the hillside. Through Murat and Tessa they had been told of her beauty and pleasant manner. That she was both wealthy and Greek was beyond their comprehension. One day in late October a group of them gathered at Tessa's cottage, eager for a glimpse of her before she had her bath. Tessa was their spokesman.

"They are wanting to know of your life in Greece," she smiled to Sophia. "They want to hear you speak in Greek."

They were large women with no waists. Their skirts hung limply around them in a range of long forgotten colors and their shoulders were just as lifeless, seeming to stoop more and more as they stared at the young Greek goddess before them who spoke easily to them and in the simplest terms, sensing their intimidation and curiosity. She described the city of Athens and she told them about her baby, Andromache. As she spoke, the women formed a semi-circle, standing close to each other, Sophia at their center. They were like children, curious about every aspect of their new goddess and through the next weeks they anxiously anticipated her arrival at Tessa's cottage with great excitement, increasingly comfortable in her presence. They brought gifts. A basket of potatoes. Two perfect green peppers. A bouquet of timothy. In time she learned their names. This thrilled them, and when she addressed one of them, they felt connected to her world in a firm bond that of itself provided a strong new sense of splendid identity. Later, after she had gone, they talked about her, reviewed what she had said, recalled what she had worn, how she had moved among them. And in the same way that Sophia brought fresh vitality into their lives, so did the peasant women of Hissarlik bring to her the female companionship she so desperately craved. Unaware that they did so, they also taught her about the Turkish Empire's overwhelming corruption and what appeared to be its total inability to maintain any semblance of patriotic fiber. Through them, she saw the weak peasant farmer fall prey to a hopeless system of bribery, ultimately manifested in the feared tax-collector who did his part within the vicious circle of self-perpetuating poverty, for he had the unique power to prevent the harvesting of precious crops until an estimated tax was paid. Unless an agreement was struck with the tax-collector, a farmer and his wife might watch helplessly as crops rotted away, unable to pay an exorbitant tax or to prevent a total loss of months of hard work. The local zaptieh (police) were in the pockets of the tax-collectors and until they received confirmation of the peasant tax payment, there was no harvest, no income. In order to pay the required tax, a beleaguered peasant farmer could be relieved of his sheep, his horses and seed. Entirely at the disposal of the tax-collector, the zaptieh were feared as puppet tools of higher authority and not as enforcers of the law or protectors of the rural populace, making it startlingly clear to Sophia that the weight of life turning the women of Hissarlik into hard, prematurely aged creatures, was largely a result of the zaptieh's abuse. Women were incidental human items, easily added to the list of chattel that could be taken away by the zaptieh at will, along with sheep and horses. It was a fact of life and through many years had led to a strong communal camaraderie among the women, holding them together in tender bonds of fear and support that in spite of horrifying overtones, brought opportunities for genuinely spontaneous humor and many practical jokes. They could laugh together heartily, sharing and relating their experiences to one another with a surprising absence of malice, but their personal feuds could be long and loud, often volatile, for the most part eventually forgiven in the deeper felt poignancy of compassion and sympathy. Since they lived with chronic disappointment, news of the most serious disaster seldom surprised them and they were imminently skilled at hiding sadness. They also lived with the eternal cycles of birth and death, their long memories amazingly accurate when it came to names and dates which they anchored only by the weather at the time and the seasons of the year. A child had been born during the harvest just as the yellow corn was at its tallest, or a husband had died of the pestilence which all of them knew came in the humid heat of late summer. They worked constantly, from dawn to dark and often beyond, expecting to be disappointed at every turn and enormously relieved when yet another catastrophe fulfilled their well-tested prophecies of doom.

Tessa was their uncontested leader. Smallest among them, she had a talent for watchful detachment and was a fiercely loyal friend, warmly encouraging within the group and openly affectionate. It seemed she never rested, remaining alert to every nuance and subtle signal that could threaten her and those around her and like her husband Murat, she saw herself as immensely capable and far from oppressed. The Turks could take the position that the peasants existed for their sakes alone, but their arrogance never angered or really reached her, for Tessa had built a convenient emotional wall through which, until the arrival of Sophia, outsiders had never penetrated. Tessa saw herself as neither slighted nor conquered and she had earned great respect in the eyes of the other women for her consistently agreeable relationship with the tax collector, Ahmet Ostrogorsky, who had never singled her out as he had some of the other women. Among themselves the women called him "Nephos," Greek for "black cloud," and they confided this nickname to Sophia, swearing her to secrecy and including her in one of their best-guarded confidences, a condition of delicate trust which she held in highest esteem.

One day, Sophia approached Tessa's cottage carrying her tapestry covered satchel. From it she produced the silver singing bird box Tag had given her in the shade of her mother's Athens garden as the women gathered outside Tessa's cottage door watched with heightened interest.

"Shortly after we were married, my husband brought this gift to me," she told them as they drew closer. Holding the silver box in her hands, she pressed the knob signaling the start of the bird's song. Slowly he rose from his deep enclosure and twirled round and round, chirping his perfect song and enchanting the women. His concluding descent back into the box elicited their gasps of amazement. They clapped their hands and begged her to make him appear once again, which she did. Sophia then handed the box to Tessa as the small golden beaked bird twirled and chirped and disappeared yet again.

"Press the knob, Tessa," Sophia urged. "The bird will sing for you." Tessa pressed the knob and waited for the bird to appear. She pressed again. And again. But the bird remained concealed. "I have broken it," Tessa said.

"Yes," several of the women chimed in, nodding their heads in agreement. "Tessa has broken it."

"No," Sophia quickly assured her. "You have not broken it, Tessa." And as Sophia pressed the knob herself, the golden-beaked bird appeared once again, chirping, twirling, disappearing, just as before. Sophia once again handed the box to Tessa. "Press the knob, Tessa," she instructed. "Press it firmly, Tessa." Three times Tessa pressed the silver knob and three times she successfully activated the singing bird as the women watched, mesmerized. Again she returned the chaised silver box to Sophia's hand and as once again Sophia set the golden-beaked bird into motion, she smiled to Tessa. "You see, the beautiful bird sings for you, Tessa."

For one precious moment, the small face above the faded, immaculately clean dress had beamed, and for once in her life, Tessa's frozen gray eyes had shone bright and warm in a rare surge of satisfied acceptance.

Within seconds of Tessa's success, the Ladies of Hissarlik adjourned the day's meeting and Sophia was alone, the air absolutely still until she heard a voice.

"That was beautiful," someone said as she looked up to see Benjamin Chadwick smiling, his arms folded across his chest as if he'd been standing there for quite some time.

"You're very nice to them. They're lucky, especially Tessa. She's devoted to you. I saw what was happening with the women."

"Tag gave this to me before we were married," Sophia said, pleased by Chadwick's interest and approval and returning his warm smile as she walked toward him with the silver box.

"It's always with me. I like having it close by, especially here."

She was unprepared for the affect of his closeness and the small contented smile she saw on Chadwick's face as she activated the golden bird and together they watched its pirouettes and twirls.

"If you were mine, I'd give you the world," he said quietly, his gaze riveted on the silver box in her hands. "And I certainly wouldn't allow you to live in a place like this while I was on some wild goose chase. You'd live in a proper house and you'd always look exactly the way you looked the first time I saw you in the Nomion," he went on without moving, "dressed in silk the color of burgundy wine, your hair like a beautiful cloud around you. Couldn't you feel everyone staring? You really don't know how beautiful you are, do you?"

Looking into her eyes, his voice had become a hushed murmur. She stepped back, astonished and suddenly she wanted to run, but her body felt frozen. All she could do was stare after him as he calmly turned and walked away.

She was unsettled and anxious for days after, Chadwick's unexpected attention a complete mystery, her own reaction to him not without its own perplexing difficulty, and it was his own impression of her appearance that left the greatest mark. She kept re-living his every word, never imagining that anyone would have remembered what she wore or how she looked at the Nomion Hotel one night at dinner a whole year ago, least of all the British Ambassador's Deputy.

"Silk, the color of burgundy wine," he had said. "Hair like a cloud. Couldn't you feel everyone looking?"

It was nothing, she told herself. It meant nothing. He meant nothing. But she kept seeing him there beside her, handsome and close, his small defiant smile as he watched the pirouetting gold bird a smile she simply could not forget.

❧ ❧ ❧

They received mail at the Dardania in Canakkale. In April there was a letter from Spiro Tassos. "I baptized Ennea Pephredo's baby daughter. The child cried constantly. We have a new litter of kittens in the chapel, six this time! I stopped in to see Andromache. She is a lovely, happy child, her nurse completely devoted to her. And your parents are there like sentinels. Do not worry. Your child is in excellent hands. I hope you don't mind, but I had to see your garden . . . . just a moment or two in that lovely place . . . . it's all young and just getting started, quite like you, but one day . . . ."

The 1871 season at Hissarlik closed in late October with little to substantiate Tag's theory that Hissarlik's hill was the Pergamus of Troy. Nevertheless, he now insisted upon referring to it as just that to the Times of London and to the Royal Geographical Society. At home in Athens during the early winter he continued to communicate with a number of European historians and academicians, inviting many of them to Athens to meet with him in the hope of generating their interest and gaining their valuable support. They came in a steady stream, graciously welcomed as guests in the Schliemann home, usually two and three at a time, gathered in a pleasant round of discussions and dinners. At first, Sophia and Tag were curiosities to many of them. Financially able to pursue an unusual experiment that although fascinating remained on the fringes of established scientific classification, at the same time they hosted an unprecedented type of international forum, offering historians and scientists the opportunity to freely share theories in a residential setting of privacy. For the most part, it was a group that genuinely liked Tag, and although his concepts for breathing life into Homer's Iliad were regarded with no small degree of uncertainty, every visitor to the Schliemann home on Vintrous Street was influenced in some way by the elegant, self-made man who stated his case with a passion and intelligence they could not help but admire. Ziegler came, and Thompson and Zucher, and Alfred Nobel. Louis Lartet came more often than the others, boring his colleagues to the limits of their patience with his monotonous repetitious tales concerning his discoveries of the remains of ancient man. He had indeed discovered the skeleton of Cro-Magnon Man from the Upper Paleolithic Age, the first homo-sapiens in Europe and successor of Neanderthal Man, but Gilbert Faraday promptly left the room whenever Lartet went off on his tangents, amusing those who pretended interest, and leaving the rest to fall asleep in their chairs. At this time, Tag also began to write the first of several books and segments of memoirs which would initially be published as a series of articles in journals and periodicals. In his correspondence to the London Times he detailed the work of the first full season of excavation at The Pergamus of Troy, acquainting the world with the tantalizing idea that the Trojan War may not have been the creative invention of an ancient bard at all.

Christmas of '71 was complete with towering Christmas tree, an avalanche of presents, and a combination of German and Greek holiday customs. The Kastromenou family came for a festive Christmas Day dinner and it was announced that Sophia was expecting a second baby. At about this same time Sophia became substantially aware of wide public interest in the place Tag was calling the Pergamus of Troy. She had first heard of plans to locate the city of Troy in 1869 in her mother's garden, but by the New Year of 1872, much of the civilized world had also heard of the Schliemann excavation in Asia Minor, and much to her surprise, she was included in the news. Not all the publicity was favorable. Articles in the London Times described both Schliemanns as idle treasure hunters, their names added to a distinguished list of wealthy Europeans who had taken to the adventurous idea of digging for treasure while on holiday, the Schliemann expedition regarded as somewhat more creative and expensive than most. Time and again, rapacious and indiscriminate probes into foreign lands had resulted in the sort of serious civil disagreements that had led directly to the need for licenses and permits, not unlike Tag's Firman, and aware of this, the Times also published an article listing some recommended procedures for securing such licenses, using the Schliemanns as examples and illustrating exactly to what lengths certain wealthy Europeans could be expected to go with such licenses in hand, even to the mythical Gates of Troy.

The shallow innuendos infuriated Tag. They hurt Sophia in more personal ways. One report said that detailed communications from the Pergamus of Troy in Asia Minor were all the more fascinating since in the winter of his life, Herr Schliemann, Iliad in hand, had not only set out to find Homer's ancient city of Troy, but had also married a young Greek woman thirty years his junior and barely into the spring of her years, undoubtedly his muse.

"The May-December couple romantically read The Iliad aloud to each other as they scour a hill in northwest Asia Minor for the signs of Homer's city and his legendary heroes," one article concluded.

That others might see her as Tag's child-bride was disturbing enough, but that a respected newspaper would regard the thirty-year difference between them as newsworthy was a source of complete mystery to Sophia.

"They do not know us. They know nothing about us except our ages and where we come from," she had said to Tag. "Why is the difference in our ages important enough to include in a newspaper? Who is interested in reading about such things?"

In spite of his careful analysis of all things printed about him, Tag had not paid much attention to the May-December characterization and it did not prey upon him as it did upon Sophia. To her it was an embarrassing negative opinion, one contrary to all the levels of moderate propriety so integral to her personality, her upbringing, and to the great strides she was certain she had made in appropriately adapting to Tag's world. She had only recently begun to feel successful in having securely bridged many difficult gaps, but no level of confidence had equipped her to deal with what she increasingly saw as her husband's obsessive need for recognition and his love for the type of publicity that had begun to focus as much on the two of them as players in an ever changing scenario as it had on the scenario itself.

The thirty-year difference in their ages had long since ceased to concern her. People who knew them and saw them together had ceased to think about it as well. Tag and Sophia were a strikingly attractive match, becoming even more so with the passage of time, his silvered hair the only external evidence of advancing years. His face did not look aged. It was not deeply lined, and the expression on his face was now one of vigor, the few developing lines around his eyes and mouth only adding distinction. Sophia's own maturity had been incredibly rapid, and while she still bore an appealing level of public shyness, she was becoming confidently aware of her genuine abilities and accomplishments. Privately though, she still sought simplicity, essentially desiring more than anything else, to please the husband she loved and conform successfully to the standards he set. Of course, neither she nor Tag understood the magnitude of this burden upon her, and it would be years before Sophia herself would realize the significance of the delicate period in which she lived at this time, for along with a world poised on the brink of enormous industrial change and its accompanying age of opportunity, came the developing age of celebrity and she and Tag bore all the markings, the essential ingredients of fame at their fingertips, all combining electrically to create an indisputable starring role for them in a world that Sophia, at the age of nineteen, could not believe was at all interested in her. She was a Greek wife and mother. It was as much as she wanted, and she could never tell Tag this was her simple wish. But he did notice that as his own vision had expanded, so had Sophia's as she quietly assumed complete responsibility for running her house, skillfully combining her own natural spontaneity with the organization he demanded. She dealt with the servants, with daily maintenance of the house and its grounds, as more and more, Tag stepped away from those daily details of the household for which he had assumed initial responsibility, grateful for Sophia's talents at them and appreciative of the freedom she gave him to concentrate solely on his work. The routine of their lives was seriously interrupted when a few weeks into the New Year of 1872, Sophia suffered a miscarriage. She remained more depressed than ill until late in February when she once again regained interest in the household and also gradually regained control of her domestic responsibilities with an increased thoroughness Tag could only attribute to sheer will.

It was at this critical stage that Tag added still one more project to the substantial range of his own responsibilities. He decided he would build a house in Athens. That decision made, he promptly engaged an architect and purchased a fine hillside lot of land on University Square.

"Plenty of room for a garden," he told Sophia. "Better than Vintrous Street. In Spring the hillside is covered in wildflowers."

Solidity. Permanence. A house built for Sophia. Grand. Large. An Italianate structure to be set into Athens' most prominent area, its completion requiring yet one more commitment. Heinrich Schliemann became a Greek citizen, thus expediting procedures for the purchase of Greek land and ensuring the orderly construction of his new home.

# CHAPTER ELEVEN

## 1872

B Y SPRING OF 1872 there was still no sign of a city, masses of dirt and endless piles of coagulated, foul-smelling debris the only measure of daily productivity, the ever-present sweet smell of decay almost tolerable when the winds blew hardest, the accompanying circling dust preferable by far to the stench. But that spring, Sophia found a refuge, and her eager escape into it had little to do with the city she was now convinced Tag would never find under the gigantic canyons at which he labored more tenaciously than ever, at times with no tools, as if empowered by nameless spirits to uncover Homer's city with his bare hands. It would end soon. She was sure of it. They would sail for home, never to return; across the sea to Athens. Greek wife. Greek mother. It was all she wanted. But the year of 1872 marked a turning point in their lives and nothing would ever be the same. Not at Hissarlik, and not in Athens. The meanings of home and work and world would change, and so would the meaning of Sophia.

It was never difficult for her to reassemble the pieces of that eventful year, or to recall exactly when the thunder and lightening had struck. When they arrived in Canakkale, earlier that Spring than usual, there had been no expectant crackle in the air, no exploding blasts or bursts of light. It was just one more inauspicious campaign season, and to Sophia, a waste of time. But bound by patience and her love and admiration for Tag, she never told him how she truly felt.

They had sailed into Canakkale aboard the D'Alaire, and although from the gangway, port activity at Canakkale appeared substantial, it was still too cold for comfortable open-air dining on the Dardania's waterfront terrace cafe and few people were to be seen. A few hardy souls braved the swift breezes coming off the Hellespont, but on the day of their arrival, Sophia and Tag stayed inside, lunching in the Dardania's cozy dining room and once again ordering the menemen and pogaça of which Sophia had become quite fond.

One of Sophia's first genuine surprises that Spring came with a dramatic change in living conditions on the hill. The familiar anxiety with which she had approached each season's return to Hissarlik melted into sheer delight when she saw the stone cottage Murat had built at Tag's suggestion. During their summer absence, Murat had gathered white stones from the plentiful deposits at hand and partway up the hill had erected what she came to call The Sheepfold. What struck her first was the grandeur of the site, the small structure clinging possessively to a flat bedrock, before it the full panorama of the plain and to the southwest, a view to the endless horizon. From the outside, the cottage looked flat and small, but inside, its two rooms were surprisingly large. The native white stones completed the interior walls just as they did outside and the only room dividers were exposed thick white stone arches. A small center courtyard separated the two parts of the construction, providing living quarters on one side, and storage on the other.

From the first, the sheepfold offered greater comfort and safety in a world that continued to worry Sophia and from which she could not wait to escape early each summer and late each autumn, but despite her persistent reservations concerning the hill's validity, the sheepfold quickly became a home and Sophia soon came to regard it with great affection, striving to make it for Tag, the same fanciful refuge he had intended for her. In its near fairy-tale setting she worked harder than ever at maintaining the fragile balance in their lives as the wholeness of her being continued to be measured by Tag and increasingly by what Tag was thinking, doing, and planning. Without realizing it, she coddled and encouraged him in new ways, filling the gaping hole of emptiness that for the first time had begun to riddle him with nagging doubt. She visited Tessa's farm less and less frequently, at Tag's side more and more as he continued his great trenches through the hill, exposing its layers in a daily drudgery of digging that continued with great energy and yet revealed all too little. Animal skeletons and bones turned up in the soil debris along with immense numbers of curious spinning whorls and the interminable pottery shards, but there was absolutely no sign of the buildings and walls Tag really wanted. The many signs of prehistoric habitation that did exist, regardless of their significance, were not what he had hoped for, and in spite of ever-increasing evidence that the layers under Hissarlik's surface had indeed been settled as prehistoric communities, one atop the other, his concentration began to waver. Sophia tried to assure him that at the very least, proof of Worsaae's stratification theory was justification for his effort, but he had already decided that this would be the last of the excavation campaigns. He told Sophia that they would not be returning in the Fall. He also told her they would concentrate instead on building the house in Athens which even at this early stage was named Iliou Mélathron, House of Ilium.

Chadwick came out on June eighth. He had become a frequent visitor to the hill, interested in surveying the proceedings and continually fascinated by what he saw as Tag's sheer tenacity. He frankly thought the digging at Hissarlik had been going on for long enough to conclude it was not to be the great discovery of Homer's Troy at all. But he could see that Tag kept pouring money into the excavation in what seemed an unlimited flow of funds. The project remained well-organized, the crew worked efficiently, the soil was being moved around every day, and Tag had even built his wife a stone cottage in the middle of it all.

"These people have no agenda," he confided to an acquaintance in Constantinople. "They are living for several months of the year under the most appalling of conditions and they seem not to mind at all. Strange thing is," Chadwick had commented with no small degree of admiration, "they have the most incredible luxuries out there. A cook takes care of housekeeping and laundry, and the crew supervisor is their bodyguard. I have been invited to dine with them and have been served the most delicious meals, complete with fine French wine poured into crystal stemware."

Tessa had learned to set the table with astonishing style, the chairs arranged by the open door and the four candles lighted, just as Sophia had instructed, this accomplished while overhead the late afternoon sky streaked red and bright turquoise. Whenever he was invited, Chadwick settled back into his chair to enjoy the rarified view, his gaze unwavering and fixed almost constantly on Sophia.

Chadwick had joined in the digging early on the morning of the eighth, impressing Tag, as he often did, with his willingness to set all formality aside as he perspired and gathered dust along with everyone else. By afternoon he agreeably assisted Tag's crew with the extension of a third platform, some forty feet below the surface. About sixty men worked at it, setting footings, hammering wood planks together and securing them alongside the freshly cut narrow trenches. It was a delicate, tedious undertaking, but an additional work area was absolutely essential if the excavating was to continue at this depth. Next to Chadwick, four men were removing soil when two of them suddenly hit on something hard with hand shovels. The sharp, ringing sound was unmistakable. Their excited, loud shouts brought Tag quickly and he immediately saw the reason for the commotion.

Jutting out from the brown-gray soil and etched in dark encrusted earth was the partially exposed mane and head of what appeared to be a marble horse. Perspiration broke out on his forehead as like one of the agile boys he quickly crossed the platform and began to chip carefully into the calcinated earth around it. No one came forward to assist. No one dared, yet the crew gathered. Some of the small basket boys scrambled onto the highest mounds of excavated soil. Sophia had seen the crew gathering and she too came to see what all the confusion was about. Inch by agonizing inch, Tag's picking continued into the late afternoon, but by the time the sun was setting on the plain, its rose-streaked rays glistened on the silhouetted head of a white marble stallion, its flowing mane and flaring nostrils clearly magnificent. As the skies darkened, Tag could not stay away. He had no appetite for dinner, and returned again and again throughout that sleepless night to marvel at the beauty and meaning of the white marble head, anxious as a lover acquainting himself with the beloved's every line and curve. He did not swim in the Hellespont the next morning and when Sophia woke at dawn, he was gone. She dressed quickly, knowing exactly where she would find him, not at all surprised when she saw the two workmen who had stood guard throughout the night still watching, fascinated, as Tag calmly began his labor anew, wielding handpick and chisel with steady precision, his hands patiently sweeping aside every small bit of crusty dirt as he went. Sophia came along the extended wooden platform, and while still at some distance, she too, stopped to watch. He wore no hat, which was unusual, and she could see his head bent over his tools, his expression serious and intense. Then suddenly, his hands moved much faster, clearing very quickly, as if he had found something else. Instinct had, of course, told him this could be much more than a horse's head. That head could be connected to a body. It could have four legs. He dug lower, quickly exposing exactly what he had expected. More white marble, covered with the gray, gauze-like soil of Hissarlik. In that moment and without thinking, Sophia came to work beside, him, scooping dirt away with her bare hands. Within an hour they had exposed the legs of the horse. But she could see something else. There were not four legs. There were five, well carved, the hooves deeply detailed. Her heart was pounding.

"It is more than one horse!" she shouted.

On the afternoon of June ninth, barely fifty feet away from Sophia's sheepfold the sun in Asia Minor set in yet another fiery blaze, and on the hill of Hissarlik it reflected on a life-size marble frieze of four magnificent, snorting, white marble steeds, their muscled power reigned in at the hands of the sun god, Apollo, who stood proudly behind them as the god of light, regally splendid in a long robe carved of deep folds, his fine head framed against a large marble disk of the sun's rays flaring out into a superb, pointed radius that had managed somehow to harness the real last rays of that June day's sun into thousands of golden beams.

Chadwick could barely contain himself. He had done absolutely nothing, but like Tag, he too was completely drenched in perspiration. In all his forays into archaeological fields, he had never witnessed a find of these proportions. Its implications had instantly captured his imagination and he was not alone in this.

They named it the Apollo Marble and it was flawless. Miraculously, not a scratch or nick had marred it anywhere. Tag assumed it to have been part of the decorative center cornice of a municipal building, most likely the centerpiece frieze of a Temple of Apollo. It was finely executed. The horses were almost stilted, but at the same time, splendidly powerful, the quality and level of artistry suggestive of a highly advanced civilization, one capable of an artistic expression and style that neither Chadwick nor Tag could categorize. It wasn't Roman, and it lacked the finesse of the 450 B.C. Greece of Pericles, but neither was it a crude, simplistic execution speaking of impoverished artisans lacking experience and familiarity with their materials. Its size and grandeur were quite moving, its mere existence setting off a new wave of interest and energy on the hill. Published newspaper photographs of the Apollo Marble set off a fresh world-wide wave of interest in the Schliemann work at Hissarlik with the understated assessment that the find was one of "inestimably high, artistic merit," as one journalist put it.

In the days following the discovery of the Apollo Marble, Sophia became a changed participant at Hissarlik. Overnight, she not only shared enthusiastically in the drudgery of digging, she became absolutely convinced that soon Tag would indeed find the buildings of the City of Troy along with evidence of its heroes, and of greatest importance to her, he would establish the validity of its Greek conquerors, and as Tag talked to her of the gold of Troy, her mind was racing ahead to victorious Greeks returning home with tales of valor, Trojan bounty, and a long, dangerous adventure from which all did not return.

At the same time, Chadwick's attention was impossible to ignore, his astonishment and enthusiasm for the Apollo Marble on a par with Sophia's own, her thoughts of him too frequent and too stubborn to pass off as harmless, his encouragement of her participation only adding to the confusion that had begun to erupt inside her.

"I never thought I'd see anything like this," he had told her quietly as the Apollo Marble was being loaded onto the wagon headed for Canakkale, "and I'm beginning to believe you didn't think you would either. Sophia, I've never seen you like this, so involved, so happy. Success becomes you, gives you a glow. I like it."

Removed from nameless centuries of entombment, The Apollo Marble was taken to Canakkale, where it was placed on view in the small square. Chadwick had taken official possession of it in the name of the Turkish government, conforming, he said, to the provisions of the Firman. Many people saw it in the square, marveling at its beauty and perfection as Tag took great pride in their praise. Once each week, usually on Sunday, with Sophia at his side, he rode into

Canakkale to stand beside his prize, eager to answer questions put to him concerning details of its discovery and its meaning.

"It is the first sign of the City of Troy," he said with complete conviction.

Greatly encouraged by the Apollo Marble, the Schliemanns returned to work together now and with a combined new vigor, Sophia especially encouraged by a remarkable and rapid series of finds that only added to the radical change in her attitude overall. First, Tag located two ancient natural springs at a depth of forty-two feet. The water no longer gushed out of them, but it bubbled up enough to be another of the Homeric signs for which he had searched repeatedly. In The Iliad, Homer described one hot and one cold spring and these were important landmarks, well known to the inhabitants of the citadel of Troy.

> "They passed the lookout point, the wild fig tree, with wind all in its leaves, then veered away along the curving wagon road, and came to where the double fountains well, the source of eddying Skammander. One hot spring flows out, and from the water fumes arise as though from fire burning; but the other even in summer gushes chill as hail or snow or crystal ice frozen on water."

To Tag, the location of these springs on the hill of Hissarlik were crucial to its verification as the site of the Trojan War. Homer had clearly said that the Trojan women had washed clothes at the springs, gathering daily to gossip at the stone walls close by. These were signs of a city, signs of life once lived within that city.

The two springs Tag found recorded almost identical temperatures, but his critics vehemently challenged the finding as soon as he reported it, insisting that one of the Homeric springs had clearly run hot, the other cold. Tag argued in turn that the river bed of the ancient Scamander River had shifted and that over thousands of years any number of geological changes: earthquake, flood, could have taken place to affect the water temperature. He wrote to The London Times and to the German Ausberg Allgemeine Zeitung, presenting his arguments at great length for what he was certain were the Homeric springs. Two days later, at the same forty-two foot depth, stones of a wall appeared. It was a circuit wall that ran on in a confusing path, about thirty feet in length. Water bubbled up at two places, about six feet apart. The morning sun was shining brightly, warming one water hole and not the other.

In the next weeks, two interesting objects were found in tremendous quantity with which Sophia had great fun, this fresh emotion of spontaneous joy by itself, one which Tag and others on the hill noticed with great pleasure, was changing her. One object was a piece of clay in a triangular shape with many small holes on its surface.

"A brush! It was once a Trojan brush!" she decided, excitedly. "Of course, all the bristles are gone. Do you suppose they used real animal hairs?"

The second object was a large hook, also of baked clay.

"A hook! A hook for hanging Trojan clothes!"

"You are getting much too clever at this," Tag said to her. "But you could be right."

Also found in tremendous quantity at the same depth of forty to forty-four feet, were arrow heads and hundreds of terra cotta vases depicting the human face in the form of an owl. Some of these vases imitated the human form, with eyes, noses, ears, and female breasts molded on. A few had arms. Tag said that they were seeing the evolution of Canakkale's native terra cotta for which the area had been famous for centuries, pointing out that even at the Dardania in Canakkale, Sophia had seen new pieces of owl-headed terra cotta pottery in rounded female shapes, quite reminiscent of these. But what had such owl-headed pieces meant to the people on the hill?

The answer to this question remained one of the most nagging in Sophia's mind and for weeks she dwelled on its significance, convinced that the owl-shaped figures and the spinning whorls frequently found to accompany them were an important key to solving Troy's mystery. The bewildering figures and whorls haunted her thoughts daily, but in time and as a result of her natural tenacity, Sophia not only unlocked their mystery and meaning, she also succeeded in finally reconciling many of the lingering doubts she had carried with her for so long. When her answers did come, they came swiftly and all were tied to what she had learned was the secret of the Palladion, its powers revealed in a brief passage from one of the series of books on Greek myth she had brought from Athens and was re-reading. According to legend, toward the last days of the war, she learned, Helen had taken still another lover, Paris' brother, Diephobos. Helanos, another of Priam's sons had wanted Helen for himself. Losing her to Diephobos, he had sulked at the fringes of the Greek camp, found there by the Greeks who interrogated him until he told Odysseus and Diomedes the secret of Troy's impenetrability.

"It is the Palladion," he confessed to them. "It protects the city of Troy and has great powers. It was crafted of wood by Athena herself, in her own image. When Zeus cast it down from Mount Ida, it fell upon Troy. Around it Priam built a temple, and around the temple he built his city. As long as the Palladion remains in Troy there will be no end to the war."

The following night, Diomedes disguised himself as a beggar and entered the city of Troy from the lower gate, meeting Helen, who in exchange for his promise that the Greeks would be told of her assistance, took him to the temple of Athena where the revered Palladion was housed. Diomedes did not tell Helen that the Greeks had already constructed a wooden horse with room enough inside its belly for fifty men but quickly stole the Palladion and presented it that night to Agamemmnon.

"It makes complete sense! Sophia explained to a clearly fascinated Tag. These female-shaped vases, the hundreds and hundreds of owl-headed terra cotta figures of every conceivable size are all images of the goddess Athena, and from deep within the hill they are being unearthed in tremendous quantity."

Of course! The known mythology explained the Palladion's importance. Athena, the goddess of wisdom and war had been the patron goddess of Troy and its guardian. The Palladion was her owl-faced likeness, the crucial temple statue upon which the safety of the city had depended throughout the long years of the war until the Greeks had stolen it away. Athena was also goddess of crafts and weaving. That explained the spinning whorls. That also explained her power and role in Trojan life. Athena was the spiritual key to safety and victory and to appease her there would have been no end to the numbers of ways in which the ancients of Troy might have duplicated their images of her: vases, pendants, charms in endless variation. Full grown and in full armor, Athena had sprung directly from the head of Zeus and was forever his favorite child and it was to Athena that Zeus had entrusted his most devastating weapon, the thunderbolt. "Gray-eyed Athena,"

Homer had called her; the embodiment of wisdom and reason, the owl her bird, the olive her tree.

৯৮ ৯৮ ৯৮

By the end of June, discoveries were made every day, and in a wide array of objects. Knives began to appear, then longer lances, and finally, battle axes of copper, well finished and of fine craftsmanship. The terra cotta pottery shards, spinning whorls, and owl-shaped figures continued to come up in huge numbers and were added daily to the mountainous deposits now in several locations on the platforms. The copper battle axes, which Tag felt were of enormous importance, were sent to the Royal Archaeological Institute in London for study. Analyses of the metals revealed that they were almost entirely made up of pure copper.

From time to time, Tessa brought her young daughter, Leda, to the hill, pressing her into service in the sheepfold with a broom or a water bucket. One day, Sophia took the little girl onto one of the excavation platforms with her while Tessa busied herself in the cabin with preparation of a stew. The child was thrilled to be able to watch the excavation activity within such close range and standing close to Sophia was fascinated to watch the small handpick come out of Sophia's pocket.

"Would you like to help?" Sophia asked as she began to pick away at a clay-colored section of soil. She handed her pick to Leda. "Here you are. Now, pick carefully, Leda and you may be lucky enough to find a great treasure box!" They both laughed as Leda took the small pick and began to tap at the hardened soil. "You'll have to do better than that," Sophia said, encouraging the child to attack the business at hand with greater energy. "You have a wonderful name, Leda. Has your mother ever told you that long ago Leda was the name of a Greek king's beautiful wife? She was the mother of two of the most beautiful daughters in all Greece, one named Helen, the other Clytemnestra and when . . . ."

Sophia did not finish her sentence. Idly picking away again and again at the same spot as she had listened to Sophia, Leda had loosened a large clay-filled crag of soil. It fell to her feet in a great mounded heap and at her own eye level, she could look into the deep crevice it had left behind.

"Look! Look!" She pulled Sophia down to see. Peering into the opening, Sophia saw a handle on part of a large terra cotta jar.

Quite accidentally and much to her delight, Leda had, during this brief time, uncovered one of the most fascinating finds on the hill. It took four full work days to clear the calcinated soil away but by the second day of clearing it was apparent that she had come onto an important ancient storage yard. Fourteen enormous terra cotta vessels lay on their sides, eighteen inches apart, all but three in perfect condition, their handles in tact. Tag placed two of them by the sheepfold door. Upright, each jar was almost as tall as he was. The jars, he was convinced, had stored food supplies, wheat, and corn in a well-ordered storage system that spoke eloquently of the nature and customs of its consumers. They were signs of a city, evidence of people who had inhabited that city. Chadwick packed up the twelve remaining jars for shipment to Constantinople.

All, along, Tag believed The Great Tower of the City of Troy would have stood on the west side of the hill where its location would have commanded the broadest view of the surrounding plain. On June twentieth, on the west side of the hill, just four feet away from his earlier roped area and more than thirty-five feet down, he uncovered remnants of a wall about ten feet thick. At first he took this fragment to be a part of a fortification wall, but as more and more stone was exposed, he changed his mind. This, he believed, was The Great Tower of Troy, this the place where Helen had stood with Priam to identify for him the Greek warriors and heroes who had come in their thousand ships.

> "Come here, dear child, sit
> here beside me; you shall see your
> onetime lord and your dear kinsmen.
>     You are not to blame,
> I hold the gods to blame for bringing on
> this war against the Akhaians, to our
> sorrow. Come, tell me who the big man is
> out there, who is that powerful figure?

Other men are taller, but I never saw a
soldier clean-cut as he, as royal in his
bearing: he seems a kingly man."

    And the great
beauty, Helen, replied:
    "Revere you as I do,
I dread you, too, dear
father Your question,
now: Yes, I can answer it:
that man is Agamemmnon, son of
Atreus, lord of the plains of Argos,
ever both a good king and a
formidable soldier . . . .

It was also on this very spot that Tag and Sophia had stood during their first visit to the hill together, Tag recalled. On horseback they had come to this same crest and had seen the Troad below, the view of the entire Plain of Troy at its best, the sea, the islands of Samothrace, Imbros, and Tenedos, the river, and the mountains in a fully surrounding panorama. Buried for more than three thousand years, The Great Tower no longer commanded a view of the entire plain and now was little more than three ruined walls of stone, but there was no question that the site itself did still stand in full view of the surrounding plain and of the critical Hellespont. The sea. The essential element. It was there, unchanged.

Discovery of The Great Tower was, for Tag, the most important of all his findings to date, and solidified for all time his belief in the existence of the City of Troy. Additional excavations in the next weeks at the base of the ancient walls of The Great Tower revealed not only more stone, but the sort of evidence he had not dared hope for. There were traces of a fire, an all-engulfing inferno that could have spared nothing in its path and in this instance, his knowledge of ancient history proved invaluable.

The catastrophic events concluding the Trojan War would have brought all citadel life to an abrupt and fiery end, men of the Trojan citadel mercilessly murdered, children hurtled over the high walls, fleeing women taken by their Greek conquerors as slaves and concubines. All was ended in a consuming fire that would successfully erase most evidence of the city's glorious existence. At the site of the wall of The Great Tower, large portions of the hewn stone were blackened, and this was not simply the blackening deterioration of soil buried in unmeasured time. The signs were unmistakable. But now there was also something else.

By July, Tag had come to an important conclusion, one that would seriously affect his work and his future reputation as an archaeologist. The Stratigraphic-Layer-Theory had been the one practical guideline upon which he had based his attack on the hill and now there was no doubting its application. At a depth of more than forty feet, the relentless scooping out had revealed seven distinct undulating layers of stone and debris and in a few places, stone accumulated in masses substantial enough to suggest the remains of ancient buildings of varying size. Of itself and discounting Homeric reference this was a highly important discovery, for The Seven layers of the hill exposed more than three thousand years of consecutive human habitation and seven separate cities dating from 3000 B.C. to 850 B.C. It was first hand evidence of prehistoric life dating back to a completely unknown age, and it would attract the attention of historians the world over, eventually requiring the rewriting of textbooks and chronologies. Now, it was this revelation, more than any other that captured Sophia's imagination. Now there was a satisfactory scope of historic reality to add to what she already felt. In its own controlling way and in its own time the hill had finally revealed its soul and naked in the sullen light it had not only found the opening to Sophia's heart, it had touched her soul as well.

In one diary entry made much later in life, when she was by the sea at Phaleron and prone to remeniscense and long reflection, Sophia wrote: At Hissarlik we adapted to our environment in much the same way all animals adapt when cornered or captured: cautiously and dependent on one another, but it was never easy. Digging into the heart of a hill is hard work. Nature fights you every step of the way. After a while, the wind and weather are the least of your worries. It's the flesh and blood of the earth itself, the soil and rock, that become your worst enemies and that you worry about and battle constantly. And the earth never gives in to you, not an inch. You give in to it, all of yourself, completely, every fiber, every breath, every inspiration, every exhalation, and until you hunger for it and need it and fall completely in love with the taste and touch and silence of the earth itself you never get anywhere.

They numbered the layers from top to bottom, the uppermost level being Troy VII, the lowest, Troy I and it was one of the layers close to the bottom that absorbed Tag's interest most. Unlike stones in other layers, its stones were badly blackened and charred and it was this second layer from the bottom that he identified as the Troy of Homer, the elite Troy of The Iliad, the Troy of Helen and Paris, and the Troy of Priam's gold. Whenever his hands touched these blackened stones he was convinced he brushed against the building blocks of Priam's golden city on a hill, and it was on this layer of blackened stone that he focused his energies and which, to a man, became the challenge of the entire crew.

Now, of course, there was no thought of going home to Athens as one eventful day dissolved into another. Tag gave Sophia a small crew of her own, and on the morning of June 26, at a depth of forty-two feet, she made her first independent discovery in a deposit of dry, bright yellow wood cinders later found to be part of the upper chamber of a stone hut. All that remained were blackened stones, but inside, sitting straight up and perfectly erect, were three skeletons. She stared at them shocked and spellbound by the flawless state of their well-preserved bones. Close by were remnants of the simple jewelry they had worn, hairpins of thin gold wire with rounded tops, six gold earrings and three finger rings of gold wire. They were women. Three Trojan women, she told herself.

"Had they hidden themselves, hoping to escape the Greeks who had entered the gates to devour the city?" she wondered. Or had they died in the confusion of the fire, horribly afraid? Perhaps the fire had not reached them at all. Perhaps they had killed themselves with a deadly potion rather than face the fate of meeting their Greek conquerors. A torrent of supposition filled her mind in a chain of endless possibilities and she worried about the fate of the women as if she had known them by name, as if she had been a friend concerned about their frantic activity in the last hours of life. Later that same week she came upon two more skeletons, these much larger.

"Warriors," she decided. Nearby were helmets and lances and of a material not yet seen in the excavations. They were heavy. Tag immediately realized they were bronze, the same substance as the few nails he had shown to Worsaae two years before.

"You will need more evidence," Worsaae had said to him. Tag closed his eyes, shook his head, and smiled to Sophia. On a June day of pristine summer beauty, on The Pergamus of Troy, Sophia Schliemann had discovered conclusive evidence of an unknown ancient Bronze Age and at first, it meant little to her. But, in fact, with the unearthing of several heavy prehistoric bronze helmets and weapons, she had uncovered the earliest traces of human life on Hissarlik; life that had existed as far back as three thousand years before Jesus would come to Jerusalem and three thousand years before the Disciple Peter would come to Rome, preaching a gospel that would cause the Roman Empire to forsake centuries of pagan gods in the sweep of Christianity that would forever alter the course of human history.

By early July, excitement grew as findings accumulated ever more rapidly. Each day, there were important items to record and catalogue and now there were not enough hours in a day. Sophia learned to use daylight wisely, often working right up to the moment when darkness surrounded her and she suddenly realized she could no longer see. She and Tag reorganized their personal schedule, deciding to have dinner inside the sheepfold later than before and lighting oil lamps long after dark. She wakened earlier in the morning, eager to face each new day on the hill with an excitement she made no attempt to stifle and although increasingly anxious as summer's heat descended, Tag delighted in catching sight of her as she seriously pursued her own diligent study of the many curious findings being unearthed, gratified in the knowledge that at last she shared his beliefs and worked at his side.

Items were collected and stored in the two storage sheds that had been erected just across from the sheepfold and sometimes they both worked at the two long tables inside the larger shed. It was a fascinating place, confusing in its array of oddities and surprises, but Sophia knew exactly where everything was, and when Tag asked about a particular item, she could put her hands on it almost immediately. She loved concentrating on the timeless possibilities crossing her hands and she sometimes held up a vase, an earring, a hairpin, or a coin, contemplating its intended use or the appearance of its owner and as the picture she began to form in her mind of life on The Pergamus of Troy became the Troy of solid structure that Tag clearly understood, Sophia's Troy also became a Troy full of colorful life and movement and a world driven by the emotions of its inhabitants.

They sailed out of Canakkale aboard the Granville on July 10, Tag reading and updating his journals as once again they crossed the Aegean, Sophia at a loss for things to do, her restlessness unsatisfied by the newspapers and periodicals she had brought on board, these mild diversions unsuccessful in erasing from her mind the unnerving memory of Benjamin Chadwick's blue eyes and the way his light brown hair fell across his forehead in the Turkish sunshine, his every word spoken to her remembered, her every attempt to forget his voice, his every nod, conquered by the mere thought of his warm, crushing glance and his lingering smile, a smile embossed on her whole being as the distance between Athens and Canakkale turned into the most unsettling separation she had ever known.

She tried not to think about what it would be like to be alone with him in a room, in a house, a place apart. She tried not to dwell on the curiosity, the ardor, the end, the rational half of her able to quickly put those thoughts aside, the irrational side quickly burrowed into consenting dreams at night. At home in Athens she would forget all this, she told herself. The distance would mean something, do something to erase this secret agony.

❧ ❧ ❧

Despite Tag's frequent communication with newspapers, scientists, and societies, no newspaper accounts had formally acknowledged a discovery of Troy as such. No single qualified individual or group came forward to verify the hilltop findings and for some time it appeared that Tag and Sophia alone understood the true scope of their discoveries. But now, they also understood the growing need for further proof. They must somehow tie Troy to Greece.

They spent three months in Athens, occupied primarily with progress on the construction of their new home. They ordered new furniture, carpets, china, and silver. Tag planned for a museum on the ground floor, a musicians' gallery on the second. Sophia concentrated on the new garden and with Niki looked after Georges, who was in failing health. Assured that Iliou Mélathron would be completed by the following summer, they returned to Canakkale in mid-October as more and more, Sophia's thoughts turned to the Greek homeland from which the armada had come to wage war across the Aegean Sea at the shores of Asia Minor, and it was Mycenae to which her attention was turned; Mycenae, City of Agamemmnon, known as an arid, mountainous region in the large peninsula of the Greek Peleponnese.

"The maps have come from Giannis and here's a letter from Niki," she excitedly announced to Tag, opening the envelopes one after another following dinner one Sunday evening at the Dardania.

"Giannis has sent us what he says he has been able to find on Mycenae."

The relationship with Giannis Kolodji continued strained, but disregarding this unavoidable aspect of life, Tag and Sophia had amicably sought his professional advice in several instances, which pleased the Acropolis curator no end. With each request, Giannis had responded promptly providing whatever information was requested, but down deep, his personal tensions remained, most kept alive by the egotistical fires periodically ignited by published reports of Tag's findings at Hissarlik. Giannis always downplayed these small triumphs, choosing to agree with the London Times, who steadfastly labeled Tag as nothing more than a wealthy, ill-advised adventurer. Under all this, however, and most important of all, Giannis was still a Greek and embedded in his flesh and blood his issue with the Turks could not be set aside nor could he forget that Sophia, his wife's sister, was spending a greater part of every year in Turkey, a fact he often drew to Victoria's attention. Now and then, however, as news developed and evidence mounted stage by painful stage, he experienced surges of remorse and guilt and small, secret episodes of genuine admiration for his sister-in-law and her galling, tenacious, and completely uncompromising husband.

Sophia remained in frequent touch with Niki, kept abreast of family news and events in Athens through Niki's long letters. Sophia's own letters to her sister were openly affectionate and bore an ease of expression that did more than she knew to keep their relationship alive. Neither sister escaped the constant underlying friction existent between their husbands, but in ways they seldom understood, they had not sacrificed the bonds of sisterhood in favor of spousal loyalties.

They had, instead, learned to write long, newsy letters which tread lightly on areas of greatest sensitivity and were confined to their children, recent occurrences, and light-hearted gossip.

"Metrios is being married next month," Niki had written. He is to marry Alexandra Lemonis. You must remember her. She was the girl who always led the processions." Sophia smiled to herself, recalling Alexandra with mild disdain. She had always been the first girl in the church procession lines; the perfect little leader with the perfect little walk and the perfect little smile. Why was it that the last girl in the line always remembered the first?

Sophia pictured Metrios and Alexandra together. They would live a simple life in Athens, in a small neat house, and they would attend church just as their parents had, involving themselves in the Greek family framework of predictability and old habit.

"I'm happy to hear of Metrios and Alexandra's marriage," Sophia later wrote to Niki. "I wish them much happiness and many tall children."

Mycenae loomed ahead as the next step in Sophia's life and she welcomed its inevitability in a way she would never have thought possible just a few years before when she herself had longed for precisely the simple life she knew that Alexandra and Metrios would soon begin to live in Athens.

Now she was relieved to have overcome the secret hesitancy she had felt as the summer had evaporated and once again the leather trunks came up from the basement, waiting open in the upstairs hall, the return to Hissarlik a journey she faced still taunted by reminders of the blue-eyed, fair-haired Benjamin Chadwick who would surely be waiting. To avoid the inevitable she had thought about insisting on remaining in Athens with Andromache. She would tell Tag she was too tired, too unprepared to face the journey, but as if reading her mind and knowing the secrets of her heart, Tag said he needed her more than ever now, wanted her at his side, respected her opinions. He made passionate love to her, his desire for her closeness to him and her surrender to his lovemaking an overwhelming emotion she handled with unspoken loyalty and inbred courage, the path ahead one that although clouded, was one she was sure she would travel in complete safety because he knew. Of course Tag knew. How could he not? He knew her better than she knew herself.

❧ ❧ ❧

"If the Greek Mycenaens can be contemporary with the Trojans of the second city, they would have lived anywhere from 1100 to 2000 B.C.," Tag said as he scanned across one of the large maps Giannis had sent. "I must write to Worsaae to get his opinion on what geological changes he thinks might have taken place on the Greek mainland since then. The sea levels and river valleys may have altered considerably. A sizable deposit of sediment may need clearing."

Sophia nodded. "We should apply for a permit immediately. Thank God, the Greek government will be easier to deal with." She suggested they seek Giannis' counsel on how best to approach application for the permit to excavate in Greece, knowing that the Ministry of Public Instruction in Athens served the same purpose it did in Constantinople as one of the municipal leftovers of Turkish rule. She wrote to him the next morning and sent her letter out from the Dardania with that Sunday's mail.

In Athens, Giannis read her letter with surprise and interest. "and we have decided that it is now time to begin thinking about the Greek mainland and the possible origins of Greek Mycenae," she wrote. "I know we shall require an excavation permit. Should we apply to The Minister of Public Instruction, or is there a new public office or Greek municipal agency we should address?"

This was an important question and Giannis knew it. He also knew that restructuring was taking place in many areas of Greek government with a heightened regard for the preservation of history and historical sites, especially in Athens, and at the same time, in the midst of construction was the Greek National Archaeological Museum. Begun in 1860, it would not be completed until 1889, but Giannis suspected it could play an important role in the Schliemanns' new plans for excavating at Greek Mycenae, its rather lengthy construction program the result of an outgrown Greek national central museum which from 1834 had been housed in Hadrian's Library and called The Tower of the Winds. With the donation of a large plot of land on Patission Street and a generous initial grant, the building began, only to be halted periodically as funds ran out or the design of the building was modified through frequent changes of heart on the parts of a frequently changing leadership. At its head now, however, was a man whom Giannis respected highly, Demetrios Panyotis, who finally spearheaded the completion of the museum with a popular community education program and a high level of expertise. Sophia and Tag had met him on a number of occasions. Panyotis was the link Giannis suggested.

Giannis responded to her letter promptly. "Panyotis advises me that the Ministry of Public Instruction in Athens is the appropriate agency through which Greek permits are being issued for the purposes of excavation. He does advise, however, that you make application soon. The laws governing such things will be changing, restricting the number of excavation permits issued in any one year. At last, some sense to all this amateur fanaticism over antiquities." His letter was signed, G. Kolodji, The Acropolis Museum, Athens.

In a world that communicated almost exclusively in the written word, it was a natural thing to look carefully at such things as one's personal letters, at the manner in which people signed their names, the paper they used, and the habits that became recognizable hallmarks of a personality.

"Giannis uses good quality rag paper," Tag had remarked to Sophia, fingering the heavy paper stock expertly and holding it up to the light. It was a rare compliment but one more indication that the friction continued.

Sophia handled the application for the Greek permit herself. Giannis sent her the necessary forms and when she returned them to him, he personally delivered them to the Ministry. She thought it generous of him, and said so in yet another exchange of letters. Plans for a preliminary visit to Mycenae were quickly put into place and Sophia looked forward to these travel plans in a way far different from her initial visit to Hissarlik. She avidly studied the maps with Tag, discussed potential for success, and sent for countless books on the history of the Peloponnese, immersing herself in its background.

At Hissarlik in late September, more men were added to the crew, bringing its numbers to two-hundred twelve. In rapid succession they uncovered large sections of a long stone paved roadway and then huge blocks of white marble slab of the same color and quality as that of The Apollo Marble, much of it untouched by the blackened signs of fire. Large foundation stones appeared, rambling on and on in a labyrinth of odd shapes and patterns, but in one particular area, a tall portion of a stone wall remained completely in tact. Each stone measured sixteen inches in length, and all were blackened.

Chadwick was drawn to the marble slabs, many of which were carved in scrolls and deep leaf-like patterns. They had a lustre and a richness that centuries of blackened earth had not destroyed. They varied in size, the largest pieces measuring six and one-half feet in length and five feet in width. In all, there were forty-three slabs collected. Chadwick took twenty-five and shipped them to Constantinople out of Canakkale, headed for storage until they could be sent "on the Road to Izmir," as he liked to say, Izmir the location of the new Turkish Archaeology Museum.

Most of the marble was creamy white in color, but a few pieces were heavily matrixed and veined in thin streaks of dark green or dark gray. With no little degree of satisfaction, Tag saw them carried away, extremely pleased with himself for being able to present these admittedly impressive pieces to the Turkish Government as mere examples of what further Trojan riches lay in the hill called Hissarlik.

As work progressed, the tall stone wall took on greater form. Some of the stones were found to have mortar between them. Periodically, Tag stepped back to look at the blackened mass, eerie in the bright sunlight, out of character and strangely sad, but at the end of a week, the foundation and walls of a large building were clearly apparent. Jagged and broken in some places, certain portions of the walls were higher than others, but clearly outlined what had once been a substantial structure. Constantly, Tag examined the interior sides of these walls for signs of painting or ornamentation which would have revealed so much, but there was nothing to be found adorning the walls. The charred blackness obliterated any traces of refinements. He tried washing some of the stones clean, but no amount of scrubbing removed the long imbedded damaging scorched residues and the persistent signs of devastation that in his heart he knew had consumed what he was certain was this great Palace of Priam. Within the following week, an additional section of the ancient building came to light, confirming his belief that this was indeed the palace itself. A long, terrace-like stone floor was unearthed, its stones well preserved and free of scorch. These stones were pale in color, unscarred, unusually large, and looked exactly like the huge stones the crew had been ordered to hurtle over the edge of the hill during the earliest cutting of the north-south trench.

The palace would have been prominently situated on the citadel, its authority and character determined by the strength of its stone fortification walls which in some places were as thick as twenty feet. Tag theorized that Priam had likely been Troy's king for many years, a monarch long established on his citadel, his luxurious palace a stronghold well known in Egypt as well as in the Greek kingdom of Pylos, seat of King Nestor, and in Argos, Sparta, and of course, Mycenae.

In his correspondence to The Times of London, he described The Palace of Priam on The Pergamus of Troy as having the same great sweeping vistas of open plain and sea as did The Great Tower, paralleling its style of construction. He wrote, "The Palace was a self-sufficient stronghold; a fortress ensuring safety and protection for its inhabitants within the thickness of its stone walls and surrounding fortifications. It would have been seen by state visitors and admired, its parade rooms setting a tone of grandeur for visiting ambassadors who sought Troy's friendship, favor and trade. Its long, open colonnades led to the royal apartments whose rooms were large enough to house the fifty sons and twelve daughters of Priam, along with their wives, husbands, children, and servants. But the glory of Priam's Palace lay at its great center core, its megaron, the heart of the kingdom and the throne room of its king."

In most sections of the palace, the blackened foundation stones barely ascended to five feet, but for Tag they were not a series of confusing building fragments. He saw them with his own unique talent for reconstructing the entire scene in detail, and what he saw was the magnificent Palace of Priam complete in every way, its walls finished, its roofs capped, its courtyards paved, its inhabitants alive. His report to The Times concluded that The Palace of Priam had not only commanded a spectacular view of the vast plain below and the sea beyond, . . . . "it was the heart of the magnificent royal citadel, rich in the natural resources of its surroundings and a desirable, hospitable link familiar to the leaders of an heretofore unknown prehistoric world."

Time and time again he recreated the great palace for Sophia, his verbal portrayals so vivid and alive that she was soon able to envision its scale and form, its very color and texture. He walked her through its ancient ruins of jet black stone just as he had walked her through the Louvre, a fountainhead of information and technical knowledge, but in this garden that was his hill he was more like Martial Caillebotte, the quintessential, sensitive gardener, expertly tending his prize specimen, certain of their ultimate yet untouched potential. Tag saw Priam's Palace not burned and blackened, but built of pale stone and fine timber, its thick, fortification stone walls enclosing a private world of royal favor and peaceful character. "These crenellated walls may have been forbidding," he said, "but inside, the courtyards and gardens spoke of human grace and true nobility."

Along with The Great Tower, the Scaean Gates described in the Iliad were items highly prioritized on Tag's list for indisputable evidence that he had discovered the City of Troy. He had searched for traces of metal gates of copper or bronze, their imprint, their hinges, but he found no sign of these metals. Digging into the area at the north palace wall, he did find two wide gaps in the blackened foundation stone. They were of equal length and he thought they might have once held doors of wood that had long ago deteriorated and that was it, of course. The gates to Troy would not have been metal at all, he realized, not bronze, and not copper! The gates to Troy were openings in the stone walls, openings made prominent by their stone ornamentation and to close off the openings, the Trojans had drawn an enclosure across them, heavy wooden planks tied securely with strong bindings of hide. It was entirely possible to believe that Troy had several timbered gates, all but one or two safely filled in with stone or marble during the long course of the war, leaving only one vulnerable, the Scaean Gate, to control and secure. "Homer says that the Greeks sailed up to the gates of Troy in their ships," Tag related to Sophia. "But this does not necessarily mean that the gates were those of the high citadel itself, nor would it have necessarily meant that those were the gates at which the wooden horse was left. Homer says that the Greek flotilla came to the point where the Scamander River empties into the Hellespont and from which a river road led to the gates of Troy. The Greeks sailed directly to them." Tag reasoned that this could indeed have been entirely possible at that time of the year when the melting spring snows from Mount Ida produced their flash floods, deepening and widening the Scamander River as they still did. He quoted to her directly from The Iliad.

> Erect on Troy's great tower, aging Priam
> gazed at huge Akhilleus, before whom
> Trojans in tumult fled, and no defense
> materialized. Then groaning from the tower
> Priam descended. For the *gatekeepers,*
> known as brave soldiers, he had urgent
> words: "When our soldiers
>
> crowd inside the wall to get their breath,
> *close both your timbered gates. bolt them*
> *again,* I fear this murderous man may leap
> the wall." At this they *pushed* the *bolts,*
> *opening* the *gates,* and the *gateway made*
> *refuge* Then Apollo flashed out to avert
> death from the Trojans, headed as they were
> for the *high wall,* men grown coarse in thirst,
> covered with dust
>
> out of the plain where they had run.
> *Troy* of *the high gates* might have fallen now
> to the Akhaian soldiers . . . ."

❧ ❧ ❧

In his notes at the conclusion of the 1872 Fall season at Hissarlik, Tag summarized the findings to date. Sophia read them on the journey back to Athens, enthralled by the thorough, vivid picture he presented and by his use of the present tense. "From the appearance of the clay bricks, I have determined that Troy's buildings are pale in color, giving the entire city a soft, rich, lightflooded radiance on its commanding acropolis. The Tower, the Palace of Priam, and the long paved roadway to it are finished with stone and some traces of timber. It is a fine, broad, gradually ascending roadway, approximately twelve feet in width. Its lower walls are quite high and are marked for wood posts which were once set into the walls every twenty to twenty-four inches. In a few places, the walls are still covered with a smooth clay finish. The roadway curves to the left. A ramp to the right leads to the Palace. The road narrows at this spot which is the likely place for a double-portalled gate. The entire road is paved, and in some sections there are the traces of a clay surface identical to that of the walls. Within the gateway opening are The Tower and The Palace. Large, buttress-like walls remain at that point, once constructed with massive horizontal beams, which extended fully across the road, supporting a ceiling which formed the flat roof of The Tower that rose above it. In the center of the citadel stood the largest building, the Palace of Priam. The southeast gate led to it. To the back of the Palace is an open space, a courtyard, or the remains of a garden leading to the interior royal apartments. The walls of the primary apartments are five feet in thickness on foundation substructures eight feet deep. All are overlaid with slabs of stone and over every few feet of brick, wooden beams were once connected every twelve feet by wooden cross-beams. Each brick is four and three-quarter inches high. The roof of the palace was horizontal, constructed of beams, wood planks, and clay. In parts of the roof interiors there is a thick layer of clay mixed in with calcinated wood rafters and rather well-preserved fragments of wood. There is a second building whose walls are four feet thick, with foundations twenty-two inches deep. This building is eighteen feet wide, with a doorway six feet wide, leading to an interior room twenty-five feet long. There is a small door leading into the last room which is thirty feet, four inches long. There are traces of flooring material, and of a pavement composed of small pebbles and clay alternating with slabs of gray slate. In the buildings lie piles of brick debris and many calcinated masses of wood, especially at doorways where a fire would feed upon a quantity of woodwork there. Yellow, hardened, sponge-like substances cover large portions of the brick walls. The Second City of Troy, unlike its succeeding settlements was not confined to the plateau, but extended on the west and south-east sides to a substantially large lower city. A masonry wall of unwrought block was built vertically, its irregular crevices filled with smaller stones. This is the part of the walled city outside the citadel. No portions of the building have been found there, but every trench sunk into the lower city has yielded countless potsherds identical to those of the second city. The lower city was likely deserted from Troy III to Troy VII, providing a source for building materials on the higher hill. The existence of this lower city redefines many Homeric images. The Scaean Gate, for example, up to which the Trojan War often surges, is in the outer walls of that lower city, and will never be found. It was situated on the west, somewhere between the citadel and the two flowing springs."

# CHAPTER TWELVE

## 1873

T HE HALCYON SAILED into Canakkale on April twentieth and once again the Dardanelles pulsated with the activity of migratory waterfowl.

A good sign," Sophia said optimistically as she picked up her binoculars to watch the wildlife spectacle as the Halcyon maneuvered the "S" straits that had come to signal a homecoming of sorts. Murat awaited them at the Dardania as he often did, but that day a stranger waited with him.

"I am Ahmet Ostrogorsky," the man standing beside Murat in the small portside vestibule said, addressing both Schliemanns. "I represent the Turkish Government and I shall be with you during your stay at Hissarlik this spring."

Ostrogorsky was immediately overly patronizing, making his presence felt with an authority suggesting he had come with an official welcome designed to extend singularly and by himself the generous hospitality of the entire Ottomon Empire. In appearance, Ahmet Ostrogorsky immediately reminded Tag of Stossel, the big burl of a man who had worked at the revolving disk machine in Berlin, hand chopping wood scraps. Sophia, however, immediately recognized him as Nephos, the "black cloud" the peasant women of Hissarlik had told her about, noticing that except for the slight indentation at its middle, his wide perspiring forehead shone just as brightly as they had said, the opaque, gleaming oval at its center one she was sure had come with years of prostrate Muslim prayer. She could not take her eyes off it.

"I have been expecting you," Tag said cooly, in a voice that conveyed only polite introduction. For some time he had wondered what was taking the government so long to get a Turkish representative to Hissarlik since his Firman clearly defined the presence of a government official as integral to its provisos. Chadwick had probably managed to delay it, he had concluded, since in five campaigns no one had appeared until now, but as if to make up for lost time, from the moment of his arrival, Ostrogorsky became the eyes and ears of official Turkey.

"So, Herr Schliemann, when will we see the gold of Priam?" he asked several times on his first day at the hill. "One half to the government and one half to you. Will the Effendi of Hissarlik spare just a small souvenir of Troy's gold for poor Ostrogorsky?" He laughed and stood before Tag like a heavy jowled watchdog who knew his territory and exactly how to maneuver within it, soon taking to the daily routine of roughly pulling some of the crew aside to examine random baskets of soil and whenever it occurred to him, which was often, to search pockets for signs of theft. His presence quickly cast a pall on the hill, affecting morale and inhibiting enthusiasm for what to all participants had thus far become a successful venture. Nephos was the perfect name for him and it was not long before Tag mentioned him in the meticulous notes he made each day.

Nephos loved the coins. Sophia said that was because they were small enough to be stolen and later used as bribes. Everyone knew he took a number of them every day, slipping a few into his pockets when he thought no one noticed at the end of the day as he walked to the cabin Tag had provided him. Tag overlooked all this, cooperating in full compliance with the terms of his Firman except when it came to the proviso that one half of the findings be turned over to the Turkish authorities. Prior to Ostrogorsky's arrival, he had sought to have the language of the proviso altered to state that he and the Turkish Government were to share equally in accumulated findings but only at such time as he had formally closed all excavation activity and not before. Chadwick had only recently expedited the change in the language of the proviso and until Ostrogorsky's arrival and except for the pieces Chadwick had taken for the museum, all items had been cleaned and stored in one of the two courtyard storage rooms across from the sheepfold. But now, Ostrogorsky demanded that the daily findings be divided each afternoon, in his presence, and that two guards be posted at the storage sheds day and night, to be paid of course, by Tag. Ostrogorsky's greedy hand was unacceptable and Tag insisted that Chadwick clarify the terms of the proviso directly with him. Although after a brief conversation with Chadwick, Ostrogorsky quickly dropped his demands, it was abundantly clear that such representatives stood for Ottomon authority in whatever framework they were placed, assuming an unbearable arrogance and augmenting their power with impossible, corrupt demands in what Tag saw as potential for sinister consequences. But far beyond the importance of the terms of his Firman, Tag saw something else that had become impossible to overlook. The fragile sense of community on the hill he had worked so hard to establish was being destroyed. The men had been spirited and capable of spontaneous humor before Nephos had arrived, their unity and concerted effort a source of great pride to Tag and to themselves. Now, like a new bully coming into an old game, he had changed the rules and because now any one of the crew could be suspected of infraction, the men likewise suspected one another. There were fierce disagreements and explosive arguments, confrontations about who worked where and for how long. Fistfights broke out every day, even among the boys. There was pettiness, quibbling, bickering over allotments of bread, cigarettes, wages. It was endless. Fortunately, Murat addressed this divisiveness with patience, humor, and a skill aimed at simply maintaining peace. After a while Tag called him King Solomon of Hissarlik, admiring the manner in which Murat managed as he did, to placate injured parties with fairness and to mete out swift penalties when called for, all with the steady admonition that greater consequences would fall upon every man as a result of the indiscretion of a few. But the Black Cloud lived up to all the attributes of his title and remained an enigma on the hill, his presence a disturbance to all concerned, just one small crack of light detected. The Greek-speaking crew discovered that his proficiency in Greek was seriously limited and that Nephos relied far more on his eyes than on his ears. They found they could actually talk about him in his presence without fear of being understood. When important visitors came, they watched him display an uncanny talent for cosmopolitan graciousness, especially toward the British, and at these times were, unknown to him, at their most offensive to him. When Chadwick came to the hill, Ostrogorsky, speaking in Turkish, a language in which Chadwick was proficient, never failed to compliment him on the progress of "his" excavation, as if it were he in charge and not Tag. Tag overheard this on several occasions, his own Turkish now almost fluent, but he made no comment, attributing Ostrogorsky's cordiality toward Chadwick as still another Turkish idiosyncrasy that defied understanding.

"I made a tour of Italy this summer," Chadwick told Sophia during one such visit, "Venice, Florence, Rome. I purchased a few nice paintings and a carpet, and were it not for the rumors of civil unrest spreading like wildfire throughout all Europe, I would have been in Paris by September."

What charming, idle madness, she thought to herself, wondering what it was about him that she disliked and at the same time craved to keep nearby and close to her.

❧ ❧ ❧

June eighteenth was a breathtakingly beautiful early summer day, warm, the sky clear, the vaulted blue overhead sparsely painted with white puffs of cloud, the peak of Mount Ida clearly visible, brilliant and regal as Sophia and Tag worked on the stone-floored terrace of the palace at a depth of forty-five feet. The day before, the last of its debris had been removed basket by tedious basket, until the surface of the stone floor was revealed as a beautiful, large open space, its columned ruins finally freed on the long west side. The terrace was remarkably in tact, its large stones and columns untouched over time but for the layers of soil in which it had been safely entombed. Both Tag and Sophia had been anxious to return to it that morning, eager to resume their search for a possible opening, an arch or a doorway into the palace, any means of access.

Tag had adjusted his gloves and turned to his work beside Sophia when with no warning whatsoever suddenly there was a loud rush of air. In an instant, the wall before them began to fall away in a tumbling wave of stone and dust, large stones tumbling onto the terrace before them, rolling and crashing in every direction. Tag took Sophia's arm and quickly pulled her away to the far end of the terrace floor where he held her tight against him. At first, the wall had crumbled in a slow sheer of bouncing stone, but then it crashed down faster and faster in louder and more terrifying surges of splintering rock and mortar. They were more than forty feet below ground in a canyon-like space, helplessly caught in a dangerous rockslide. But it stopped as abruptly as it had begun. Quiet returned, the gray dust rose in dense, silent clouds, and when it cleared, they saw a second layer of identical stone in the very same place where only moments before a wall had crumbled away. Something shone out of it. It was about the size of Tag's hand and it appeared to be a triangular piece of bright metal caught in a hardened mass of fire-blackened stone. He ran to it and slid his hand back and forth over the bright triangle. Whatever it was, it was deeply embedded into the wall and it would be too dangerous to attempt to pick at the calcinated layers around it. The whole wall could fall in, setting off a landslide or worse, a cave-in.

"It's copper of some kind," Tag said. "I'll need help. Get Murat, but try not to let Ostrogorsky see you. Just get Murat here as quickly as you can."

Sophia hurried to the wood ramp connecting the west palace wall to the platform above, her heart racing. She remembered that Murat worked the tower that day and from the platform she saw his crew of about fifty men digging into rock-hard soil. Another forty or so men passed baskets of dirt and debris from one man to another, on up a platform and beyond to the high ground of the hill. Now she could see him. Murat was at the top, thank God. She waved him toward her with beckoning hand motions, all the while on the lookout for Ostrogorsky, who by some miracle was nowhere to be seen. Murat saw her and came quickly.

It seemed to take an eternity to reach Tag and when they did he stood at the far edge of the palace terrace, the wall that minutes before had exposed a shimmer of copper covered over with wood planks. Such planks were stacked everywhere on the hill, used as walkways and bridges over the dirt piles that accumulated, but there was no sign of the tantalizing metal glimmer.

"Where is Nephos?" Tag asked them.

"He carefully counts the baskets today," Murat said, smiling. "He would not have noticed the goddess Athena herself."

Tag quickly removed the wood planks and together he and Murat began to pick around the copper triangle. Once a small section of calcified soil had been removed, the stones surrounding the copper object came away with surprising ease. There was no mortar holding them.

The object when freed was a strange shape, not a triangular shape at all, but an oblong. There were deep indentations along the oddly curving sides. It was a lidded copper container, some twenty inches in length, with the remains of a chunk-like clasp, also made of copper. The broken clasp had long ago ceased to keep the lid firmly in place and although still partially attached, it was badly bent out of shape. There were no hinges, but clearly, the heavy shallow lid had, at one time, fit tightly onto the flanged edge of the container.

"It must be the copper liner for a box of some kind," Tag suggested, holding it in his hands. "The wood has disintegrated of course, but the copper is beautifully preserved." He held it up to examine the bottom which was roughly pebbled in texture, as if it had set on small stones for a long period of time. He then opened it.

Some forty-five feet below the surface of the hill of Hissarlik, Heinrich Schliemann's lifelong dream came true. In the copper coffer of what had once been an ancient wooden box he found more than he had come to his hill to find and it was unlike anything even he could have imagined. The copper casque was filled with gold. He called it Priam's Treasure. The gold was jewelry, pieces of the most exquisite quality and artistic design. And this was not all. That same day, a short time later, from farther back in the same wall and not more than a foot away from where the copper container had lain imbedded, Sophia removed a large silver vase. In it she found two gold diadems, in perfect condition, of fine workmanship and in a remarkably fine state of preservation. In the same vase were golden earrings, hairpins, and six magnificent gold bracelets.

Without being seen by Ostrogorsky, Sophia returned to the sheepfold to look for anything in which the pieces could be carried without suspicion. She rifled through the trunk at the foot of the bed. In it she found exactly the right camouflage.

"I've never used this," she said to Tag as they wrapped the copper liner in the blue silk shawl that Niki had given her sister as a wedding present. "It has always seemed too elegant for Canakaale, but this shawl has been everywhere I've been. I always think I shall be needing it and at last I really do."

It was entirely in character for Sophia to be seen with a shawl, albeit not one of blue silk. She often wore one draped around her shoulders in the damp of early morning. That day she made five trips back and forth between the sheepfold and the palace terrace where Tag remained on the lookout for Nephos who briefly caught sight of her only once. She hid everything. A priceless treasure buried through centuries was hidden under the bed, in the trunk, anywhere out of sight and Sophia remained in the sheepfold for the remainder of the day knowing that Tag would continue at his work, giving off the appearance of complete normalcy. It was the longest afternoon of her life.

When at last the pointed rays of sunlight hovered over the Hellespont and slanted in the west, the crew was dismissed, ending the day as was the established custom, standing in line, ready to be paid for the day's work by Murat who did his part in preserving the customary daily routine by joking good-naturedly with a few of the men and admonishing the small boys for little legs that simply must learn to move faster, or little hands that simply must grow larger. When this procedure was completed, Murat joined Tag, and as was also the established custom, accounted for equipment and storing tools. Murat asked nothing about the copper casque and Tag volunteered nothing. Murat returned that night to his farm and to Tessa.

At last, to be alone in the sheepfold to savor the treasure, to touch it, hold it, was beyond belief. In one spectacular find they had come upon an array of gold and silver fashioned into objects of spectacular beauty and artistry. Everything in the silver vase was solid gold, the most outstanding piece one of the golden diadems, a splendid headdress made of thousands of individual pieces of gold worked together into hundreds of chains which would have draped the brow of its wearer, cascading into long, thick tassels of shoulder-length gold beading. In the silver vase there was a second diadem, its draping chains of gold designed of rings on a pear-shaped leaf and finished in campanula pendants which would have fallen below the ear, the whole ornamented in finely worked repoussé. Two pairs of earrings were made in the same finely worked gold chain and pendant design. The silver vase had also held hundreds of solid gold signet rings, most of them etched in scenes of a charging bull and embattled helmeted warriors on horseback, their shields held high.

Of the six bracelets, five were shaped of a twice-wound golden circlet embellished at each end in two golden knobs. The sixth bracelet was a single thin gold wire, circle-shaped and also finished in two gold knobs. The knobs on the six bracelets were soldered on, "an astonishing accomplishment," Tag said. Closer to the bottom of the vase were great numbers of gold chains and small loose gold pieces: links, prisms, discs, and small, straight bars of solid gold.

In the copper container they found six flat bars of gold resembling large knife blades. They were leaf-shaped and quite smooth at the edges. Tag was convinced they were examples of the Homeric "talent," the monetary currency of Homer's time and frequent description. The talents were in three sizes and yet, when more carefully examined later, were found to be of similar weight, varying from six ounces to just over six and seven-eighths ounces. To Sophia, the talent appeared more like a long pendant meant to adorn a girdle, but none had holes by which they would have been attached. Under the talents were hundreds of gold beads of several sizes, some flatter than others. There were also gold linked chains of varying lengths and three gold cups, each with a single handle. Two of the cups were pure gold, the third later found to be of electrum, which was composed of four parts gold to one part silver and so light in color that it was called, "white" gold. Near the bottom lay gold signet rings, gold earrings, and twelve bracelets similar to those in the silver vase but much larger double circles of gold finished in large, rounded gold knobs, and at the very bottom, there were single beads of pale golden amber, unstrung.

Sleep did not come that night. Who had owned such wonderful things? Whose hands had touched them? Against what skin had they lain? Whose lips had touched the rims of these golden cups?

The next day was Sunday. The Greek crew rested on Sunday and even Ostrogorsky stayed away in Canakkale. Given a precious day alone, Tag and Sophia returned to the palace wall at the northeast end of the stone-littered palace terrace. There, after about a half-hour's hand picking, Tag removed three sixteen-inch stones from the wall at the same level from which the copper coffer had come. Miraculously, from this same opening he removed four additional silvered vases, the largest with a single handle. There was also a smaller pure silver vase and a beautiful sphere-shaped golden bottle, narrow necked and perfectly cylindrical. A copper object was also removed, about five inches in length and oddly shaped. Tag thought it could be the old clasp to the disintegrated wooden coffer. A small cup of the same copper lay alongside and what Sophia would always remember as the prize of the day came in the form of a pure gold, boat-shaped, two handled cup, the handles soldered onto the body of the cup, a spout at one end. There was also an assortment of copper daggers designed with broad, leaf-like blades, curiously curved into thin narrow tangs at their bases and two large battle-axes, which later analyzed, were found to be almost entirely of copper.

The next day, making his rounds, Ostrogorsky noticed the remains of splintered rock piled on the terrace. Tag and Sophia worked there, clearing the area with a crew of twenty men, hoping to finish before Ostrogorsky saw it. He had just asked about the strange new deposit of rocky debris when Sophia heard the same sound of rushing air she had heard two days before. She looked up to see the remaining stone wall falling away, and this time not in one section. Removal of several large support stones had loosened the wall considerably and now it was plummeting away entirely, huge tumbling stones and clouds of circling dust sending Ostrogorsky and the crew scattering to every available wood plank leading away from the work platform, Tag and Sophia swept away with them in the frightened commotion.

In a duplication of the previous rockslide, it again ended quickly, but this time the dust rose more slowly, ascending in a thick gray darkness that hovered for the longest time. It was very quiet, strangely still in a way that was unusual for the hill now so accustomed to the energetic din of daily activity. Impulsively, every person on the hill remained constantly alert to the sounds that meant danger and the loud impact of tumbling rock meant only one thing. Everyone had heard it. Many came running and now, much against Sophia's urging, Tag rushed to the palace terrace, anxious to survey the damage. His immediate view as the dust cleared left him briefly stunned. Stepping back onto the platform, he could see that the ancient palace wall had crumbled away completely, now leaving a large, ragged opening. Through it he saw a small room, a chamber, and it was littered with the same type of yellowish wood cinders that Sophia had found in the hut where she had discovered the skeletons of the three girls. Stony debris was scattered about, and the now familiar blackened stone, but towards the far wall of the small chamber there was another glimmer and this time, there was no question of its identity or purpose. It was clearly a copper shield. Tag shouted for Sophia. Ostrogorsky was not far behind. As the three climbed through the opening to stand inside, other discoveries were made. Some three feet away from the shield lay a two-handled copper cauldron and strewn nearby were a vase of pure gold and a cup of pure gold. There was also a silver goblet, five double-edged daggers, and a bronze helmet.

Tag and Sophia concluded that a Trojan guard, perhaps a trusted personal bodyguard, had attempted to secure some of the royal objects into a secret chamber. The guard had been required to move with great haste in secreting away what little he could carry alone, but either the overwhelming fire or the attack of an enemy Greek warrior had brought him down before he was able to complete his task. Eager to escape the engulfing fire and dense smoke, a Greek warrior would not have noticed a box or a silver vase, nor would he have cared much about its contents. His war was over. He had entered the gates to Troy. There would be time enough for looting and for plundering treasures of far greater value: women, wine, grain, horses.

Under Ostrogorsky's supervision, the contents of the chamber were placed in the sheepfold's largest storage room along with Troy's other artefacts, but the contents of Priam's Treasure were not added to it. The golden jewelry, the diadems, the bracelets, the gold talents, the vases; all remained hidden in the sheepfold, wrapped into Sophia's clothing, packed under filthy rags and even under a layer of brown dirt Tag had shoveled into the trunk at the foot of the bed. If Tessa saw any of this in her housekeeping routine, she never mentioned it and of course as a result could not have shared in the great anxiety Tag and Sophia now experienced daily.

Tag wanted to keep his kingly treasure in tact, fearing outright thievery on the parts of Ostrogorsky and the Turkish public officials whom he suspected could never be trusted to keep the treasure together for eventual exhibition in their Archaeological Museum. But if there was anything he truly wanted to keep for himself, it was this evidence of regal life on the Pergamus called Troy, this treasure of Priam about which he'd dreamed and that at last breathed life into the human beings of Homer's ancient song. In his mind he clearly saw the draped headdress worn by the beauteous Helen, her white arms circled by the gleaming gold bracelets, her ears adorned by the gold he had held in his own hands. He would never turn such a treasure over to the Turks. He would never divide the treasure equally with them. This was his own reward. It was due him, intended for him, and he devised an ingenious means by which he would eventually succeed in spiriting it out of Turkey and into his Athens home.

It could be, that in the back of his mind, Tag had decided to hold on to his treasure for just a short time, perhaps for a few years. He would show it off, prove to the public's satisfaction that he had found Homer's Troy, and then he would ceremoniously offer it to the Turks for their museum. This prospect soon led to an ambitious list of possibilities for the future of the treasure, none of which Sophia found acceptable. His first suggestion to Sophia that eventually he would make a gift of Priam's Treasure to the Turks led to sharp differences of opinion between them on its ultimate dispersement, even affecting conversation regarding terms of his will and its ultimate provisions. Sophia could not understand her husband's wish to deal so generously with the Turks and she adamantly opposed him. She felt that at some point he should legally satisfy the Turkish Government's half and half proviso as stated in the Firman, and that his remaining half rightfully belonged in Greece, specifically in the new Archaeological Museum in Athens. At about the same time, Tag also considered the possibility of presenting the treasure to Berlin. Germany, was, after all, his birthplace. The idea of a Schliemann Collection, permanently exhibited in special Berlin Museum rooms would focus on his German heritage, providing an opportunity for recognition in his homeland and the satisfaction of an emotional void he could explain to no one but Sophia. But, he would decide all that later.

For now, the Treasure of Priam must be kept hidden and secret, no word of it in reports or articles, no announcement, no hint of its existence. It was a near impossible feat for Tag, but the importance of keeping the treasure a secret could not have been more strongly emphasized than it was only a short time later when he overheard Nephos asking Chadwick how sales were going. It was a devastating moment for Tag, and in many ways, a turning point.

"Souvenirs of Troy must bring good prices," Nephos had commented to Chadwick one morning as he smoked a cigarette.

"Souvenirs of Troy?" Tag shot back, startling the two as he approached them. "What souvenirs of Troy, Benjamin?"

Chadwick had lowered his eyes.

"Benjamin, do not tell me you are one of them! Do not tell me such a thing!" Tag took a deep breath as he looked away.

"It got a bit out of control," Chadwick said quickly, as Nephos disappeared almost on cue. "Tag, I never expected you would find all this. Never! I was going to right it, really Tag. I had every intention."

It came out that Chadwick had been at it for quite some time, dealing in the corrupt Turkish official atmosphere he found "strangely compelling," as he put it. The challenge excited him, he confessed, and he had never feared the risk. There actually was none, he said. Tag could not believe what he was hearing. He felt his blood boiling.

Benjamin Chadwick sold antiquities unearthed in several parts of Turkey to eager European collectors with the full knowledge and cooperation of the very Turkish officials who could have stopped him and who pocketed their share of profit.

"Roman antiquities are plentiful, and frankly, European collectors are insatiable," he smiled, "when it comes to marble statues, carvings, and artefacts of almost any age and nature for their homes. You know, they're building these immense houses as if there's about to be a shortage of bricks and mortar!"

Chadwick's original fifty-fifty arrangement with the Turks was modified somewhat as he saw that Tag and others were providing him with important, often extremely valuable finds on his Turkish land leases. Never dreaming that the findings at Hissarlik would prove to be of such significance, the Turks had seen an expanded opportunity to continue a covert sale system of all Trojan discoveries, using Chadwick as their agent. In fact, Chadwick now openly admitted that he had made a handsome commission on the sale of the marble friezes which Tag had prized so highly, and that ten of the large terra cotta pots little Leda had come upon had been sold to an Italian Count for his new villa at Lake Como. Acting as an agent for the Turks in Europe, he was expert at finding qualified European buyers for antiquities that Tag and others essentially paid him to find in a treacherous circle of high land lease fees, clandestine meetings with officials, and outright bribes such as those Tag had voluntarily paid in Constantinople when he had first met Chadwick. The last puzzle pieces fell into place when Tag realized that from the beginning, he had been led directly into Chadwick's hands and straight from the government official who had stopped his first digging operations, asking to see his non-existent Firman in 1870. Once he had made it known that he wished to purchase outright the hill called Hissarlik, they had him. Chadwick had known all of it well before Tag had ever called on him, introducing himself and even making mention of mutual friends. Tag had never worked so hard at holding his temper in check.

"You mean to say that I pay excessive land lease fees to you so that you can hold on to the land and pocket the difference between your fees and mine?" he asked, incredulously.

"Tag, it really isn't the way it seems. In the long run, you get what you want, and I make a decent living. Who could have predicted the success of your campaigns here? I plan to work you into the system so that you can continue to enjoy yourself here with Sophia and at the same time, turn a handsome profit of your own."

"Enjoy myself? You must be insane!"

Chadwick made it sound completely feasible; perfectly workable, and above all, perfectly acceptable.

"And what of the new Turkish Museum on the Road to Izmir?" Tag asked, sarcastically. "Do you plan to have anything left of what I have found here to put into it? Anything at all?"

"Now, Tag, you're behaving like a temperamental artist. The Museum will receive two beautiful terra cotta pots from Troy as well as a goodly number of marble friezes and half of everything else you and I decide to give them. But the museum does not have to be filled with every piece in duplicate and triplicate. Really, a few good examples are best. Public imaginations are best treated that way. Trust me, Tag, the Road to Izmir will have enough representation of your findings here to give you a permanent place in the big book in the sky."

The surprising success at Troy had provided Benjamin Chadwick with a rare twinge of conscience. He liked Tag and was in love with Sophia, but there could be no turning back. It was too simple an operation, with a highly profitable market for antiquities that was growing daily. The smallest things were desirable: insignificant fragments of cracked and broken marble figures, the faintest suggestions of the ancient past. And all sold at exorbitant prices. Chadwick lit a cigar. He puffed at it two or three times. He brushed his hair away from his forehead.

"Too bad you told the Times about the Apollo Marble, Tag. Now that the world knows about its existence I couldn't possibly sell it. It would have brought a few thousand pounds – maybe fifty. Could be you want to give that sort of thing some thought, for the future, I mean."

Tag wanted to lunge for Chadwick's throat, but they were too close to the end. He and Sophia had come too far. Tag clenched his teeth.

"In a few weeks my work will be finished here and we will be leaving for Athens," he said, managing to remain calm. "I don't expect anything dramatic to turn up in that time. When you come out next week we should divide things up and start the shipment of my pieces to Greece. Then that's the end of it."

Tag had already decided exactly how he would get his treasure out of Turkey and he needed Chadwick just a little longer. They said good-bye civilly and as gentlemen, Chadwick with the conviction that they were still friends, and that nothing was changed, but a few minutes later, as Tag locked the door to the sheepfold, he found its intended use as a refuge never more uniquely required. Inside, he angrily put a handkerchief up to his mouth. He had clenched his teeth so hard, his tongue was bleeding.

"The marbles and the damned pots may be gone forever," he said to Sophia, infuriated, "but they will never get what belongs to me, not ever!"

Chadwick's position with the Turks seemed incredible, but as they talked and thought about it, it was easy to see how, with the growing number of Europeans interested in antiquities, an Englishman on Chadwick's diplomatic level could be seen as a highly desirable ally by the Turks; one to be cultivated and encouraged. He had command of the language, spoke beautifully, had the appropriately detached manner about him and was possessed of an irresistible social charm as Sophia knew too well, her whole being paralyzed by feelings of remorse and guilt as she chastised herself for her foolish, romantic infatuation with the man who had betrayed them. How had this happened?

"A number of things should have alerted me to what was going on," Tag blurted out to Sophia. "I've been stupid! For one thing, Ostrogorsky frequently referred to `Mr. Chadwick's business.' I overlooked the remark every time, thinking that Ostrogorsky referred to ministry procedures of some kind. But the ease with which certain formalities were taken care of should have been a clue. That it had taken so long for Ostrogorsky to appear on the scene should, in itself, have raised a question, and especially so when it came to other requirements of the Firman, which at the beginning Chadwick discussed almost constantly with attention to what the Turkish Government "must have as evidence." Chadwick had reiterated that point any number of times, especially as he had personally supervised the packing of the twenty-five marbles."

It was true that Chadwick fit rather handily into that category of British career diplomat who found conditions at Constantinople irresistible enough to allow a rare exclusive freedom. But the Turks admired the British, in many ways striving to duplicate their manner, their dress, their social traditions. The elegance and intellect upon which Chadwick prided himself was exercised in a climate highly receptive to his suggestion and cooperation without need for written agreements or documents tantamount to contracts. Chadwick had seen Tag merely as his next victim, ripe for the taking and he had moved accordingly and with the Turkish government's full support.

He made a full fifty percent profit, sometimes more, and there were no records. Ministry assistants expedited transactions and shipments until objects either rested in private hands at a number of locations around the globe or were deemed destined for inclusion into the new collections for the Turkish Archaeological Museum on the Road to Izmir. Chadwick was kept busy, consorting with an ever growing number of unsuspecting amateur archaeologists who found

Turkey an attractive place for whiling away their time. He had relationships with hotels, cabarets, and prostitutes. Any source likely to expend a sizeable investment of time and money was a fair target, and better than anyone else, Chadwick knew full well that the Turkish Government's half of the findings at Troy sitting in the storage hut atop Hissarlik was not earmarked for the new museum collection at all. Everything was to be sold, he had been told, already hotly pursued by a long, world-wide list of breathless confidential buyers ready to pay handsomely and in secret for a small piece of the ancient fable. There was hardly one person among his group of privileged European friends who had not acquired a piece of antiquity through Chadwick. He attended their country house parties, supported their causes, and exuded the same sort of elegance with which they identified. His taste was impeccable. He was one of them, and because he was one of them, they entrusted him to select just the right pieces for their private homes and to enrich their life environments with the proper cultural accessories.

Tag's worst disappointment came in the knowledge that his own ethic had been compromised for the sake of his own ends, and that he had voluntarily paid bribes twice and without being asked. And over and over again, he thought of the beautiful ancient marbles he had painstakingly removed from deep in the earth, marbles from the buildings of ancient, legendary Troy. He had allowed Chadwick to take them away. No questions. No resistance. It was the same with the huge storage pots of terra cotta. They were flawless and no one would ever see them again, not as they should be seen – together and complete, as they had been found. They would stand here and there, isolated in scattered obscure houses whose owners would tell all their visitors that they had been dug up at ancient Troy.

The following week, the contents of the storage cabins were divided in the presence of Sophia, Tag, Chadwick, and Ostrogorsky. Before the arrival of the others, Tag and Sophia had spent long hours by themselves, sorting through the sizeable collection of items and they had divided it, not with what originally would have been an honest, forthright or altruistic eye toward the future Turkish Museum, but rather with a satisfaction for what they knew must become their own attempt to preserve a completely representative collection of the many and varied items they had found. When Ostrogorsky argued for the bronze shield and helmet from the small palace chamber, Tag insisted on keeping those, offering in exchange, almost all the coins, a bargain to which Ostrogorsky quickly agreed. But it was Tag's last decision that would be best remembered and ultimately turn the tide of history against him.

In a final stroke of glowing personal revenge, Tag asked Benjamin Chadwick to ship some wooden crates of personal items separately to Piraeus for him.

"They're mostly Sophia's clothes and things she needed on the site, you know, plates and cups and a few pairs of gloves, that sort of thing. They are all packed up and ready to go. I just wouldn't like to have the port officials rifling through her things; underclothes, cosmetics, women's things."

Benjamin Chadwick nodded, "Of course, of course," he quickly agreed as he personally cleared all the Schliemann crates at the Port of Canakkale on departure day, the impressive scarlet seal of the British Embassy applied to the wooden crates which remained tightly closed, received preferential treatment, and arrived in Piraeus just a few days after the Schliemanns.

Tag was at Piraeus to receive the crates. He had them loaded onto his horse-drawn cart, and slowly lighting his pipe, sat back to enjoy the scenic drive home to Athens. For the rest of his life, Benjamin Chadwick never knew that he had acted as Tag's accomplice in smuggling Priam's Treasure out of Turkey, but this remained one of Tag's favorite personal triumphs and for many years he saved the wooden crates emblazoned with the great scarlet seal of the British Embassy at Constantinople in the basement of the house on University Square.

In Athens, even as he and Sophia settled into their new home, Tag wrote and communicated his excitement to a world public he refused to interpret as anything but admiring of his great success and feeling confident of a wide circle of support, he decided that the Treasure of Priam could no longer be kept secret. "The world must be told!" he insisted. The gold was the most important of all findings and he boldly included its full description in his published reports and many articles, arranging to have a photograph taken of Sophia wearing one of the elaborate Trojan diadems as well as the earrings and the bracelets and hairpins found in the silver vase.

"The Jewels of Helen of Troy," the caption under the photograph read as it was published in newspapers around the world. The photograph caused a sensation and although the recognition Tag had sought was his at last, it was Sophia's face that launched hundreds of news stories and at the same time raised many embarrassing questions. The photograph was breathtakingly beautiful, Sophia at ease in the regal headdress of draped chains and links to which her lovely face seemed so perfectly suited, its thick tassels cascading attractively to her shoulders. The expression on her face was beautiful as well, and had the circulated photographs been in color, the overall affect would have carried even greater impact, the lustre of gold along her forehead and cheekbones highlighting her face now lightly bronzed by hours in the Turkish sun, the magnificently sculpted brow utterly luminous through the photographer's camera lens.

Surprisingly, announcement to the world that Priam's Treasure had been unearthed in Asia Minor was met not with the excitement and distinction Tag had fully anticipated, but with apathy, criticism, and unleashed Turkish wrath. In news articles quickly circulated by the Turks themselves, the Schliemanns were called thieves and charlatans. Who had seen the treasure? How had Priam's Treasure left Turkey undetected? They demanded its immediate return.

Heinrich Schliemann's Catalogue of Trojan Treasures soon appeared in print and included complete published descriptions of the Treasure of Priam. It first came out in newspapers, but Tag quickly announced that he was preparing to publish a complete book on the treasure and his discovery of Troy. His catalogue listed all ten thousand items taken out of Hissarlik's earth and gave a description of each, documenting the date of discovery, the exact location in which it had been found, and his conclusions on its purpose or usage within the scope of ancient Trojan life. Included with the extensive catalogue were his personal memoirs on the excavation campaigns as well as personal observations and conclusions. Although he named and credited each person who had played a major role in the Hissarlik campaigns, Chadwick and Ostrogorsky were treated in the most perfunctory terms. Nothing in his published work hinted at their true functions and the Turkish Government as a whole, was recalled as "cooperative" and "interested."

Once the book was published, the Turks promptly applied pressure on the Greek Government to have Priam's Treasure returned and the Greeks were left no choice but to appoint a Greek representative to negotiate with Heinrich Schliemann. In an ironic twist, they appointed Giannis Kolodji, Curator of the Acropolis Museum and Heinrich Schliemann's brother-in-law.

# CHAPTER THIRTEEN

## A House In Athens

### *1874*

F OR THE REST of her life Sophia carried the scars of those actions and although she eventually succeeded in camouflaging their significance, she could, whenever reminded of their pain, recall in precise detail, every aspect of their drama. Prominent in her memory of that unhappy period and central to her invariably clear response whenever reminded of its poignancy was the quality of life she and Tag led in Athens at the time, by then, the impressive house they had built on University Square, their one true home and the place where Sophia felt safest and most loved. Standing at the foot of the stairway she could always remember the grand occasion Tag had made of moving day, so happy to have provided a home for her in Athens. The smile had not left his face all that afternoon. How could she forget his childish delight, his anticipation, or the gleaming new carriage filled with flowers?

The driver had brought them slowly from Syntagma Square, through the tall iron gates and along the gravel drive on a sultry early July morning, the house imposing and stylish against the cerulean Greek sky. Abundant in grand continental detail, the

Schliemann house, like the Adelphi Hotel, was somewhat overwhelming to the Athens of its time, and set into its distinguished residential area on the hills in sight of the Acropolis was a house to engender more enemies than friends. Nonetheless, it was a house to which Sophia had immediately responded and adjusted, her kingdom, her palace, the haven into which she installed herself as if born to its arrogant walls.

On moving day she had held Andromache, and with her child in her arms had walked into the rooms of her house, proud and happy, every detail pleasing to her eye, perfection greeting her at every turn: the stairway at the end of the wide, paneled foyer, the marble steps ascending in a fluid turn, the balcony above from which she could see the pattern of the lathwork below. She had moved from room to room of the house named Iliou Mélathron, upstairs and down, filled with satisfaction, her delight more uninhibited with the sequential unfolding of each ambitious room, spacious, hospitable, light-filled rooms in which to linger, inviting alcoves in which to be drawn and become acquainted, generous cupboards, storage rooms in which to place the precious belongings of a family: a child's first toys, her infant clothing, a lace christening gown, a cradle, blankets and pillows, table linens and silver, luggage, books, a ball of twine.

There is a power about great houses. Some transform their inhabitants into the beings they hope to become and from first introduction house and house lover are united in bonds of reciprocal fidelity. The bonds are never broken. Not in a lifetime, not by distance or absence, not even in the face of misfortune or at the moment of death when a well-loved house is the embodiment of hope. Iliou Mélathron was such a house, its potential for solace and inclusion never more dangerously tested or more truly comforting than during those lonely weeks of waiting when, barely settled into her new surroundings, Sophia had helplessly looked to its windows and walls for strength and signs of hope. And of course, everywhere she looked, she saw Tag. He had, from start to finish and in spite of the magnetism of Hissarlik, overseen the decorating and had selected furnishings, superb French and English pieces on Aubusson and Savonerrie rugs, many from the late Empire, Napoleon's famous laurel wreath liberally scattered on creamy damask upholstery and drapery fabrics, massive figured ormolu mounts glinting from chests and tables displaying rare porcelain bowls, tall silver candlesticks, and vases filled every day with fresh flowers. But the garden had always been Sophia's, left from the beginning to her design, her mood, her whim, and long before moving day, she had selected a shapely young mulberry tree to be planted at its southwestern corner where the land abutted the sloping hillside with its magnificent view and its carpet of grape fern and woodbine.

From the broad terrace, she had loved to gaze in the direction of the mulberry, envisioning the happiness of the future stretching ahead through long rows of young, silver-leaved olive trees shading delicate calendula and eglantine, and it was on that same mulberry that she had focused her gaze that afternoon when Giannis had come. From that day forward, like a testament to torment, every time she glanced its way, Tag's loud, angry voice rang in her ears.

"And what will happen if I do not comply?" he had shouted. "Tell me exactly, Giannis!"

"The Turkish Minister insists that the collection of items you unearthed at Hissarlik be returned in its entirety! He wants it immediately!" Giannis shouted back.

The mulberry had acclimated itself to the comfort of its soil, revealing early signs of the solid, sheltering strength Sophia herself had known under a similar tree in another Athens garden, and as voices thundered around her she wished she were there again; wished time had stood still, frozen in days of backgammon played in the shade of an Athens summer and tall tales told in undamaged light.

"Tag," Giannis went on, his voice controlled, his words prolonged and strained with impatience, "I am most uncomfortable with the position in which the Greek government has placed me. You must know that. I pleaded with them to exclude me from this matter but I could not convince them that our family relationship makes this difficult. There will be a lawsuit. It will be initiated here in Athens by the Greek government. Tag, please return it. Our family will be hurt by this. Victoria worries about the talk. Tag, it is not that important!"

"Not that important? How dare you say such a thing to me!" Tag flared. "I did not invent Troy!" he bellowed into Giannis' face. "I found it! Yes, found it! And from the start I have been forced to deal with weak-minded people like you, Giannis, small, petty impostors who pretend to understand the great heritage of Greece better than anyone else. Live your little life in your little world, Giannis, but do not come to me with the common touch of apology in your meager voice! Clearly, you have chosen your position! I have chosen mine! The treasure will remain in my possession until the day I die! Now take those democratic principles back to your model of Periclean Government and leave my house!"

Bank accounts were frozen. The house on University Square was watched and eventually searched. The embarrassment was overwhelming.

"They should be praising me, congratulating me, telling me how grateful they are," Tag said to Sophia. "Instead, they are suing me, gossiping about me, ridiculing me, searching my house, humiliating me."

❧ ❧ ❧

There were enormous spaces in the basement beneath the house on University Square, big, empty spaces in which nothing lay stored, no forsaken furniture, no trunks of discarded clothes, no bins of vegetables. Just the unopened crates sealed with the impressive scarlet insignia of the British Ambassador to the Ottomon Port of Constantinople which it was impossible to believe the Greek authorities had overlooked in their search.

At first, standing in the foyer they had seemed uncomfortable, three embarrassed Greek officials anxious to complete their required investigation of the distinguished Schliemann residence as quickly as possible. But as they began their unescorted house tour, their steps had slowed and their inquisitive eyes had roamed and lingered. Their intrusive hands touched the fine paneled walls and swept over the pair of marble columns at the drawing room entrance. They moved silver vases and porcelain bowls, lifted mirrors and paintings off the walls, opened cupboards and doors, and last of all, they descended the basement stairs, only to ascend a short time later and agreeably compliment Tag on the solid workmanship of his fine house as he showed them to the front door and out into the brilliant Athens sunshine.

Had they not been intimidated by the house that due to the notoriety of its inhabitants was generating an increasingly high degree of curiosity in the Athens community, the three Greek officials might not have left empty-handed or so hastily. And had they realized for a moment that the fine, paneled partition they admired behind the basement stairs was not a solid wall in a basement at all, but a well-constructed partition dividing the two major architectural core spaces of a large house, they would surely have claimed Tag's Trojan treasure. In the service pantry, just steps beyond the borders of the huge Savonnerie dining room carpet Tag had purchased from Claude Archambault, had they ever so slightly moved the magnificent tulipwood chest with the ten fitted drawers at which they marveled, told it was once the property of the Comte d'Artois, they might have noticed the deep notch carved into a panel of the freshly polished oak floor, which when lifted would have revealed the narrow, winding stair leading from the pantry to the wine cellar below, a cool spacious area whose lower basement door had only recently been artfully concealed. And, in addition to itemizing the contents of the wooden crates therein bearing the eight impressive scarlet Ottomon seals, they might also have been required to count the thirty-one bottles of rare 1851 Chateau d'Estille, the eighty-eight bottles of assorted vintage Bordeaux, the one hundred-twelve bottles of 1860 Redon, the eighty-one bottles of Zein-Münden, and the ninety-two bottles of Aurore Champagne lining the walls, also required to have reported that Herr Schliemann stored no Greek wines and not a single bottle of Greek retsina.

"Just Sophia's work clothes, some personal items, cosmetics, things women need," Tag had told Benjamin Chadwick at Hissarlik as Sophia's heart had pounded wildly. But it had been done. No examination of contents necessary. Effortless. Painless. Later, Tag had met the freighter at Piraeus and claimed the crates, arriving back at the house on University Square calm, smiling, and pleased with himself and with his success at having breathed life into an impossible dream.

In April of 1874, the affair came before the Greek Court in Athens and for the next three months they waited for a decision. Secluded. At home. Rarely venturing out. And in spite of the strain and with the miraculous strength often born of adversity, they continued to discuss prospects for an excavation at Mycenae the following year, Sophia methodically keeping daily notes and plans in the top drawer of Tag's desk, often complimenting Tag on his tidiness since their move into the spacious new house, the pens, pencils, and writing paper he usually scattered here and there on the desktop and tables now in neat stacks and rows. The study's shelves were also neater, she noticed with increased admiration, Tag's treasured books in pristine order, arranged alphabetically, row after row, and not at all in the haphazard stacks to which she had grown accustomed.

Every day, a group of curious gossip mongers gathered outside the house on University Square, hoping for a glimpse of one of the controversial Schliemanns. And every day, from behind the draperies, Tag saw them as they pointed to the windows and waited.

"Could the treasure be estimated as worthless if the site of Hissarlik is proven not to be that of Troy?" Giannis was asked as he testified against Tag at the hearing.

"The treasure cannot be entirely worthless," Giannis had answered in the courtroom, his face white and pinched. "But, there is not a shred of evidence to substantiate it as the treasure of the king Homer names Priam since Homer himself, and all the characters of The Iliad are not universally accepted as real people who lived in a real world."

"Our thanks to the distinguished curator of the Acropolis Museum!" Tag called out in the courtroom before storming out its doors in a human whirlwind oozing anger and contempt.

One of their few visitors in those lonely months was Spiro Tassos who came to see them regularly.

"You have accomplished something extraordinary," he said to them on more than one occasion. "But now the test comes. You both have the strength to endure it, to manage it together as I know you will, and you must not be discouraged. Not for a single moment."

One day in May he came with news. "I am to be elevated as Bishop," he announced to them. "How wonderful to hear such joyous news!" Sophia said. "We need this kind of happy news, don't we, Tag?"

Tag congratulated his old friend, embraced him warmly and shook his hand, recalling that under different circumstances they had done this very thing at the Adelphi Hotel just a few years before.

Sophia asked when the ceremony would take place. "We will host a reception for Father Tassos, won't we Tag?" He didn't answer, staring instead toward the window where through the panes of sparkling glass he could see the group of curious people gathered that day by the scrolled gates outside his house. "They're here every day now," he whispered under his breath. "For hours."

"It will be over soon," she said to him. "And everything will be fine. Then we will go on. Mycenae will be different. It is Greece. It is our home."

A home in Athens. Greek citizenship. Permanence. Solidity. It didn't matter. In late July, the Greek Court decided against him. He was fined two-hundred-thousand francs, payable to the Turkish Government and most astonishing, that was the end of it. There was nothing else, no restriction on travel and most important of all, no demand for the return of his treasure. The decision shocked him and for a while there was the incomparable euphoria of personal victory. He would keep what rightfully belonged to him and savor his triumph, but feelings of victory did not last. On every corner and in every Athens shop the most popular topic of conversation was focused on the Schliemanns. In coffee houses and in taverns, Tag and Sophia were under attack as every day, gossip and rumor gave way to exaggerated stories, jokes, and embarrassing innuendo. Where was this great treasure of gold which no one but Schliemann had ever seen? Still in his dreams! Ha! And how could Schliemann have smuggled such a great treasure out of Turkey? There was no treasure! It was all lies! Ha! All the fabrication of the madman who thought he could come to Greece, marry a Greek, and prove something. Prove nothing!

Spiro Tassos was elevated as a Bishop of the Greek Orthodox Church in September and as she intended, Sophia hosted a festive reception following the ceremony at Saint Demetrios. Tag had not attended the ceremony, but that was not unusual. He subscribed to no organized religion and had not attended a church service since the day of his marriage to Sophia. Sophia, however, had accompanied her parents, and together they had met Giannis and Niki at the church, proudly watching their closest family friend rising to his well-deserved rank in the midst of the parish families he dearly loved and in whose esteem he occupied a singularly important place. The blessings and benediction included all of them in strong bonds of abiding support and reinforced the warm relationships that all his life Spiro Tassos had successfully nurtured and maintained.

The house on University Square was readied for its guests, its gates and finely carved doors flung open to receive visitors in somewhat more than a celebration to welcome and congratulate an old family friend. It was the first entertaining they had done at Iliou Mélathron and Sophia had taken great pains with preparations. Flowers filled the tall crystal vases. Musicians played from the second floor balcony. Servants passed silver trays of food. Wine was poured. The receiving line flowed onto the terrace where Bishop Tassos stood proudly in new vestments with his three sisters, two brothers, and four priests from Saint Demetrios. Sophia looked for Tag. Surely he would want to congratulate his old friend and propose one of his clever toasts. But he was not out on the terrace.Not in the dining room. Not in the living room or in the garden, or upstairs in the bedroom.

The pristine ivory envelope with her name scrawled across it almost leaped out from the mantel in his study, and sinking into Tag's desk chair, she slowly ran her fingers over the fine heavy vellum and closed her eyes, dreading the words she somehow knew she was about to read.

"I never imagined that I, of all people in the world, would bring you this humiliation and embarrassment. I never imagined I would bring it to myself. You, of all people, Sophia, must know I cannot continue here, pretending to be the same person I was before all this. Forgive me."

Aching pain had immobilized her for days as she tried to grasp the fact that he had left her. She could not understand why he had turned his back to everything; to her, to Andromache, to their home. What did he mean, he could not pretend to be the same person? Could not continue here? Could she? Did she mean nothing to him? A thousand times he had said she was tied to everything he hoped to achieve, her Greek heritage, her dedication to his purpose. He had whispered it, smiled it, kissed it into her every fiber. Why was it not enough? Why had he run away?

She did all she could to find answers, and during sleepless nights, engulfed by question after reckless question, all she explored was confusion. What had she done to force him away? Why had he not confided in her? Why had they not talked about the seriousness of his concerns the way they had always talked about the smallest, most insignificant things? And under all her questions, only one consideration seemed sensible and she knew it was not a complete answer, but more and more she reprimanded herself for having hosted a reception for Spiro Tassos, Tag's closest Greek friend and a man elevated in the midst of the very adulation and respect she knew Tag himself deserved and hungered for. In his own house, in the rooms he had planned and furnished, he had felt like an outsider and she had assisted in the rejection.

The anguishing emptiness, the regret, the self-recrimination seared at her relentlessly. The rain did nothing to help. It had poured for days, the normally sunny warm month of Greek September turned sour and oddly gray, Athens draped in an abnormal pall of dark clouds and periodically flooded in wet torrents. She laughed when one of the servants informed her that there was a storm hovering over the Aegean. How true, she thought, watching the small rivulets of water run down the grassy hill that sloped away from the house and toward the square, the rain trickling down window panes more accustomed to the pleasant accommodation of September's sparkling sunshine. Yes, long yellow rays of it. Bundles of it. Washed away. Rivulets of water vanishing down the hill. Just as he had vanished. How ironic to think now that her parents had been their very first visitors on the July day she and Tag had moved into the house. They had come late in the afternoon, Victoria carrying two trays of her fresh baked pastries, insisting that Georges enter the house ahead of her. "For good luck!" she said.

The space, the size of rooms had overwhelmed Mamma Victoria and she had tiptoed silently alongside Sophia as she was taken on her first tour. Georges had come to the building site with Tag on many occasions and was familiar with the floor plan, but Victoria had declined numerous invitations to accompany him and now the generous proportions of the many rooms in her daughter's new home elicited comments of disbelief, the formality of the high ceilings, the bronze chandeliers and French crystal wall sconces, all the residential ingredients with which Tag was supremely comfortable and with which she had no experience, eliciting the observation, "Sophia, you will never be able to clean this house in one day!"

The smell of fresh paint and plaster had hung in the air. The last of the kitchen's mosaic tiles had been grouted just the day before and Sophia, not knowing how to tell her mother about the expanded staff of servants recently hired, blurted out, "Mamma, we have hired a few extra people to do the cleaning and cooking. They are relatives of Metrios from Adrotos Street." She could not bring herself to add that they would be living in the new servants quarters as of the very next day.

Sophia had simply stood, passively quiet and extremely uncomfortable with this show of wealth in her mother's presence, the quiet, unassuming wealth to which Tag had introduced her in Paris, her untested memories of its tenderness carefully framed in lovelocked images of French marquetry and old gilt and as yet unlinked to the realities of her rapidly expanding world. In Paris, caught up in unprecedented style and swirling romance, there had been talk of a fine house in the French countryside, perhaps at Yerres, near the Caillebottes' La Casin, a country place to escape to and love. Martial would make inquiries, keep Tag informed should a suitable property come on the market. There was reverie and talk of padded arm chairs, patterned carpets, country things, walking sticks by the door, old shoes, old hats, window curtains faded by the sun, long herbaceous borders, enormous fireplaces, bundles of kindling. Wait. "Soon," he had said. "First, Paris." And she was lovely there, born for flowers he told her, for wild orchids, for summer's warm rose petals, for autumn's purples and golds, for a thousand Arcs de Triomphe, for avenues in twelve directions, for music and dancing, and most of all, for his love. And alone at last, far from Kastromenou Athens, aboard the Valoir bound for France, he had confessed that love, gathering her to him on that memorable night, tracing the long-loved amber cheek, whispering against the jaw curved hard, and kissing the lips no longer out of reach. She was spring rain and laughter in the sun. She was valor and pride and all that was missing in his life, and as if designed by fate to accept his love fully and without reservation, her arms had closed him in, her long legs pliant and yielding, all the world held fast in lovers' hands, in lovers' hearts, the struggle of urgent, blinding dreaming at an end.

❧ ❧ ❧

Every day she passed Tag's desk, everything on it just as he had left it, impeccably neat, impossibly nonfunctional. She sat in his chair behind the desk and ran her fingers along the silver letter openers, the magnifying glass with its intricately carved ivory handle, the inks, the blotters, the pens and pencils. One day, from the top drawer, she took the maps and drawings of Mycenae and spread them out on the desk. A list she had written drifted down to the floor. "Write Worsaae. Write Ziegler."

Tag had been gone for more than a month and had not contacted her. There were no letters, no messages. She had lost weight and the dark circles under her eyes had returned. The aching pain deep within would not subside, and adding to her misery, Andromache was ill with a lingering cold and a nagging cough that made sleep impossible. Sophia remained confined to the house with Andromache and the servants until late in September when Charles Demours sent her two generous checks drawn on Tag's Paris bank. In Athens she opened a bank account in her own name, knowing as she did so that there was gossip about her, about Tag, and about her marriage. A few days later she asked Niki about it, begging for honesty.

"Yes," Niki admitted. "I suppose it is known that you are living here in Athens alone now. You know how people love to talk!"

She tried not to cry so much, especially when she was with Andromache, but with her sister it was different. She talked to Niki for hours, confiding in her and reliving the past months in a catharsis of tears and self-pity so repetitious that by late autumn, even though he was never far from her thoughts, when Niki encouraged her to talk about Tag, Sophia quickly changed the subject.

ॐ ॐ ॐ

News of the discoveries at Hissarlik had a residual effect, reaching the world public in a gradually intensified series of reports and articles that for many months after the official close of the 1873 excavation campaign continued to gain momentum, ultimately reaching the farthest corners of the globe. On any given day between July and December of the following year Sophia could have read about herself in world newspapers, becoming re-acquainted with accounts of her unique historic adventure, so fresh and new to some, and now so painfully etched into her lonely being.

Some few scholars applauded the Schliemanns' sheer tenacity in print, singling out Tag's courage of conviction as future archaeology's strongest tool, but at the same time they also discounted the likelihood of a place called Troy. Pinder in Berlin said, "As impressive as Heinrich Schliemann's findings are, their validity will remain impossible to prove."

At the very least, scholars as a group, could not discount the evidence found at Hissarlik as anything but conclusive in proving the existence of a mysterious prehistoric civilization spanning thousands of years with countless examples of human habitation. And there was the nagging matter of signs of a heretofore unknown Bronze Age, exemplified for the time being in the bronze lances and helmets found in the hill, photographs of which were also published worldwide. Of course, the Schliemanns had their admirers, people who had become very much taken with their exciting discoveries, eager to accept the authenticity of Troy, confirmation of the Homeric myths, and fascinated by the idea of prehistoric lives lived on a grand scale. Many of these same people saved the published photograph of Sophia wearing what they were convinced were the jewels of Helen of Troy, but in terms of scholarly opinion as a whole, supporters were few in number and not at all the selective group that could have substantiated findings with the authority and expert credibility Tag had expected all along.

Spiro Tassos visited Sophia regularly. She was grateful for his company and not at all unmindful of the many subtle attempts he made to combine sympathy with fatherly advice.

"I think something happens to people when they participate in a dramatic event with a shared emotional sense," he said to her one early evening. "They keep a wonderful comforting secret and it takes their relationship to a new level, a place where no one else is welcome. They rest secure in fresh insulation against future storms, no matter how many miles may separate them."

"Thank you for that, Father," Sophia said to him, "but I'm certain that Tag finds it far easier than I to share with others the emotional sense you may think is ours alone. Need I remind you that Tag is the highly gregarious one? You know how he loves to talk. I like my privacy."

But there was more wisdom to Spiro Tassos' perceptions than Sophia could begin to consider at the time. He never once asked about the treasure or its whereabouts, and it indeed remained a strangely comforting secret between just the two people in the world who had ever seen Troy's gold and knew that once it had arrived at the house on University Square, Priam's Treasure had remained hidden in soiled work clothes, enfolded in layers of the Hissarlik soil with which it had been comfortable through nameless centuries. The wood crates shipped from Turkey still rested safely in the dark and otherwise empty basement, the impressive official seals of the British Embassy still unbroken.

In the day's mail on the last day of 1874, two envelopes arrived, both addressed to Sophia. One was in Tag's familiar handwriting. "Forgive me. I cannot face your world. Charles Demours will handle any financial needs you may have." It was dated December 25 and signed "T." The second envelope contained the official Greek permit to excavate at Mycenae. It was assigned to its applicant, Sophia Schliemann.

❧ ❧ ❧

Victoria was devastated by what she saw as the failure of Sophia's marriage. At first she pretended even to herself that nothing at all had happened and that Tag was away attending to new excavation opportunities or business matters. But as the months passed, it became more difficult to convince her friends and acquaintances that this was indeed the case. In the world press, the Schliemanns continued to be highly popular topics and Sophia's photograph in the gold headdress was reprinted a number of times, especially as news of the lawsuit was circulated. All Victoria's Athens friends had seen it.

Concerned with appearances, it took some time before Victoria suggested that Sophia come home to her with Andromache. When she finally did make the suggestion, Sophia thanked her, but both mother and daughter knew Sophia would not agree to such an arrangement as long as she remained financially independent and Tag continued to be generous, sending regular bank drafts to her through Charles Demours. Money was one thing Sophia did not worry about. The Athens house was free of debt and entirely hers, the deed of ownership in her name. But even with this knowledge Victoria struggled with her own disappointment in a serious deluge of self-recrimination that ultimately affected her health, a series of odd maladies at first resulting in severe headaches and later in disabling fatigue that often lasted for days. She had strongly encouraged Tag and Sophia's marriage and now saw the embarrassment of its failure as largely her own fault. Nothing the family said to the contrary altered her opinion on this, and she carried her burden of remorse with increasing sadness. If there were any benefits at all to her periods of reckoning, they were manifested in increasingly selfless acts of generosity to Sophia, and indeed, to the whole family as Victoria became openly affectionate, offering in countless ways to help with Andromache and with the cooking and housekeeping, knowing full well that Sophia had servants to attend to such things. She also visited Sophia more frequently than she had in the past, seeming genuinely to enjoy her daughter's fine house and its lovely garden in a maternal display of warmth that left Sophia openly appreciative and grateful for her mother's company, the relationship between the two women dramatically improved by the start of the New Year of 1875 when the family celebrated the holidays at the Kastromenou house on Andromous Street much as they always had before Heinrich Schliemann had come into their lives.

Paris was freezing in January. Every day the air startled him with its bite. He tied a muffler around his neck and wore his gloves and heaviest coat, but still the sharp cold chilled him to the core, forcing him to walk more quickly than he had intended, and by doing so to conclude his daily solitary outings too soon. He turned onto the gravel path of his garden. Even in the dead of winter it was beautiful, the circular flower beds now clear of plantings and dormant in the hard, cold light, cooperative foils for the hardy grace of tall bare trees mottled against skies that threatened snow. There was hardly ever a full day of sun, the sky as bleak and angry as he was, no warm, crystalline blue sea to soothe him, no sunset worth watching. On Rue Victoire, people came and went, rushing into big houses and to the big roaring fires awaiting them, oblivious to his loneliness as behind elegant limestone facades and under slate roofs encircled with chimney smoke they escaped the cold he could not escape no matter how warm the fire. But none of them had ever dreamed long dreams of warm sunshine dancing over a beautiful ebony head on a day of pristine beauty, or been touched by endless memories that no matter how one tried, could not be buried away in the deepest, most sheltered crevices of a bruised and deeply wounded spirit. He would concentrate on the book, he told himself. It would be a good way to spend the winter. Perhaps the spring and summer as well.

Mornings at his desk. One o'clock luncheon. Santini's for cafe noir. The old practiced solitary routine. But it was not the same. The old Paris he sought was no longer there and the old pleasures eluded him. Lampierre was gone. And now, gone also was his most trusted confidante. Martial Caillebotte had died on Christmas Day. Sadly, there had been no time to talk things out with him. It would have helped. Following an aimless month in Italy, wandering through Venice and Rome, he had returned to Paris in October. He did not like Yerres in autumn and hadn't visited with Martial as he had considered. The heavy rain and purple Montgeron hills would have depressed him further, he had told himself, but he should have gone. Martial would have listened to him, would have been sensitive to his disappointments, would have understood his rage. His intelligent assessment would have done so much to unscramble this terrible jumble of suffocating defeat.

"I would have measured Martial's thoughtful opinions," he told himself. "I would have sifted through his advice. I would have asked him how to deal with bitterness. Martial's objectivity was never compromised for the sake of his personal opinions. How fortunate Gustave was to have such a father! If only he had been mine."

"I wish you were taking another sort of risk," he remembered Martial had said to him in the slender spring shadows of young budded maples when his enthusiasm had bubbled over like quicksilver. "And what will you do when this Troy business is over? And make no mistake, it will be over one day. Will you then sit at one o'clock luncheon as before and later each afternoon bore Santini's patrons with your repetitious tales?"

It was just as well that Martial would never know the truth, he told himself. And the truth was, that no one asked. Not in Santini's, and not in the Royale, not at the Capoulade and not even in the chandeliered Beyarde, which despite its reputation as the intellectual elite's preferred cafe, had recently become little more than an attractive stage onto which successful Paris merchants and bankers paraded their expensively dressed deminonde paramours and engaged in empty conversations bordering on gossip. Contrary to Martial's far-sighted prediction, no one in Paris provided him the slightest opportunity to bore the smallest audience with tales of life on a wild prehistoric hilltop as in the aftermath of the Franco-Prussian

War, the Louvre, no longer connected to the Tuileries Palace, stood strangely symbolic of a new brand of cosmopolitan independence and in the Capoulade there were long discussions related to its future. The Empire was history, Eugenie's last waltz with the Tsar as rapidly fading a memory as were her nightly candlelight balls, but in the Beyarde there were still long, prattling discussions about the Bonapartes. He, Heinrich Schliemann, had held on to a clearer vision, a firmer conviction, and most of all, he alone had generated the power to carry it out to the end, but in the cherished city to which he had returned to find peace and sanction, he was ignored, betrayed by the environment, painfully deceived by the times, and as winter progressed he grew angrier and lonelier than ever before.

But if Paris did not recognize his greatness, it was still a city that defined high living. Perhaps he could skillfully lose himself in its spirit after all. Marienne came into his life once again. Dining with him at La Poussin. At Granville. In his skillful arms. In his skillful bed. "Save me!" his spirit cried out. "See me! Touch me!" But Marienne did not hear him. No one did. He bought her another house, more furs, jewelry. She was lovely in green, he recalled, emeralds, citrines, beryllines, tourmalines. Again she suggested marriage and again he skillfully fled. "Divorce her! That Greek!" Marienne had unskillfully shrieked once too often as once again the house on Rue Victoire became his sanctuary and he locked himself inside for days on end, writing. He wrote of all he had seen, all he had accomplished, poured out page after page of all he had ever hoped for on the poignant hill that had effectively lacerated his heart, anger and bitterness occasionally lost to catharsis, but for a few hours each day he could slip on his reading glasses and live contentedly once again in the only world he loved, with a crystal-clear memory of the exquisite masked bandit whose voice still rustled through him in the night and still filled him with passionate desire. She had closed sheepfold doors behind her and cast her spell over heaven and earth, her mask removed above the peaked ivory hills of Thracian horsemen and over the sea waves swelling to Lemnos. Like Hera of the golden chair, she stood apart and he remembered that to know her love in tinted twilight at the breaking shore was to wrap one hand in lush warm earth, the other in a flowering sea.

❧ ❧ ❧

At her request and at this time, Spiro Tassos introduced Sophia to several Greek historians in Athens, some of whom she met frequently for informal discussions at the University and in her home, her cordial relationships with these few scholars enabling her to explore a multitude of possibilities as unknown to them, her excitement grew daily. They would never have guessed that Sophia was beginning to plan her own excavation on the Greek Peleponnese at Mycenae and that every morning she was being awakened with fresh purpose and a resolute single-mindedness. They saw her as a lovely, intelligent young woman who displayed a remarkable affinity for the history of her native Greece and a person who one day, with the proper guidance, might just become a noted Greek historian herself.

Tag was never far from her thoughts, but more and more she resigned herself to the real possibility that she might not see him again. As time passed, every day she expected to receive documents of divorce from a solicitor, and when they had not arrived in that particular morning's mail, she went on, forcing herself to redirect her thoughts and focus her energies on the viability that had begun to consume her imagination, which was Mycenae. For centuries, the shadowy legends of a fabled land of ancient Greek warrior kings and their splendors had hovered over the mountainous peninsula called The Peleponnese, their reflections lingering long enough to perpetuate a vaguely remembered history of opulence that had simply vanished almost a thousand years before the Periclean grandeur of Athens, and now that the secrets of Troy had been revealed Sophia remembered her own prediction that once Troy was found that would not be the end and that if there was a Troy, so must there be the Mycenae from which the Greeks had come to wage war. The most famous warrior chiefs of Homer's Iliad were said to have lived in the many scattered kingdoms of the Peleponnese, the names of Menelaus, Ajax, Odysseus and Nestor forever entwined in fables of the seafront kingdoms of Sparta, Ithaca, Aulis, and Pylos. All were legendary, but none had carried with them through time the imposing illusion of riches and power of the citadel between two mountain peaks on a hill called Mycenae and no king had exerted greater influence than its king, Agamemmnon. It was his name that had remained eternally linked to the power of Greek military leadership and it was his citadel that had remained synonymous with glowing tales of glorious golden riches and the resounding victory over Troy.

Several things were known and Sophia was well aware of their nature. First, a history of the area had been written by the Second Century Greek traveler and historian, Pausanius, and second, Agamemmnon's tragic return from the Trojan War to his citadel had been dramatized for the Greek theater, its story deeply woven into the fiber of classic Greek literature and theatrical tradition, adding strength to the classic tale, and known not for years, but for centuries. Pausanius had written a carefully detailed account of his own visit to Mycenae, describing its enormous stone walls said to be the work of the Cyclops, the race of giants who had also built the Herculean wall of Tiryns.

"On the remains of those walls of Mycenae," Pausanius wrote, "stand two carved lions of stone and in the ruins of Mycenae are a fountain and the subterranean building belonging to Atreus, father of Agamemmnon, in which are stored the treasures of the king."

Pausanius also said that the tombs of Agamemmnon, his daughter Electra, and his charioteer, Eurymedon, all lay inside the great walls of Mycenae. He clearly named all those buried and the combination in which they had been entombed. With Agamemmnon lay Eurymedon, the charioteer, Agamemmnon's daughter Electra, and the infant twins born to Cassandra, Agamemmnon's great war prize, the daughter of Priam, King of Troy. It was believed that the twins, Telemadus and Pelops, were fathered by Agamemmnon and that they had been born in the year following the war, most likely during the victor's return journey to Mycenae. According to Pausanius, the whereabouts of Cassandra's body was unknown.

At the conclusion of the Trojan war, its Greek victors set sail for homes in the kingdoms of the Peleponnese and throughout the Greek Archipelago, Nestor, the Elder, sailing back to his magnificent turquoise kingdom of Pylos, Odysseus embarking upon his long adventurous return to Penelope at Ithaca, and Menelaus, reunited with Helen, returning to Sparta. Determined all along to kill Helen, Menelaus had instead forgiven her, so overwhelmed was he by her bare-breasted beauty, appropriately clad as she was when he found her, not in the silvered robe of a Trojan princess, but in the open-bodice gown commonly worn by the beautiful royal women of

Greece. Agamemmnon returned to Mycenae with Cassandra, his royal Trojan concubine, his ships laden with the rich plunder of Troy and its horses and slaves, but Agamemmnon was not to enjoy the plentiful spoils of war. In his ten-year absence, his wife Clytemnestra, had taken a lover, Aegisthus, with whom she conspired to kill Agamemmnon, thereby satisfying the deadly vengeance that had raged from the day she had watched Agamemmnon sacrifice their daughter, Iphegenie, for a favorable wind. During the great ceremonial banquet honoring the victor of the Trojan War, Aegisthus murdered Agamemmnon, along with Cassandra, her infant twins, and Agamemmnon's guards and charioteer. Clytemnestra proclaimed Aegisthus new King of Mycenae and she his queen, but in a final act of vengeance, Orestes, son of Agamemmnon, avenged his father's murder soon after and killed both his mother and her lover in the last of the human tragedies connected to ill-fated Troy.

Giannis was surprisingly helpful to Sophia during this time. In addition to a number of rare books, he also gave her a series of maps by Colonel William Martin Leake, a nineteenth century topographer who in the manner of Pausanias had traveled extensively through Greece and Asia Minor. Leake was the founder of the science of topography and the leading topographer of the Greek world. His maps were precisely detailed and he made it well-known that he worked with a reliance upon the ancients, using the works of Pausanius and Thucydides as guides. Leake had successfully identified the precise location of the ancient Athenian Agora as well as the Piraeus Gate, and Giannis Kolodji had come to rely upon him as the ultimate authority for his own study and planned restoration of the historic monuments of Athens.

Leake maintained that the legendary Peleponnese, located in the southern peninsula of Greece, was named by the ancients and known by them to be divided into six distinct districts. They were Messinia, Argolis, Laconia, Elis, Arcadia, and Achaea. Leake also relied in part, on mention of the Messinian (Mycenaen) kingdom in the Iliad and on several sixteenth-century chronologies and writings that named Thebes and Orchomenos in Boetia, Iolkos in Thessaly, and the minor northern kingdom of Athens in Attica, but he insisted that the power and greatest Greek wealth were known to be in the Peleponnese, its entirety controlled by Mycenae.

Sophia left for the Peleponnese in late April. Andromache remained in the care of Nurse Phillips and her doting grandmother, Victoria, who agreeably encouraged her daughter's wish to travel as just the right tonic for sagging spirits. Niki and Giannis accompanied Sophia and the three quickly relaxed into a congenial, leisurely pattern which allowed an unusual opportunity for them to become better acquainted. This was of particular consequence now that Sophia and Niki were away from Athens and the familiar settings in which they had been raised, but in a surprising emotional compromise, Sophia had begun to deal with Giannis in a truce bordering on forgiveness. He had refused to compromise in the difficult months of waiting for the Greek Court's decision and still refused to acknowledge the work on the hill of Hissarlik as one of significance, but he was still family and her beloved sister's husband and as such, Sophia decided to set past differences aside.

They spent a few leisurely days at a small gulf-front inn at Corinth, on the southern end of the isthmus linking mainland Greece to the Peleponnese where Sophia had time to reflect and to observe her sister at close range, newly aware how very much like their mother Niki had become. Like Mamma, she fretted and fussed over the details of daily life, readily assuming the role of expert, especially when it came to ordering meals. She made suggestions for appropriate seashore attire and questioned the innkeeper's charges for food and lodging. Giannis interfered in none of this and seemed to make few demands of his wife at all, relying on her natural ability to organize these small details of life, guided as he knew she must be, by an inherited talent for such things. Sophia did notice that it was a great source of pride for Niki to be able to refer to her husband as the Curator of the Acropolis Museum, the title alluding as it did, to the ancient heritage all Greeks claimed proudly. For Niki, however, Giannis' title created an important identity, one that she felt elevated her community standing somewhat above that of other young married women she knew in Athens whose husbands were engaged in less prestigious work. It was not always an attractive trait or one she handled with poise or charm, but it was the same air of superiority

Niki had inherited from her mother, just as she had inherited selfishness and vanity and peering at the world from small, spiteful eyes with hardly a smile anywhere in her.

❧ ❧ ❧

Sophia's first view of Mycenae conformed exactly to everything Leake showed on his maps. It rose to a height of nine hundred twelve feet between two peaks called Prophet Elias and Zara, the two peaks separated by a ravine known as the Ravine of the Chavos. A second ravine, Kokoretza, curved westward, and it was at the angle formed by these two ravines that the citadel of Mycenae had stood, connected to Elias by a narrow saddle. Behind the saddle rose a spring said by Pausanias to be the celebrated Fountain of Perseia which provided the citadel's water supply, and exactly north and on the Kokoretza side, Sophia could see traces of the ancient road he said had led from Mycenae to Corinth in three distinct paths. But there was no need for corroboration on what she could plainly see for herself, for the ancient fame of the citadel of Mycenae had come not only from the wealth of its shining gold, but also from the reputation of its golden light, a liberating, impartial light that washed the world in honest candor, offering endless clarity to distant woods of clustered eucalyptus in the lower valley and brilliant, fire-sparked, opal sunshine to the ever-present sea. It was along and with these eternal tides that the sea-faring Greeks had lived, their intense passion for the sea second only to their passion for combat. In the light of clear outlines and razor-sharp edges they had established the code of fraternal warriors and in this same setting Sophia was captivated by the powerful impact of her view to their sea, to their small rocky island of Aegina, and to all that had been basic to Mycenaean life which was the sea. The sea was their element, their intense passion for its life-enhancing role matched only by the Trojans' passion for horses, and as her mind filled with radiant images of the Greek warrior chieftains who had gathered in their glorious pageant of departure, sails hoisted and unfurled at last, Sophia understood what lay ahead, its setting just as Homer had catalogued, real ships, real men, the panorama just as he had written it.

❧ ❧ ❧

The Greeks had set sail for Troy in a thousand ships. Launched in the gift of fresh, buoyant winds, their sails billowed up slowly and gracefully, then roared in gusts of wind filling the spirit of every man with the towering excitement of approaching battle. The Boetians led, Homer said, in fifty ships of one hundred twenty young warriors each, commanded by Leitus and Peneleos from Aulis. Next came the men of Orchomenos, led by Ascalaphus and Ialmenus in thirty long, curving ships. Following them in forty long black ships came the men of Pocis, carrying hundreds of seasoned captains in column after column. Out of Salmis, the great Ajax came to lead his twelve armed ships. The men from Athens were led by Menestheus, the famous field strategist who led his bronzed array of shielded fighters and teams of horses in ships just ahead of the red-haired Menelaus in his sixty ships of Sparta. Respected Nestor, King of Pylos, the oldest warrior and advisor to Agamemmnon, sailed in his complement of ships, carrying to the battlefield his own golden goblets, bowls, and wine pitchers. And behind him came the men of Argos and Tiryns led by Diomedes, and from the great walled citadel of Mycenae, came Agamemmnon, son of Atreus, who, in a sudden windburst from the north, took the lead, in command of the largest number of ships, his warriors armed in a blaze of gleaming bronze.

In his ships, Eumelus brought the best of the chariot-teams; horses swift as birds in flight, matched in age and size. And Philoctetes, the master archer came in his seven ships, each one with fifty trained archers aboard, their departure marked by a spray of arrows cast high into the air from polished bows as grateful acknowledgment to the gods. Odysseus led the island men of Ithaca in twelve ships whose prows flashed bright crimson in the sun, and the great spearman, Idomeneus, led his Cretans in eighty long, black ships. From Arcadia came Agapenor in sixty ships of the most highly skilled sailors, his ships a gift from Agamemmnon of Mycenae, and in countless ten-ship flotillas, their decks surging with bands of Epean fighters, came the companies under Thalpius and Amphimachus, Diores, and Polyxinus. In forty of the longest of the black ships came the ocean men of Dulchion and the Holy Islands, commanded by Meges.

Thoas led Aitolia's units, soldiers in forty ships, and Heracles' own son, Tlepolemus, led nine fine ships of Rhodes in three divisions from Lindos, Ialysus, and Camiius. And Nireus from Syme, said to be the handsomest of the warrior Greeks, sailed just ahead of the ships of all the fighters called Achaeans, Hellenes, and Myrmidons, in fifty ships led by the warrior of greatest fame, the golden Achilles. Achilles, one of the warrior gentry esteemed not mortal, but godly. Senior member of the exclusive small fraternity of famous fighters who confined energy and talent to opposing equals, far too proud and valuable for the weariness of indiscriminate battle. Powerful enough to determine the outcome of wars. Aware of the long warrior tradition of egalitarian authority he was pledged to maintain.

At the entrance to the citadel, the great Lion Gates of Mycenae stood before Sophia just as they had stood before Pausanias in the second century, known even at that time as entrance to Agamemmnon's private world, a secretive world defended by the imposing strength of facing stone lions set high above the entrance gates at the great inner wall surrounding his city. Now confronting them herself, she was moved to her final decision and by the time she had returned to Athens with Giannis and Niki, Sophia knew exactly what she wanted. Evidence of Agamemmnon. A grave. A tomb. Proof that Agamemmnon was the powerful, Greek king who had led the great pageant of ships to Troy. And just as Tag had used Homer and The Iliad at Troy, so would she use Pausanias and his history at Mycenae. But unlike her earlier doubts concerning Homer who had lived six hundred years after the Trojan War and had never been to Troy, Sophia was sustained by the knowledge that Pausanias had seen the actual location of the graves of Agamemmnon and his companions with his own eyes. He had come to Mycenae and the lion gates still stood as he described them in his writings, their location never quite forgotten. Even Thucydides knew the gates. He too had come to Mycenae, referring to it in his own history as the unquestioned capital of the Mycenaean Empire. But how would Pausanias lead Sophia to Agamemmnon? Although he had described the royal tombs as lying inside the stone city walls, ancient stone walls also still surrounded a large portion of the lower valley, once likely an agricultural settlement. A few small farms were still to be seen, functioning in the midst of old stone ruins. If Pausanias had specified having seen the tombs inside the city walls, did he mean the walls of the high Mycenaean citadel, or those of its valley?

Of course, Sophia learned that others, fascinated by Mycenae, had preceded her to its gates, and some had come not so much to glorify the past as to enrich the present, one of the more noteworthy visitors to make his way to Mycenae, Lord Elgin, British Ambassador to Constantinople who, touring Greece in his official capacity and as the marble cornice of the Athens Parthenon was being dismantled for inclusion into his home in Scotland, had come to Mycenae in 1802 with an official Turkish Firman to begin an excavation. Inside what was called the Treasury of Atreus, an underground tomb in which nothing had ever been found, he had unearthed and carried off five pieces of red and green marble that had fallen from a decorative frieze at the tomb entrance. He also found two massive fragments of a limestone frieze depicting a lion, which he sold to the British Museum. For himself, Elgin removed the main portions of the marble half-columns which had flanked the doorway to the Treasury, selling what remained of the columns to the Marquis of Sligo in 1810 who installed them on the imposing south facade of Westport House, his home in County Mayo, Ireland.

The modern-day Pausanias, William Leake had come to Mycenae, preparing a description of the site for his Travels In The Morea, the only published contemporary account of the area, which until his time, had not appeared on maps, and which would remain absent from charts and geographies for years to come.

Many encouraging factors were at work to propel Sophia, but in a gesture reminiscent of the traditional olive peace branch, Giannis provided the final spur. Making a tenuous excursion into the unfamiliar realm of apology, he gave her a rare copy of Edward Dodwell's 1834 Grand Folio in which she found interior illustrations of the "tholos," the beehive gravesite of Mycenae in which Agamemmnon and his companions were believed to have been entombed. Although she had seen the tholos site herself during her short visit to the Peloponnese, these were accurate drawings she could study at her leisure, pictures that set a stimulating stage and repeatedly tempted her imagination. But willing as she was, Sophia was also troubled and genuinely worried about her prospects at Mycenae, and with good reason. She would be a woman alone. How would she hire and assemble a crew? Would they work for a woman? How would she get supplies into camp? Would she really be able to look after herself? And now another nagging doubt came to haunt her. Was Pausanias a believable, accurate historian, or in his enthusiasm had he seen

Mycenae with the same vivid imagination through which Tag had seen Troy? Had Pausanias implemented similar reconstructive powers? Had he been clinically objective or had he written about Mycenae as he thought it to be? The worry was endless, but finally she decided to methodically address one concern at a time and several major problems were solved all at once when she decided to contact Murat Narjand. Perhaps he would come to help her. She wrote to him through the proprietor of the Dardania in Canakkale. Murat could neither read nor write, but through friends at the Dardania he read her letter and sent his reply in two weeks.

"Yes, Murat Narjand will come," was his response and it was the best beginning she could have hoped for. Murat would hire the crew. He could supervise the logistical problem of supplies. He would protect her if the need arose and best of all, she could trust him. Of that she was certain. She was to contact him with details concerning payment of his passage from Constantinople to Piraeus and she was to let him know when he was expected to arrive.

Another major concern was not so easily addressed. One of the provisions of the Greek Permit to excavate at Mycenae specified that all findings were to be turned over to the Greek Archaeological Society, not one half, as was the case at Troy. This technical aspect of the provision, although of little concern to Sophia at that time, did further specify that a Greek representative from the Archaeological Society was to be present on the site at all times. The representative, she was informed, was to be paid by her, since the "cost of keeping a representative at Mycenae would never possibly be repaid by her findings." In an unusual display of governmental flexibility, however, and Sophia assumed because she was a Greek citizen, she was given the opportunity to name a representative of her own choosing. If she chose not to name her own representative, the Society was to appoint one for her. Had Sophia applied the retrospective wisdom of a seasoned old age to these early decisions, she could not have begun more auspiciously or skillfully. She chose Giannis Kolodji. He was not only a respected member of the distinguished Greek Archaeological Society and the Athens community, he was family and he owed her something.

⚭ ⚭ ⚭

The Saros brought Murat into the port of Piraeus, and Sophia watched excitedly as the ship came closer and closer toward the harbor where she waited. She saw him almost immediately, his tall, muscular frame towering over all the passengers crowded onto the decks, his sharp eyes scanning the dockside for a familiar face. He spotted her and waved in instant recognition, his wide smile restoring her confidence as it reminded her of his unfailing kindness to her at Hissarlik. But something moved beside him. It was a small hand on a small arm and it waved furiously at Murat's side. It was Tessa!

"How did you get enough money to bring Tessa?' Sophia asked in disbelief as she warmly hugged them both. "I would have sent more if I had known she would come!" Sophia said to Murat, touched and delighted by this unexpected surprise. "I thought I sent enough only for your passage and a few expenses."

With assistance from Spiro Tassos, Sophia had secured Murat's travel document, one she did not know included provisions for a wife and Murat cheerfully explained that he had not needed expense money. He had used what money Sophia had sent, which he insisted had been enough for two passages, and he still had "enough left over for coffees." Of course, in her typical fashion, Tessa had packed enough bread and light foods in a basket to last through the four day voyage.

With Murat and Tessa at Iliou Mélathron, Sophia's study continued more confidently now as preparations were made for departure to Mycenae, but Greek history was not her only source of reading material. Intending to continue her language study she had arranged to have the London Times sent to her in Athens. By the time it arrived, the news had developed age, but she studied the columns from beginning to end, using them as a daily English reading exercise. She noted that the Prince of Wales was visiting India and that Georges Bizet, the French composer, had died. She also read that Heinrich Schliemann was about to publish a book he called TROY. Her name, she discovered, would be prominently mentioned, the text giving her a great deal of credit for the success of the campaigns at Troy and for unlocking the secret of the Palladion and its relationship to Athena, patron goddess of Troy. Her picture, wearing the jewels of Helen, was again published.

ॐ ॐ ॐ

# APRIL 1875

La Casin was as beautiful as ever. It had not seemed possible at the time, but damage inflicted by the Prussians had been minimal. The maples had been replaced. The lawns, badly burned in some places, had been seeded and restored, and now the young green of spring was everywhere. Elm and sycamore wore fresh leaves, and at the river's edge, branches of lacy willow draped the ever-gentle waters, just as he remembered. Martial's prized purple and yellow iris were in full bloom. Cones of wisteria drifted from braided vines covering pergolas, and along the edges of the great meadow, thick clumps of the Dutch tulips he had lovingly planted the past spring carpeted the ambling corridors under pine and spruce. Celeste seemed to be in full control, her calm, gracious smile as ready and warm as ever, both her face and her house free of the sadness Tag had fully expected to find.

"I have no regrets. Only that he could not live forever and I with him," she said with a smile. "But I accept things as they are. Martial remains here at La Casin. I see him in every living thing, in every corner of the gardens, in every blade of grass. It is Gustave I worry about. He has an apartment in Paris but he insists upon painting here and looking after me. I do not need looking after. I think Gustave comes to La Casin only to hold his memories together. He has taken his father's death very badly. They spent several wonderful months together in Italy last year. He did some painting there and I am sure he has told you that he has been accepted at Beaux-Arts. Perhaps that will be the best thing for him. Come to the studio. Gustave would welcome your visit if he were here."

Tag did not let on his genuine surprise at Celeste's news. Gustave had said nothing to him about having been accepted at the Beaux-Arts when they had met for dinner in Paris a few weeks before. It was so important an accomplishment. Entrance to the Beaux-Arts required a competition, a formal announcement, and yet all he had talked about was his father. And of course now, in the surroundings he knew so well, Gustave was painting the gardens, the river, the landscapes of exquisite balance, all the windows to the sensibilities of nature those to which his father had introduced him. A short time later, Tag saw his latest canvases, all of them pictures of the gardens and the house at La Casin, all of them really portraits of Martial.

But in the studio there were other paintings, clearly not by Gustave, Tag told they were painted by friends, a few of them currently houseguests of Ernest Hoschede, the well-known Paris merchant and art collector who frequently invited the renegade band of painters known as Impressionists to work at his beautiful Chateau de Rottembourg at nearby Montgeron. Edouard Manet and his wife, Suzanne, were spending two weeks there. Manet was working on a portrait of Hoschede.

Tag stayed on at La Casin that spring, and far longer into the summer than he had planned. He wrote, walked, slept. Occasionally he gazed to the misted purple hills of Montgeron and wondered about Gustave's painter friends at Hoschede's chateau. It was close by. He could have visited and if he had, he would have been warmly welcomed by the immensely hospitable Ernest Hoschede and his wife Alice, a charming woman from a family of distinguished Paris clock makers. Hoschede would have satisfied his curiosity and would have shown him the four panels Claude Monet had executed, paintings inspired by the park on the property. He would have seen the first panel, in which the serene facade of the chateau was painted and against which a flock of white turkeys paraded. He would have seen Hoschede's flower garden and his ornamental pool, and he would have seen the lake with trees reflected in The Pond. In the last panel, he would have seen Ernest Hoschede himself, hunting in the Senart forest, contentedly involved in one of his favorite country pursuits and never dreaming for a moment that one day soon his Alice would become Claude Monet's wife.

# CHAPTER FOURTEEN

## Alone

### *1875*

IT WAS AUGUST, the late ripe time of summer when fields of red poppies wave lazily in the warm winds on the Peleponnese and the wild grass grows tall and blue-green in the valley. With Murat and Tessa, Sophia rode slowly on horseback through patches of bell-shaped campanula and wild amaranth toward the mountain peaks of Mycenae. The three friends, whose affections and loyalties had been cultivated and tested in the long eloquent shadows of Turkish Hissarlik now rode together in the land of the Greeks, relying upon little more than a mutual heritage and an abiding faith in each other and the strength of shared experiences. But now, in contrast to the peaceful calm which she had felt when first approaching the hill at Troy, Sophia approached Mycenae with intimidated awe. At the bottom of its ascending hill, campanula and amaranth had disappeared in a dry rocky terrain ever more graceless and arid, and as they approached Agamemmnon's austere citadel, the enormous stone walls seemed to have actually grown far beyond the size she remembered from her past visit. They seemed gigantic and their daunting size filled her with pangs of doubt and uncertainty. But as if there to encourage her in a moment of doubt, she could see the gates and the pair of regal lions gazing directly toward her in the clear morning sun, their silently eloquent bodies of ancient strength and determination not unlike her own.

Sophia had come to the Peleponnese well-prepared for a demanding excavation and emotionally better equipped than she realized. She had diligently studied, she had read, and she had Murat and Tessa. Giannis in his capacity as official Greek representative would arrive in a month's time, giving her enough time to set up camp and begin. The three would work with and not against her, providing at least some peace of mind, and allowing her the freedom to be herself. Her confidence did not come overnight, but with every passing day, Sophia saw more reason to carry on and no one knew that in her bed at night she prayed long prayers, not so much for her own success, but for Tessa and Murat's safety. Nothing must happen to hurt them here. Personal disappointment was far more preferable. She would never be able to live with the knowledge that she had put them in danger. This was yet another worry, adding significantly to the constant strain of uncertainty with which she now lived.

For one thing, she had expected difficulties with the men of the crew who might not take orders from a woman, but because of Murat, these fears never materialized. More engaging than ever, he told them the stories of Hissarlik, long compelling stories of the unearthing of Troy, of the part Sophia had played, and in a short time Sophia had gained the generous support of a small crew of Greeks who looked to her as the best qualified guide possible to revelations concerning their own heritage.

In a week's time the supplies she had ordered from London and Athens began to arrive, shipped into Charvati, about four miles away and brought up the mountain by oxcart. From Athens came food supplies: tins of olives, dried apricots, raisins and prunes, tins of sardines, salmon and hams. There were sacks of potatoes, onions, flour, sugar, tea, and bottles of retsina. Crates from London were marked with the seal of Wesson and Durleigh, the suppliers Tag had used at Hissarlik. They contained hundreds of spades and shovels in several sizes, pickaxes, wheelbarrows, baskets, hammers, saws, nails, lengths of wood plank, rolls of canvas, everything Sophia could remember put to use at Hissarlik.

She had planned her strategy well in advance of her arrival, reviewing it again and again as she lay awake at night, and on the morning of the nineteenth of August, her excavation began with a westward trench just fifty feet inside the Lion Gates, directly on the high citadel, and not inside the lower town wall that Pausanius had seen. By the end of August, and at a depth of twelve feet, Sophia had uncovered a Greek "stelae," a marble grave marker bearing the carved images of helmeted warriors in chariots. Directly beneath the marker was bedrock. Her heart sank. If this was the rock bottom of the hill, there would be nothing found beneath it. But, examining the area directly under the "stelae" she saw a peculiar, shallow cutting into the surface of the rock. It was a split and jagged crack, three feet in length and it became the focus of her concentration, the crew working at it through the entire month of September and into early October, chipping away relentlessly at the rock in painfully slow days of exhausting, unproductive drudgery.

The rains came, turning the earth into mud measurable in feet in some places near the worksite, but she stubbornly continued on. The rock became slippery and dangerous to tread, but by mid-October it was clear that she had not hit bedrock after all. The cracked rock had to have been placed there by human hands, Sophia reasoned. Soon, it was found to have covered piles of stone-filled debris and dark brown soil, and farther down, at a depth of nineteen feet, there were fragments of what she remembered from Troy as being the same kind of calcinated wood fragments mixed with broken stone. When removed, the wood and stone revealed a narrow door, tall enough for a human to pass through. It was made entirely of stones, each one about five inches square, the whole held together with mortar. The stones had been randomly painted in a blackish color with the outlines of two winged birds, back to back. There were no other markings. The door had been completely sealed. She ordered it removed.

Every effort was made to preserve the door with minimal damage and miraculously, just one corner was broken as it was cut away and found to open into a long, narrow corridor. Broken pieces of stone had fallen from its once smooth and unadorned walls onto the corridor floor, which was uniformly covered with small white pebbles. The dark corridor gradually descended to a depth of twenty-five feet, and at its end were five, unmarked, upright stone grave markers, or

Greek "stelae," standing in a large, perfect circle, some eighty-eight feet around, under a huge, beehive shaped dome formed of gigantic stones held completely without mortar. It was a "tholos," or underground treasury, and it had been constructed in regulated layers of enormous individual stones, expertly fitted together. It was a magnificent and remarkably rapid find.

The Grave Circle, as Sophia immediately called it, was numbered, the first of the five graves lying some fifteen feet inside the entrance and to the west. The digging began at the first grave in late October and at a five-foot depth, the crew cleared debris away from still another gently sloping passageway, this one shorter than the first, and narrower yet, but at its end stood still another door, this one smaller than the first, also of stone, and also sealed, but undecorated. The accumulated dirt and stone were removed from the passageway and four workmen stood awaiting Sophia's next instructions.

Fresh torches were lighted and Sophia stood at the opening with only Murat behind her. She had dismissed the others, knowing that whatever might or might not lie behind this door would be a fresh topic of news for the crew, more than likely spread in an emotional exaggeration of pure conjecture. Taking one of the flaming torches she stepped inside, unafraid, walking slowly onto fringes of the world she had come to find. Murat stood beside her, speechless, then quickly left to stand guard outside the narrow chamber doorway It was a small, dark chamber, the air inside noticeably cool and dry. As her torchlight swept over the darkness she could see pebbles underfoot, and as her eyes grew accustomed to the dim light, she saw the unmistakable shimmer and glitter of gold. It was everywhere. The chamber fairly glowed in its incandescence, and on the floor paved of flat, white stone, on orderly piles of small pebbles, lay human remains, completely covered in gold.

The air was clean smelling and fragrant with some unnamed gentle scent of spice and as she realized she was not in an ominous, fearful chamber of the dead at all, but in a place of serenity possessed of a compelling life spirit, she also noticed that some things looked as if they had been brought inside just that morning. Three branches of oak lay on the floor, dried into long, well-shaped stalks of transparent golden brown onto which two unblemished oak leaves miraculously remained. Objects had been carefully arranged and were startling in their scale and beauty. Most startling of all were the large gold crosses carved of laurel leaves at the chamber entrance. Sophia counted fourteen of them, arranged on the white floor stones and set about three inches apart, great sentinel crosses, their pointed golden leaves fastened at their centers with golden nails. The floor was paved in large, hewn, immaculately white stones. She estimated the walls rose to sixteen feet. She walked slowly toward the center of the chamber, toward the piles of uniformly small white pebbles and the human remains of three adults whose heads faced east. The beauty and fine workmanship of the golden objects close around them revealed a staggering splendor. It appeared the bodies had once been wrapped in fine linen shrouds onto which had been sewn or fastened, a complete covering of gold rosettes, each one the size of a teacup saucer. Portions of the bodies were mummified and beside each lay a neatly coiled and braided crystal knot. All three heads faced to the east and beside one of the bodies, amber beads still in the form of a necklace appeared just at that hour to have been removed from the wearer's neck and placed at arm's length. In spectacular grandeur lining the walls of the chamber lay countless vessels of magnificent gold, silver, copper, and feldspar.

The bodies lay three feet from one another, and nearby lay three gold diadems, each of similar shape and formed in a golden oval, twenty inches in length and ornamented in magnificent repousse work. They were decorated with circles of varying sizes, the largest in the center, the succeeding circles tapering off and becoming gradually smaller in size at each end. Close to the diadems were a large number of oval shaped gold pieces, lying separately. They were similar in design to the crowns, and Sophia assumed they had once been attached to the larger pieces. There were some cylindrical pieces of deep blue colored glass with holes pierced through their centers, likely once strung together as a necklace and there were dozens of terra cotta objects: small female figures with their heads broken, their arms raised, under the breasts and around the neck slanted hatchings and two dark lines painted at the waist. All along one wall there were terra cotta vases of fine yellow-brown clay, thin at the sides, very pale in color and delicate in appearance. The terra cotta vases were all painted with a lustrous varnish. A tall vase stood out from all the rest. Narrow at the neck, it had a deep spout and around the body of the vase ran a wide band of several narrow brown lines, alternating with similar lines in red. On the neck of this vase were two broad red circles, and between them, in front and opposite the one handle, two imitations of the female breast.

Sophia spent the remainder of that day and well into the night slowly examining every magnificent piece, tenderly savoring moving hours that knew no beginning and no end and when at last she finally emerged from the chamber tomb in the darkness of night, she was surprised to be greeted by the watchfires of official armed Greek guards illuminating the skies. It had been written that nightly circling watchfires had awaited Agamemmnon's victorious return to Mycenae from Troy. Now, they apparently awaited him once again. Completely exhausted, Sophia smiled.

Earlier that day, it had taken only a simple nod from Murat to let Giannis know what Sophia had found. The expression of complete awe on his face had said all the rest. In a move that he would never be able to explain, Giannis had sent messengers to Athens when the first stone door had been discovered, demanding that the Archaeological Society request Greek military assistance for the protection of the finds of value that he felt absolutely confident were about to emerge at Mycenae. Military guards had been dispatched almost immediately, reaching Mycenae at precisely the right time, an incredible three days later. And the watchfires continued thereafter on the citadel of Mycenae, night after night, in a demonstration of protective security that was also a substantial source of encouragement to Sophia as they faithfully marked the end of each subsequent day's slow, careful progress. It was a breathtaking sight, the fires illuminating the black skies and slowly igniting as they did, the world's interest in a part of Greece that still could not be found on many maps, the watchfires of Mycenae a symbol, not only of the rich mysteries of the ancient Greek past, but of the young Greek woman who had come to solve them.

The news of a fabulously rich find of gold on Mycenae spread quickly, attracting peasants from miles around who came every day, at first to watch from the Lion Gates, and after the arrival of the militia, to wait for news at the lower walls. Many came with offerings. Long oak branches such as those they had heard were found on the chamber floor were left at the foot of the mountain, along with random bunches of amaranth, campanula, and even cabbages and onions. Nothing went unnoticed. Sophia received a full report from Tessa each evening before dinner.

The watchfires of Mycenae quickly became more than symbols. They also attracted the attentions of packs of wild, silver foxes who scurried down from hillside dens and through the guard camps in the dark of night, carrying off food, and surprising the night guards who stood assigned to their watches completely unprepared for the intrusion of silver streaks who ran off with anticipated suppers and whole loaves of much loved bread. A number of the foxes were shot and killed and some of the guards skinned them and kept the lustrous fur pelts as souvenirs.

Delayed copies of The Times of London continued to come to Sophia at Mycenae through the inn-keeper at Charvati. A series of cartoons had appeared, one of them depicting Sophia Schliemann as a draped goddess emerging from a circlet of flame, holding the war helmet of Agamemmnon high in her hand. Again, her picture wearing the jewels of Helen, was circulated, accompanying the cartoons.

Sophia found the chamber tombs at Mycenae to be rock-cut graves, constructed in a circular form, each approached by what had once been a gradually descending corridor that had been sealed and filled in following funeral ceremonies. The Greeks still called such tombs "tholoi." Within a week after the opening of the first grave in the high-domed central tholos, a physician came from Athens to supervise the removal of one of the corpses for examination. The wrapped remains went to Charvati in an oxcart and were then transported to the Archaeological Society in Athens. Physicians there confirmed the skeletal remains as masculine, estimating the man to have been forty-five years of age at the time of death. Of greater importance to Sophia was the date they attached to him. It was the year 1600 B.C.!

Later, in conversations with Father Tassos in Athens, she would say, "Think back to the Emperor Constantine, praying on horseback in the Hagia Sophia in 1434, A.D. Now go back farther to Marco Polo and to the Crusades. Now go back farther to the Apostles Matthew, Mark, Luke, and John, and the crucifixion of Jesus. Now go back farther to the poets, Horace and Virgil and back farther yet to Alexander the Great, to Plato and Aristotle, to Socrates and Hippocrates, to Xerxes and Darius and to King Solomon; to his father, David, and now go farther back to the Great Pharaohs of Egypt and to Moses and the Ten Commandments. Now you have reached the time of golden Mycenae, and the time of the great, long dynasty of Agamemmnon and the origins of the House of Atreus."

This backward sweep through history became her favorite game and over time she cleverly and quite expertly learned to add many other historical events and more than a few humorous incidents as well, creating a poignantly realistic chain through history that left her audience spellbound and very much aware of its own fleeting existence.

Although the Greek Archaeological Society had attached the date of 1600 B.C. to the male remains in the first tomb, the date of the war with Troy had been established as having occurred sometime between 1100 to 1250 B.C. Sophia accounted for the four hundred to five hundred year difference in dates when she determined the first tomb to be one of an earlier ancestor of the royal house of Atreus, one pre-dating the great war. Encouraged by her premise, accurate or not, to Sophia this meant that the remains in Grave One were not those of Agamemmnon or his companions if the Society was correct in its dating, but four tombs still remained to be examined and Sophia's confidence in her ability to find Agamemmnon was never at a higher level.

Tag arrived unexpectedly on The Peloponnese on November first, making his way on horseback into the valley and slowly on up to the citadel. As he came into view of the great Lion Gates, the familiar din of excavation greeted him with the punctuated rhythm of its unique sound effects, pickaxes chiming with the percussive sounds of metal spades thrust into rock and soil. He stopped and listened, drawn back to his memories of Troy and its similar ancient music. Guards were posted at the gates. Recognizing neither his face nor his name, they asked to see his identification and in a memorable touch of irony, it was only when he produced his travel papers listing Sophia Schliemann as his wife that he was allowed to pass. It was late in the afternoon. Rain threatened. Large, ominous gray storm clouds had gathered. Streaks of white lightening flashed across the skies. He found her just outside her cabin where she removed her canvas gloves and shook the caked dirt from them, the profile of her body in the gray light jarring his memory back to days exactly like this they had shared, days ending long, dust-filled afternoons at the door to the sheepfold and signaling an end to another long day of hopeful, fruitless work. A heavy sadness swept over him in an aching surge of regret and self-recrimination as he watched her.

She had seen him. He approached her slowly as she stood shocked and frozen, her hands suddenly thrust into her pockets. He stopped, folding his arms over his chest as they faced each other like two horned rams testing the air of combat between them.

"I read that you received the Homeland Medal in London," Sophia blurted out suddenly to him, unable to think of anything else to say. "The story was in The Times with your picture. Congratulations."

"Thank you, Sophia," he said to her, "but half that honor belongs to you. I said that in my acceptance speech."

They almost circled each other, unable to stand still as they marked off their territories, sniffing at the air, all the while silently struggling in the vast deep canyon of mistrust between them. Sophia looked up into the menacing gray skies and then to the deep trenches of Mycenae that carried the distinctive mark of her own doing, her determination and her exhausting labor, knowing that the balance of power had changed between them in the passage of too many days and nights of lonely pain and disappointment. They both felt it.

Tag also looked to the deep trenches and admired her progress, attempting to make conversation, anything to fill the silent void between them. He complimented her on everything he could plainly see. It was not enough, of course, but she did not send him away and he spent that night in Tessa and Murat's cabin. The next morning she invited him to dine with her later in the afternoon but she did not invite him to join the excavation and he did not volunteer.

Tag had come to Mycenae seeking forgiveness, but the words would not come and now everything had changed. More than anything else, she had changed he quickly realized. And she was impossibly beautiful, more so than ever, he thought. In fullest bloom, the flawless, once pale amber complexion had turned deeply golden in the Greek sun he knew she loved, the cheeks and forehead highlighted in reflections that only called attention to her magnificently expressive face, its planes, its wide range of all-too attractive appeal. He could think of a dozen young men in Paris who would have struck a Faustian pact to have her.

Had Sophia been aware of her status in Tag's eyes, she would have tarried a bit longer and lingered to enjoy his fresh interpretation more fully, but lacking the easy playfulness of more experienced European women, and deeply hurt, she had become deadly serious when it came to understanding the basic human chemistry she felt in those around her. Now, with the development of a rigid set of personal requirements requiring no voice, Tag was well aware of a very different Sophia, one whose principles had somehow become commensurate with her height. But she was not oblivious to his powerful presence or to the unmistakable impact he still made on her, but she had concluded that he had realized his error in marrying her, and she presumed this visit was the word she had been waiting for. It would end in an agreement to divorce so that he would be free to marry someone else. Sophia had already decided she would agree to a divorce.

They were cordial at dinner on Tag's second night at Mycenae, entirely too strained and polite with one another. He admired her fine china and crystal. She thanked him. He said she looked well. She returned the compliment. He liked the chicken with tomatoes. "Where did the wonderful fresh vegetables come from out here?" he asked her, the urge to reach out and hold her overwhelming. Curious situation. Involved in the drama of spectacular discoveries in the grave circle of Mycenae, Sophia was at the same time confronting personal difficulties for which she saw no completely happy solution as Tag sought only harmony and total definition in his own life. Perhaps he would stay just one more day, she thought as the evening ended on the same superficially cordial note with which it had begun. He said, "good-night" and turned to Murat and Tessa's cabin where he would sleep all of six feet away from her as they each laughed audibly and proceeded to their cabins, separated only by a short, connecting passageway that neither of them knew how to cross.

The next day, Tag began a fresh courtship. "I brought this. I hope you won't mind," he said, smiling as he produced the same backgammon board on which they had played in her mother's garden. She laughed so elegantly, he observed. He loved so much about her, and at least it was a beginning as once again they were forced to face each other across a backgammon board in the way they both clearly remembered. They had slowly accustomed themselves to one another then. She had stolen glances at him in the leafy Athens shade of years passed, and now she stole them once again. She had not forgotten how to play the game of backgammon, but in an interesting turn Tag did not let her win now as he had in Athens. She lost every game that afternoon, but still, she did not ask him to leave. The next morning, she returned to her work, concentrating more intensely than ever as in the continuing stand-off Tag neither joined her, nor did he offer advice.

The rains came again, turning the freshly excavated areas into pits of mud. Giannis returned from Charvati, where he had spent a few days making arrangements for shipment of excavated items to the Archaeological Museum in Athens. Everything from the first grave would be taken under guard from Mycenae to Charvati in horse drawn wagons and shipped to Piraeus where it would be received by authorities of the museum and studied. Giannis was totally unprepared for Tag. The rain had pelted down as he made his way on horseback up toward the walls of Mycenae, wearing a black hat and a dark canvas cape intended to keep the rain off. It didn't, and he was wet and uncomfortable by the time he caught sight of the Lion Gates. Once past the posted guards, Giannis headed directly for his own small cabin, looking forward to a change of clothes. He almost collided with Tag just a few steps away from his door. They stared at one another in stunned glacial disbelief, nodding courteously and unsmiling, each walking on, neither asking the other the reason for his presence on Mycenae. And even as the day wore on in its persistent storm, neither Giannis nor Tag approached Sophia on the subject. Finally, it was Murat who explained Giannis' position to Tag.

"He is the Greek Government's representative assigned to us. You must understand. Just like Ostrogorsky at Hissarlik. But this is not exactly the same thing. Mr. Kolodji is more of a gentleman. He is not a 'nephos'."

"No, of course not," responded Tag as the small muscles along his jaw quickly constricted into a hard line.

There would be no easy way to resolve the strained relations between Tag and Giannis, just as there would be no easy solution to the problem of communication as it existed between Sophia and Tag. If anything, all was more complex at Mycenae, but in a second, surprising turn of events, all this was forgotten and set aside when word arrived that Victoria had suffered a stroke in Athens. Sophia left Mycenae immediately and Giannis accompanied her. The last thing Tag said to her was, "I will be here waiting for you."

Sophia arrived in Athens too late. Niki met her at Piraeus to tell her that their mother had died just hours before. Victoria's death had come quickly and in the same scope of overwhelming power she had controlled in life. It was fitting.

Sophia mourned her mother's passing in a confusing haze of tearful days and nights spending long hours acquainting herself with death's finality. She and Niki went through all the motions of accepting condolences from the many friends and family members who came to call and pay their respects, all the while more deeply concerned for their father and his utter despair. And every day, as is the lot of those in mourning, Sophia tried to find moments alone to search her memory for as many images of her mother as she could possibly recover. In one moment she saw her in her immaculate white kitchen, where every day she had reasserted her personal worth through an impressive repertoire of Greek dishes, extensions of herself which she never failed to judge as "even better than the last time," and in another there was the garden, where Victoria had made her way along paths formed and hardened by the sheer frequency of her steps as she had moved in and out of her house time and time again, throughout the course of any one day. All her life she had loved her family with a controlling and domineering love, and they knew it, and now each of them stepped forward to assume with no little hesitation, one or another of the responsibilities that would unquestionably have been left to her as a matter of course. Saying good-bye to her was, for Sophia, the most painful of farewells, the realization that too late in her mother's life she had become her friend, a heavy burden to bear.

Giannis made the funeral arrangements, most of which he left in the hands of Bishop Tassos, concentrating on the small details as he contacted all those he thought would wish to attend, which was of course, the entire neighborhood and the extensive church community. Niki took charge of the household, preparing platters of food for the family that for the most part went uneaten. They all comforted Georges as best they could, but it was an impossible task. He was devastated, his tears shining constantly on his expressive face. He hardly spoke, his sadly dejected eyes mirroring his great sorrow. Much of Sophia's own grief was soon suppressed in concern for her father. How would he manage without Victoria to take care of life's details? How could he possibly take care of himself? He had never cooked. He had never washed his own clothes. Niki suggested he come to live with her. Her house was close by. She would cook for him and look after him. But Georges would not agree to leave his home, insisting that he would be just fine in his own house.

Bishop Tassos officiated at Victoria's funeral and visited with the family privately and often, offering what comfort and emotional support he could. After the funeral, the house filled with people. Relatives and friends came, many bringing trays of food. Sophia had just thanked Spiro Tassos for all he had done, when she looked up to see a familiar figure. It was Tag. Stunned, she watched him as he slowly and graciously paid his respects to Niki, to Giannis, and lastly, to Georges. Georges would not look at him and would not take his outstretched hand. Tag stood before him, waiting for some acknowledgment. Again he said to Georges in Greek, "My condolences." Georges looked up directly into Tag's eyes finally, and said, "You killed her, you know. You killed her with the life of worry you brought to Sophia." Georges' voice then bellowed at Tag. "You killed her! You, you . . . . !"

Sophia rushed to them. "Papa, please, please. Tag did not kill Mamma. Please, Papa! Please, stop!"

Georges had broken down into a pitiful heap. Giannis and Niki supported him, leading him to his room. The house had fallen silent. Sophia had run into the kitchen, hurt and mortified by what she had heard from her father. Tag followed after her.

"I see I have succeeded in embarrassing you once again. I'm sorry. It was not my intention, Sophia. I only came to do what I thought was proper." Tag lowered his voice.

"Proper? And what do you know of propriety?" Sophia shouted to him, the normally well-modulated voice rising to a suddenly explosive tone. "Is it proper to abandon a wife? A child? And what would you have me properly tell Andromache? That her father has decided he cannot properly live in her world? And now you come here to pay your proper respects? Leave us alone!" Sophia's voice had pierced the hushed silence of the stunned, mourning house as in her mother's spotless kitchen she was filled with a fury she had never known. Her whole body shook as at long last she boiled over, an erupting human volcano spitting out her pent-up ash and lava and facing her tormentor squarely. "My mother called you my opportunity! Imagine it! You are nothing more than a coward!" She picked up a plate from the freshly washed stack on the table and threw it at Tag with deadly force. It whizzed past his head, missing his left temple by a hairsbreadth. It was followed by another. And another, Victoria's best white plates, propelled with a vehemence of which she would never have imagined her beautiful baby daughter capable.

"Go back to wherever you have been! Leave us in peace!" Sophia shouted at him, angry, burning tears running down her cheeks. And instead of turning to escape the rage around him, Tag went directly toward her, disregarding the barrage she could not stop, disregarding her shouts and her hands beating savagely against his chest and his arms as he reached for her and forced her close to him. "Liar! Coward! she blared into his face. "Imposter! Fool!" And still he did not let her go.

"I love you, Sophia," he said over and over again, rocking her in his arms as at last she cried out in the huge wrenching sobs she had hoarded deep within her. "It's all right. Everything is all right. We must make it right. Please."

જી જી જી

He had taken his usual rooms at The Adelphi Hotel. He loosened his collar, stretched out on the bed, and fell into an exhausted sleep. He awoke early the next morning, took a hot bath, and dressed with care. It was not yet eight o'clock as he walked out through the Adelphi's highly polished oak doors, but the day was warm, the trees lining Syntagma Square full and green. He stopped in at a shop that sold handmade dolls, examining all of them carefully before choosing one with a pink-cheeked porcelain face and a dress of ivory cotton lace. He paid the clerk, took the doll under his arm unwrapped, and continued on.

The gates to the curving drive on University Square stood open, and passing through them he looked up to the house he had built for Sophia when nothing had seemed impossible, not a fine house in Athens' best residential area, not fame, not the admiration of the entire world. He stood before the pair of hand-carved doors he had ordered from Berlin. A servant answered the bell, held the door open for him, and suddenly small Andromache had flown across the hallway and into his arms. Clutching at the doll in the ivory lace dress, she hugged him hard, her chubby arms locked around his neck as he whirled her about on the polished floor in the sunny foyer, the doll pressed between them.

"Papa! Papa come home!" she shouted happily. "Papa come home!"

Sophia, still in her dressing gown, watched them as she walked slowly down the marble steps.

"Mamma look! Papa come home!"

"Yes, darling," Sophia said to her. "Papa has come home."

With that, and no additional fanfare, Tag and Sophia resumed their lives together. It was not a dramatic reunion, nor was it passionately consummated, for they both knew that the mending would require far more than one physical encounter. But mending and healing was what they both wanted and somehow it had begun. The Christmas holidays were spent at Iliou Mélathron and few weeks into the New Year, Tag and Sophia left Athens for Mycenae.

In the weeks that followed, people scattered and life after Victoria's death slowly resumed its routine. Giannis joined them in his official capacity, Niki left in Athens to run back and forth between her own house and her father's, bringing food, looking after his house as well as her own and finding time for her young son. It was exhausting and she knew she could not continue for long. With Spiro Tassos' help, Niki convinced her father to live with her for a while. He would not sell his house, he said, but yes, perhaps he would lease it for a short time. Eventually, Georges did lease the house with the lovely garden to Metrios Stamakis and his wife, Alexandra. Metrios was still employed by the Adelphi and had been promoted to the position of Chief Usher, Georges oddly comforted in the knowledge that the people who would live in his house were not strangers. Metrios and Alexandra had been his daughters' playmates. Victoria's house would be in good hands. "Temporarily," he insisted.

Sophia returned to Mycenae still mourning her mother's death, but her interest and energy were quickly restored, and on her second day back she ordered the passageway to Grave Three opened. Tag's presence at Mycenae was assimilated into the scheme of things with calm acceptance as with no dramatic change in their relationship, Sophia and Tag slowly began to work together once again. It seemed perfectly natural to both of them and in many ways Sophia was grateful for Tag's advice. He still did not volunteer it, but she sought it unhesitatingly. Murat and Tessa were delighted to see Tag and Sophia together, and Tessa immediately took it upon herself to enrich the daily meals she prepared for them with what she remembered as Tag's favorite dishes, for a short time each day, happily observing scenes similar to those she vividly recalled on the cabin terrace at Hissarlik, the china, glassware and flat silver arranged just as she had been taught on the Trojan citadel.

Her romantic enthusiasm aside, Tessa's culinary talents were taxed appreciably at Mycenae. Fresh produce was scarce and although nearby farms provided an abundance of chickens and occasional geese, they also provided what she saw as consistently inferior tomatoes and beans. The supply of fresh milk barely met her standards, the goat milk for the preparation of feta cheese was unacceptable, and in spite of these adverse conditions she managed to turn out one delicious meal after another as like an experienced nomad she took to foraging through the nearby countryside for suitable greens, on one occasion, actually stealing four of the irresistible green peppers and two of the cabbages left at the foot of the hill in homage to Agamemnmon.

Sophia made no such sacrifices in Tag's behalf, frequently including his adversary, Giannis, at dinner with a second Greek representative who often came to the excavation site to join him, and although she had given little thought to solutions between them, there could have been no better way to proceed. Tolerance on all sides was the unspoken order of the day, and guided only by Sophia's strong and overriding will, it was sustained. She ignored past differences and concentrated on one thing: moving ahead. Tag marveled at her objectivity. Giannis responded to the neutrality. And again, the galvanizing ritual of food provided its unique salve as Tessa's delicious robust Greek and Turkish dishes appeared on the table day after day, one of her most amazing culinary accomplishments emerging from the outdoor stone oven which Murat had built for her and in which she baked bread. Every day the tempting fragrance of warm bread filled the remote confines of ancient hilltop Mycenae, eliciting comments of shared pleasure and playing no small part in nurturing the deeply bruised spirits of the three people whose lives had become irrevocably entwined and who now shared lasting impressions, dependent one upon the other, breaking bread together at mealtime every day.

Sophia maintained a highly cordial relationship with the Greek government officials who visited the site and Tag watched her with great interest in these encounters. She easily assumed the role of catalyst, her intelligence and relaxed manner with people leading to lengthy and stimulating conversations, especially at mealtime. On a personal level, exchanges were not as effortless between Tag and Sophia as they had been in the early days of their return together to Mycenae following Victoria's death. They maintained a delicate brand of kindness toward one another as they enjoyed a renewed cordiality, but it continued to matter very much to Sophia that Tag had hurt her. The past would not easily be swept away, but Sophia made a conscious effort not to equate her hurt with Tag's presence on Mycenae and as a result, her work went on in one spectacular success after another.

By March, with no less wonder and anticipation than she had experienced at Tomb One, the grave Sophia had numbered Three, was opened, its contents of gold exceeding that of the first tomb, its relationship to it apparent at its very entrance where six, large, gold crosses of laurel leaves, identical to those in Grave One welcomed her, again set on an immaculate white stone floor, three inches apart. At the centers of these laurel crosses, smaller laurel leaves had been added, also in gold and attached with broad center pins. This chamber contained the human remains of three full-grown women and the bodies of two infant children, all once again, on mounded white pebbles. The children's faces had been entirely covered with tiny masks of pure gold leaf. In one mask, the eyes had been cut out, the small hands and feet also covered in gold leaf formed of perfectly shaped fingers and toes. Again, all heads turned eastward and feet to the west.

The remains of the adult women were covered in magnificent gold ornamental jewelry. Predominant, were two large, gold diadems. They differed from the crowns of Grave One, and also differed from each other. One was designed of ornate circles, re-encircled with interlacing spirals, the other composed of circles filled in with designs of rosettes, pointed leaves, and smaller spirals. Near to the adult female remains were six earrings in a smaller facsimile of the larger laurel leaf crosses at the tomb entrance. The earrings appeared to lie in pairs, attached to small rings intended to pass through the earlobe.

There were large, heavy hairpins of gold. One was shaped into a female figure supporting an encircling frame, ornately designed in a succession of small leaves and lotus blossoms. Beside each of the bodies were small balls of rock crystal, hollowed out, with traces of a linear pattern in bright red and white, likely the pieces of a necklace. There were many amber beads in several sizes, some cracked, along with other beads of richly colored amethyst, carnelian, and agate.

Of particular interest were three gold ornaments which had probably been threaded together in a necklace, adorned with human figures and animals in intaglio. On one, a man was fighting a lion, thrusting his sword into the lion's throat. In the second intaglio was a scene of two warriors in combat, the conquered man almost completely covered by his large shield. He wore a helmet of crest and plume. The third intaglio ornament was a lion looking behind while running forward, under him a number of rocks.

There were tiny figures fashioned of gold plate, once attached or stitched onto garments as trimming. Some showed a naked female figure with hands crossed over her breasts. Her head and feet were to the left, but the remainder of her body faced to the full front in the manner of archaic Greek drawings. On her head was a diadem which closely resembled the large diadem of the first adult male grave. Above the fixture hovered a small dove. The pieces were perfectly finished on both sides, fastened together by small rivets visible in the bodies. These pieces may have formed the head of a hairpin. There were many more similar pieces formed as houses, leaves, swans, eagles, foxes, the sphinx, and a flying griffon.

Above, around, and below the bodies were two-inch gold circular disks, seven hundred eventually counted in this tomb. Sophia thought they had once been attached to the burial garments in some manner, perhaps covering the garment entirely in gold. The disks were exquisitely made, shaped as butterflies, palm leaves, and again, spirals, circles, and waves.

There was a flawless alabaster spoon, a bronze blade, and a magnificent golden cup decorated with two rows of fish. The cup was in one perfect piece of gold, its handle riveted on. There was a gold lidded box, its lid fastened with knotted thin golden wire, and there were three small vessels of gold. One was a round box, the other two shaped as amphorae, one decorated with the pattern of a leaf, the other smooth and free of design. Since they were lying next to the children's corpses, Sophia assumed they were specially crafted miniature copies of similar adult pieces.

There were vases of silver, copper cauldrons, and everyday utensils. On a small interesting piece of porcelain was the painted head of a warrior, his face in profile, the nose large, the eye staring out, and the pupil painted black. The warrior's helmet was worn low on the head, composed of several bands, each separately plaited. Over the ear was a chin strap, and at the top of the helmet and to the front, a curving horn. One vase was very beautiful, its body painted and lustrous, encircled in bands of palm leaves within circles.

℘ ℘ ℘

The third of the tombs to be opened a few weeks later, was numbered Two. It was the smallest, measuring nine by ten feet and it contained one corpse, a man. The fragments of a bronze sword lay next to him, along with a bronze spearhead. Also close to this body lay a very fine gold cup, made of one piece of gold plate, its one handle riveted onto it. Around its upper portion ran a border ornament of pointed arches, and circling its center was a slanted herringbone pattern.

This chamber contained a fine golden diadem, shaped quite differently from those in the women's tomb. It was narrow, broadened slightly at the middle, and could have encircled a large man's forehead. Subsequent findings produced more of these narrow diadems, some twisted as they would have been when worn as arm decorations or bands on ankles or knees. They were all decorated as was this one, of gold palm leaf with rosettes and slanting pointing leaves.

Other objects in this chamber included a small knife, three vases of the same porcelain type found in the tomb numbered, three and later verified as Egyptian porcelain, and two painted vases. One of the painted vases had no handle and terminated in a sharp, pointed bottom that was pierced with a hole, as in a funnel. It was decorated with reddish-brown varnish on a yellow ground of clay. Large painted spirals filled the center spaces. The neck and middle of the vases were painted in dark, simple bands.

The fourth chamber was the largest, and in every respect, the richest. Its floor measured sixteen and one-half feet, by twenty-two feet, and on mounds of small, white pebbles, lay the bodies of five men. Three lay with heads to the east, and two lay with heads pointing north. Items suitable to both male and female were present. Hairpins and a massive gold bracelet lay near the bodies, but no woman's earrings or breast pendants were found, the dress bodices of ancient Greek women known to expose naked breasts across which they draped chains and ornamental pendants, fastening them to the fabric at their sides.

There were eight gold diadems of exquisite workmanship and in a variety of styles, some executed in circular form, and others in square shapes on gold rosettes, leaf crests, circular gold bosses, and repoussé work.

Two large gold signet rings were found near the bodies, each with small, richly carved intaglios, likely left as funerary gifts. The intaglios portrayed fascinating scenes of life. On the first signet ring were two men in a chariot, hunting a stag. Their four-spoke wheeled chariot was drawn by a pair of horses. In the chariot were two men, one of whom leaned forward to kill the stag. The other man stood erect, his hands half raised, to hold the reins which could not be seen.

The second signet ring showed a battle scene of four warriors, one of whom had seized his opponent by the hair, about to kill him with his sword. In both rings, the men were clothed with aprons. The warrior with the shield also wore a helmet decorated with a long, flowing plume.

Along the wall of this chamber stood five large copper vessels. In one, were more than one hundred large wooden buttons covered in gold and near to them lay the most beautiful item in the tomb which for Sophia would remain the most magnificent of all findings at Mycenae. It was a silver rhyton, a drinking vessel in the shape of a bull's head with two long golden horns. The head was perfect in its replication, even to the wide muzzle and spacing of the eyes, but it was the workmanship of the two long, slightly curving horns of gold that chilled her spine and set her finger trembling.

In this small chamber, she found two more bull heads, these rhytons of gold plate with a double-axe between the horns. Here, also, were found more than twenty bronze swords, as well as a number of lances. Later, when exposed to the air, the lance shafts crumbled away in her hands. The two bodies whose heads pointed north wore face masks of pure gold and a third gold mask was on the face of one of the bodies pointed east. A fourth heavier gold mask was found at the head of another of the three bodies facing east. Shaped like the head of a lion, it appeared not to be a human face mask, but more likely a device for a shield.

The remaining two bodies facing east wore large gold breastplates of superb design. One was massive and of unadorned gold. The other was of much thinner gold, decorated with repoussé work along borders of small circles. This breastplate had holes in it for fastening to the body.

The gold masks were renderings of the human face, life-size facial expressions of the ancients, precious portraits of the deceased, and they raised many questions. How had these masks been made and to whom had they belonged? The gold plate was too thick to have been molded directly over the faces of the dead, and yet, how could they have been beaten out of a wooden mold? Two were remarkably alike, both bearing faces of moderate size with straight noses and small, full-lipped mouths. The closed eyelids were set close together and noticeably slanted. At each eye, the lashes had been emphasized by small, incised strokes, somewhat stronger stroke marks at the frontal bone. The ears on the second mask appeared not to be so far from the eyes as those of the first mask, and they were much more carefully shaped.

The third mask had an entirely different physiognomy. The nose had been pressed grotesquely out of shape, and the eyes were much bigger, wide open, and very prominent, not slanted even slightly, but perfectly round. The eyebrows were not emphasized, but the mouth was marked by a curve. Deep lines extended from the corner of the nose. This man may have had a mustache, and certainly a beard, perhaps a short beard, possibly indicating a younger man. The lower lip was very narrow and the ears appeared to be upside down, their cavities pointed downward and not forward.

Among the objects found here was a golden gaiter. Around the knee of one of the corpses, this golden gaiter had served to hold up leather gaiters, predecessors of the leg greaves which Homer described as being worn by the brothers, Paris and Hector, in preparation for battle. The band of the gaiter had been tied around the leg, just below the knee, by means of a golden wire.

The remaining objects in Grave Four, were weapons and drinking vessels. Here also, were found numerous swords, daggers, spears, and arrowheads. The sword blades were dazzling in their artistry, exclusively of bronze, and in fact, no iron at all was found in any of the tombs. The swords were double-edged and tapered from a broad width to a narrow point. Some of the blades were decorated along their entire lengths with running animals in gold and silver. One had, along each of its edges, a long row of identical griffons. When the dagger blades were later cleaned, six revealed magnificent inlaid work. On one was a lion hunt, the dramatic action finely inlaid on a thin bronze plate. The lions and men were of gold, the shields of silver, shield straps and clothing patterns in a black substance, likely ebony or lapis lazuli. On the opposite side of the same blade were a lion and five gazelles. The lion had captured the last of the gazelles and the others had run off.

On a second dagger, were three running lions, completely inlaid in gold, their manes in a red gold, the lines on their legs a lighter gold. The finest examples of the great civilization of Mycenae before Sophia's eyes, she would never again doubt that this was the Greek culture underlying the Homeric descriptions, every gentle detail dwelt upon with exquisite attention. A highly discerning civilization had produced these things of beauty, and to have described them, Homer must, himself, have seen or known similarly beautiful things, she determined.

Many other warrior accessories came out of Grave Four. There were hilts, sheaths, and the baldrics from which they had hung. The sword blades were fastened to the hilt by means of three or four rivets beautifully plated in gold. The sword hilts ended in pommels of gold. The sheaths, like the hilts, were made of wood, and had decayed, but some still bore remnants of thick folds of linen in fragile particles stuck onto the blades. The quantities of round wood buttons plated in gold had likely decorated these sheaths.

She found three shoulder-belts, or baldrics, all of the same shape and length. One carried no ornamentation, but the best preserved of the three measured five feet in length, was two inches wide, and decorated with a row of gold rosettes. At one end, two holes had been cut. Some lances, which were found in absolutely pristine condition, crumbled away in the air. She found gold bands which had once been attached to the lance shafts. There were thirty-five lance heads, all of stone-hard obsidian.

The lion mask was fixed to a shield at one time, she concluded, its edges later found to have been perforated and covered by a deposit of green oxide, proof that it was once set into a bronze border of some kind, which had held it in place. The lion's head was split in two.

There were many impressive vessels in this chamber. Nine were gold cups in two shapes. One was a simple, footless goblet, its one handle riveted in place. Five of the cups were of this design, decorated in twigs on vertical borders. The second shape was slender footed, and of moderate height. It bore no ornamentation at all. The third shape was the most interesting, and of silver. It was adorned with inlaid gold work in a pattern of leaves, and in three places there were flowerpots containing lotus plants. The flowerpots pointed to a cultivation of flower gardens which had never been known to exist in Greece, but were highly developed in Egypt.

The prize among the collection of vessels in Grave Four was the gold, double handled cup on a tall stand with a flat based foot and two handles riveted first to the sides but further connected to the foot by a band of thin gold strips. Two birds sat on the handles. For Sophia, this cup recalled Homer's description of the golden cup Nestor had brought with him to Troy. She called it Nestor's Cup.

> "a rightly good cup that the old man brought from home, embossed with studs of gold, and four handles there were to it, and round each, two golden doves were feeding, and to the cup were two bottoms. Another man could scarcely have lifted the cup from the table, but Nestor the Old, raised it easily."

One of the most surprising objects was a large, translucent, alabaster vase, in perfect condition, its three handles curling gracefully at the top into lovely spirals. There were also two very beautiful jugs, one small and golden, and a third of silver with cut out ornamentation.

There were thirty-four large copper jugs and cauldrons. Five lay at the south side of the grave at the feet of the two gold masked male bodies, and five others were found on the east side, behind the heads of the other three bodies. Ten were on the west side, at the feet of those same corpses, and fourteen were against the north wall.

These vessels were reproduced in two shapes, one with a large, upright handle, and a second horizontal handle lower down, facilitating the lifting and tilting of the jug when pouring from it. The other shape was that of a large, shallow cauldron, with two and sometimes three handles. Among the vessels was a beautiful head of a stag cast in lead and silver. It had strong antlers, and from its back rose a short funnel, probably for use as an oil flask. Unlike the other pieces, this stood out in its unsophisticated awkwardness.

She went back time and time again to the golden-horned bull, admiring its amazing execution. True to nature in its form, its ears, eyes, and mouth had been gilded and the gold was not plated directly on to the silver. Later it was found the silver had first received a plating of copper, over which the gold had been laid. On the forehead was fastened a large, gold rosette, also on copper plating.

Appearing again, the knot shape was present in this chamber, but slightly altered in appearance from the crystal knots of Grave One. These were alabaster knots, two and one-half inches in length and realistically scaled, the lower ends finished in low relief, the rest of the knot ornamented with a checkered pattern formed by white lines on a smooth, green ground. There were three perforations in the middle to indicate that they had likely been attached to some object. Egyptian wall paintings would later reveal similar knots in the hands of kings and high priests, usually interpreted as the earliest symbols of initiation into religious mysteries and cults.

Grave Five was the last of the chambers, and in its darkened confines, as September cooled, Sophia found the proof she had come for.

The fifth chamber was of the exact same dimension as the first and third. In it were three bodies, about three feet apart, once again, heads pointed eastward. All three were unusually large, and all three were men. Two of the bodies wore magnificent large gold masks, but the third wore none, lying between the other two. This middle body wore very little gold.

One of the gold masked bodies had a round face. Its facial flesh was quite well-preserved under its heavy gold cover. No hair remained, but both eye sockets were undamaged, as was the mouth, which was wide open under the weight of gold, eventually exposing thirty-two teeth. The nose was gone, and the body remains had been reduced to a thickness of two inches.

The funeral offerings were similar to those of Grave Four, one of the male bodies appearing to have far simpler furnishings than his companions who, in sharp contrast, were richly and ornately adorned. Among the adornments of one corpse was a large breastplate of smooth gold, completely free of decoration. The breastplate was perfectly matched by a wide sword belt, also of undecorated gold.

The most richly adorned of the corpses wore a superbly executed gold face mask, commanding in its design and artistry. The mask was bearded, its features uniform and strong, its expression stately and benevolent. There was a long nose above thin lips. The eyes were double-rimmed, the closed eyelids, marked.

This large boned body wore a beautiful breastplate of gold, its whole surface covered with interlacing spirals and bands of bluest lapis lazuli. Still encircling one of the body's arm bones was a large, gold band, decorated with rosettes and spirals, and near this body were a number of perforated large amber beads. Nearby also, were thirty-seven circular pieces of gold leaf, and twenty-one fragments of the same saucer-sized pieces resembling the gold ornaments found in the women's grave. Such gold ornaments would have been applied to the burial garments of both sexes, but unlike any of the others, the garment worn by this corpse had been drawn over the head.

Sophia gently removed the bearded gold mask to find under it, a plain round leaf of gold ornamenting the forehead. A larger gold leaf lay over the left eye. There were a large and a small gold leaf at the breastbone, just under the large golden breastplate, and another large leaf had been placed just above the left thigh.

This was Agamemmnon. She was sure of it. Next to his body lay two silver vases and one large, perfect vase of alabaster. Inside the alabaster vase was a collection of thirty-eight gold buttons and a gold funnel. To one side of the body, five round golden discs had fallen. They were etched in double-eagles, birds back to back, just as she had seen on the first door to the central tholos. They had once been strung together in a necklace of imposing size, in the manner of seals of high office.

Near to this body she found another gold signet ring and on it was a deeply etched figure identical to the owl-faced terra cotta figures of Troy which she had identified as the image of Pallas Athena, the tutelary goddess of Troy and Troy's secret of survival. On this ring, Athena was depicted in the very same manner, with the face and horns of an owl. But why would Athena adorn a Mycenaean ring? The patron goddess of Mycenae was Hera, defender of the Achaeans, wife of Zeus, and protector of marriage. Hera was the queen of goddesses among the immortals, forever enthroned on a silver-studded chair and forever remembered as the goddess of Mycenae.

Sophia held the signet ring in her hands for the longest time, searching its softened lustre of gold for some clue, some reason for the presence of Athena in a Mycenaean tomb and the simple answer came to her as she again recalled the story of the Palladion, its powers often overlooked in tales related to the Trojan War, but, as she now believed, the Palladion had been the decisive spiritual pivot in the ultimate turn of the war, and now she clearly understood its great significance within Mycenae's walls.

Could it be that the Pallas Athena clearly depicted on a golden signet ring found in a rich Mycenaean chamber tomb was the personal symbol of a great victory over the city that had held Athena as its tutelary goddess? And who would be entitled to wear such a ring? Certainly, one of its greatest victors. Certainly, Agamemmnon.

Twelve large gold plates lay near the bearded masked corpse. On one, a lion was shown, avidly pursuing a stag. The space above and below the lion was filled with palm trees and other foliage. These twelve gold plates belonged to two exquisite, small boxes, whose hexagonal wooden bottoms were also found in the chamber. The long sides of the boxes corresponded exactly to the size and number of gold plates to which they had once been attached. Near to this body also, were three gold cups in flawless condition. Two were of the simple, single-handled design, flat at the bottom. One was decorated with a frieze of running lions and sat on a pedestal base, with a handle, again riveted as the others. One additional cup was of alabaster, footed, and with a perpendicular base.

A sword belt to match the simplest of the gold shields was found near the beardless body at the north end of the grave. One end of the belt had remained fastened to the end of the sword, and also still attached, was one of the round gold discs that decorated its sheath. A great many buttons were found, numbering three-hundred forty in all.

There were sixty swords in this chamber, several of exceptional design and beauty, one in particular, fashioned with a long blade in a frieze of galloping horses worked in low relief on each side of the central rib. Another beautiful design depicted feline animals hunting wild ducks in a marsh. The felines appeared to be panthers and wildcats. Between and under them was a winding river in which fish swam and papyrus grew. The cats, plants, and the bodies of the ducks had been inlaid in pure gold, the wings of the ducks and the river inlaid in silver, and the fish of very dark enamel. On the neck of one of the ducks was a single droplet of red blood fashioned of a drop of colored gold. The whole was powerfully worked, the papyrus another reminder of Egypt.

A very different type of porcelain was found in this chamber, but like the alabaster knots of Tomb Four, this porcelain was also smooth and flat at the back, indicating it to have been fastened, or attached at one time to another object.

There was an impressive quantity of terra cotta. One well-preserved vase appeared to have been a large water jar with two handles. It had been well-painted, with bands and half-circles in white, painted on red clay.

Seven large copper vessels stood together at the feet of the bodies. Two were large water pitchers with a single handle joining the rim to the body, and another handle lower down, by which to tilt the vessel and pour from it.

A large wooden object had miraculously survived. It was a portion of a shield; one end of a large shield that was pinched in towards its middle, forming the figure eight. The Figure Eight Shield had often been described by Homer as well as other Greek bards as the classic warrior symbol.

Two charming little marble slabs belonged to the small boxes, both in the same design worked in relief, of a lion, and another unidentifiable animal. There were a number of oyster shellsand boar teeth, likely once used for bridles on horses and decorations on helmets.

The large ostrich egg was of great interest. It had fallen into fragments, but all the pieces remained, and Sophia later reassembled it whole again. There were perforations at both ends, for blowing the egg out, she assumed quite reasonably, but all she wanted to dwell upon just then was the great Greek king, Agamemmnon; his preparation for battle; his armor of gleaming bronze as Homer had described it.

❧ ❧ ❧

The son of Atreus cried out, "Troops in arms!" and clothed himself in armor of bright bronze. Upon his legs he fitted beautiful greaves with silver ankle straps. Around his chest he buckled on a cuirass, long ago a pledge of friendship from the Lord Kinyres, who heard his fame at Kypros, on the eve of the Akhaian sailing against Troy. To please the Akhaian king he made this gift, a cuirass with ten bands of dark enamel, twelve of gold, twenty of tin. Dark blue enamel serpents, three on either side, arched toward the neck, like rainbows that Lord Zeus will pose on cloud as presages to men. Across his shoulder and chest he hung a sword whose hilt bore shining golden studs, and bands of silver glinted on the scabbard, hooked to a gilt baldric. Next he took his shield, a broad one and work of art for battle, circled ten times with bronze; the twenty studs were pale tin round the rim, the central boss dark blue enamel that a fire-eyed Gorgon's horrifying maw enclosed, with Rout and Terror flanking her. Silver the shield strap whereon a dark blue serpent twined – three heads, put forth by one trunk, flexing every way.

Then, Agamemmnon fitted on his brow a helmet double-ridged, with four white crests of horsehair nodding savagely above it.

Last, two tough spears he took, with brazen spearheads whetted sharp, and that clear bronze reflected gleams of sunlight far into heaven

When Sophia emerged from the Fifth Tomb it was dawn. The sun had come up suddenly in a flashing yellow light quickly softened into a flood of whiteness. She had lost all track of time but Tag heard her come into the cabin.

"Is everything all right?" he asked, his voice heavy with sleep. "Everything is fine, very fine," she answered before falling into her own bed, exhausted and absolutely convinced that these were the graves of Agamemmnon and his companions. There were five graves, just as Pausanias had said. There were two infants, just as Pausanias had said. And in the fifth grave lay the great king, just as she had hoped. A man of the Heroic Bronze Age, large boned, bearded, his fine shield and sword at his side, his face a visage of gold, his remains, she knew deep in her heart, vastly older than anything ever found in Greece.

When she awoke near midday she was immediately aware of an odd stillness on the hill, and an uncharacteristic quiet. She quickly dressed and stepped outside into the cool breeze where the entire crew and the Greek guard stood somberly outside her cabin in their small groups, waiting for her to appear. She faced them and smiled, understanding their presence and appreciative of their show of affection. There was no need for an announcement. They knew what the last of the tombs had held, their own silent vigil eloquent in its austere pronouncement which she accepted as the highest of compliments.

❦ ❦ ❦

The rituals surrounding Greek traditions of death played an important part in all the considerations at Mycenae and bore significantly on the findings at Mycenae. Before Sophia's chamber tomb discoveries, it was commonly believed that Greek death demanded full cremation of the body. Numerous examples of cremation existed in Greek drama and literature, and some of the most descriptive of these came from Homer himself, who described both the cremation of Patrocolus and that of Hector, detailing their ceremonial funeral fires with attention to the locks of hair that Achilles had placed upon the flaming pyre of his beloved friend. At Hector's cremation, "all in tears placed his dead body high upon its pyre, then cast a torch below." In the final lines of The Iliad, Homer ends his tale with the last tribute to Hector.

> "In a golden urn they put the bones
> shrouding the urn with veilings of soft purple.
> Then in a grave dug deep they placed it and
> heaped it with great stones. The men were
> quick to raise the death-mound, while in
>
> every quarter lookouts were posted to ensure against
> an Akhaian surprise attack. When they had finished
> raising the barrow, they returned to Ilion, where all
> sat down to banquet in his honor in the hall of
> Priam King. So they performed the funeral rites of
> Hektor, tamer of horses."

No urns of ashes were found in the rock-cut beehive tombs of Mycenae and there was no sign of a consuming cremation fire, this fact becoming a difficult hurdle to overcome as scientists and historians first reviewed the findings, firm in the conviction that all prehistoric Greeks of prominence had been entombed in urns of ashes. In time, however, Sophia was able to present a hypothetical account of the funerary rites of a high royal personage at Mycenae, and it contrasted quite sharply with the more common historic beliefs of Greek tradition.

"The procession bearing the royal body would have moved slowly down the descending ceremonial ramp to the large central beehive tomb. This tomb itself, built of the best quality stone, was impressively constructed with colored marble door lintels and great attention to detail. In its large triangular overdoor was a decorative stone or marble piece, now disappeared, but not unlike the triangular shaped opening above the Lion Gates." Sophia maintained that the great domed, central beehive vault was never intended to be blocked or sealed off but impressively built, to be visited and admired and remain accessible to survivors after the interment of bodies within its similar but smaller beehive chambers. The vault had probably also functioned as a setting for ritualistic cults of the dead where sacrifices had been made, and in fact, Sophia had found remains of animal bones within the depths of the central beehive. The Archaeological Society had identified them as rams, sheep, horses, and other beasts.

"The funeral cortege most likely entered the doors of the great beehive amidst chants, burning incense and dirges for the dead. The body was then gently placed in its regal burial robes of gold, resting for a time on a stone slab in the center of the floor so that all present might pay homage. This ceremony completed, the body was then taken down into the smaller chamber which awaited it, already prepared with mounds of small pebbles on its stone floor. Upon and around the deceased in the chamber were laid personal possessions that would serve to identify the dead; royal diadems, weapons, jewelry, and seals of office. Utilitarian vessels of favorite foods, jars of fragrant oils, wine, personal adornments, and gifts to the deceased provided all the necessities required for the sustenance of the soul on its final journey."

It was believed that favorite horses of the deceased, or those horses bearing the funeral chariot would have been sacrificed in the central chamber. To Sophia, this type of sacrifice seemed entirely possible within the large chamber, and all the more likely if, indeed, one of the corpses in the tombs of Mycenae was that of a king's charioteer.

A highly important key to her final conclusions lay with the knowledge that the Greeks who came much later, had firmly believed that the soul of the dead remained attached to the grave only so long as bone and flesh stayed together. Once the flesh was dissolved, the journey was complete and the spirit was released from this world, never to return again.

Day by day, Tag and Sophia began to mend their lives as professional colleagues. Some days there was no time at all for private conversation, but with others around them and especially at mealtime, it was easy to pursue objective topics. Under these circumstances, an unbiased framework was created through which they could amicably discuss the work at Mycenae and even disagree, which they often did, especially on one particular point.

The idea of confining the excavation activity exclusively to the Grave Circle inside the Lion Gates did not set well with Tag. He felt that a second crew should simultaneously be at work at the fortification walls of the lower city. Unwilling to divide her own time, Sophia encouraged Tag to begin an excavation of his own there, which he did and almost immediately.

During Sophia's absence and her return to Athens when news had come of Victoria's stroke, Tag had studied her work on the citadel, impressed again and again by what she had managed to accomplish in so short a time. He thought a great deal about the realities of what she had initiated, and he studied the histories, maps, and excavation drawings that she had quite openly invited him to examine. But it was the areas of the lower fortification walls that he returned to again and again, firmly convinced that these were the walls Pausanias had seen, even though they were not the walls inside which a king would be found. Sophia had stood firmly by her decision to seek Agamemmnon within the protection of the high walls and she would be proven right. Of that he was certain, and she had explained her reasoning to him in the simplest terms. "Agamemmnon was murdered. The murder of a Greek had to be avenged. It was a matter of honor then, and to some degree, it still is."

She told him that in the Athens of her own lifetime, she had often heard of an entombed murder victim being ceremoniously guarded for three days, or until the murderer was apprehended and brought to justice. It was still a custom commonly observed in the absence of natural death. Only when the deceased was truly at rest, free of disquieting anger, and allowed at last to lie avenged in peace, was he no longer in need of guarding. What greater measures would be taken for a murdered king whose next of kin was responsible for seeing justice served? Sophia theorized that Agamemmnon's body could have lain temporarily entombed and ceremoniously guarded at the outer wall of his great city, until he could re-enter, his murder appropriately avenged by his son, Orestes, and that this was the nature of the ancient legend passed on to Pausanias.

ॐ ॐ ॐ

Tag's excavation began with a crew of thirty men and ten basket boys. He concentrated on a small tract to the south of the Lion Gates and in a direct line with them. By the end of the first week, he had come upon walls built of quarry stone and clay. Houses, he said. At the beginning of the second week, marvelous objects appeared, and at first he was sure he had discovered a gravesite. There were numbers of fine golden vessels; cups, signet rings, and bowls. But these contents were not of the funerary type, nothing to comfort the deceased into the after life. But everything was solid gold, and each article served some real life purpose. All the objects were found in a space two feet long and ten inches wide, a space that could have been occupied by a storage chest, possibly in the lower level of a house.

The pieces were magnificent in their quality and scope of utilitarian purpose, most prominent among them four beautiful golden goblets with curving bowls and high stems. The handles were finished as dog's heads whose open jaws connected to the rim of the vessels. There was a gold ring. On its large signet a woman sat under a tree, her right hand in her lap, flowers in her left hand. To the front of her were two female figures and a third smaller one gathering fruit from the tree. Each of two small figures stood on a pile of stones. The women's eyes were protruding and they had long, thin noses. Their dresses fit tightly at the bodice and fell to the ankles. Their heads were adorned with diadems, from which rose a cluster of three flowers. In the background were the sun and a crescent moon.

It was the last piece Tag discovered here that would reveal, more than any other, the most convincing evidence of warrior life at

Mycenae. Found broken apart in several large fragments, from the beginning it was called The Warrior Vase and its great importance was to lie in its graphic pictures of the human being. Tag's meticulous notes on its removal described it in clear, clinical terms, but its importance to him was of great emotional significance on several understandable levels. He wrote,

> "The Warrior Vase is shaped as a large amphora. A series of human figures form its center border all the way around its circumference. On one side, five warriors are departing, watched by a woman. On the other side is a combat scene of several warriors. All of them have pointed noses and large, protruding eyes. The departing warriors wear coats of mail, close-fitting and covering a chiton which reaches to its fringes mid-way down the thigh. The legs are protected by gaiters. At the feet are pieces of leather or cloth, bound in thongs. The heads are covered by a helmet with two projecting horns in front and a plume hanging down at the back. White dots are sprinkled over the helmet, depicting their bosses. On the left arm, the warriors carry round shields with a small segment cut away at the bottom. In the right hand they carry a long lance with an object resembling a small sack fastened just below. It appears to be a gourd-bottle or knapsack. The woman behind the warrior raises her hand to her head, distressed by their departure. In the battle scene, the men wear skin caps, not helmets. Their shields are circles with nothing attached to them. These could be the opposing enemies of the warriors on the opposite side. The design of the Warrior Vase is in a dark brown varnish on a painted yellow ground. The clay is coarse. The inside is painted red. The vase was found broken in several large fragments. All the pieces were found simultaneously and all at the same location."

Discovery of The Warrior Vase not only depicted the prehistoric human form in great clarity, it also carried with it a recognition for the timeless and harsh universal reality of what it meant to go to war and for the first time Tag considered what the ancient Greek warriors might actually have thought about a war with Troy. What would a victory have meant to them? To whom would it have meant the most? Homer had called war "tearful," but he had also glorified the exhilaration of the fight and the nobility of the battle. For the Greeks, war was filled with the brutal thrills that tested a man's every effort. It embodied the highest principles by which that test was measured. To be brave and strong was the goal of the common warrior, but the common warrior was not the victor of record. The victor of record was the rare and exemplary Achilles-Hero.

Achilles was the greatest of the Greeks to go to Troy and a figure central to The Iliad. He concerned himself with an assessment of the physical and intellectual attributes of the enemy and the lesser warrior strove to imitate him, for Achilles had everything. He was strong and beautiful, courteous in his manner, and he aimed to fulfill his father's charge that he ever be the best and surpass all others. The few Greek heroes who shared Achilles' golden circle fought for the glory and honor they brought to their families and to their homeland but they also fought to maintain their own glorious reputations, well aware of their own legends and impatient to satisfy their own desires for added fame and increased recognition. The field of battle was never far from their consciousness, its unpredictable exploits the true measure of a man, its lessons applicable to every other aspect of their lives.

෨ ෨ ෨

It would be very difficult to withhold conclusive judgment as she knew she must, until all the notes, articles and evidence were collected, examined and re-examined, confirmed and reconfirmed in Athens, but Sophia knew that many of the pieces of the great puzzle were in place. It all made perfect sense to her, but how long must she wait before being able to say, "This is Agamemmnon! This is his funeral mask of gold, his shield, his golden shroud, his sword and baldric, his gold ring, his symbol of victory. This is the world he loved, this hilltop citadel where he breathed its air and gazed out to his beloved sea."

She now understood Tag's incurable tendency to jump to dramatic conclusions, as he had at Troy, and she sympathized fully with the enthusiasm he had shown in such ample measure, but now she also knew the loneliness of his beliefs as the outside world and most of the people he cared about had struggled to catch up with him. Pythagoras would have admired Sophia's fifth virtue, recognizing patience as the most rapidly sacrificed of all the cardinal virtues. But slowly, her harvest began.

First, the large envelope from The Royal School of Mines arrived in Athens in December. In it were the several pages of the required analysis report, a copy of which had also gone to the Greek Archaeological Society. "the gold contains a fair amount of silver, varying from eight to twenty-five percent in the pieces of gold plate," the introductory narrative began. She read on, thrilled to find that the silver in several of the vases was pure, and that the largest of the utilitarian copper vessels contained almost pure copper, tested at ninety-eight and one-half percent. The swords were found to contain eighty-seven percent copper and thirteen percent tin, the accepted content of bronze alloy.

Shortly after, the Greek Archaeological Society announced its belief that the findings at Mycenae represented the largest and most important archaeological discoveries in the annals of the science of the spade. They were correct. Nothing would ever parallel its richness and there would be very little to compare with its resounding implications as the world's first undeniable evidence of a Great Bronze Age. It would take years to study all of the rich findings officially and to assign accurate meaning to them, but Sophia drew her own conclusions very early, most of which were eventually proven accurate.

Of course, the scientific community as a whole would never agree that these were the tombs of Agamemmnon and his companions, but it was generally agreed and published that the human remains and objects found by Sophia Schliemann at Mycenae were those of important persons dating to early prehistoric times, and more importantly, that the findings served as irrefutable evidence of the existence of a heretofore unknown Bronze Age dating to three thousand years before the Birth of Christ. Later verification of the Bronze Age would place it specifically between the years of 3200 B.C. and 1100 B.C. It would also be called The Aegean Civilization, and in subsequent years, many additional supportive discoveries would take place throughout the Greek mountains and valleys of the

Peloponnese and in the beautiful Greek Islands, in the twentieth century, the magnificent palace of Nestor found above a turquoise bay at Pylos, and on the Island of Crete, the Minoan civilization at Knossos uncovered in glorious richness, the advanced technologies of the twentieth century providing unlimited possibilities for its validation and reconstruction. Others would follow in Sophia's footsteps as Mycenae opened its magnificent lost secrets to the world with additional treasures and signs of ancient life that would only add credibility and precision to the first discoveries made by the beautiful young Greek woman who had gone to Mycenae with a broken heart and left it a legend. Many official honors would come to her, but none ever compared to the satisfaction her heart knew in having tied Troy to Greece so indelibly that in later years further study and excavation would continue, unwinding a thread through the Greek past that would forever bear her stamp.

The facts themselves were impressive. Statistically, Sophia had uncovered the skeletal, and in some cases, the mummified remains of seventeen Mycenaens, but apart from this important achievement and above all, she remained acutely aware of the very real fact that the first expeditions to Hissarlik with Tag had succeeded in adding a new dimension to her perceptions of her own Greek heritage, allowing her to dream in much the same way he had dreamed, and it was this realization that finally freed them both to cross the last fragile line remaining between them. That each of them had made the dream come true sealed their union with permanence, succeeding in healing them as nothing else could. Greece had been tied to Troy, just as Tag and Sophia were irrevocably tied to each other.

There had been so much Tag had wanted to say to her all the while, about his love for her, about his own feelings of self-recrimination, feelings which at times still filled him with the painful darkness of guilt and long moods of depressing disappointment. The time never seemed right to tell her, or she would not let him. She was concentrated on her work and there was little time to be alone. Everything else had assumed greater importance and the distance between them had remained.

Once, on a rare evening when they had been alone at dinner, he had begun to tell her how much he had worried about her and about Andromache during the months they had been apart but she had not allowed him to finish, setting the direction of the conversation abruptly aside and quickly turning the subject to something so inconsequential he could no longer remember its topic.

Giannis had quite expertly organized the procedures through which all the Mycenaean artifacts reached the Archaeological Society, and under the difficult circumstances of deeply rutted dirt mountain paths and unpaved roadways, he had done a masterful job. But Sophia worried constantly. Fearing things would be damaged unless properly packed and blanketed for the arduous journey to Athens, she took great pains in personally wrapping almost every piece that had crossed her hands in the semi-darkness of the five chamber tombs almost thirty feet below the surface of the earth. One afternoon they had walked up to the cabin together, she and Tag, exhausted after carefully supervising the packing and loading of yet another wagonload of Mycenaean treasure bound for the port of Piraeus out of Charvati.

"Do you think everything will be all right?" she asked, seeking his honest reassurance as they made their way along the hard packed dirt that had become her own path to the small complex of cabins just east of the Lion Gates. "Yes," he answered. "It all looked fine. I believe Agamemmnon's mask will reach Athens in one beautiful piece," he had teased.

Tag had willingly joined in the tedious work of packing and loading onto the ox-drawn wagons which for more than a week now, had occupied the better part of every day. "I just would not want to see anything improperly handled, you know, battered about and dented. I would feel it was happening directly to me," she said to him, looking into his face as they walked on.

And then in a voice touched with an unfamiliar anxiety, Tag said, "I would not see you battered, dearest. It would hurt me . . . ." The ancient Iliad lines they both knew well returning with a meaning neither of them misunderstood.

" . . . . . and yet I could not help you, not a bit," he went on, his voice almost a whisper. "The Olympian is difficult to oppose. One other time I took your part he caught me around one foot and flung me into the sky from our tremendous terrace. I soared all day! Just as the sun dropped down I dropped down too, on Lemnos nearly dead. The island people nursed a fallen god." Tag looked away, unable to go on.

"He made her smile," Sophia continued, the Iliad's remembered lines returning to her. "And the goddess, white-armed Hera, smiling took the wine cup from his hand, then dipping from the wine bowl, round he went from left to right, serving the other gods nectar of sweet delight." Sophia had reached for Tag's arm, holding onto it tightly, as both their voices went on together in the memorized lines.

"And quenchless laughter broke out among the blissful gods to see Hephaistos wheezing down the hall. So all day long until the sun went down they spent in feasting, and the measured feast matched well their hearts' desire. So did the flowless harp held by Apollo and heavenly songs in choiring antiphon that all the muses sang."

They stopped. They had reached the cabin door as the ancient music became their own, at last sounding the tune they recognized as unsung too long.

Inside Sophia's cabin, Tag kissed her. He brushed his lips along her warm, smooth cheek, finding her mouth again and again as he pushed the door closed. They reached the bed and as he tenderly gathered her close to him in the twilight silence they were new lovers, filled with the fire and wonder of fresh discovery. And later, in the dreams of her half-sleep, Sophia opened her eyes to see his face coming towards her's, his lips covering her mouth once again. He wound his fingers into her thick, tousled hair, and this time she leaned up to him, leaving all her questioning doubt behind in a freedom and desire renewed and equal to his own.

In the simple austerity of the tiny cabin on Mycenae, towards the last of the days they would spend together there, complete renewal came, not in an avalanche of fresh promises, but in the silently impassioned fulfillment of an earlier prophecy made by Georges who had been first to notice them standing together in what he alone had recognized at the time as an "indescribable strength, upon which, one day, nothing would intrude."

❧ ❧ ❧

At Mycenae, Sophia Schliemann had uncovered thousands of pieces of ancient gold, silver, copper, and bronze wrought into objects of great beauty, the thriving socio-economic culture sophisticated enough to place emphasis upon the fashioning of such objects also sophisticated enough to have sailed to and traded with other civilizations of its own time.

Within the next fifty years, evidence of this visitation and trade would be found as a result of archaeological excavations in the Egyptian Valley of the Kings at Luxor, revealing similarities not only in cultural development, but also in customs of entombment. Unlike the Egyptians, however, the Greek Mycenaeans had employed neither coffin nor sarcaphogus for their dead. But in the tombs of the Pharaohs, not only were the same Mycenaean crystal knots seen on wall paintings and held in the hands of the pharaoh, but the same types of alabaster urns were also found entombed with the pharaohs, along with the same types of porcelain jars.

It was entirely possible to believe that the Mycenaeans knew of the many grave robberies in the Egyptian tombs long before the pharaohs were entombed in the Valley of the Kings. By the time of the Eighteenth Dynasty there was hardly a royal tomb in all Egypt that had not been vandalized and aware of this, the Mycenaeans could have placed their royals well within the guarded safety of the inner citadel. Long before his own death, Egypt's Tutmose I had selected the Valley of the Kings for his totally hidden burial chamber. Learning from the Egyptians, the Mycenaeans may have felt better served by capitalizing on their well established royal tradition of remaining on a protected, lofty acropolis in death as well as in life.

The findings at Mycenae brought the Schliemanns worldwide fame. It also brought the credibility that had eluded them at Troy. Not all scholars and academicians were prepared to put aside the beliefs of a lifetime, but the combined discoveries at Troy and Mycenae rewrote histories, changed time frames, and forever altered the chronologies of man's development. Now added to the prehistoric knowledge of civilization was the Great Bronze Age, where from the years 3200 to 1100 B.C., life had been lived on the Peloponnese and in a northwest corner of Asia Minor in a lavish opulence further gilded by the language of the poet.

# CHAPTER FIFTEEN

## Return To Troy

### *1877*

T HE ANCIENT GREEKS knew there was nothing to compare with the elation of victory. To be tested and to win; at war, at games, at love, was to live life to its fullest and be called heroic. Old scars were shown off with pride. Suffering was recalled in waves of bliss. New wounds incurred in fresh battle were badges of honor, proof of having been there, of having surmounted the insurmountable. And in the end, against all odds, the vocabulary of test, trial, peril, and duty was privately defined in the consoling festival of the heart that is joy. It came as they left Mycenae for Athens, a sense of well-being Tag had never known and as he and Sophia disembarked the Deschamps at Le Havre, the London Times was publishing his serial reports on the findings at Mycenae and their connection to those made at Troy, barely two years earlier. A few days later, the following dispatch reached Leipzig: "Sophia Schliemann has discovered a great treasure of gold and other precious objects in the tombs of which the Greek historian, Pausanius wrote, and which he described as those of Agamemmnon, Atreus, Eurymedon, and their companions. The bones and teeth are of large human beings. The swords beside the bodies bear handles of gold. The faces were found covered in masks of pure gold and the bodies of two infants were also discovered, their small bodies enveloped in gold."

The fame he had wanted. The recognition he had sought. The vindication. He and Sophia had triumphed with a dream. They had all the proof they would ever need. Let the world go on assuming and presuming and undermining and destroying. That world was small menace to all that was now his and Tag returned to Athens a changed man, interested not in proving himself further, but devoted to the pleasures of daily living and the pursuits of simple family life. Sophia had never been happier. At last it was over.

He spent long hours with Andromache, devising new games they could play and planning outings they could enjoy during leisurely afternoons. He gave her a pony. They spent an entire morning deciding on a suitable name for him, finally settling on Ajax. She was a beautiful child, miniature of her mother, now the absolute center of his undivided attention. With Sophia, Tag spent long uninterrupted mornings on the terrace where they sat in a pair of chairs, drinking coffee, talking about the maturing garden and planning little more than an afternoon outing. And as if he had not noticed them before, he took particular pleasure in Sophia's flowers and trees, in the extended vistas from the garden to the hillside, and to the Acropolis beyond. From his terrace, Tag could see part of the Parthenon and all of the Turkish tower still standing amidst ongoing restorations, and in a gesture considered by many as generous in the extreme, he offered to pay for the tower's removal. Giannis was shocked, but gratefully accepted and made the necessary arrangements, typically insensitive to understanding that for Tag, the tower was one last remnant of emotional debris to be cleared as he took up a newly balanced life as a Greek citizen in Athens. The last vestige of Turkish occupation removed from the Acropolis efficiently and with no small degree of fervor, the Greek government went so far as to send Tag a lengthy official letter of thanks, citing his kindness to his adopted homeland. It did not go unnoticed, of course, that Giannis Kolodji wrote no such letter to Tag in his official capacity as Curator of the Acropolis Museum, his office in a building not fifty feet away from where the tower had stood.

Further visual assessment of his environment led Tag to still another significant decision. He unpacked the Trojan Treasure and arranged all of it on the shelves of new library cabinets made to order for display of every item unpacked at last from the basement crates whose British Embassy seals he deftly sliced open only after ceremoniously uncorking a bottle of fine old Bordeaux and savoring its velvety contact on his tongue.

The brass locks on the new library cabinets were uncomplicated. Anyone could have broken them to examine or even steal the golden headdresses, the vases, urns, bronze helmets and shields, the arrowheads, lance points, pieces of diorite, the cups, cauldrons, the bracelets, signet rings, hairpins, and earrings. But no one, not even Sophia, trespassed between Tag and these fruits of his long labor. The treasure was his in every sense, and although he invited many people to view and enjoy it with him, few visitors touched a single piece. Everyone who saw it was impressed. Most were astounded as they looked, then listened to Tag as he reconstructed every small detail of discovery, the order in which pieces had been found, the way copper shines in bright June sunlight. His many audiences loved his alluring story-telling style, and in a way that would matter very much to the manner in which the future would judge him, the display of Priam's Treasure came to represent dramatic change, not only in Tag's own private life, but in the means by which the future community of archaeology would conduct itself. More and more, haphazard treasure hunting would be left to a shrinking group of dilettantes as archaeology began to look at itself as a respectable science, taking many examples from the difficult experiences of Heinrich Schliemann.

Although this was a deeply reflective period, Tag's instinctive understanding of the most fundamental requirements of excavation continued to motivate him and he continued to write and publish the results of the campaigns at Troy and Mycenae, drawing from his voluminous notes and records. ANTIQUITIES OF TROY was published in 1876, in French and German, and he and Sophia collaborated on MYCENAE, published in 1878 and extremely popular in Europe that year. Its critical reviews were glowing. In America, it was published by Scribner, Armstrong, and Company of New York, who sent a letter which stated in part, " . . . . your MYCENAE has met with the most flattering reception by the press and the public, and it is, and bids fair to remain, the leading publication of the year."

In 1877, Iliou Mélathron became home to a new baby. A son, named Agamemmnon, was born in September and the contemplative, happy years continued as satisfying family life took precedence over all other activities.

There was travel throughout Europe, and there were many extended visits to Paris where the family periodically took up residence in the house on Rue Victoire. The children were introduced to Paris parks, licorice sticks, puppet shows, and merry-go-rounds. Andromache learned to tell time by insisting they arrive early enough at Saint-Cloud to watch for the attendants who, promptly at noon, opened the sluice gates of the fountains with their gigantic keys, activating the enchanting spectacle of water cascading down the tiered structure of spouting urns and open-mouthed gargoyles to the clover-leafed basin in the lower esplanade.

Tag had never quite forgiven Paris for ignoring him, for turning its head away from his Trojan success, and although he enjoyed his time in the city with his family, energized by its sophisticated shops, its theater and music, the intense love he had once felt for Paris had diminished considerably. But in October of 1878, the sudden death of Celeste Caillebotte altered his feelings. La Casin was for sale and Gustave suggested he buy it.

A house in the country. His own two children running on paths carpeted in velvety moss, on familiar terms with Martial's spring ranunculus, celandine, and the hill where the wild orchids grew, resting on thatch-roofed benches, then to the dairy, to the orangerie and the hollow by the Ha – Ha. Sophia seated under the elms, at luncheon in the mural-paneled dining room, asleep beside him in the Empire bed he had helped Martial select. All of it in place just as Martial had suggested when he had said, "You need a wife, a family, a home like La Casin to love and nurture. Put all this history, ancient and otherwise, behind you."

Sophia loved La Casin "Yes!" she enthusiastically responded the first time Tag raised the possibility of ownership. "I would love the gardens! The children! It would be wonderful for them!" But Tag hesitated and said he would think it over. There were other decisions and choices to be made, he said, and during the return voyage from

Marseilles to Athens that April, Sophia found out what those decisions and choices were.

"I want another opportunity at Troy," he announced to her one morning in their stateroom aboard the Fécamp. "And I want you and the children with me."

Sophia refused. Adamantly. No, she would not go. And no, she would not allow the children to go. And inwardly, the old anxiety festered, not her crooked line of defense this time, but a straight, unwavering nettle of resentment. How could he possibly think she would agree to expose herself and her children to the deprivations of a hilltop that had brought her so much pain? He defied understanding. His mission had been accomplished. He had proven enough, and so had she. She had thought it was over, really over, and now that they had the opportunity to live life at peace, to delight in a house and gardens in the French countryside he said he had loved for years, she saw it was not over at all.

"Can we not do both?" she suggested in compromise. "Leave me with the children at La Casin and go to Troy if you must. When you return, it will all be here for you. We will be here for you."

"No," Tag interrupted. "Expenses are much too high to consider doing both and we shall always keep Iliou Mélathron which is a major expense by itself."

"You have already chosen, haven't you?" Sophia knew him well. "You just won't come out with it and tell me forthrightly that the decision is made."

There was no point to ranting and raving, nothing to be gained by nagging and insisting. She recognized the old restlessness. Weeks ago she had seen traces of the old unflinching resolve in his eyes, the distraction of something like a shadow she had not quite understood. He had not been concentrating on conversations she had with him. He was not completely attentive to the children. Yes. Of course. It was even in his walk, which was freshly energetic, sparked with something new. It was in his speech, noticeably more rapid, and most of all, it was in the hard line that had returned to his often clenched jaw when he was lost in thought.

"I must get it right, Sophia," he said looking deeply into her eyes. "I must go back to where I left it and put the last pieces together in better order, or at the very least as I now understand it. And I do understand it now. Do you see what you have done for me? You have made me realize that I can be seen not only as credible, but as accountable, and I simply must make a last attempt. Sophia, I'm no longer a young man and I know my dreams are gathering age along with the rest of me. But now, with the success of Mycenae and all it means, I often ask myself what else could be out there on the hill, buried and waiting, ready to link together the final pieces of this splendid puzzle which you and I have only begun to understand. And something else. Sophia, a citadel such as Agamemmnon's was not its own creation. It did not exist alone in that vast land, its warriors alone, sailing through those islands. There had to be others like it, related to it, other Greeks living other lives on other sea-front hilltops, on other promontories overlooking other sands; an entire Greek Mycenaean world connected by the realities of commerce and active trade, by water and fishing rights. And if you look at the map, the Aegean Sea, loved by the seafaring Greeks, is a mere stepping stone not only to Asia Minor, but to glorious Egypt. Even your old decrepit Pausanius discusses it. Sophia, I have good reason to believe that on the island of Crete, just perfectly located between Egypt, Syria, and mainland Greece, we could find the most important link of all. The hill of Kephalia Tselempe is not unlike the hill of Hissarlik and I would venture to say it is stratified in exactly the same way. A prehistoric palace is said to have existed there. Next year we shall go to see. But first, Troy. Just one last time."

In the spring of 1880, the excavation party traveling from Piraeus to Constantinople was vastly changed from that of the past ten years when the burden of proof had lain on one pair of shoulders. The group numbered a diversified eight: five men and three women: an engineer, a field geologist, a draftsman, a photographer, and two Belgian archaeological assistants led by their ever-charming catalyst. Completing the unusual traveling party whose curious-looking piles of baggage composed of odd shapes and bulky pieces had attracted a good deal of attention as the group had boarded ship at Piraeus, was the catalyst's equally charming wife, the tall, stately young woman he introduced to them as Sophia. When one of the young Belgians asked what equipment Sophia hand-carried in her tapestry satchel, she produced a pair of binoculars she said were suitable for the study of migratory birds, a silver box she said was intended for diversion, and two dozen cotton squares that she said at the last minute, before kissing them good-bye, she had asked her children to fold into triangles.

As the Andelys sailed into the Dardanelles and Sophia once again watched the annual spring spectacle that by now she had come to regard with great sentiment, she heard exclamation and delighted comments from the six specialists in the group traveling for the first time to Asia Minor, now observing for themselves Homer's nations of "wild geese and arrow-throated cranes over Asia's meadowlands and marshes in tumult on that verdant land," and as the port of Canakkale came into view through her binoculars, she smiled and recalled Achilles' words. "Oh immortal madness, why do you have this craving to seduce me?" Unexpectedly, her heart pounded wildly with anticipation, and knowing what she now knew of Mycenaeans who had sailed into these waters long before her she also knew there would be no turning back now. No idle rest. No simple family pursuits. Not ever again.

# CHAPTER SIXTEEN

## The Hero's Heart

### *1880*

U NCHANGED, THE HILL of Hissarlik still moved her, the same awkward jumble of scarred earth and long trenches bordered by the terrible beauty of accumulated soil they had left behind two years before. Turkish sunsets were the same, still fiery red, still awe-inspiring, but Turkish authority had become far more cooperative. A new Firman was issued almost immediately, allowing for a few days in Constantinople where, with his group Tag played a favored role of host and tour-director. He was typically over-informed, full of energy, articulate, humorous. They all dined together late in the evenings, and later yet, the congenial company of eight drank ouzo in cabarets and quickly adapted Tag's habit of attracting the waiter's attention with two claps of the hands. Sophia watched her husband with a mixture of admiration and concern. How much longer could he continue this? He was tireless, but he was also driven now, pushing himself and compelling those around him. But as the hard work on the hill began anew, her anxiety was set aside as she watched, the haphazard approach of the past replaced by a novel, fast-moving system of efficient procedures. The combined professional efforts of geologist, engineer, draftsman, assistants, and photographer produced clear and rapid evidence of the hill's stratigraphy, proving beyond a doubt that the effects of natural disaster such as earthquake and tornado had indeed resulted in topographical complexities of enormous significance in the successive stratigraphy of the seven cities. By early summer, the last objects were uncovered in the elite second layer of Troy and they were the most magnificent of all. Six crystal scepters and four carved and polished stone axes appeared. Three of the axes were of lustrous blue lapis lazuli, one of green nephrite. Tag said they were the most precious of all his findings. "Homer was not blind!" he told Sophia repeatedly. "He saw everything there was to see in a world equipped to interpret beauty."

More certain than ever that Troy had once stood as a proud and royal citadel, the home of a king called Priam, Tag gathered enough material to publish still another book, LAND OF THE TROJANS. It appeared late in 1881 in English and German. The book established the antiquity of Troy and accompanied by photographs, it presented a clear picture of its stratigraphy. And although he knew people would forever doubt the authenticity of The Iliad, with so much more evidence in hand, he still reduced his conclusions to the simplest denominator, and it remained the sea, the citadel's proximity to the sea as ideally suited to his final conclusions as it had been to every aspect of his earliest theories more than ten years before. "It will just take time for people to get used to the idea," he often said casually to family and friends, and in fact, he began opening his talks and lectures with, "I am going to give you something to think about for a long time. Perhaps, for the rest of your life."

The invitations to speak poured in. Lectures, symposia. Audiences enthralled, informed, doubtful, inspired, curious. And finally, an invitation to present a paper before the Royal Geographical Society in London. In 1873, David Livingstone had addressed the membership of the Society with reports on his explorations into Central Africa. Burton and Speckes had also appeared, bearing vivid accounts of conditions along the Congo as they sought the source of the Nile. The Society Journal had published several of Tag's articles, but his personal appearance was far more important to him. Sophia was invited to attend and to receive the Century Medal in recognition of her work at Mycenae.

Benjamin Chadwick, a member of the Society, was present in the august hall, entirely at home in the company of his titled contemporaries.

"How exquisitely turned out they are!" he thought to himself admiringly, watching them as they arrived together. Under these circumstances it was difficult to imagine the articulate steel-haired gentleman in the well-cut morning coat and soft cravat digging into the heart of the earth, his beautiful young wife beside him, now elegantly attired in a blue, long-skirted suit with fashionable striped leg-o-mutton sleeves. During the final weeks on Hissarlik they had been inseparable, he recalled. But for her baths at Tessa's cottage and his morning swims in the Hellespont, they were together constantly, he remembered with renewed interest. Toward the end, she was constantly at his side throughout the long, exhausting days, digging, sorting, cleaning. And living under the worst possible conditions, catching the blowing dust in every fold of her clothing. But he had never heard Sophia complain. She still impressed him as one of the most loyal human beings he had ever known. Perhaps the only one, he mused. Sitting there, in the prestigious chamber smelling of seasoned wood and old leather, Chadwick was not alone in observing that Tag directed his remarks almost exclusively toward Sophia who sat in the front row. It was as if she were the means by which he had organized his presentation and the sequence in which he had placed his thoughts, and remembering several occasions at Hissarlik when Tag had excitedly discussed certain findings, all the while looking to Sophia, Chadwick knew that she was indeed, the muse.

❧ ❧ ❧

Gradually, Sophia began to share Tag's enjoyment of the limelight, which she herself had tasted in 1880, not with the level of Tag's egocentricity, but with her own natural reserve and with the unpretentious candor for which she had no idea she was already loved. For almost a full year, she had enthusiastically supervised the preparation of an extensive Mycenaean catalogue for the Greek

National Archaeological Museum in Athens. Her stunning work in the Peloponnese had resulted in the creation of the museum's Mycenaean Collection, every piece discovered at Mycenae; every cup, every sword, every mask, every diadem, every ring, every piece of gold, all of it, to be exhibited in a permanent collection in the largest of the new rooms of the National Museum, seen over the years by hundreds of thousands of international visitors in a never ending public fascination with the legendary kingdoms of prehistoric Greece and the fabled lives of its heroes.

Sophia wrote all the first individual descriptions herself, working from her copious notes as well as from the highly vivid personal memory of her findings. Tag liked to watch her in that pursuit. At her desk, unaware of his frequent presence, she concentrated for hours at a time, completely at ease in the mysterious world she had brought to light, already successful in a science which was still vastly misunderstood, and although she could not know it yet, Sophia had already woven much of the tapestry of her life into its fiber, adding as much elegance to it, as ultimately it would bring to her. The Mycenaean Collection was officially opened with a formal dedication ceremony on October 20, 1880.

At the time, the museum building was far from completed. There were still many areas of exhibition and storage to be added, but enough was in place to give off the appearance of a serious municipal building and the central room, known as Room Four, was complete. The Schliemanns had been invited to arrive early so that together they might privately view the newly mounted exhibition at their leisure and prior to the official ceremony.

On the way, seated in the carriage, Sophia was extremely nervous. She fidgeted constantly with her leather gloves and pulled at the black braid on the cuffs of her new dark green jacket, unable to sit still.

"They were such familiar objects," she thought to herself. Each one had passed through her hands and she found herself proud of them in an uncharacteristically possessive way. She almost regretted the arrival of this day. She had last seen everything in storage rooms, being studied, cleaned, recorded, prepared by strangers, but of course, according to the terms of the excavation permit, none of it had ever been her property. Under those circumstances she likewise had no authority over its exhibition, and although she had worked closely with museum officials in its lengthy documentation, she had not been involved in the final preparation of the exhibition. She had no idea what to expect. For months, a multi-national group of experts had clinically pored over every item, analyzing, taking measurements, assigning a museum number, reviewing and validating her carefully written descriptions. She was almost afraid of what she would see.

"I should have been more involved with the final exhibition," she said to Tag, aloud, as they rode in the freshly polished carriage. "Tag, you should have taken a stronger role in this! You really should have!"

Tag smiled, shook his head, and looked to his unsettled Sophia, lovely enough even in her ruffled state to remind him, as he explored her troubled face, of what it was like to love her amidst beautiful chambers built for immortals or under wide violet skies she could still drain of color at the long seashore. He wanted to take her in his arms, but instead, he gently took her hand in his.

"It will be fine. It will be more than fine. You'll see." He reassured her until they alighted from the carriage at the museum doors.

Her hands quivered as the new Ephor of Antiquities welcomed them and handed her the freshly printed catalogue. On its cover was a drawing of the beautiful silver rhyton she loved; the silver bull head, its graceful horns of gleaming gold, its forehead rosette formed of sixteen gold petals. She could hardly look at it. Tears burned in her eyes, and she had to glance away. He had lain there through ages, in the long darkness. So perfectly. So flawlessly. His beauty had reached out to her as few other things had, and it still did. The Ephor led them to the entrance to Room Four as she swallowed hard, standing just inside the doorway, unable to move a single step further, her feet feeling glued to the floor.

It was all there. In tall cases and low, along every wall, and in glass enclosed cases in the center of the room. Everything. The entire room, filled with the magnificent array of ancient Mycenaean gold and silver she had found; terra cotta and porcelain; alabaster and crystal; golden cups and hundreds and hundreds of pieces of jewelry; diadems, bracelets, hairpins, earrings, signet rings.

"How wonderful! How perfectly wonderful!" she repeated, breathlessly entering Room Four, her eyes glistening, her apprehension dissolved, completely relieved in the realization that the treasures of Mycenae had received their well-deserved honor.

In a simple room, elegantly white and constructed of marble, the entrance marker read, The Mycenaean Collection, 3200 B.C. to 1100 B.C. Sophia approached each of the display cases with the greatest affection, lovingly running her hand over the new gleaming glass. Tag watched her with enormous pride, folding his arms over his chest, sensing her satisfaction and approval. She saw the gold diadems from Grave III. The small card read, "belonging to a dead princess." Each piece was accompanied by a printed card carrying a description. The place of origin. A date.

The Alabaster Vase was called, "excellent Middle Sixteenth Century, B.C." "Four Bronze Swords with precious handles," "Gold Sheets from Grave III used to cover the entire body of an infant, Mycenae Twelfth-Thirteenth Century B.C.," and her favorite, the beautiful bull head in a place of prominence, where he rightfully belonged. "Silver Bull Head, 384, with gold horns and gold rosettes, used as rhyton." She looked to Tag and smiled. The Ostrich Egg, " . . . . a rhyton with faience additions, a drinking vessel . . . ." The Warrior Vase, the vase of warriors, number 1426 . . . . "Gold Death Masks from Mycenaean Tombs;" numbers 253, 259. No. 624, called the "Mask of Agamemmnon."

The Gold Lion Head that had been "found split in two," now repaired, gleaming and glorious; dated, first half Sixteenth Century, B.C.; The Gold Signet Rings: in a central glass case; The Gold Cup of Nestor, . . . . "known as the Cup of Nestor, King of Pylos; answering the Homeric ILIAD Book Eleven." " . . . . Copper Dagger from Grave Four, . . . . Sixteenth Century, B.C.," gleaming now in its glass enclosure, the black etching now officially identified as "niello." The Hexagonal Wood Box from Grave Five; what she had called the small casket, now labeled a "pyxis," Sixteenth Century, B.C. The Grave Stelae of Mycenae, its bas-relief decoration of warriors and chariots, authenticated as " . . . . Chariot Races Held In Honor Of The Dead" . . . .

Marked and assembled as it was on that day, The Mycenaean Collection was a spectacularly impressive array of rich prehistoric Greek treasures, both ceremonial and utilitarian. Sophia was thrilled to see it in this manner, but she alone knew how it had lain within the chamber tombs through the ages, and at what cost she had searched for it; how it had felt to find it, and what it meant now to essentially, give it away, which she did, simply and graciously, in her brief remarks during the dedication ceremony.

> "It was my hope to find some historic connection to my own Greek heritage, enlarged as it has been by long centuries of myth and legend. The Schliemann discoveries at Troy and at Mycenae are a beginning, for I am certain that in coming years, others will establish still firmer connections between Mycenae and Troy as we understand with increasing clarity, the conditions of The Heroic Age and the great poet's relationship to it."

Christina Stamakis, who remembered being taken many times as a small child to the National Museum, had been born in the Kastromenou house just a year after her parents had leased it from Georges Kastromenou, following Victoria's death.

"She was the Greek woman I wanted to be," Christina said of Sophia. "Everything about her was beautiful and sincere, and I had the great honor to live in her childhood home. It made me something of a celebrity, I suppose, but no one I knew came even close to achieving the kind of Greek honor that she did. We thought it had all died off with the old heroes."

Into the year of 1880, Tag received many requests for guided visits to the sites of Troy and Mycenae. These came from distinguished private citizens, but they also came from European heads of state and a number of well-known dignitaries. King George and Queen Olga of Greece were the first he took on a guided tour of Mycenae and soon after, the Queen of the Netherlands was also escorted through the Lion Gates to Mycenae. But it was when William Gladstone came as emissary of Queen Victoria of England to visit Troy that Tag saw the earliest possibility for wide public acceptance and the recognition he once again sought so stubbornly. The Prime Minister was himself an Homeric scholar, knowledgeable, and greatly interested in the Schliemanns' work at Troy. With a strong common interest, he and Tag quickly became good friends, so much so, that Gladstone wrote the preface to the last of Tag's published books on Troy. He visited Athens and saw Priam's Treasure in Tag's library cases at Iliou Mélathron, and through Gladstone's enthusiastic efforts, the Treasure of Priam at long last went on public exhibition for the very first time at London's South Kensington Museum. It was the first opportunity for the public to see the great Trojan Treasure about which so much had been said and written, and people came in great numbers for the next full year.

Preparation for the Kensington exhibition prompted several visits to London. Sophia did not accompany Tag on these brief trips, but she did come for the formal opening which was well attended by members of both the Royal Geographical Society and the Architectural Society. Once again, Chadwick was in attendance, now escorting the widowed Kate Franklin, an American who had married a descendant of the Bruces, ironically the family known as the Lords Elgin of Elgin Marble fame. It was well-circulated that Chadwick loved Kate to distraction and that he had begged her to marry him. And it was true.

"I love everything about you, my darling Kate," he was known to have whispered to her again and again. "We were made to be together. You know it and I know it," he had repeated to her, often and within calculated earshot of interested observers, some of the better informed among them considering it a marriage made in heaven, what with Chadwick's acquisitive nature.

It was also well-circulated that Chadwick's idea of loving everything about Kate Franklin included the fact that she came with quite a bit of attractive baggage, most of it luxuriously confined to the splendors of Wingate Park, her magnificent country house in Northamptonshire. There could be little questioning Chadwick's sincere affection for Kate, but he did have an insatiable appetite for beautiful things and along with his impatience to pledge his troth, Chadwick had fallen headlong into the thick sweetness of Wingate's honey jar, fairly drowning himself in the taste of its abundant riches. Horses in parks. Paintings. Silver. Exquisite furnishings. An army of servants. Income from one of the largest of all English estates, Wingate's several thousand acres functioning like the smoothly managed self-sufficient community it was. And all of it in the hands of its recently widowed and quite lovely mistress.

Sophia was introduced to Kate at the Kensington opening, having read about her in the tattler and gossip columns she still scanned in the English papers, in a continuing effort to exercise and hone English reading skills. Sophia had been amused to read that far from being an impulsive person, Kate was apparently taking her time in deciding on Benjamin Chadwick as her next husband, but the consideration of Chadwick aside for now, and along with many others who met them, Kate Franklin immediately liked this attractive and charismatic couple who had chosen to breathe life into the myths of unknown ages with such serious and complete dedication. Her prediction soon after to Chadwick that they would become extremely popular was proven true, as into the next few years, Tag and Sophia were invited to European capitals as distinguished guests, establishing warm relationships with a number of prominent Europeans and Americans.

These events of popular interest, touched with the stylish flourishes Tag and Sophia enjoyed, added significantly to the climate of acceptance into which Tag felt their work had moved, and with the success of the Kensington Exhibition and as pleasurable contact with a number of world figures occupied an increasingly time-consuming part of their lives, so did additional requests for guided tours to Troy. None was of greater consequence than that of Otto von Bismarck, the Iron Chancellor of Imperial Germany who came into their lives with the arrival of a letter requesting Tag's personal attention on a guided tour of Troy. Also a credible Greek scholar totally enamored by the feats of The Iliad's heroes, and himself the architect of the Franco-PrussianWar, Bismarck could hardly wait to visit the site of the Trojan War.

The two met in Constantinople and traveled on to Canakkale together. Each man conscious of the other's most apparent strengths, they got on famously, Bismarck well aware of Tag's German background, his wealth, and the freedom it had allowed him to pursue as he had, an experience allowed few men. For his part, Tag admired Otto von Bismarck's overbearing insistence upon immediate action, likewise well aware that in the years between 1871 and 1880, Imperial Germany had become the fastest growing, most patriotic country in all Europe and that under Bismarck's watchful eye, a generation of

Germans was plunged into an unparalleled period of prosperity. Napoleon's ambitiously planted seeds of bitterness had been sown in the widely fragmented Germany of the early nineteenth century and nowhere more noticeably than in Prussia where the word "Fatherland" was heard for the first time. Bismarck loved the sound of that word and had used its power to great advantage in his personally designed unification program, its resonant message supported by the short, hammering phrases in which he proclaimed that the unity of Germany was to be brought about "by blood and iron!" and of course, by the Kaiser's superior army and its 1871 victory over France, the event that more than any other had galvanized the German people with a jolt of intense national pride, something Bismarck knew full well they had never experienced. In an amazingly short time, the world began to wonder exactly when the poverty-stricken Germany that Queen Victoria had called "little" and "dear," had become the dynamo of all Europe.

By the time he visited Troy, Bismarck had grown a thick mustache and was losing his hair. His watery blue eyes were emphasized by deep bags which lay under them in two pockets of loose flesh. He and Tag spoke exclusively in German, which pleased the statesman enormously. Bismarck was fascinated by what he saw at Hissarlik as Tag conducted his tour with graphic descriptions and with his unique picturesque references, enthralling the Iron Chancellor, who could also quote long passages from The Iliad from memory, which he did expressively and repeatedly between puffs from the dreadful smelling Caporal Rose cigarettes he still ordered by the pound every month from Paris. Standing on the sun washed promontory overlooking the Troad, he became particularly excited as he relived the fateful moments of combat between Hector and Achilles, entirely accurate not only in recounting the manner by which Achilles had killed Hector, but also in describing how he had dragged the beautiful Trojan body three times around the battle arena. Bismarck was captivated by Tag's stories of life with Sophia in the sheepfold which continued to stand partway up the hill on its flat bedrock and he listened, clearly enchanted, as Tag described the daily ritual of dining with Sophia on the citadel of Troy as the sun set upon the Troad in ancient splendor.

"The world must know more about this," Bismarck had said to him in parting. "The world must see it."

Before the conclusion of his first visit with Tag, Bismarck had already suggested that Berlin was the only place worthy of housing the great Treasures of Troy. "Your country is proud of you," Bismarck said to him. "We must do something to honor you." It was the earliest seed. Greek acceptance and Greek rudimentary honors were all Tag had wanted, and now The Reichschancellor of the new German Empire was suggesting Imperial honors. It was irresistible.

The Reichschancellor's impressive letter arrived promptly. It said that the Emperor himself, was interested in honoring the German son who had "brought the ancient City of Troy to light." Bismarck cited Tag's German heritage, the pride his homeland felt for him as a native son, and the honor it would bring to Germany to have the Trojan Treasure permanently exhibited in museum rooms that bore his name. Once planted, the idea grew and developed rapidly, often out of control and reaching gigantic proportions in Tag's thoughts.

Sophia was beside herself. "The Germans had nothing to do with this; nothing to do with Troy or with Mycenae; not in its origins, not in our discoveries, and not now." But, try as she might, she could not convince Tag to change his mind and offer the treasure to the Greek Archaeological Museum where she felt it belonged.

Tag met with Bismarck in Berlin to discuss the conditions and terms of a permanent exhibition in Berlin. Every one of his many demands was agreeably met and every question received an affirmative answer. Yes. The Treasure of Troy would be on permanent display at the Museum fur Volkerkunde in Berlin. Yes. It would be catalogued as The Schliemann Collection. Yes. The Schliemann name would be etched into eternity. Yes. There would be a formal dedication attended by the Kaiser.

In view of the harsh treatment he had received at the hands of both the Greek and Turkish Governments, Berlin grew more and more attractive as the permanent home for the treasure, and much against Sophia's wishes, Tag finally made the decision to give Priam's Treasure to Berlin. It was no small moral victory when Greek museum officials came to him after learning of his decision to gift Germany with the Trojan Treasure, "hats in hand" as he liked to say, "begging me for it." Although Tag most certainly enjoyed this encounter with the same Greeks who had helped to defame him, they did not change his mind, and if anything, their interest accelerated the finalization of his plans. A letter from Emperor Wilhelm I confirmed the conditions stipulated by the generous benefactor and expressed the "nation's gratitude for the preservation of the treasure as a testimony to the benefactor's patriotic gift to the fatherland."

In the winter of 1881 Tag traveled to the Kensington Museum in London to supervise the packing of his Treasures of Troy into sixty packing crates marked for Berlin and at home in Athens, he and Sophia began preparing for the Berlin exhibition.

# CHAPTER SEVENTEEN

## Reconciled

### *JULY 1881*
### *IMPERIAL BERLIN*

A S CAPITAL OF the German Empire, Imperial Berlin was a city of one million people, one of Europe's most elegant capitals, and with Paris, ranked as a world leader in the development of the arts and sciences. They arrived on the fifth, with the children and Nurse Phillips.

The ceremony was conducted in the Hall of Heroes on July Seventh as filled with German dignitaries, and standing before the Emperor of the German Empire, Heinrich Schliemann received decorations as an honorary citizen of Berlin, an honor bestowed upon only one other German citizen, Otto von Bismarck. A citation was read, announcing that the German Empire recognized its beloved son as one of its heroes; that the great fruits of his work, the Trojan Treasure, was received gratefully by its people, and publicly accepted with pride and thanksgiving. The formal opening of the Exhibition Room followed. The Emperor led and the others followed him into the large chamber lined with massive glass enclosed cases.

All had been arranged in the order it was found. There were more than ten thousand Trojan objects, including wall fragments, soil and rock samples, and the last swords of nephrite and lapis lazuli found with the crystal scepters which had been taken from Turkey by special permission. In special cases were Tag's journals, his notes and hand-drawn maps. Two old and tattered copies of THE ILIAD belonging to him and which had served as his earliest geographic guides were also in the case. His handwritten marginal notes could be read on the open pages of the well-worn bindings. Passages were underlined, words encircled, and page corners turned down. The books had lain on his desk in Paris with many other personal items, and as she examined them, Sophia made a mental note to herself. During the next visit to Paris, she would collect Tag's desk items and send them for inclusion in the case here. The silver letter openers and eyeglass cases still in Paris were among his oldest possessions.

Wearing his medals, Tag stood beside Sophia, looking to her for the final accolade only she could now provide. What he found in her face was a great struggle to resist tears of pride that once again threatened one of the most important occasions in her life and he quickly looked away, totally gratified to know what was in her heart. How natural it had seemed to dream long dreams about such things; to imagine what it would be like to secure untold riches and the love and admiration of the most beautiful princess in all the land; to be proud of these superhuman feats.

In The Reichsanzeiger of late 1881, the donation of Heinrich Schliemann was acknowledged in the official government bulletin as a "gift in perpetuity" to be kept inalienably in the Imperial Capital. Its ten thousand items were listed in their entirety in an accompanying folder.

Tag and Sophia viewed the Berlin exhibition somewhat ceremoniously in the official company of the assembled dignitaries and promising themselves to return the next day for a more leisurely tour, they left the Museum Für Volkerkunde, moving outside and through a crowd of onlookers to their waiting carriage. As they proceeded, an attractive, middle-aged woman stepped out from the crowd. She made her way directly toward Tag. "Hello, Tag," she said to him, looking up and smiling. "I am Herta, your sister, Herta!"

Tag stopped abruptly and stared at the woman, unable to comprehend what he had just heard. His little sister, Herta? Impossible! Impossible!

"Herta, is it really you? I had no idea I would ever see you again. Herta! Oh, my!"

They had been so young when they were separated. Tag introduced Sophia, really quite unable to believe that this woman could be his own sister, but yes, there was something in her face he recognized. "Please come back with us to our hotel, Herta," Sophia suggested. "There is so much to talk about!" Over cups of hot tea at the Hotel Kaiserhof, Tag and Herta spent the remainder of the afternoon filling in the years that had passed between them, brother and sister.

Herta had been the youngest and along with their other sister, Anna, had been sent to live with relatives after their mother's death. An aunt and uncle had raised the two girls, along with two of their own children in a poor, but far less impoverished household than that of Pastor Schliemann. The girls attended church, went to school, and each of the sisters had married before the age of eighteen. Anna had moved away to Saxony with her husband and shortly after, Herta had come to Berlin.

"For a time I lived right here in Berlin myself," Tag said to Herta. "It is unbelievable that you and I were living in the same city and did not know it!"

"We read about you in the newspapers," Herta said to him. "We have been so proud of you Tag, and of your wife. It is a wonderful thing you have done together, and now, to have all of this in the museum right here in Berlin! I cannot wait to see it. It is something our family will be proud of forever!"

Tag smiled at his sister, appreciating her compliments, but really wanting to know more about her life. "Do you have children, Herta?" "Yes," she said nodding her head. "I have three; two boys and a girl. They are grown and married now. They all live in Berlin. Tag, I have two grandchildren!" Herta said, shaking her head in disbelief. "Now at home I only have my husband and Papa."

"You have Papa? Your husband's Papa?"

"No, Tag. Our Papa."

"Our Papa?"

"Oh yes, Papa has lived with me for a long time," Herta said to him. "About twelve years, I think." Tag was astounded, speechless and unable to grasp the idea that his father could still be alive. He sat back in his chair and took a deep breath.

"And how did you find Papa, Herta?" Tag asked, his voice noticeable stiff and tense.

"I did not find Papa. He found me," Herta smiled. "I was already married and living here in Berlin, when Mamma's sister, who had raised me, told Papa I had come to Berlin. She gave him my address. "Tag, I know I cannot speak for you, but Anna and I were much better off growing up with our relatives. Papa was sick for a long time after our mother died and the woman he married just ran off. She put all Mamma's furniture in a cart one day, and just left! Papa knew that Anna and I were well cared for, and he even came to visit us sometimes, but he just let us be. He let us stay where we were, but he told us he had looked for you Tag. He wanted to know where you had gone. He went for you at the farm you were sent to near Hamburg, but they told him you had run away. He tried hard to find you after that, Tag. He looked and looked. He asked everywhere. Then, when Anna died, he just stopped." Herta paused, visibly moved by her own clear recollection. "He stopped many things when Anna died, but later, when we started reading about you in the newspapers, I wrote to the Allgemeine Zeitung to ask if they could give me an address where I might write to you. They said they had no residential address; that your dispatches came through one of the ministries in Constantinople. I wrote anyway, Tag. I never received an answer, so I thought you must not have received my letters. Sometimes I thought that perhaps you did receive my letters and just did not want to remember me."

"No Herta," he said to her. "I never received your letters. I would have answered."

"Tag, come to my house, you and Sophia together. Come to meet my husband, my children. Come to see Papa, Tag."

"Thank you, Herta," Tag said, too quickly, "but Sophia and the children and I must be getting back to Athens tomorrow. Our travel arrangements are made, and we have an engagement this evening. Perhaps the next time we come to Berlin . . . ."

Tag had no desire to see his father, no desire to unravel the past over which he had triumphed so successfully, especially here in Berlin where now the evidence and accomplishment of his lifelong challenge was to remain forever. He had begun to wish Herta had not said hello.

"Tag, you would enjoy a visit with your father," Sophia suggested calmly, knowing exactly what he was thinking. "We could stay one more night here in Berlin. The hotel will accommodate us and change our travel arrangements."

"No, Sophia, we cannot change our plans. We must go home tomorrow!" He was emphatic.

"Tag, you must make your peace. This is the opportunity for it. Please do it. Please," Sophia whispered. "It would make everything so much better." Sophia looked to Herta who had not missed her meaning.

"Papa is very old now, Tag," Herta added. "Please come. I would bring him to you, but he gets so tired. Tag, I must tell you, you look just like Papa, younger of course, but the same eyes, the same build, everything is the same."

"I am nothing at all like my father!" Tag blurted out. "Nothing! Nothing at all like him!"

"It is all right, Tag," Herta said sympathetically. "I understand. You and I can still be in touch and perhaps visit again sometime later." Herta could see it was too much to expect more of Tag. Perhaps it was best after all these years, to leave things as they were, she thought. She did not press him further, suggesting instead, that they exchange letters. Promising to write, she gave Sophia her address and said good-bye.

Later, after dinner that evening, Tag and Sophia sat on the sofa in the sitting room of their hotel suite. "Tag, my dearest, you have lived with this hate, this hurt, for so long, too long." She stroked his forehead, her cool fingers moving along his hairline and down his cheek. "Please put it aside, now. Your dreams have all come true, but a corner of your heart continues to ache. I know it does. Go to see your father. Take him to see the fruits of your dreams."

"Take him to see Troy? How could I do such a thing? Even if he were able, I could not take him there. You heard Herta tell us how easily he tires."

"No," interrupted Sophia, "Not to Troy. Take him to the exhibition; to the museum right here in Berlin!"

ॐ ॐ ॐ

The old man's hair was white as snow, thinned out with age. He sat in Herta's parlor in a wooden wheelchair, his lap and legs covered in a brown, wool blanket. His gnarled hands grasped the armrests of the chair expectantly.

Sophia was first into the room. She walked over to the old man with a pleasant smile on her face. "I am Sophia, Tag's wife," she said to him, leaning over, reaching for his hand.

"I am so happy you have come," he said to her, gently pulling her close to him and looking deeply into her eyes. It was then that Sophia saw where Tag's expressive eyes had come from. The old man's brown eyes carried exactly the same expression. They were faded and dulled, but there was no missing the similarities between father and son. It was exactly as Herta had said.

"Is Tag coming? Where is Tag?" he asked her, almost plaintively. "I would like to see Tag. I wish you had brought him with you." His voice was pleading with her, seeking in her face an explanation of Tag's whereabouts.

"Hello Papa." Tag walked slowly across the room toward his father.

"Ach, mein liebchen! Is it you, Tag? Come closer. Come closer to me, here. Here, let me see you better. Yes. Stand here in front of me."

The white-haired head looked Tag up and down, slowly from head to toe and over again. He explored his face and stared into his eyes. Finally he nodded, at last assured that this was indeed his son. The old man stretched out his arms and Tag went into them, not reluctantly.

"Bring that chair here so you can sit by me, Tag," the old voice wavered. Tag sat down, facing his father, just to one side of the wheelchair. "Herta says you found Troy. It is amazing to me. She read all the newspaper articles to me. I saved this for you, Tag. You must have wondered what happened to it."

The old man's face crinkled up with delight as from under his lap blanket he produced Tag's childhood book of Troy.

"I saved it for you, Tag. I knew you would want to have it."

Tag's hand shook as he slowly reached for the Christmas present his father had given him long ago. This was the book that had motivated his very life, formed its dreams, the same book that had brought him more shades of happiness and unhappiness than he could ever have thought possible. He had never been quite so astonished in his life. The cover of the book was still beautiful, still in surprisingly good condition after all the years. None of its pages were torn and all the picture drawings were still clear. He couldn't speak.

His throat had tightened up and his eyes burned. He blinked over and over again, but the burning would not go away.

"Papa, you saved it," he finally said in a voice cracked with overwhelming emotion. "Papa, you saved it for me. I never thought you would save anything for me."

સ્ર સ્ર સ્ર

As was the case with so many people worldwide, Herta had followed newspaper accounts of Tag's discoveries with great interest. It had been so difficult to believe that this was her brother; the same insistent brother who, in the middle of winter, had forced her as a little girl, to play the part of Helen of Troy, standing tall on a pile of stones he had gathered by the frozen stream to portray the walls of Troy just as he had shown her in the illustrations of his book. Reading about Tag in Ausburger Allgemeine Zeitung, she had told their father about his amazing discoveries, but she had never shown him a newspaper photograph of his son. The old man had enough regret to live with. But when Herta had learned that the Trojan Treasure was to be permanently displayed in Berlin, she saw an opportunity to set things right.

Looking up from his old book, Tag could see that his father had grown very tired. "You must rest now, Papa."

"Herta says you have found Troy, Tag," the old voice repeated. "It is amazing. "She reads the newspaper articles to me. Will you come back to see me, Tag?"

"Yes, Papa. I will come back tomorrow," Tag answered.

The next day, they bundled the old man into a carriage, wheelchair and all, and a short time later, Tag slowly guided his father's wheelchair along the gleaming museum floors. He stopped at the entrance to the exhibition wing that bore the name, Schliemann. "Do you see our name, Papa?" he said, pointing proudly to the bronze letters. "Schliemann."

Large numbers of people had come to view the exhibition that morning. The news of its dedication in the presence of the Emperor the previous day had been the lead story in the papers. People crowded into the entrance. Escorted by a museum official, Tag stepped beyond them and took his father into the room now known as The Schliemann Collection, Treasures of Troy. He explained the contents of the cases to his father, again telling his stories of discovery in complete detail, and again attracting a group of museum visitors who listened to his narration with fascination.

"So much gold, Tag. So much, so much, so much gold. It is amazing," the old man repeated over and over, in a tired voice.

"Tag, does this mean we shall not be a poor family anymore?"

"Yes, Papa, that is correct," Tag assured his father, unsmiling. "We are not a poor family anymore."

Two months later, Tag's father passed away, peacefully, in his sleep. Tag did not mourn his father's death, but he did have his childhood book of Troy placed in one of the Berlin museum display cases that held his books and notes and the many things that had led him to Troy.

"My war at Troy is now ended," he wrote in his personal journal shortly after. "For more than ten years I have labored with the hill called Hissarlik. I have proven that in a distant, prehistoric time, there once was a citadel on a vast plain in Asia Minor. That citadel conforms exactly to the Troy of Homer's ILIAD. I shall forever believe it to be the site of his Troy and the setting for the heroes of the Great War fought between the Trojans and the Greeks. I further believe that my discoveries of Troy's palace, tower, gates, and walls, and of the great fire that consumed them, are evidence of its inhabitants, some of whom bore the names of Priam, Hector, Helen, and Paris."

How natural it had seemed to dream long dreams about such things; to imagine what it would be like to secure untold riches and the love and admiration of the most beautiful princess in all the land; to be proud of these superhuman feats.

# CHAPTER EIGHTEEN

## Distractions

### *1883*

D ELAYED BY SEVERAL years, but nonetheless true to his word, Tag traveled to the Island of Crete and Sophia accompanied him. But in five years, the proposed itinerary had grown more ambitious and in addition to Crete, they also visited three additional areas Tag now focused upon with serious plans for excavation: Tiryns, legendary home of Hercules just four kilometers from Mycenae; the Apollo Oracle at Delphi; and Orchomenos in ancient Boetia, known for its tholos tomb built of hewn limestone blocks.

In Crete, Tag learned that the land at Kephalia Tselempe, where he believed the great palace lay, was owned by one man, and once again he attempted to purchase and own a piece of history. The owner set an exorbitant price of one-hundred-thousand francs, which Tag refused to pay, his counter-offer of fifty-thousand francs likewise refused. In the meantime, word reached him that permission to excavate at Delphi had been granted to a team of Belgians and that according to the terms of the official Greek excavation permits being issued to him for Tiryns and Orchomenos, all finds were the property of the state and there would be a waiting period of six months before he would be allowed to begin. Crete, in Turkish hands, was under no such jurisdiction, and typically eager to begin work as soon as possible, he wrote to Benjamin Chadwick, requesting his ambassadorial assistance in securing an immediate Turkish Firman. Chadwick's prompt reply reached him in Athens.

" . . . . we can reduce the price to sixty-thousand francs and a Firman could be issued today, but you should be fully aware that you will be closely supervised. The Turks have long, rather inconvenient memories where you are concerned, and I am told that whatever you find, belongs to them. No exceptions. More importantly, however, many feel a revolution is imminent on Crete, and on a purely personal level and as a friend, I would advise you to exercise patience and wait until the island is under Greek sovereignty, which many feel it soon will be."

"We will work at Tiryns!" Tag happily and in a sudden change of mood announced to Sophia, placing Chadwick's letter in the top drawer of his desk.

"Perhaps Crete will hold its secrets for us until the Greeks take charge."

And in the next weeks, his heart and mind raced. He would again do battle and shake the earth at the beachhead, but this time he would bear warning to the god of sleep and like the streams of Lystros, he would run high and full, and like the Trojan horses cut down dry declivities into the swollen sea. This time, all would flee headlong, gasping into the hills while their cultivated fields eroded away.

That autumn, as they waited impatiently for the required six-month waiting period to pass, Tag and Sophia's attentions were diverted as they participated in one of the most noteworthy events of the year. On October 4, 1883, they sat in the first of the six varnished teakwood carriages slowly pulled out of Gare d'Est, the departing Paris railway station for points east in the inaugural run of what was to become the grandest tradition of railway luxury ever known. Over the next six decades, the gold-lettered cars of the Compagnie Internationale des Wagons-Lits et des Grandes Express Europeans, best known as the Orient Express, would touch the lives of a long list of glamorous passengers. The luxurious appointments Sophia and Tag admired in their car, Number 2419, included walnut paneling, handcrafted marquetry, and the fine china, crystal, and linens that several times each day marked the arrival of impeccably served food prepared by French chefs. A select group of dignified Austrians, French, Belgians, Germans, and Turks boarded the gleaming cars in what was compared to a maiden voyage of a fine new ship of the line, and although the list of English, French, and German titles was impressive, the inaugural itinerary of the Orient Express would prove somewhat less so.

Out of Paris, the train passed through Strasbourg and continued on its scenic route to Vienna, Budapest, and Bucharest, terminating its elegant journey at Giurgi on the Danube in Romania. At Giurgi, passengers left the gold-lettered cars of the Compagnie Internationale to warily board an aged ferry boat which took them to Rustchuk where they boarded the old Austrian Eastern Railway trains and finally, miles later, made one last connection at Varna where they boarded the antique ESPERO for an eighteen-hour voyage to Constantinople. It was widely circulated that one of the passengers had said that by the time the Golden Horn of Constantinople came into view, it was very difficult to recall the moving beauty of the costumed Rumanian troubadours who had come aboard back at Giurgi, playing their obscure folk songs for more than three hours. Of course, that passenger was Tag, and Sophia often reminded him that the troubadours had actually finished their performance with a spirited rendition of the French National Anthem in which one full stanza was quite capably sung by the executive chef of the Compagnie des Wagons-Lits himself. The completed journey to the aptly named Ottoman Port of Happiness took five and one-half difficult days, and five years would pass before Sophia and Tag could travel from Paris to Constantinople entirely by Orient Express, all the necessary miles of track at last laid. Thirty-five years later, in an interesting twist of history, Sophia would remember Car Number 2419 as the car that Marshall Foch moved to Compiegne, near Rethondes, twenty-five miles outside Paris, the car in which the French Armistice with Germany would be signed. Later yet, in June of 1940, Adolf Hitler would insist that 2419 be taken back to precisely the same spot at Compiegne to receive the surrender of the French, and just prior to the capitulation of Germany in 1945, the SS would destroy 2419 in a move planned to prevent its implementation in yet another historic turn of events.

# CHAPTER NINETEEN

## Tiryns

### *1884*

IT WAS TO Tiryns, neighbor to Mycenae, whose massive walls Pausanius had said were as impressive as the pyramids of Egypt that their full attention was turned that March. Tiryns: Home of Hercules, strongest man in the world and subject of the Twelve Labors laid upon him by Eurystheus, King of Argos.

Four friends rode into the bluegrass land of Argos in the springtime sun of the Peleponnese, their staunch loyalty to one another renewed and as essential to their mission as were the vast numbers of new pieces of excavation equipment, ordered once again from London's Wesson and Durleigh.

Little had changed on the arid plain, the wide, irregular bands of blue campanula that Sophia now easily recognized as the ancient flower of Mycenae captured in the artistry of many objects she had uncovered several years before, comforting in their familiarity. Seeming unchanged, the campanula still wove itself into wild amaranth amidst patches of powder-dry earth, but the party of four had changed in more subtle, human ways. Although at forty-six, Murat

Narjand rode with as much authority as he had at thirty-one, predictably tall and solid in the saddle, his eyes constantly alert to everything around him, he had taken to wearing a narrow-brimmed Greek fisherman's cap which above his graying mustache and full beard, gave his strong, handsomely lined face a playful, rakish look. His substantial presence could hardly be interpreted as capricious, however, his still massive chest and strong arms fortified and enlarged over the years by hard work and liberal quantities of Tessa's delicious breads and the richly satisfying potato dishes he favored.

Amazingly, Tessa appeared to be the same person Sophia had met in 1870. Except for her gray-streaked hair, which she wore pulled back in a severe bun, in many ways she still looked like a young girl, small and lithe, and surprisingly quick in her efficient movements. But as much as she had looked forward to yet another excavation campaign with the Schliemanns, aware of her important personal role and eager to return to Greek soil, unlike Murat, Tessa had made few friends in Greece, staunchly maintaining the carefully guarded exterior that she felt protected her and which for most of her life had successfully kept the friendliest strangers at a distance. At Mycenae, with the many Greek officials who had visited the site and complimented her culinary skills, as well as with members of the Greek crew whom she genuinely liked, she had either involuntarily or wisely and by design, conveyed a consistently cool detachment, her vulnerability and good sense of humor rarely seen by anyone but Sophia with whom she laughed often and openly. But in the company of a third party, and except for Tag or Murat, Tessa was known to quickly assume the highly protective role over Sophia for which she was known, and in spite of Turkish retaliation for the parts she and Murat had played at Hissarlik, she had continued to augment her powers of survival with a rock-hard determination.

The Turks had made life miserable for all the impoverished inhabitants of Hissarlik, whether or not they had worked for Tag, and convinced that as crew chief, he knew the whereabouts of the treasure of gold, Murat had borne the brunt of their suspicion. Tessa had endured the interrogations. Just after the official closing in 1875, as Tag's reports were published world-wide, describing in detail the treasure of Priam, Tessa had been questioned repeatedly, especially regarding the means by which the Trojan Treasure had been smuggled out of Turkey. She was the Schliemanns'cook and housekeeper. She had access to everything in the sheepfold. She would know where the Schliemanns had hidden things. The Schliemanns confided in her, trusted her. What had she seen?

She had, in truth, seen nothing, so well had Tag and Sophia concealed their treasured objects in the trunk at the foot of the bed which Tessa never opened. Tessa maintained she knew nothing about the treasure, as did Murat, but it was impossible for the Turks to believe either of them. Murat continued to insist he had never laid eyes on the treasure which, of course, was true and at the same time, also difficult, if not impossible, to believe. In retaliation and for three successive years of labor and loyalty, the Narjands and other Hissarlik peasants had been punished with exorbitant taxes levied on their farm crops. Unable to comply with the zaptieh's unreasonable financial demands, three times they had watched their crops rotting in the fields, unharvested. Tag had offered to pay their taxes in full, but his letters and attempts at intervention went ignored. Livestock, wagons, and farm tools were confiscated. There were two fires at Murat's farm, and had it not been for many friends in nearby villages and as far away as Constantinople who provided food, a horse, and no small degree of comfort, Murat and his family would have suffered irreversible harm. But, as Murat had for so long extended his own generous brand of friendship and concern, it was returned, and the very support that he and Tessa had offered to others on many occasions, was reciprocated in full measure.

Tag had paid Murat well, but no amount of hidden resource could satisfy the corrupt greed of the Turkish zaptieh who took pleasure in watching the gradual decline of this strong, popular Greek of Hissarlik. But under Turkish domination, the faithful ethnic dynamics of a near-tribal Greek community had worked in Murat and Tessa's favor, coming to their aid in a highly charged support system which for some time and completely unknown to them, had extended well into Constantinople and beyond into the Greek community above the Golden Horn with which Murat was so familiar. An openly aggregate and often vocal Greek support of Murat Narjand and Heinrich Schliemann, whose wife was also Greek, came to the attention of Turkish officials who saw a dangerously fertile ground of growing opposition which they had quickly and wisely moved to halt. Suddenly, the harassment ceased and Murat, Tessa, and their neighbors planted again, assured that their taxes would be minimal at harvest time. The Turks kept their word and the ensuing years had remained peaceful, not only for Murat, and Tessa, but for the entire peasant population of Hissarlik, many of whom said it was no coincidence that the settled Turkish lawsuit had allowed Heinrich Schliemann to keep his treasure.

℘ ℘ ℘

Organized, meticulous, and no longer prone to unfounded conjecture when faced with stone wall fragments or crumbled tiles, Tag directed the excavations at Tiryns with new circumspection, and in the southeast corner of the Plain of Argos, he and Sophia once again savored the taste of archaeological success. In the depths of a site commanding spectacular access to the sea from a sun drenched turquoise bay, they uncovered the well-preserved remains of a prehistoric Greek palace corresponding to Homeric descriptions, its color-rich floor plan of magnificent rooms, apartments, colonnades, and sweeping terraces an eloquent reflection of the lives of its prehistoric inhabitants. The Palace of Tiryns revealed a splendid warrior chieftain life clearly illustrated for the first time in colorful wall paintings, frescoes, and expressive scenes of human life that confirmed the existence of a great period of prosperity and active commercial relationships between many coastal communities on the Greek sea. Said in legend and myth to have been built by the Cyclops, the enormous three-foot thick fortifying wall stones individually measured from six to ten feet in length, more than three feet in height, and in twelve trenches close to the surface of the earth, fragments of vases and vessels for the storage of food were quickly exposed. When reassembled, the terra cotta vases revealed ornately painted surfaces decorated and covered in lustrous varnishes. Many were painted with human figures in a wide range of pursuits: hunting, socializing in groups, preparing for battle, offering sacrifices. But above all, the Palace of Tiryns revealed exactly what Tag had hoped to find at Troy: the household of the royals in color, the intimacy of their life environment rich in personal decoration, highly developed in artistry, and most important of all, exactly as Homer had described.

If Sophia had ever doubted the wisdom of her decision to leave the fashionable comforts of Paris and the potential pleasures of leisurely French country life, the tangible revelations at Tiryns validated for all time her concept of the work to which she and Tag were now irreversibly committed. This was their home. All of Greece. All these, her houses.

The palace at Tiryns had been superbly situated on its promontory, and all her life Sophia would regard it as the work of a master prehistoric architect who not only understood the requirements of his monarch, but one who had brought a breathtaking scope of interior decorative artistry to the ancient world. Limestone was used almost exclusively in the building, its walls evenly covered with plaster, the scenes of life painted in splendid scale: a hunting party, a procession of women, red-lipped, their long ornamented dresses close fitting, their arms, necks, and fingers encircled in exquisite jewelry of gold. Clearly, the king and his household had lived in rooms alive with activity, the busy public rooms on a first-floor level, private royal apartments on the second, reached by a magnificent staircase of stone.

The large central room of the palace, the "megaron," held a spectacular, central circular hearth, sunken into the floor and bordered in well-finished stone work. Four stone columns found in fragments, had once soared upward from the megaron, the hearth at their center. The upper column capitals were painted in a surprisingly bright red and yellow geometric pattern. To the far right of the hearth was the king's throne, of which only its ornate stone base remained, still a marvel of the ancient stone cutter's skill, precisely bordered in deeply carved spirals. The interior plan of rooms revealed that the formal aspects of royal life had revolved about this central megaron, its paintings of life-sized animals and birds in woodland scenes serving as impressively executed backgrounds, and in only four unshaded colors: white, red, blue, and yellow. Floors and ceilings had been completely covered in stones arranged in geometric patterns of painted squares, chevrons, rosettes, and stripes and some rooms were bordered in painted stones of brilliant hues.

On the upper level, separate megarons for men and women revealed the more private aspects of royal life. All were decorated with wall paintings. In the women's, elegant ladies carried small boxes or caskets of gold, identical, to those found in the tombs of Mycenae.

Their hair was long and entwined with ribboning. They all wore gold jewelry; neckpieces, bracelets, and rings.

The bathroom was a most surprising discovery, its large sunken stone tub complete with a step-down platform and a water drain reminiscent of The Odyssey's Telemachus, who was bathed in a similar tub by the lovely Polykaste in the Palace of Nestor at Pylos. The Tiryns bathtub drain was found to connect to an impressive system of terra cotta and stone drainage pipes leading directly through the underground center of the palace courtyard and further down its paved roadway into an elaborate system of cisterns.

Of all the paintings at the Palace of Tiryns, one scene, well-preserved on seven slabs along the entire length of one wall in the men's megaron, stood out and became famous, revealing a favorite pastime of the ancient Greeks, acrobatic bull-leaping. Sophia called it the Painting of the Bull Leaper and later it would come to be known in museum records as the Toreador Fresco, dated 13th-14th Century B.C.

The bull-leaping fresco of Tiryns depicted a powerful bull galloping at full speed to the left of the viewer. On his back was a human acrobat, balancing himself. Painted in yellow, the bull was spotted in red, his curving horn held in the acrobat's right hand, the acrobat's knee barely touching the bull while his left leg was thrust high into the air. On the acrobat's knee and above his ankles were several bandings. The background of the fresco had been painted blue, the contours of the bull outlined in a thick blue line, the whole scene framed by a border of white horizontal bands crossed by red vertical lines. Future coastal findings would confirm the popularity of Aegean bull-leaping as a spectator sport attracting the interest of large numbers of ancient Greeks throughout the Aegean. The agile acrobats were found to be both males and females who performed athletic tumbling feats as they repeatedly jumped from the ground onto the moving bull's back, balancing themselves in death-defying somersaults and mid-air antics. As Sophia came to understand that wagers were placed on the better known acrobats, tempting them to refine their courageous powers of duration and stamina, at the same time encouraging them to compete between themselves, she was reminded of the small basket boys on the hill of Hissarlik who, now that she thought about it, were themselves natural acrobats, agile, flexible, consistently fearless in their attempts to defy gravity and terrify her.

Other relationships to Troy were at times overwhelming. In the style of Troy, a tall tower containing two chambers commanded a panoramic view of the Plain of Argos, and approached from the same type of forecourt and exterior courtyard, the pottery found in and around the palace complex ranged from five-foot-high pithoi and large tubs to flawlessly preserved vessels for wine-making, pots for cooking, lamps and stands, incense burners, and jugs with many painted patterns of papyrus and geometric motifs of Egyptian style. Numerous terra-cotta figures similar to those of Troy and Mycenae came up, again representing the female figure with arms raised or clasped together, some in a circle. One of greatest charm was a headless female kneading bread. Another wore long robes and an elaborate ornament across her breast. The same types of spinning whorls found at Troy were also found at Tiryns, as well as the same types of terra cotta cups with perforations through which a string was passed to serve as a handle. Similar arrowheads of obsidian and beads of cobalt were also found, and in this atmosphere Sophia had little difficulty reconstructing the patterns of Tiryn's ancient monarchial life; banqueting from its bowls and goblets of fine gold, its wine poured from pitchers of gold and silver, its beautiful women well-groomed, adorned in fine robes and body ornaments of gold, fragrant with rich oils of myrica and tamarisk.

"Such an existence would have inspired and encouraged the creative artist in many forms," she concluded to Tag one evening in one of the two rooms they took at the small inn at Mauplis. "It would have required skilled resident craftsmen to execute the royal utensils of the monarch's household and it would likewise have required entertainments to match royal tastes. A bard, a singer of songs, a poet summoned to entertain the king and his guests, recounting tales of Greek valor and victory in the king's palace where he would have seen for himself the most beautiful objects in the Greek world."

Now it was abundantly clear that the Mycenaean Civilization was not to be confined to the citadel of Agamemmnon, but that just as Tag had suspected, it would come to include a far wider representation of kingdoms, and beginning with Tiryns, he would also conclude that the seafaring Greeks had indeed absorbed the many citadels of the Greek Aegean into their expanding world, creating an empire of strength and the strong coalition he plainly understood. Its traces would be found in future years throughout the entire eastern coast, from Lacedaemon through Mycenae, Tiryns, Mauplis, and Attica, through Sparta and Menidi, to Boetia and into Thessaly. It would extend to all the islands of the Archipelago; to Cos, Carpathos and to Syra and Thera and most importantly, to Crete and Rhodes, and even to the far coasts of Asia Minor where further remnants of Mycenae would be found in excavated jugs and vases, along with Mycenaean knives and arrowheads, suggesting exactly what Tag had envisioned from the beginning and what twentieth-century archaeologists would call a common federated market supplying both European and Asiatic coasts.

Of course, it was from these combined Greek kingdoms that Agamemmnon had drawn his mighty forces, but the age-old question of motive remained. "Why," Sophia asked Tag repeatedly, "why had the great Mycenaean Empire gone to war against a small coastal rival in Asia Minor?"

Tag's conclusion: "Acts of piracy. The many Greek tribes, all members of the coalition, were very likely targets of Troy's increasingly daring interference with expanding trade and fishing rights and the abduction of Helen of Sparta was the final insult. Let us say, from what we now know of the locations of Troy, Mycenae, and Tiryns, that for a time, control of trade was in the hands of greater and lesser Greek kings who supplemented their wealth with spoils of war, thus obtaining added resources to be exchanged for goods. For the Greeks, Troy's strategic location would have constituted the tail-end of the vastly rich trade routes to and from the East and well-aware of its vital location, Troy could, by itself, have assumed complete control over navigation through the Dardanelles, its deep natural harbor set on a protected site opposite Tenedos, the last anchoring station for the many ships who would have waited for a favorable wind to pass them through the Dardanelles. And of course the gods would be called upon to assist them, just as Agamemmnon called upon them at Aulis. Sailing into the wind was unknown and waiting for wind shifts could have taken miscalculated days, weeks, even months. The Trojans could have decided to capitalize on this dilemma, levy taxes, show favoritism, exchange bribes. And the longer the wait, the better. Did the ancient Greeks finally figure out that for an annual period equivalent to that of July to January, that the North wind blows, while from February to April routes can be calculated in accordance with the South wind? Did they attempt to strike an agreement, a contract of sorts with the Trojans, enabling seasonal, perhaps preferential access through the Dardanelles? And were their demands denied? To this day, Troy lies at the very mouth of the Dardanelles and that is its secret. Troy's destruction had everything to do with the power of its location."

Tag's good friend, the nineteenth century German archaeological historian, Carl Shuckhardt, would say in his book on the Schliemann excavations, that the second layer of Troy "represents the only great and important period of its history, coming to an end directly in the midst of the period of greatest Mycenaean prosperity. The explanation is not far to seek. The end was brought about by the advance of Mycenaean Civilization. In this light, the Trojan War finds a substantial foundation, and Homer speaks in a new light."

⟊ ⟊ ⟊

At Tiryns, Tessa's role was altered considerably and her experiences were not without touches of humor. Only years later, when some of them were gone, did she understand how the unique camaraderie formed on a hilltop and forged in the land they all loved had taught her that the sweetest memories ebb and flow to teach what is most lasting.

The Inn at Mauplis served food and Tag decided that all evening meals would be taken there, not on the excavation site. Ignoring all the fashionable boundaries of social protocol, he promptly included Murat and Tessa in his dining plans, and although noticeably uncomfortable in their first public dining experience, they adapted quickly, much to Tag's amusement and Sophia's genuine delight. Relieved of her mealtime responsibilities, Tessa became more companion and personal maid to Sophia than cook and housekeeper, and in fact, summarily dismissed the Mauplis' capable chambermaid, refusing to allow her to so much as touch Sophia's things as she herself took up the tasks of laundering and ironing bed linens, towels, and even the white napery Tag insisted be twice-creased just before being placed at the table.

The dish most frequently served at the Mauplis was mutton fried in liberal quantities of olive oil. Sophia hated it, but adequately smothered in vegetables, especially onions, Tag said it was delicious, and he said so each time the dish was placed before him. Hearing such praise for food she herself had not prepared for him, Tessa became visibly indignant whenever the curling fried mutton was served, and from the bottle of rezinato placed each evening within Murat's convenient reach, she took to the habit of pouring herself a full cup of the Greek resinated wine for which she knew Tag, in spite of his love for all things Greek, had never developed a taste. She downed it in three gulps as she stared at him and said, "delicious!" after each swallow. Seated across from her, Tag talked on in his customary streams, reviewing progress, noting the next day's plans, oblivious for a brief moment at least, to Tessa's rezinato-inspired humming which began softly, her unmusical monotone soon becoming loud enough, however, to compete favorably with her employer's considerable oratorical powers. It was a strange duet, neither of the two allowing the other so much as a brief solo.

No other menu item served at the Maulis during the Tiryns excavations provoked such behavior or encouraged so much consumption of rezinato for that matter, but since mutton appeared to be the Mycenaean meat of choice, served more frequently than anything else, such duets were frequently performed and thoroughly enjoyed by Sophia and Murat who openly maligned all the food served at the Mauplis, gaining much favor from the hummer and frequently falling from the grace of the orator. They were learning to have fun, all four, to enjoy living and working together, which by now had, of course, become the same thing.

# CHAPTER TWENTY

## Journey To America

### *1886*

I N MAY OF 1886, the Schliemanns were invited to attend The Liberty Ball in New York City. Scheduled for the following October, it was planned to celebrate the formal dedication of The Statue of Liberty and to be held in the ballroom of The Franklin Court Hotel. Accompanying the engraved invitation was a personal note from White Franklin, the Franklin Court's owner, who suggested the Schliemanns consider spending several weeks visiting New York as his guests. They declined, the work at Orchomenos now a demanding priority. Later that summer, however, White Franklin was in Paris. As American representative to the International Committee for the Statue of Liberty, he had come to meet with his French counterpart in making final arrangements for the French-American observances marking the dedication. Through mutual Paris friends, he met Tag and Sophia who had just arrived in Paris themselves. Franklin spent time with them at the house on Rue Victoire, and before returning to New York, completed transactions which made him the owner of a lovely, smaller house in the same courtyard of Rue Victoire, some three doors away from the Schliemanns. In the course of his visit to Paris, White convinced Tag and Sophia to come to New York for the Liberty Ball. It was to be a gala occasion, and "one to which you both would lend great prestige," he said. Having taken a liking to White Franklin, Tag and Sophia changed their minds and accepted his invitation, anticipating a trip to America and intending to take full advantage of their visit, Tag wasting no time in contacting Henry Adler at the American Institute of Anthropology, hoping to arrange an American lecture tour or a series of American Symposia at the same time. But it wouldn't be easy. Archaeology in America was still tied to anthropology in an overlapping of principles that focused primarily upon the development of cultural history and it would not be until Alfred Kidder who worked extensively in the discovery of the Pueblo Cliff dwellings in the southwestern United States, that some clearer perspective would be brought to American archaeology as a science of itself, Herbert Spinden taking the first American broad view and studying the farming and pottery techniques that would later be further enlarged within the overall concepts of prehistoric life on the American continent.

Henry Adler had visited the Schliemanns in Athens and had been a guest at Iliou Mélathron. He knew their fame had reached America in the level of admiration and curiosity that provokes a good deal of interest, and that their book on Mycenae had been popular. But, in truth, that fascination had been quickly overshadowed by a burgeoning series of simultaneous events and developments of far greater interest to an aggressive, young country hurtling at full speed into the twentieth century. In the years between 1869, the year of the Schliemanns' marriage, and 1886, John D. Rockefeller had founded the Standard Oil Company, the gunsmith firm of Remington and Sons began to produce typewriters, the Brooklyn Bridge had been opened, Alexander Graham Bell had invented the telephone, Edison had invented the phonograph, the United States National Baseball League had been founded, and large parts of America were powered with electricity. American corner grocery stores were stocked for the first time with canned fruits and canned meats, Americans had discovered tennis and golf, and George Eastman had perfected a box camera. A long, leisurely look into the dust of prehistory was not a priority on the American agenda. In fact, those few Americans who were interested in prehistoric archaeology or anthropology were collectively a small group, and for a time were regarded with no little degree of suspicion in a society totally focused on its present and eagerly anticipating its future.

Well aware of all this, Tag and Sophia came to America with some apprehension, at first deciding they would enjoy a purely social visit; a quiet, well-deserved holiday, but Henry Adler surprised them with a proposed speaking itinerary that would have taken them from New York to Boston, Philadelphia, and Baltimore. Deciding instead to confine their engagements to New York, Tag accepted only two speaking engagements; one at the New York Historical Society, the other before the annual meeting of the American Association of Journalists where he did not escape the attention of James Gordon Bennett, the flamboyant editor of the New York Herald and later, the Paris Herald, who, toward the end of the 1860's, had become similarly attracted to Henry Stanley's interest in the fate of David Livingstone, the popular Scottish explorer who opened Africa to the outside world. During the New York visit, Bennett met the Schliemanns, first at the American Journalists meeting, and later at several social functions. He was interested enough to send two reporters from the Herald to interview both Tag and Sophia at the Franklin Court Hotel, and later to send them to accompany the Schliemanns on several site visits at both Troy and Mycenae. Their stories were published in the New York Herald in a series of provocative articles that focused as much on the Schliemanns' lifestyle and tenacity as it did on their accomplishments, and irresistibly drawn, as the American public was, to the sort of adventure that placed beautiful, wealthy people in situations fraught with danger, much of the historic significance of Sophia and Tag's work was lost on a reading public far more fascinated by living conditions on the hill of Hissarlik and by what the local Turkish peasants had to say about Sophia's bathing habits than by the signs that tied Hissarlik to Homer's Iliad, or that tied Troy to Mycenae.

The speaking engagements were enormously successful, Tag and Sophia confidently self-assured before a burgeoning American society that had only recently fallen in love with elegant Europeans and looked to them for examples of how to live. The Schliemanns were seen first as refined connoisseurs. That they had embarked upon serious excavation campaigns together was fuel for a fire romantically flamed by a circle of men and women who essentially strove to emulate their glamour, and in America that year, Sophia and Tag had their first real taste of international celebrity. Unexpected, it came with such a surge of curiosity about the highly attractive couple who had "discovered Troy," that their days and nights were suddenly crammed with luncheon parties, dinners, and balls. The fact that they both spoke English, and with "the most divine accents," as Henry Adler put it, only added to their popularity within a circle of New Yorkers to which White Franklin became instrumental in introducing them and through whom many of them had their first opportunity to understand anything at all about archaeology.

℘ ℘ ℘

White Franklin loved New York. He was one of its earliest image makers, and he had helped to shape the city's national architectural reputation in an era when much of America looked to it for examples of grandeur. He had served on the American committee for the completion of the large pedestal supporting the copper statue erected on Bedloe's Island in New York Harbor called Liberty Enlightening the World. His American committee had raised two hundred, eighty thousand dollars for the construction of its massive granite and concrete pedestal, and his friend, the American architect, Richard Morris Hunt, was its designer. Another friend, Joseph Pulitzer, publisher of the New York World, stressed the importance of the statue in his newspaper, urging American donations for its pedestal, not only from the rich, but from all the people of the United States. The French had donated two hundred, fifty-thousand dollars for the construction of the statue sculpted by Auguste Bertholdi. The colossal monument that would keep alive the republican ideal in France and embody the meaning of American opportunity and prosperity was to be dedicated on October twenty-eighth by Grover Cleveland, President of the United States, its very completion a symbol of the new supporting the old.

In accepting White's invitation to attend The Liberty Ball, Tag wrote to him and said, "Since I have made a French donation to its construction, and since I understand there will be a replica here in Paris along the Seine, it seems appropriate that Sophia and I see the genuine article." On October 20, the Schliemanns sailed into New York Harbor aboard La Liberte. The great copper lady was a moving sight. Her torch illuminated by a mercury vapor lamp, she cast a beacon of light over the waters, sweeping all who saw her into the heartfelt meaning of life lived in freedom and friendship. It touched Tag deeply.

He shared his feelings with White in the carriage that took them to the Franklin Court. "It was the most moving sight!" he said. "I had not expected this great surge of emotion when it came into sight. I am very proud; very proud, indeed . . . ."

White had met them at the dock in New York. It was not simply a gracious gesture. It was the sort of well-bred behavior that came easily to him. The Franklin family had long occupied a comfortable place in the quiet, unpretentious annals of American aristocracy. On the surface they had lived in an atmosphere of simple rural interests, but for White, those interests had been enlarged by proximity to a bustling, metropolitan city, ready at a moment's notice to provide a rich background of experience through the talented practitioners who supported its art, its theater, music halls, saloons, and the endless entertainments he loved. At a time when a New York gentleman's wealth was often measured by the memberships in his clubs, White Franklin was very much at home. He and his circle were connected not only to the exclusive private men's clubs of New York, they were also connected to its theater and art worlds through a chain of childhood and school relationships that endured a lifetime. The Riverway Club at Fifth Avenue was "their" club, one of its few membership requirements being a three-year residence at a college or university. They all, more or less, conformed to this requirement, finding the amenities of private dining rooms, lounges, billiard rooms, and a swimming pool, more than equal to the drudgery of at least three years of academic discipline and an annual dues of seventy-five dollars.

White had always loved the dining room at The Riverway. It was paneled in English oak and was one hundred, forty feet long. In many ways it had inspired his first concept for the Franklin Court Hotel, and he brought many of its amenities to it, including the same types of rooms for lounging and dining. But White added something else for which he could not have planned. The location and public rooms of the Franklin Court offered New Yorkers one of their first opportunities for people-watching, something that the newly defined upper classes had refrained from doing. But it became very much an activity of the times in an American society that was beginning to learn how to live, mainly by observing life outside the private home, and people of note made an occasion of their arrivals and departures, aware that they were being watched by curious bystanders. Eventually, the Franklin Hotels contributed significantly, not only to the social and architectural profile of the city, but to its real estate as well, increasing the value of their surroundings by many millions of dollars.

He did not always like to admit it, but White shared with his widowed sister, Kate, a love of beautiful settings and a natural ability to create them. His talent exceeded Kate's when it came to architectural concepts and an unfailing eye for scale, but he had to admit that Wingate Park thrived under her supervision. She was dedicated to its maintenance and since her husband Thomas' death, had enlarged her art collection with a number of paintings that White decided he rather liked. Inherited money and a good education had made him a part of the developing society that called New York its home and although the manners and demeanor of a gentleman may have allowed him an expanded view of his world, White had a knack for recognizing an opportunity for making money on his own, which he did, regularly and with amazing success. He had started rather inauspiciously with theaters in Times Square, adding a few small, conveniently located hotels that catered to the theater crowd. The Chanticleer was the most popular, with an oak paneled bar that became a favorite meeting place for his crowd. White did not see himself as flamboyant, but he was. Some people said he invented New York celebrities. Some said he was one.

## OCTOBER 1886

## NEW YORK

The Grand Ballroom of the Franklin Court occupied the east portion of the building. It was filled with sparkling Austrian crystal chandeliers and sconces and gilded white paneling. If ever a setting had been created to show off beautiful women, their gowns, and jewels, it was the ballroom of the Franklin Court, and this would never be more apparent than on the evening of The Liberty Ball.

Although the entrances and promenade had been decked with festive red, white, and blue bunting and with American and French flags, the gold mirrored elegance of the Grand Ballroom was swept in one prevailing color. White. White roses. White gladiolae. White orchids. White lilies. White trailing stephanotis formed huge bouquets. White's well-known guests may have lent a convenient notoriety to his lavish setting, but from the moment they entered his beautiful ballroom many of them realized that New York had never seen a party quite like this one. Although officially called The Liberty Ball, it was remembered as The White Ball, not only because of the abundance of its fresh white flowers, but because of White Franklin himself, who had supervised every opulent detail. He had nothing to do with the abundance of pearls, diamond clips, and diamond and pearl stomachers the women wore, but he had anticipated the effect, and in the softened evening candlelight it was a memorable sight. Beautiful rustling gowns were accentuated by soft ropes of pearls held in clasps of gleaming diamonds, many with matching hair ornaments. The men in black evening clothes dramatically offset the white background, their dark mustaches and beards elegantly outlined against white ties and stiff collars.

With no possible way of anticipating the room's decor, Sophia chose to wear a spectacular white gown. Its wide, cuffed, portrait neckline set off her shoulders, the thick white satin falling from her waist to a long, full skirt of lustrous folds. At her neck she wore a necklace of pearls, and at her ears, clusters of matching pearls set with diamonds. Her shining dark hair was swept away from her face, thicker and more luxurious than ever. The music and dancing continued late into the night, and Tag and Sophia enjoyed themselves enormously, socializing comfortably and quickly establishing themselves as utterly fascinating. They said goodnight and reached their rooms on the third floor well after three in the morning. White had watched them throughout the evening, attentive to other guests, conversing with them, but constantly aware of where they sat, to whom they spoke, his interest in them uncommon, his view of Sophia, the most pleasant of the evening. Had he suggested what she wear, she could not have looked lovelier, he thought, her profile silhouetted against the background of white lilies and orchids, her beautiful dark hair gleaming in the soft light, her slender fingers occasionally tapping on the table in time to the music. They did not waltz together, he noticed, did not dance at all. Her dress was made for dancing. Much later, when he returned to the suite of rooms in which he lived, he opened a drawer and removed one of his many boxes of newspaper clippings. He collected news items on people just as he collected furniture, clipping out and saving anything that interested him. He rifled through the box. Yes, there it was. There was Sophia Schliemann wearing the jewels of Helen of Troy. And there again, the same photograph of her and an article on Mycenae. And just under that, a news photograph of his sister Kate, pictured just after her marriage, "leaving London and headed for Wingate Park," the caption read, "the former Kate Franklin, widow of Lord Thomas Bruce, bride of Sir Benjamin Chadwick, newly appointed Ambassador to the Ottoman Court of Constantinople."

# CHAPTER TWENTY-ONE

## Orchomenos

### *1886*

**B**Y THE TIME late Autumn came and they had returned to Athens, the path of least resistance, the one of silent resignation and cooperative conformity, had vanished from Sophia's thoughts, her focus clear, her goals balanced, even clearer as she met ambition face to face, on friendly terms, in a warm inviting place where the conventional expectations of the past were forever set aside and actually dissolved in favor of the reality she could at last identify. She was an archaeologist. She had ability, experience. She had the heart for it, the passion for it, the creativity it took to imagine the unimaginable. And Tag had known it long ago. He had watched her remarkable tenacity at Mycenae, knew the depth of her determination which was not unlike his own, and even if she had never been successful there, her carefully laid plans, her clear objectives, her stamina and endurance had convinced him that eventually her triumph would have come on some other significant stage.

"Promise me that when I am gone, you will continue with this," he requested, not once, but many times. "You are the one gifted by nature far more than I, more capable of patience, more disciplined. Promise me."

She could never agree, nor could she disagree whenever she knew Tag attempted to prepare her for what he said was the inevitable time when she would be without him and still young enough to pursue a fulfilling life. She always looked away in silence at these times, waiting for the awful present moment to pass so that life could continue on as she knew it and preferred it to remain.

In the spring they journeyed to Orchomenos, in northern Boetia, to the tholos tomb built of hewn gray limestone blocks, and there they found the Treasury of Minyas erected in the manner of the great tomb of Mycenae. It consisted of the same type of great vaulted ceremonial dome, its most unusual feature its color; the entire interior of the central tholos constructed of a green stone quarried in nearby Lebadeia and never before seen in Greece. The beautiful green ceiling of the Treasury of Minyas made Orchomenos famous, resulting in one of the earliest successful attempts at reconstructing an ancient work of architecture in its entirety. Found fallen in large fragments, the ceiling slabs had originally been sculpted in the Mycenaean pattern of rosettes and spirals in the manner of a modern-day carpet, a centerpiece medallion of spirals framed by a widening design of rosettes and alternating palmettes, additional rosettes, and spirals, all worked together, the whole forty-six-foot ceiling then edged along its entire border by an enclosure of dentil, the design providing the guide to its reconstruction.

The one grave chamber found at Orchomenos was identical to the shaft graves of Mycenae, also sunk directly into the rock. The Orchomenos tomb differed only in the location of its chamber tomb, which was alongside, and not below the great ceremonial chamber. This had allowed easier access to the actual graves of the dead. But it had also allowed easier access to grave robbers who had stripped the graves of all their valuable contents, leaving behind only a few pieces of pottery and clay figurines. The few items left behind were, however, of great significance, not for their beauty alone, but for what they clearly verified in the ancient use of bronze. Within the central chamber, at a height of four feet, every stone had a hole in it and some of the holes still held a bronze nail. The nails formed a perfect horizontal line around the circumference of the tholos, equidistant one from the other. They had once held highly ornate pieces of additional bronze which had decorated the thick, interior stone walls, as well as two doorways, one an imposing large entrance, the other, a doorway off to the side. Additional ancient bronze nails were found preserved in the stone work of the tholos structure, some in the doors. Fragments containing these bronze nails were removed to the Archaeological Museum at Athens, where they were displayed with many other pieces now rapidly accumulating from the Schliemanns' extensive Bronze Age finds.

In an interesting and revealing gesture indicative of the esteem with which their work was now held, all the wall fragments collected at Orchomenos were exhibited with the excavation labels Sophia herself had attached to each piece, and on which she had written in her own hand. A visitor to the museum could read, " . . . . head of a nail, of the type used to attach the bronze plates covering the walls, not only at the interior of the treasury, but at the great entrance as well as at the entrance to a side chamber." For a bronze handle she wrote, " . . . . sheet of bronze found in the earth fill of the treasury on the W side; perhaps the remains of a bronze nail with which the bronze plaques were fixed to the inner walls of the treasury . . . ."

Accurate labeling became Sophia's trademark, completed as quickly as possible at the site, and in an increasingly fastidious manner. She had heavy card labels made, in three sizes, each with a hole at its top through which she could lace a string or wire and attach it promptly in a secure knot. The additional findings of bronze at Orchomenos not only added greater credibility to the likelihood of Greek capitals which Homer had listed in his Catalogue of Ships, they also further verified the travels and historical writings of Pausanius with convincing life and color. Again and again, this second-century historian would be proven highly accurate in his descriptions, geographic locations, and in the specific names he had heard given to those people who had inhabited the civilization of the Aegean Sea. Sophia also found that Pausanius was not above reinforcing the principles of his ancient Greek pride. He wrote " . . . . and distinguished writers are at much pains to give an exact description of the Egyptian pyramids, and say not a word of the Treasury of Minyas and the walls of Tiryns, which are no less noteworthy . . . ."

Of Minyas, ruler of Orchomenos, Pausanius said, " . . . so far as we know, he was the first who built a house in which to store his treasury. It is a round stone building, ending in a blunt, conical point; it is said that the topmost stone acts as a keystone to the whole building . . . " Pausanius saw the building in a fine state of preservation even in the second century, and said " . . . it was of bee-hive form, exactly like the Treasury of Atreus at Mycenae, which it closely resembles, both in dimension and arrangement."

It had indeed been erected, Sophia found, just as the great domed tholos at Mycenae, consisting of a great domed vault with an added chamber, and just as at Mycenae, she again found evidence of the Englishman from whom she could not seem to escape. Lord Elgin had also found his early nineteenth century way to distant Orchomenos, apparently attracted by Pausanius' description of its reputation for being "rich in gold." There was no gold found at Orchomenos, but extensive evidence of Roman habitation was found in Roman statuary, marble pedestals, and layers of ashes and animal bones left from sacrificial fires.

Evidence of the Emperor Constantine was also found at Orchomenos in the form of a bronze coin, called a "follis." On the face of the coin was a bust of a bearded Constantine VII. In his right hand he held an "akaida," and in his left, a "globus," surmounted by a cross. The coin had been minted during the very short interval in which the mature Constantine had reigned alone. It was authenticated to A.D. 913-959, and in its later exhibition it also bore Sophia's distinctive handwritten excavation label. But more important than any separate object, Orchomenos provided still one more link in the newly emerging understanding of relationships between the ancient coastal capitals of The Aegean.

The Acropolis of Orchomenos had lain on the east side of a large lake with an outlet to the sea, found to be in perfect accord with the now familiar Mycenaean custom of placing its strategic capitals on the coasts of the Archipelago at some distance from, but always within view of the sea. From Orchomenos at Boetia, had come fierce Askalaphos and his brother Ialmenos to join Agamemmnon in the great pageant of ships. Homer called them the sons of Ares, "both conceived in Aktor's manor by severe Aktyokhe, who kept a tryst with Ares in the women's rooms above, where secretly the strong god lay beside her." "In the women's rooms above," Sophia repeated aloud. Just as at Tiryns, where she had seen both men's and women's megarons on the second level approached by the great stone stair.

As excavations at Orchomenos were closing, a fresh, new demon attacked with strange vengeance as suddenly Tag was aware of damaging pamphlets and newspaper articles being circulated in the capitals of Europe. In Berlin, Paris, and London he was being accused of fraud and misrepresentation.

"The traces of fire found at Hissarlik were nothing more than evidence of the truth he refused to face," he read in Athens, "the hill of Hissarlik nothing more than a fire necropolis, a crematorium for the burning of animals as well as humans."

Schliemann had exaggerated his findings, several London pamphlets reported. He had falsified what he had known all along to be the truth, had manufactured walls and rearranged stone to his own design and will. Troy was not at Hissarlik and existed only in Schliemann's own madness. Sophia was implicated of course, and Benjamin Chadwick was said to have been in his pay. Tag should have ignored both the attacks and the attacker, but he could not, and against the advice of Sophia and many supporters, he embarked upon a public counter-campaign that further fueled the considerable energies of an amateur archaeologist and former German Army captain, Ernst Bötticher, as he successfully engaged Tag in the most trying controversy of his life.

Public opinion had never favored Tag, but now, with the slightest suggestion that doubt and reticence might be rewarded, a growing critical mass emerged, its negative opinions ignited with the cooperation of several of the most respected periodicals and newspapers of the time. And Bötticher seemed unstoppable, amazingly well-received as a speaker before numerous academic and professional groups as he reinforced the belief that Heinrich Schliemann had made absolutely no discovery at Troy at all. Schliemann was a liar, Bötticher said. He had manufactured a great hoax. The ashes found at Troy in funerary vases and urns were evidence of the truth. The so-called jewelry, gold, and evidence of warrior-life had been put there by Schliemann and his accomplices. He had bought them at a Turkish bazaar.

Letters flew, communications were exchanged between Tag and Schuckhardt, and between Grempler, von Duhn, and Bey, all in support of him, all urging him not to respond to the unqualified distractor. The facts spoke for themselves, he was told repeatedly. But even as his letters flew to scholars and historians across Europe, he was flashing furor, the peerless brand of negotiable charm vanished, replaced by the old, cold hostility, his mind increasingly sharpened by this fresh challenge, all his wits about him as he planned his strategy and prepared to do battle with the new enemy, the fellow-German he could hardly wait to confront face to face. This time there would be no running. Not to Rue Victoire. Not to anywhere. This time he would defend his beliefs publicly and in the open, to the death if necessary.

The Anthropological-Archaeological Congress was meeting in Paris and Tag was scheduled to speak. He requested that Ernst Bötticher be invited to attend, and as expected, Bötticher eagerly accepted, "deeply complimented to be included in so august a circle of archaeologists," he stated in his letter of acceptance. The room in the French Anthropology Society's building was packed, every chair occupied, many people standing and crowded at the back, shifting from one foot to the other in order to get a better look at the famous, controversial Heinrich Schliemann. His address had continued for no more than five minutes when Bötticher made his move and struck the blow Tag had hoped for.

"What did you do with the cross-walls of the crematoria?" Bötticher asked in a booming voice as he stood in the fourth row. "And what of the so-called strata of the hill which are not the results of human habitation at all, but of cremation? Your strata, Herr Schliemann, are bones of men, women, and children, horses, sheep, and birds. The numerous urns and vases you found with shapes of human faces are funeral urns exactly like the Egyptian canopi, and the city from which these humans and animals came stretched into the plain of northwest Asia Minor and to the edges of the sea. Your so-called citadel is but one of the Hellespont's many hills."

The anticipated public engagement with Bötticher was off to exactly the proper start and Tag met him head on, cool and controlled and every inch the gentleman.

"You are Herr Ernst Bötticher, I believe," Tag began, preparing himself.

"I am," Bötticher replied, his voice self-assured.

"And what proof have you, Herr Bötticher, of your charge that the strata of Hissarlik represent what you say? Have you brought samples or objects to show, documents perhaps?"

"Prehistoric cities were known for their funerary mounds and the ancients always cremated their dead. According to ancient historians, the crematoriums were consistently located at a distance from the general populace. Over the years, a fire necropolis could grow to great heights as the result of invasion and war."

"Then have you, Herr Bötticher, settled on a more appropriate location for the Troy of Homer? Where might it be, if not at Hissarlik?"

"If the Troy of Homer existed at all, Herr Schliemann, it would not have lain atop a fire necropolis. It would have existed in the seclusion of Bunarbaschi, known by Julius Caesar, by Alexander, and to this day believed by any historian worthy of the name, to be the most likely site of Homer's greatly romanticized war. You have not found Troy at Hissarlik, Herr Schliemann. And you have not conclusively proven that any city has ever existed there."

"Have you been to Bunarbaschi, Herr Bötticher? Or to Hissarlik?

"No, I have not! And I need not see evidence of your haphazard work. One need only read your books and repetitious articles to conclude that you, sir, have found nothing at Hissarlik as a result of your many energetic campaigns. Archaeology is not the physically taxing challenge you made it to be, Herr Schliemann. It requires intelligence, education, map skills and calm, rational assessment. Contrarily, you would make it a creative process, in your own case, full of the romance you are known to attach to Homer. Archaeology is a logical process, sir. A logical process of elimination."

"Yes, Herr Bötticher, I must agree with you on that last consideration. Given the odor of the many masses of debris my wife and I have encountered in our work, I would say that archaeology could indeed be compared to a study of elimination." Laughter broke out in the hall and Tag could hardly be heard as he said, "I delicately call it waste, of course, but you know what it really is, do you not, Herr Bötticher?"

As the room quieted, Tag delivered his final coup.

"In this company, Herr Bötticher, I extend my personal invitation to you to participate in a study of the site I call Troy. I am prepared to assume all expenses, and I am sure you will agree that others should be included in our study: Dr. Grempler of Breslau; Dr. von Duhn of Heidelberg; Dr. Schuckhardt of Hanover; Dr. Humann, Director of the Berlin Museum, and of course, Dr. Bey, the distinguished Director of the Constantinople Museum."

They met at the Dardania in late March of 1889, Bötticher insisting upon having his picture taken with the entire group before riding out to Hissarlik. He stood between Murat and Dr. Bey, his army officer's cap a distinctly militaristic touch that did not go unnoticed by Tag's assembled coalition of scholars. "To wage war at the gates to Troy," Dr. Grempler muttered under his breath, "but missing his helmet and horsehair!"

As hoped, Dr. Grempler had come from Breslau; von Duln from Heidelberg; Dr. Humann from Berlin; Dr. Babin from the Academie des Inscriptions et Belles Lettres in Paris; and from the Smithsonian Institution in Washington, D. C., came Dr. Waldstein, Director of the American School of Classical Studies in Athens. They spent five days in study and consultation, their conclusions summarized and written by Dr. Schuckhardt, appointed recording secretary only because his was the only handwriting deemed legible enough to accurately transcribe the decisions and deductions of his illustrious colleagues. When the time came for each man to sign his name to the document Schuckhardt had prepared, Bötticher refused, but all the others affixed a signature.

In eight parts, the final document first described the agreed geographic and physical aspects of the hill of Hissarlik, specifically its dimensions, its visible fortifications, and the circuit walls of the second layer, or "settlement," as Troy was technically called.

Bötticher observed the investigative procedures with interest and insisted a cutting be made through an exposed wall section, convinced it would reveal a series of artificial terraces in the ruins, each stage smaller than the one below it. To his surprise, each of the seven layers in Tag's great North-South trench exposed not less but more space than the one below it.

When it came to inspection of the debris Tag playfully called "Bötticher's elimination," the debris of Layer One was determined to have held nothing but parallel walls. Layer Two contained ruins of buildings, the most important of which resembled, Dr. Schuckhardt himself verified, "the palace of Tiryns in every respect, which I saw during my visit to the excavations there." The layers immediately above consisted of houses, small dwellings built on one another's ruins at differing times, a great number of them containing large pithoi. In the highest layers were foundations of Greco-Roman buildings and numerous masonry fragments of the period. The pithoi of the third layer were still in their original upright position, some alone, others in groups. Several contained carbonized traces of exposure to fire.

"In general," Schuckhardt wrote, "we have found a fortified place, uninhabited for thousands of years. We are encouraged by the fact that during our conference, we were visited by more than one-hundred other scholars and antiquarians who all rejected the theory of fire acropolis and several have since made their views known in speaking and writing. Should Captain Bötticher continue to explain the Pergamus as a fire acropolis and raise suspicion in the mind of any sensible man that the world of learning is wrong and he alone is right, we invite such a doubter to visit us at Troy during our next excavation, which is to take place between March 1 and August 1, 1891, and to convince himself of the facts on the site."

It was more than Tag had hoped for. Bötticher would be silenced, work would continue on his hill, and now Sophia would have a lifetime of protection regardless of future dissenters. Like Helen's father, Tyndareus of old, he too had set a coalition in place. It would grow and no one would forget. Bötticher had been a blessing in disguise.

In the following months, supportive writings were published by other scholars, among them Dr. Joseph Durm of Karlsruhe who wrote an essay titled, "The Trojan War." Along with the document prepared by Dr. Schuckhardt, it remained among Tag's most treasured possessions since it represented further evidence of what he now knew would be continuing study of the site of Troy. Dr. Durm said that in spite of the small size of the citadel of Ilios, he found nothing improbable in the view that Priam found room for himself and his kin on the hill of Hissarlik. "No doubt, the common people here as elsewhere, lived outside the citadel, which would have enclosed a smaller space than one would naturally have expected, a close parallel to this found in the town of Lachish recently discovered and partly excavated by Mr. Flinders Petrie. Lachish, now called Tell Hesy, is situated in Palestine in the district of Daromas, an old Canaanite royal seat taken by Joshua. Mr. Flinders Petrie in the Contemporary Review, describes the site as a hill sixty feet high, composed of towns built one upon another, containing an area of forty thousand square feet, only two-fifths as large as the Pergamos of the second town of Troy, which has an area of one-hundred-thousand square feet. As the river which flowed at the foot had carried away some of the ruins, a vertical section of the mound of debris was exposed. In the upper part, Mr. Petrie found archaic Greek pottery of the Fifth and Sixth Centuries, B.C., and half-way up, he found Phoenician terra-cottas which his Egyptian experience enabled him to date to 1100B.C. The most important town of all is the lowest, which he dates to 1500B.C. Its circuit wall, like that of Troy, is built of unbaked bricks merely dried in the sun. It is twenty-eight feet, eight inches thick and still twenty-one feet in height. The house walls are of the same material. Just as at the Pergamos of Troy, settlement followed upon settlement in the royal city of Lachish, the method of building the same. New buildings were erected on the ruins of old, and in the course of centuries, a mass of debris accumulated which is even greater than that of Troy."

So fruitful were results of the first conference, that several followed. "Our intention, is," Schuckhardt wrote to Tag, "to expose all the house walls of the second city, a work requiring great care. To the west, we hope to leave standing the buildings of the third settlement, but even here, we may lay bare enough of the house walls of the second city beneath them to prepare a plan of them." In December of 1889, one last letter came to Athens from Dr. Schuckhardt before Tag and Sophia departed for Italy. The letter never reached Tag, but its contents revealed some of what the future would hold for his northwest corner of Asia Minor.

"It was possible to fix exactly, the alterations made in the buildings during the different periods of the second settlement. The great resemblance between the Trojan buildings and the prehistoric palace of the kings of Tiryns, excavated in 1884, should be carefully noticed. The plan is exactly the same for the two buildings. We also discovered at Troy, a ramp ascending at the side of the fortress walls, like the one excavated at Tiryns, the wall marked, which we once took for a wall of the lower city, proved to be this ramp. It is built, like that of Tiryns, of great unhewn stone blocks bonded with clay. There must, as at Tiryns, have been a gate in the north wall at the top of the ramp, and this gate, we hope to discover in the course of next spring. The steps found at the bottom of the ramp are of highest interest. For thousands of years, the ascent to the Pergamus was on this spot, and to this day we can see high above the southeast gate, the remains of two propylea dating, the one from Greek, the other from Roman times. Several marble fragments of Corinthian columns belonging to the Roman propylaeum have been found. In other side walls may be seen the holes for the bolts which served to fasten wooden posts which we found charred, in large fragments. The following will be of special interest to you: In addition to the two inscriptions of the Age of Tiberius, there was found, built in a Roman wall, a slab two feet, six inches long and just over seventeen inches broad, inscribed on both sides with a list of proper names. It seems to be a fragment of a full list of the burgesses of the town and it is interesting because of the frequent occurrences of Homeric names upon it. Instances are: Skamandrios, Teukros, Memnon, Glaukos, and Menestheus. These names seem to point to the fact that the Ilians were proud of the deeds of their Trojan ancestors whose renown had been immortalized by the divine poet."

Later, an excavation conducted by Schuckhardt would bare the whole south and southwest of the citadel of the second city, two towers discovered on the west side, their lower part well- preserved in heights that suggested fifty-five original feet. "It is therefore conceivable," he wrote, "that its building should, in accordance with the legend preserved to us by Homer, have been ascribed to Poseidon and Apollo."

At a depth of more than fifty feet in trenches 325 feet long, and at the foot of the citadel to the south, Schuckhardt also found walls of the massive buildings of Ilium and many Corinthian columns.

# CHAPTER TWENTY-TWO

## Winter Ploughlands

### *ITALY*
### *DECEMBER 1890*

IT DID NOT surprise Sophia that Tag saw most of Italy ripe with potential for future excavation. But she did chastise him for describing the Basilica of Saint Peter, not as the respected seat of the Holy Roman See, but as the grave of Saint Peter under Bramante's great dome and likely covering a fantastically rich, unexplored funerary shrine. At the entrance to the Vatican Museum, she could not help but smile, when at the statue of Augustus from Prima Porta, he duplicated the emperor's sweeping arm gesture and like a distinguished stage actor, welcomed her, not to the museum, but to the "malarial Vatican Fields, site of Peter's Martyrdom."

"We shall be struck by lightening!" she said to him, embarrassed that other visitors had heard him but at the same time well-aware that he had not heard her comment at all. It was not that Tag had ignored his wife's admonition. He was completely deaf in one ear and reluctant to admit that his hearing was rapidly failing in the other.

"And these, The Vatican Hills!" he loudly continued on in the role of tour guide, gesturing with his other arm. "This is the very place where charming Caligula began his construction of the circus, that large public arena completed by the equally delightful Nero, who drove his own custom – made chariot in the games. Right here, you stand upon the stage of Tacitus, creator of the popular sport of persecuting Christians with large hungry lions. Right here, where Peter was crucified!"

Sophia adamantly maintained that Tag's ear troubles were the result of water in the ear from his almost daily swims. "Mild infection. Never completely goes away," she had repeated over the years, periodically reminding him of her mother, whose medical powers had, with the passage of time, become the stuff of family legend. Grandmother Victoria had performed many miracles, Tag's children told him. "Is it really true, Papa?" they asked him again and again. "Yes," he affirmed on each occasion, nodding his head. "She herself, was a great miracle to me!"

Sophia had, over the years, given him several pairs of earplugs to wear during his swims. He had consistently refused them, but had tidily stored them away in a dresser drawer's remote confines, recalling their exact location when Andromache began her piano lessons with Madame Vera, who every week came to the house on University Square "to torture me!" Tag said. "The child has no talent for music! Can you not hear it?" he implored Sophia, offering her one of his several pairs of earplugs as little Andromache valiantly struggled on with the Minuet in G.

Now, in Rome, Sophia affectionately took Tag's arm and led him toward the first of the rooms in the Vatican Museum housing marble Roman statues, many of them likenesses of historic figures she knew he recognized, and as he attempted to introduce her to Julius Caesar and Cicero, again attracting the attention of others, she silenced her overqualified tour guide by placing her fingers across his lips. Once or twice, she resorted to staring him into silence, her huge dark eyes flashing under the same menacingly arched eyebrows with which, over the years, he had seen her skillfully silence the children. He knew she was increasingly worried about returning to them in Athens in time for Christmas. In both Florence and Venice, they had extended their stay by several days, and although she had not seemed to mind at the time, he knew that now she wished they had adhered to their original itinerary. But the Bötticher affair well behind them, travel in Italy was the genuine pleasure Sophia had hoped for. Recovered from the hostile cloud of recent months, Tag was rested and relaxed, often playful, and like others on the Grand Tour, they visited museums, shopped for gifts, and leisurely browsed the galleries and antique shops. In Florence, Sophia had purchased a beautifully matched pair of large silver ducks fashioned as tureens, and in the little town of Imprunetta, on the old road leading from Florence to Siena, Tag expertly examined samples of Italy's terra-cotta from which for years at Imprunetta, the vases ornamenting the gardens of Italy's most beautiful villas had come. Although since their arrival in Florence the pain in his right ear had worsened daily, he smiled and made comical faces as Sophia took pictures of him with the Kodak box camera she had purchased in the United States and which, along with her binoculars, silver box, and cotton squares, had become standard travel equipment.

In 1890, deeply enamored of the cultural splendor of its own past, the newly formed Kingdom of Italy was barely thirty years old, its personality as yet unaffected by international trade or statecraft. Destination of choice for a generation of musicians, artists, poets, and connoisseurs, Italy was the fascinating romantic idyll of Shelley, Byron, Wagner, and Liszt, Venice and Florence the magical stopping points on their own grand tours where, in some cases, they stayed not for days or weeks, but years. Vestiges of Medici Renaissance Florence and a Venice whose nostalgic lagoon readily inspired remembrances of centuries past, made as deep an impression on Tag during this visit with Sophia as it had several times before when he had come alone to Italy, but now Crete was very much on his mind, and as from Florence and its crown of hills they had come through the rose and ochre of the Tuscan countryside to Rome and further south to their final destination in Campania, he could talk of little else, the ruins of Pompeii which they had come to see, of particular interest to him as yet again the power of the poet took hold, Homer again the natural resource, this time his Odyssey. "One of the great islands of the world in midsea, in the wine dark sea, is Krete; spacious and rich and populous, with ninety cities and a mingling of tongues. Akhaians there are found, along with Kretan hillmen of the old stock, and Kydonians, Dorians, in three blood-lines, Pelasgians – and one among their ninety towns is Knossos.

Here lived King Minos whom great Zeus received every ninth year in private council – Minos, the father of my father, Deukalion."

Like Pompeii and Herculaneum, Crete also lay in an area susceptible to earthquake, tornado, and sudden storms, and like Italian Pompeii, was located less than seventy miles from a volcanic site: the island of Thera, which lay directly north, and just as proximity to the sea remained his most compelling argument for the location of Troy, so now was Crete's proximity to its neighboring volcanic island of Thera, Tag's overriding consideration in understanding the disappearance of its legendary royal city of Knossos.

In Italy, though, with a glorious view to the Bay of Naples from aboard the Passero, and with his great sense of arrival, Tag was well in command of the factual preparations he had made for just this moment.

"This entire area was colonized by the Greeks," he began to Sophia, pointing to the shoreline in the distance. "Even after the Italic tribes moved down from the mountains, Campania never lost its Greek roots and as power moved to Rome, Campania enjoyed great prosperity with the arrival of many upper-class Romans who owned seaside properties here. Gaius Marius had a villa at Misenum, Sulla near Cumae, and Cicero owned not one, but three: at Cumae, Puteoli, and Pompeii. By the time Augustus was in Capri, the Bay of Naples was fringed with the "villae marittimae" of the rich.

Was it during his travelogue aboard the Passero that she had noticed something was wrong? An empty, almost blank expression crossed his face. His eyes seemed glazed. Or was he simply lost in concentration? Yes, that was it. Typical. Of course. He was at Cumae with Cicero.

In Pompeii, the exhibition, true to the immediacy of the tragedy, conveyed a moving sense of intimacy; people caught completely unaware, like Tag himself, that they were living out the last moments of their lives. A table was set for a family meal in one house. A poster announced the date of the next municipal election at another. And in still another, a young mother nursed her child. Life-size casts of the victims had been made, exactly as they had been found preserved for centuries in ash and pumice.

"Pliny the Younger saw the entire mess," Tag said to her as they reviewed houses and streets in the exhibition. "He was with his uncle who commanded the Roman Fleet at Misenum at the mouth of the Bay of Naples. It was one o'clock in the afternoon when his attention was called to a gigantic cloud in the sky which he later described in a letter as looking like an umbrella pine tree with a tall trunk, rising high and spreading its branches. Uncle Pliny the Elder, headed his ship straight for the coast at Herculaneum, but it was impossible to land. He came instead, into Stabiae, and to the villa of Pomponiaus where he spent the night. In the early morning, a fresh succession of violent earthquakes awakened him and the steadily falling ash drove the household down to the beach where Pliny was overcome by fumes and died."

Tag's voice was strong, unforgettable, as he proudly recalled his Latin. "The Romans loved their inscriptions," he went on. "And as you know, they loved to see their names inscribed in stone." When "cognomina" were first adapted, the practice in aristocratic Roman circles of adding a third name, it quickly spread to all social levels, but not before Pliny the Elder was Caius Plinius Secundus, his nephew Publius Caecilius Secundus, and Cicero, M. Tullius Cicero."

"Let me linger here. Just a little longer," he suddenly said, commenting to Sophia with interest that the dominant feature of the typical Pompeiian house was its central hall, its atrium.

"Let me stay here in the past I love. Just a bit longer," he said, more enthusiastic than ever about the many Hellenistic touches he saw around him: the house built around a rectangle, cloistered, its colonnaded peristyle, its outdoor dining rooms, and always, the garden.

In the House of Jason, he stood for a long time before the wallpainting of Europa riding the bull, Europa, daughter of the King of Phoenicia, bare-breasted, three handmaidens beside her. "You, see, the legend was known even here!" he said. "Even in 79 A.D.!" And he proceeded to recount the Minoan Myth of Crete.

"Europa walked by the seashore gathering wildflowers. The God Zeus watched her and felt profound love. He appeared to her as a beautiful chestnut bull, a silver circle on his brow, horns like the crescent moon. Attracted to him, Europa mounted his back and raced off astride him, across the winds of the sea to Crete. There she bore famous sons: Minos, Rhadamanthus, Sarpedon, and gave her own name to a continent."

Arm in arm they had left the exhibition. They were crossing the square when it happened. In one moment he talked nonstop about a town on a hill kept alive only in folk memory and in the next he had collapsed onto the cobblestones. Two men who had witnessed the collapse rushed to help. They carried him to the small inn nearby. Throughout that afternoon and into the night she kept a vigil beside him, and as doctors came and went, she watched.

"Stay with me," they heard her whisper to him. "Please stay with me. Just a little longer." The minutes ticked by and became hours. His eyes were closed, his lips looked dry. Occasionally, he raised his arm and stretched out his hand as if he were reaching for something. She stroked his forehead, then silently, as if at last resigned to the preference of his trodden course and path, she took his hand and journeyed with him. Across the winter ploughlands veiled in white, past the high ground of the windy hill, into the royal shade of Zeus' golden oak, dazzling over yellow-haired Demeter dividing chaff and grain. And she did not leave him until the hour the woodsman takes his lunch in a cool grove of the mountain pine when he has grown weary chopping the tall timber.

She could hear the night wind outside, gusting across the square. At midnight she heard churchbells. She went to the window and looked to the square below. A group of children wearing crisp white collars hurried past on the cobblestones. She then turned and reached into the tapestry-covered satchel which was never far from her side. From it, she removed the old silver box, still as beautiful as on the day he had given it to her and still, like him, her favorite traveling companion. She sat down in the chair beside the bed where Tag lay still, and she placed the box on the bedside table, pressing the silver bird-shaped knob just as she had, hundreds of times before. The small golden-beaked bird appeared, turned and pirouetted as he chirped his song, then disappeared into his familiar enclosure.

"May life's hidden treasures be of greatest joy to you always," he had written in perfect Greek. She had watched him leave her mother's garden. There was something about the way he walked, like a churning human velocity she was sure could lay waste to the north wind, this adventurer who smelled smoky sweetness on misty faraway hills and heard silver bells on snow-white rams. It was Christmas Day.

# CHAPTER TWENTY-THREE

## Particles Of Emmer Wheat

*ATHENS*
*1891*

C OLORS WERE IN all the wrong places, hours of the day and night just as incoherent. Faces drifted past; eyes, noses, mouths, a blur of disconnected human features. The mouths formed words and there was no sound. She burrowed into bed.

Solemn pacts on open ground. Hands joined, fingers entwined. Contemptible war surging to my gates. Friend of my heart and soul. Strands of hair twirled through her fingers on his cloud – soft pillow. Pull. Long slim fingers ringed with gleaming bands of jet-black hair. Pull.

"Why does she pull at her hair?" Giannis asked as he and Niki walked home together after one of their almost daily visits with Sophia.

"I watch her and I am reminded of old classic mourning rituals. The grieving females hold both hands to their heads and seem to be pulling at their hair in a protocol intended to appease the soul of the deceased. I wonder if Spiro has noticed it?"

"She's not herself right now," Niki offered, articulating the intensely protective attitude she had assumed over Sophia since her grief stricken return from Italy. "It will pass."

But it did not pass and Sophia was still not herself by late summer when one rose-streaked afternoon Spiro Tassos sat across from her on her sun-flooded terrace, shocked to suddenly notice that her beautiful black hair was no longer the familiar thick mass of gleaming ebony she was known for. With the bright light behind her, he could see through it, the thinning hairline along her temples receding, small patches of her scalp clearly visible in places. Through the past months he had watched her unconsciously twisting her hair tightly around her fingers as she talked, a nervous habit, temporary, he was certain. But now he could plainly see what she was doing. Giannis was right. It was the ancient Greek lament. The grief-stricken widow was actually tearing her hair out.

"Sophia, this reclusiveness must end soon," he said gently, searching her face for just a trace of the old determination. "You have arrived at the stage of your life that both you and Tag always knew would come. Sophia, you are just thirty-nine years old. There are wonderful years ahead and you must begin to face them. He wanted you to. You know he did."

She said nothing, took a deep, impatient breath and clasped her slim hands as she stood away from her chair, clearly dismissing her most loyal visitor just as she had for months whenever he had urged her into the inevitable future. But now, deeply distressed by the disturbing evidence of Sophia's private torment, Spiro Tassos offered a parting challenge as she abruptly turned and left him standing alone.

"A change of scenery does people worlds of good, Sophia!" he called after her. "No one knew that better than Tag. Do you remember how he loved to plan even the simplest voyages you took together? Just a few weeks in Paris was a great event. Do you remember, Sophia?"

Spiro Tassos was becoming a cruel old man, Sophia decided as she crossed the mosaic tiled foyer of Iliou Mélathron and climbed the stairs to the shadowed safety of her room. How dare he remind her of such precious times! And how dare he recall memories that were hers alone; that wonderful Paris house she had gone to as a bride, sunshine pouring into the dining room window bay, Marie and Henri, life on glorious boulevards and avenues.

And he did not let up. A few days later, Spiro Tassos returned, this time determined to leave a more lasting impression.

"Sophia, I have been thinking about you," he began, slowly settling himself into the cushion of the terrace chair from which he admired the mature grace of the flourishing garden where he knew Sophia worked for hours every day, "and it occurs to me that Athens may not be the best place for you right now. Too little to occupy you here, too little stimulation. Think about a change, just a brief one, Paris for a few weeks, perhaps a month or two. Look out onto the world from that lovely Rue Victoire courtyard. Walk in the garden. See old friends . . . ."

"I know exactly what you are trying to do, Spiro," Sophia interrupted, her voice rigid and cool, "but I am simply not ready to consider such a thing. Perhaps next year. After Christmas."

With some resistance, Spiro Tassos' suggestion took hold, and although until the moment of her departure for Paris in the spring of 1892, Sophia seriously questioned the wisdom of her decision to leave Athens at all, however briefly, she saw it through. The voyage was, as she had fully expected, a lonely one, constant reminders of Tag all along the way, all her perceptions vastly diminished without him. Where he had enjoyed striking up spontaneous conversations with fellow – passengers, interested in where they were going, how long they would be staying, and offering a cigar to a gentleman with whom he might play cards in the ship's card room that evening after dinner, she spoke to almost no one aboard the Roule, disinterested in remote, irrelevant destinations and caring less to engage in polite conversation with those few passengers she encountered while walking along the deck, many of them intrigued by the appearance of the tall, striking woman who wore dark turbans and close-fitting cloches over her hair during her walks each morning and afternoon, then vanished.

Paris was a homecoming of sorts, Henri and Marie meeting her without a word about how oddly she looked to them without restless Tag at her side, full of his immediate, endless questions. "Had the cracked pane of glass in the drawing room window been repaired; the balcony's iron rail painted; the carriage polished?"

There was a young new concierge at Rue Victoire's entrance gates and once the carriage had passed through the arch, it took a conscious effort to look squarely at the pale gray limestone house she had come to as a young bride, eager to know its every corner, impatient to identify with Tag's world. At first she did not venture far, the fashionable Rue Victoire of heavy doors and secluded gardens an adequately nostalgic domain, the Arc de Triomphe seen from the courtyard entrance and the Seine just a short walk away, enough contact with outsiders. But just as Spiro Tassos had suspected, once her old friends heard she was in Paris, invitations began pouring in.

Dinner on the tenth? I think so. Yes. Tea on Thursday? Yes. Yes, a week in the country. Yes, the races at Longchamp. Out of widows-weeds. Into new dresses, suits, silk shoes. She forced herself to speak only French, renewed her love-affair with French food, adored champagne, and whirled through a long breathless season of nonstop socializing. The Pinets, the Duboises, the du Moires, the d'Ennerys. Deauville, two weeks in Monte Carlo, and to Nice. And by October, "yes" continued. A ride in the Bois at ten? Riding costume. Tea at four? Lace tea gown, matching gloves, enormous hat, satin-lined Belle Epoque Paris immersed in a new golden age of luxury and indulgence, new ideas in the air, rapid change at every turn, all of France in love with motion and mobility. The first automobiles. Flying machines. Balloons. Bicycles.

"Study your instrument!" admonished the Paris Herald Tribune's Counsel for Lady Cyclists. "Attend to the bicycle and nothing else!" Sophia read, incredulous. "Do not attempt to talk, and look well ahead of the machine, remembering that the bicycle will go wherever the attention is directed. A new balance must be acquired and other muscular combinations than those familiarly called upon."

The Erikson air-ship. The Freyman flying machine. Mr. Ryder's amazing aerial bicycle in a twenty-mile wind. In her circle of friends she attended the first automobile races from Paris to Amsterdam and back, as excited as any of those assembled in the little village cafe at La Fourche-de-Champigny to watch Monsieur Peugeot's Petroleum Victoria speed past Messrs. Dion and Bouton's Remorqueur.

Furs in late autumn's chill. New velvet-collared suits, billowing evening dresses, her hair growing healthy again, thick, shining brilliantly, the color returning to her cheeks, the hollow under her heart skillfully concealed by a smile that came more often and more easily in an intoxicating Paris of peace and plenty.

China and Japan at war. Cuba fighting for its independence. The end of the Hawaiian Monarchy. Americans in Europe as never before, living in the grand style, marrying their daughters to titles. The new white stone apartments rising on the Champs Elysee. Sophia's daughter, Andromache, married. Her younger brother, Agamemnmon, at school in Switzerland, a tall version of Tag, both children bright, accomplished, Andromache a talented water-colorist, Agamemnmon a fine horseman.

For a time, White Franklin was a frequent escort, the American owner of the Franklin Court Hotel and Sophia seen together at the theater, at art openings, at dinner. Tour d'Argent. Broussard. Notes. Flowers. His letters from New York signed, "Tout a vous."

No one could really say when the romance peaked, but White was seldom seen in Paris after Christmas of 1893, the house he had owned since 1886 not far from Sophia's on Rue Victoire, sold to Lenore d'Ennery, who said she thought White had asked Sophia to marry him, which of course, she could not do. "But they were made for each other," Lenore said candidly. "They both spoke French and English, had such style, each of them strong and decisive, so attractive together, seen even in their fast-moving sophisticated Paris circle as people of enormous charm and intelligence. He made her laugh and taught her to waltz. And I think she was probably the only woman he had ever known without a shred of pretense about her. But their roots ran deep in vastly different worlds, a pity really, but Sophia went through all the motions; the balls, the parties, and at the noisiest, most crowded events I would catch her staring out, preoccupied. By the time we returned together from the spa at Aix-les-Bains, I could see that she was terribly restless. She began refusing invitations and stayed home more often, saying she had some reading to do. Of course I know now that Sophia's period of mourning was over and that she had to return to her real life, to herself, to something that even those of us who loved her and knew her best could never be a part of. She had developed this huge hunger I never really understood, almost a yearning, really, and I suppose I was not at all surprised when she returned to Greece without saying good-bye to anyone. But she was unforgettable, with that skin and hair. Even in her beautiful Paris clothes she had an exotic elusiveness about her. It made people stare. You had the strangest feeling she was really just dropping by for a quick look at the universe before proceeding on to some splendid secret. Then of course, after a time we heard about her work at Sparta. There, above the banks of the Eurotas River, another ancient Mycenaean citadel emerged, a massive building with a central room and a throne to one side. They say the pottery was beautifully painted and still filled with particles of millet and emmer wheat."

# THE END

# AFTERWORD

ARCHAEOLOGY HAS BEEN called the sweet food of the mind, an applicable truism as I studied Sophia and Heinrich Schliemann's compelling determination to breathe life into a legend and encountered questions that even a century after their discovery of the Great Bronze Age remain capable of stirring opposing views.

Their story is true. Archaeological sites and findings are accurately described in SOPHIA, the flexibility of the historical novel allowing me to explore considerations such as: Why did the Turkish government allow the Schliemanns to keep the Trojan Treasure after its lawsuit was settled? And how did Heinrich Schliemann smuggle the Trojan Treasure out of Turkey (Asia Minor) and into his Athens home?

I have added fictional characters and events to illuminate relationships, motives, and the times in which the Schliemanns lived, and although they are real to me now, Niki and Giannis Kolodji, Father Spiro Tassos, Benjamin Chadwick, Lampierre, White and Kate Franklin, Ostrogorsky, Murat and Tessa are my creations. The Impressionist painter, Gustave Caillebotte and his father Martial are themselves in fictitious settings. La Casin and its gardens are real and belonged to the Caillebotte family. The French villages of Yerres and Montgeron are also real, as is the Schliemann mansion in Athens, which exists today as a municipal building. Although the Schliemanns also owned a house in Paris, I have taken imaginative license with its address, its staff, and its furnishings. Captain Bötticher and the Bötticher Affair are real, Bötticher's conversations with Tag and others obviously made up. In fictionalized aspects of Heinrich Schliemann's youth, career, and first marriage, the Schwanns and Muellers are supporting characters cast to illuminate the historic and cultural background of the period.

Dr. Carl Shuckhardt's SCHLIEMANN'S EXCAVATIONS, published in 1891, was invaluable to me as a guide to the findings at Troy, Mycenae, Tiryns, and Orchomenos, but disquieting at times, knowing as I did, that the Trojan Treasure Heinrich Schliemann gave to an Imperial Berlin in the late Nineteenth Century was lost in the final days of World War II and that the pieces described by Dr. Schuckhardt might never be seen again. In late summer of 1993, however, and coincidental to the completion of my manuscript, announcement was made that the treasure had been located in Moscow and that an exhibition of Heinrich Schliemann's Trojan Treasures was being prepared by the Pushkin Museum. The Mycenaean Collection remains on exhibition in Athens.

After Heinrich Schliemann's death and for the remainder of her life, Sophia financed studies and continuing excavations at Troy and Mycenae and served on the governing board of the German Archaeological Institute in Athens which her husband had founded. She never remarried and died in 1932. Like her husband, she was given a state funeral, the blue and white Greek flag draped over her coffin. The Schliemanns rest side by side on the Hill of Colonus in an Athens mausoleum of Heinrich Schliemann's own design.

In the years after her marriage to a distinguished Greek military officer, Andromache had three sons and seldom left Athens except in summer when she and her family took up residence in a rambling stone house by the sea at Phaleron. Agamemmnon shared his father's love for Paris where he made his lifelong home. He married twice and had no children.

N.R.J.